SAINTS AND SINNERS

Stacy Rush

Saints & Sinners

Copyright © 2023 by Stacy Rush

Cover by CentralCovers
Internal formatting & page edges by Painted Wings Publishing Services

ISBNs:
eBook ISBN 9798989427413
Paperback ISBN 9798218288334
Hardcover ISBN 9798989427406

WARNINGS

This book has dark themes and matter. If you are sensitive to any of the triggers below, I suggest you pass on reading this book. You have been warned...

TRIGGERS

Non-Dubious Consent

Dubious Consent

Explicit Scenes

Substance Use

Kidnapping

Knife Play

Homicide

Violence

Assault

Blood

DISCLAIMER

TABLE OF CONTENTS

SAINTS AND SINNERS

Stacy Rush

ONE

Prologue

"Sign on the dotted line, Kitty Cat."

His words are on repeat in my head as the vision of me signing away my freaking soul to the Lords of Sin in my own blood plays back.

I shudder at the memory.

I can still feel the knife slicing through the tip of my finger, going deeper than necessary, and my blood beading at the tip. Putting my finger on the contract, I sign my life away for the Sinner's help.

"That's a good girl, Kitty Cat. Remember, come to the Frat house at seven o'clock on the dot. We wait for no one; never forget that."

"See you around, Lovely Lina," his friend smirks before shoving his hands in his pockets and walking away.

I don't know where the last of the Sinners is, but I don't care at the moment. I need to get out of here before any of my sorority sisters see me associating with the Lords.

Tossing my bag over my shoulder, I shove my finger in my mouth to try and stop the bleeding as I hastily flee the library where I met them. I can feel eyes on me, and when I glance over my shoulder, *HE* is still standing there watching smugly as I make my escape.

"Oh, God, what have I done?"

Nothing good can ever come of this.

They are twisted and depraved.

They enjoy seeing others suffer.

Even the devil's spawns can't be as wicked as these boys are, yet I want them. I want all three of them, but I'm scared of how much they will ruin me mentally and emotionally. I am insane for thinking it, but I've never wanted anything as bad as I want the Lords of Sin.

They will eat me alive and then spit me out, or so they think, but that's where they are mistaken. I am desperate enough to take whatever they want to dish out, but I won't make it easy for them. I will fight them every chance I get, only giving them just enough to keep them helping me; that's the plan anyway.

Hurrying around the corner, I slam into a brick wall, or at least it feels like one. As I focus on the wall, I realize it's not a brick wall at all but a wall of chest belonging to the missing Lord.

"If it isn't the sexy Little Saint. Is the deed done?"

"Deed?" I raise a brow, watching the sexy smirk form on his lips.

"The contract...did you sign it?"

"What do you think?" I ask cockily as I raise my finger, which is still bleeding.

"So, we own you now..."

"Nobody owns me!" I glare at him.

"The Lords do, and I can't believe you have the guts to stand here and talk to me like this, Little Saint." I lean against the wall as he cages me in with his body.

He lifts my hand and sucks my finger with the cut, moaning before I snatch it away, "Oh, the fun we will have with our new little toy." He licks his lip with a trace of my blood still lingering on it and then bites the ring pierced through his bottom lip.

"In your dreams, perv!"

"We will see about that..."

He pushes himself off the wall, and his eyes do a sweep from my head to my toes, sending tingles throughout my body. I cross my arms over my chest and continue to glare until he turns and starts walking away.

He turns and walks backward, throwing me a wink, "I will see you real soon, Little Saint."

My body trembles at his last words, and I know I am undeniably in deep shit. Saints and Sinners can't associate with one another; it's in the Sorority rules. It's a good thing that I've never been a fan of rules, because regardless of how much the Lords scare the shit out of me, I'm drawn to them like a moth to a flame, and I'm very much looking forward to getting burned.

1 Month Earlier

"Congratulations, and welcome to the Saint's Sorority!" Felisha Howard, President of the Sorority House, smiles at each of us as she sticks our Sorority pins onto our shirts.

Eight made it in, with only two of us being legacies. Dani Richards is the other Legacy Student and my new Saint's Sorority House roommate. Like me, she is nowhere near being a saint; she's a rebel after my own heart, and I know that we will be the best of friends...maybe. I don't really do besties or BFF shit.

"Catalina Scott!" Felisha calls out, and I roll my eyes before stepping forward, "There you are! I should have known it was you; you look just like your mother!" She points to the giant portrait of my mother hanging on the wall with the rest of the alumnae Sorority Presidents, "I just wanted to give you an extra warm welcome. Seems as though our mothers were best friends back in college. Who knows, we may become great friends as well."

Her cheerfulness and fake smile make me want to gag, but I can fake it with the best of them, so I give her a matching smile, "Oh, that would be so perfect!"

She then spins and calls out to Dani, moving away from me but not far enough, because I can hear the same speech she gave me. I scoff, "Great, I've landed in the middle of the Stepford Sorority."

I never wanted to be part of this Sorority, but as a Legacy, my mother made me promise to try it out, so I'm doing this for her. My father is also the Provost here at Helshire University, so I'm stuck here, regardless, and

I had better make the best of it. It's practically a free education, and it's only four years of my life. How bad can it really be?

I head back to my room to review my class itinerary tomorrow. As I'm sitting on my bed, I hear some commotion outside my window, so I get up to take a peek. I do a double take and then quickly hide behind my curtains as I stare out at three of the hottest guys I've seen on campus so far. They look older, maybe Juniors or Seniors, so they would never give a little Freshman the time of day.

Watching them like a creeper through my sheer curtains, I notice how the girls who pass by them as they sit on the bench across from the Sorority House all stare, and some giggle when one of them winks or nods at them.

Out of the blue, a door slams below, and out comes little Miss Felisha on a mission. She marches over to where the guys are sitting and starts yelling at them to leave. I'm trying to make heads or tails on why she is being a total bitch when all they were doing was sitting there, but then I hear it when she yells at the top of her lungs.

"Sinners have no reason to sit outside the Saint's House! Leave now before I call campus security!"

They are Sinners, belonging to the Sinner's Fraternity House and off limits to the women living within the Saints Sorority walls. My father told me a story about the Saints and Sinners, but I paid little attention back when he did. Now, I wish that I had hung on to every word.

When I finally notice that it's quiet again, I turn my attention back to the bench below, and all three Sinners are staring up at me, each with their own little smirk. I remember my mother always saying that it's easier to ask for forgiveness than it is to ask for permission, and I can tell you right now that I'm going to be asking for quite a bit of that forgiveness business, because this little Saint plans on doing a lot of sinning if at all possible. Smirking back down at the three Sinners, I step away from the window, removing myself from sight.

Two

Catalina

"Come on, Dani; it's already almost ten! All the good parties have already started!" I stand at the door to the room we share as I watch my roommate toss clothing out of the closet as she searches for her lucky bra, "Seriously, just pick a bra and put it on already!"

"Are you kidding me? I never go to a party without this bra. As long as I'm feeling in the mood to get lucky, I wear it, and believe me, it's been a very long, dry spell for me. I plan on hooking up tonight, and I need my lucky bra!"

Shaking my head laughing when she dives back into the closet, I walk over to her dresser, casually pull out the top drawer, and move a few items around. I pick up the black and red lacy bra and let it dangle from my fingers.

"Is this the one you're looking for?"

Looking back at me, her eyes widening in excitement, "YES! Oh, my God, where did you find it?"

"In your bra and panty drawer with the rest of your underwear," I say dryly but then grin.

"I could have sworn that I looked in there." She strips her robe off and finishes getting dressed. "Why are you in such a hurry anyway?

Nobody really starts showing up until about ten; it's not like we are missing out on a lot," Dani states as she looks at herself in the full-length mirror.

"I know, but this room just feels stuffy. Besides, I want early dibs on the guys." I wink at her, because she knows that I'm not like that.

I'm far from being a virgin, but I'm also not one to have a new flavor of the week, and neither is she, but sometimes you just feel in the mood. The guys I want to see are never at the parties we go to, they throw their own, and Felisha is always there to remind us to stay away from the Sinner's Frat House. She's like a broken record every Friday and Saturday night when any of us plan on going out.

"Okay, ready. Let's go." Dani grabs my hand and practically drags me down the stairs. I'm so happy I decided to wait to put my heels on until I get downstairs, because I'd probably be tumbling down the steps right about now.

"Sheesh, where's the fire?" Felisha giggles as she stands at her post by the door.

"No fire, just need to get to the good men first!" Dani uses my own words to answer.

The President of Saints Sorority House chuckles, "Well, have fun, and remember, no sinning!"

"Yeah, yeah, yeah, we know!" Dani and I are in sync as we respond back.

"Bye, Felisha!" I chuckle because that saying never gets old.

The first party we get to is at the Phi Beta Kappa, A.K.A. the Jock House. Typically, the guys are good-looking, but they are such meatheads, and they are more interested in getting drunk, but every so often, a partygoer may catch an eye, but not tonight. At least not for me, but Dani, on the other hand, has got her eye on two different guys.

I leave her as she talks to one of the two, to go into the kitchen where the beer keg is at. I'm not one for heavy liquor, so I stick with the gut rot, as I like to call it. I stand in line to wait my turn, and when a guy, who I'm sure is just being polite, hands me a solo cup that he just filled, I politely decline it.

"Sorry, but I pour my own drinks. You know, I'm not too fond of being roofied, so it's safer this way." I smirk at the guy, who then shrugs and drinks from the cup he tried handing me as he walks away. "Thanks anyway!" I call out sarcastically.

"That was a smart move. You must not be very drunk yet." A blonde guy asks. He's casually leaning against the counter, people-watching, "Catalina, right?"

I lift my cup in the air, "That would be me, but most just call me Cat." I walk over and lean against the island across from him, "So, are you usually the creeper at all the parties?" I ask jokingly, "Hanging out in the kitchen, looking for your next victim."

He chuckles, "Nah, I barely go to parties; I'm not huge on drinking."

I eye his glass, "I suppose you're going to tell me that that's just club soda."

"Oh, gross! No, it's Sprite, actually."

"Ah, I'm sure." I grin and lift my own cup to my lips.

"Want to taste it?" He holds it out to me.

I raise my brow at him, "You watched me turn that glass down from the guy who I watched pour it, and you think I'm going to take a sip from a guy's cup who is creeping on innocent women?"

He shrugs, "Something tells me that you're not so innocent."

"Touché," I lift my cup, and he follows suit. After taking a sip, I study him for a moment, "So, if you don't go to parties, and you don't really drink, what are you doing here? Are you a D.D. or something?"

He chuckles, "It's hard to get studying done when there is loud music and people having sex in the room next to where you are trying to study."

That's when it hits me, "Oh shit, you live here! So, you're a jock?"

"Yeah, I guess you can call me that," he grins.

I look him up and down, "Hm, you don't look like a football player, but let me guess. You are a tennis player."

I must offend him, because he pushes away from the counter and flexes his bicep, "Does that look like the arm of a tennis player?"

I have to admit; his arms are slightly bigger than most tennis players I know, "Okay, so not a tennis player or a golfer."

He laughs, "No, neither. I'm captain of the Lacrosse team."

"Ah, that was my next sport," I grin, "Which position do you play?"

"I'm a Midfielder but can play any position if needed. Do you go to many games?"

"Me? God no, I don't participate in any sports, including watching them." Taking another drink from my cup, I look out the window just behind the guy I'm talking to, and I see him. Oakley Harris, the President of the University's son, and also a Sinner; he's one of the Lords of Sin.

"I think I just saw one of my friends out back," I say to the guy I've been talking to, "It was nice to meet you..."

"Kaden Miller, it was nice talking to you too, Catalina Scott." He grins, and now I feel a bit sheepish for not knowing his name.

"Well, that isn't creepy or anything. You know my name, but I've never met you." I smile as I start walking toward the door backward.

"Everybody knows the Provost's daughter. See you around, Cat." He walks away first, so I turn, open the back door, and head outside, where it's just as loud and obnoxious.

I glance around, looking for a particular Sinner, who I have no business trying to talk to, but hey, YOLO, right? You only live once, so rules need to be broken occasionally. When I go to turn back, I run into another body, spilling some of my drink.

"Oh shit! I'm sorry, my bad." I look up, and all I want to do is crawl under a rock, "Oakley, I am so sorry!"

He looks down at the wet spot on the front of his shirt and then cocks a brow at me, "Do you know how much this shirt cost?"

Looking at it, the shirt just looks like a plain white t-shirt, but knowing him, he probably paid nothing less than a hundred for it, "I am sorry, I can pay for the dry cleaning if you need me to." I look at him, trying not to show how nervous I am.

He looks me up and down, "Nah, I'm good." He then turns and walks away from me.

Fuck! I screwed that one up! Now he thinks I'm nothing but a klutz. Maybe it's a sign that I shouldn't be talking to him. I roll my eyes and picture Felisha cursing me for accidentally spilling my beer on him when I shouldn't have been near him.

"Shit," remembering my now empty cup, I head back inside to stand in line again.

"Let's get out of here, Cat." I look up at my roommate from the cozy bean bag chair I'm sitting in.

"I thought you had two prospects for tonight?" I struggle to stand from that low until Dani gives me her hand.

"Yeah, me too. That is until some redheaded floozy stole the first one, and it turns out I don't have the right equipment for the second one I had my sights on." She pouts.

I throw my head back and laugh, "Too bad you didn't meet Kaden. Now he's probably someone I may consider adding to my list at some point." I continue to grin.

"Ugh! Why do you always find the good ones?" She links her arm with mine as we walk out of the front door.

"It's the other way around, sweet cheeks. The good ones find me, but I'm too gaga over the bad ones to see the good ones." I chuckle.

I keep my eyes open to see if I get another glimpse of a certain Sinner who was at the Jock House earlier. As we turn onto the sidewalk, I look back at the big Victorian-looking house and see someone watching us from the top floor. They salute me, and I realize that it's Kaden, and I salute him back.

As nice as he was earlier, he's a bit creepy, but it's not like I ever see him, so I push him out of my mind and hug Dani tighter, "So, which house party are you wanting to go to next?"

"Well, let's see, the Emos are having a party, and then there is a house party two blocks away, so you pick."

"The Emos?" I cock a brow.

"Yeah, you know, the students that dress all goth-like..."

"Seriously, Dani?" I shake my head.

"What? That's what others call them!" She snickers.

"Yeah, well, they sound more like my people, so we are going to that one." It also happens to be next door to the Sinners Frat House.

"We better keep watch, make sure Felisha doesn't have her spies on us. The last thing we need is her grilling us when we return." My little friend chuckles.

When we turn the corner, we can already hear the loud music and yelling coming from behind the house. I grin; they are definitely the kind of people I'd rather hang out with. I glance over at the massive stone house next door, and it seems pretty quiet, with only a few lights on. No wonder Oakley was out slumming earlier.

We enter the house, and it's utter chaos with disco lights flashing and strobe lights flickering. A DJ is set up in the corner doing his thing, and the living room is packed with people dancing. This seems to be the place to be tonight, and although I don't drink hard liquor, I do love Jell-O shots, which are being passed around as we walk through the house on the way to the kitchen.

I lean in close so Dani can hear me, "I know what parties I will be attending this year!" I yell.

"You aren't kidding; look at all the hotties that are here!" She looks around, and she isn't wrong. They may have tattoos and piercings, but they are hot, and I'm sure not all of them are bad boys.

We grab a few drinks from the kitchen, along with some Jell-O shots, and head out back to where a bonfire lights up the whole area. Beer pong and flippy cup are being played in one area while some are tossing bean bags at boards with a hole in them. Lawn chairs are scattered about, so Dani and I grab two and pull them just to the outskirts of the fire where it's not too hot and sit to watch everyone.

"Now this," I look around the yard, "Is what I came to college for."

"What? You didn't come for the education that one can only get at one of the most prestigious universities in New England?" Dani giggles.

"Oh please, this isn't Yale or Cambridge. Helshire is just more of a private school. It is one where all the rich kids come to so they can party and get away with it, because their family money keeps them here. Why else are we all rebellious?" I rim the plastic condiment cup and loosen the Jell-O enough to suck it out.

"Oh, my God! That is so true; I've never thought of it that way!" my friend looks around, "Wait a minute, so does that mean that my parents sent me here to get me out of their hair?"

I nod, "Pretty much, but hey, now you have me." I lift my cup, and we toast each other, giggling.

"What are you two fine ladies doing all the way over here? The games are this way." A guy wearing a stocking cap with a nose and lip piercing nods toward the beer pong table.

"We are just taking in the scenery right now," I say, "Besides, you all looked like you were having way too much fun. I didn't want to come and ruin your night by kicking your ass at pong." I smirk and take another drink of my beer.

"Oh, is that how it is? How about you put your money where your mouth is?" The guy smirks.

I shake my head, "Nah, I never play for money."

"Yeah, that's what I thought." He goes to walk away, and I call out to him.

"I will play for your clothes, though." I wink at Dani, who is staring wide-eyed at me.

The guy turns around, "You want to play strip pong?"

"What, chicken?" I challenge him.

He licks his bottom lip and then bites it, "I'm game as long as your friend is." He looks over at Dani.

"You're on!" I stand up.

"What!? I can't play beer pong!" My friend starts to freak out.

I shrug, "I can't either..."

Dani chases after me as I head over to the table where the stocking cap guy is setting up the cups, "I can't believe you got me into this, Cat!"

"Hey, at least you're wearing a great bra." I tease, "Now they will all get to see it."

"Fuck you, Cat! I'm so going to pay you back for this!" She gives a cute little growl.

I swing on her, "Will you relax, Dani! Unless they are better, I was the champ of my high school all four years. Nobody could beat me."

"But you said..."

I roll my eyes, "I was fucking with you!" I grab her arm and pull her along, "Tell you what, if you're that scared, then we will play one-on-one, but Dani, I think he is crushing on you, not me."

"Ugh, I can't believe I'm letting you talk me into this." She says as she allows me to drag her behind me.

"Oh! Jakey, one more shot, and you will be down to your undies." I learned the stocking cap boy's name when his friends started to laugh that he was getting his ass whooped by a girl.

"Jokes on you, Cat, because this is the last thing I have left on." He grins and then winks at Dani, who blushes.

"Ah, a man who goes commando? Nice." I aim my ball, "Prepare to show that treasure of yours..." I let the ball fly, landing it in the last cup.

Jake tosses his head back, laughing before he does a little strip show as he takes his ripped jeans off. His eyes are on Dani the whole time. There is no shame in his game as he stands up and takes a few laps around the table. He's actually in decent shape and has nothing to be ashamed of in the department below.

"I'm playing the winner." We all look over at the newcomer, and I freeze.

"Yes! Jett, my man! Win back my dignity, will you?" Jake says as he fist bumps Jett Pelletier, a member of the Lords of Sin and one of Oakley's best friends. Beside him is the other Lord and Sinner, Fynn Morin, and on Jett's other side is Oakley himself, smirking as he stares right at me.

"Lovely Lina, are you game?" Jett asks as his eyes wander over my body.

His nickname for me sends chills down my back, but I refuse to show them what they do to me. Cocking my right brow, I toss a pong ball into the air and catch it, "Jett, is it? I hope you can keep your clothes on longer than Jakey, here, did."

"Oh, this game is on!" Jett states with a wicked grin.

THREE

Oakley

Catalina Scott, the Provost's daughter, and Saint's Sorority House member. She's going to be an issue for us; I can already tell. As Juniors, and the highest classmen in the Sinner's Fraternity House, Fynn, Jett, and I are the Lords of Sin on this campus. We own this campus; nothing gets past without the three of us knowing about it. So, when word came that the Senior Academic Administrator's daughter was starting her freshman year, and she's a Saint's Legacy, we knew that she would be our next victim.

What we weren't expecting was the gorgeous bombshell that stared down at us from her window at the Sorority House just after Queen Bitch came out acting like a lunatic.

"Do you suppose she's as saintly as Felisha?" As he looks up at the now empty window, Jett asks, "I mean, why else would she join this Sorority if she wasn't like the rest?"

"Does it look like I fucking care? Kitty Cat will be bending to our will in no time." I smirk as I start walking away.

"I think it would be hot if she were a saintly virgin. I would have so much fun watching the two of you devirginizing the little Saint." Fynn grins devilishly. He's not into virgins himself, so Fynn saying this tells me just how demented my friend is.

"We will have to keep an eye on her," I say, "Watch her actions for a little while before we proceed with our plans."

"You know, your dad may not be too happy if he finds out that our new play toy is his Provost's daughter," Fynn states, "Hell, it may be a bad idea all around, and you know I'm up for it; I just wanted to make sure you are." He smirks at me.

"Please, it's my dad. Like both your fathers, he's got so many skeletons in his closet that he can't say shit. I'm pretty sure Devlin Scott may have the same skeletons as my dad," I grin.

Yeah, I've done my digging after hearing rumors about my father had started circulating. Seems that he and the Provost, along with Fynn and Jett's fathers, were the Lords of Sin when they attended the University. It's also when Mr. Scott met Mrs. Scott; although she wasn't Mrs. Scott back then, she was just a Saint that sinned a lot.

Back at the Frat House, the regulars are there waiting for us. When I say regulars, I mean the groupies that sit around waiting and hoping that we will pick them to use for the night. We may be sick bastards, but the girls love us and what we can do for them. So, as we walk past the sluts of Helshire, Fynn and Jett fall into their laps and get right to it. They don't give a fuck if anyone else is around; they get off on that shit, making the girls they are with take their cocks in front of others.

I just keep going, not picking any pussy this time around. All I want is my solitude, a bottle of Jack, and a nice fat joint while I plan Catalina Scott's initiation into being the Lords of Sin's whore.

"Hey, Oak, where are you going?" Jett calls out.

I wave my hand at him, "You fuckers have fun with all that used-up pussy. I'll be having a little party of my own."

"Fuck you, Oakley. You're such an asshole; you know that?"

I stop in my tracks as gasps echo through the room. Turning, I stare at the bleach-bottle blonde with the fake tits hanging halfway out of her shirt. I walk right up to the slut and look down at her tits. Collecting as much as I could gather in my mouth, I spit down into her cleavage.

"There you go. I gave you my wad; now get your fake ass out of my fucking house!" The bitch swings her hand at me, and I catch it mere inches from my face, "Let me go, you sick fuck!"

My smile doesn't quite reach my eyes, "If that was meant to insult me, it did the exact opposite. I may be a sick fuck, but then what are you? I believe you got off on being fucked with a beer bottle and some used condom rolled onto it." I look over her shoulder at Fynn, "Do we still have the video of Beer Bottle Betty here?"

"I believe we do, Mr. Sick Fuck." My friend grins.

I give the girl my attention once more, "As you were saying?"

She yanks her wrist out of my hand, which I let her, and she backs away, "I don't know what us girls see in you guys! You all are sick and depraved!"

Me and my friends chuckle, "Because you love our cocks and how we bring out the whore in every single one of you. Now, get the fuck out and don't come back. If you come back, the video will be released for the whole school to watch." I turn and head for the stairs, forgetting all about Beer Bottle Betty.

As I pass one of the blondes with long hair, she reminds me of our newest conquest, and I grin, pointing at her, "You just got lucky. Get your ass to my room, now."

The girl smiles and jumps up, following me up the stairs. She's already obedient, because she doesn't run her mouth a mile a minute. She keeps it closed and follows, almost like a lost puppy dog. When I get to my room, I stop before opening the door. Grabbing her jaw, I make her look at me as I pull out my phone and press record. "What is your name, blondie?"

"Katelyn Damper," she says so nicely.

"Well, Katelyn Damper, do you consent to everything I'm about to do to this delectable body of yours?"

The bitch licks her lips, "Yes, Oakley, I consent."

"Good girl. Now, get your ass in there and strip the fuck down." The moment I open my door, she flies inside and begins to strip. Because I'm a bastard, I don't close my door, so any of my Frat brothers can see little Katelyn in all her glory. I don't want to fuck her, but if she's lucky enough, I will let her suck me off while I relax and smoke my shit.

Word has it that Kitty Cat will be out and about with her roommate, so I'm going to tail her and see where she ends up. Up until now, she's been boring as fuck, and I've been tempted to fuck with her just to make her life a little more interesting.

As I wait for our girl and her friend to leave the Sorority House, I light a smoke and take a few deep drags from it, making rings as I exhale. I throw it to the ground as soon as I see my target leave, and I keep my distance until I know exactly where they are going.

"Jesus fuck, seriously, the Jock House?" I should have sent Fynn on this mission; he'd fit in better than I will but fuck it. It's not like they are going to kick me out. I keep to the shadows, only talking to people if I really have to.

I watch as my Kitty Cat talks to some bullshit jock in the kitchen, and I come up with an idea. Heading out the front door, I circle around back, planning on heading in and 'bumping' into her or some shit like that. Luckily, I don't have to set foot in that fucking house again, because she comes outside to me.

Forcing her to bump into me was genius, and yet, the dumbest thing I could have done, because now that I've been in her space, it makes me want to be up inside her even more. I'm fucked, but not as much as she will be by the Sinners.

Now that we've had this initial meeting, I know she's not the Saint Felisha hopes she is. Call it a sixth sense, but I believe that this little Saint will be the biggest Sinner of all, and the Lords of Sin will have front-row seats. Hell, we'll be in sniffer's row.

An hour after our initial meeting, I could hardly believe that our girl shows up at the Emo party next door to the Sinner's domain. It appears that Kitty Cat doesn't regard the Saint's rules as she should, and for that, she deserves a reward. I wonder just how many sins she's willing to commit before she realizes that her Saintly status means shit to us. If anything, the downfall of a Saint turns us on, but she will soon realize that it's not the downfall of a Saint that is our end game. No, it's owning that Saint's mind, body, and fucking soul.

Jett

"Oh, the game is on!" I grin wickedly at the blonde bombshell across the beer pong table.

I've been watching her, and she's good, but my Lovely Lina is no match for me. I will have her stripped bare naked like the day she was born in no time at all. Her smirk will be wiped right off her face in just...one...quick...second. I toss the ping pong ball, landing it in the cup I called.

Lovely Lina raises a brow, "Really?"

She now has to make the same glass as I did; otherwise, it's off with an item of clothing. I step back and stand with my feet apart and my arms crossed, letting my bulging, tattooed biceps peek out from the sleeves of my t-shirt. Looking over my shoulder at my boys, Oakley and Fynn are in the same stance and wearing the same smirk.

When I turn back to the game at hand, I see she's waiting for me to give her my attention before letting the little white ball fly, landing dead center just like mine. I can slowly feel my smile fade as the crowd around us cover their mouths and snicker.

"Okay, okay," I run my tongue over my bottom lip before biting it as I look at the blonde, now wearing a smirk of her own, "I see I finally have a worthy opponent to play this game with."

Pulling my shirt over my head, I let my pecs flex one at a time, showing off just a tad bit. Yeah, just like all the other women standing around, my Lovely Lina is gazing at the ink painting my upper body, which just so happens to be stacked.

"You've got a little drool dripping, Little Saint!" Fynn calls out, chuckling.

Our girl sure has some balls as she lifts her hand and flips my friend off. She will pay for that later, but when I look back at my fellow Sinner, he's grinning. I know that grin, and I can tell you right now, it won't be pretty for this bombshell.

She takes her turn first this time, making it in the far-right cup. It's an easy shot, and I roll my eyes and step forward. Lining up the shot, I start to toss it just as she decides to adjust her fucking breasts in her dress. She's got to be a D, so of course, it will draw my attention, making me miss my shot.

"Bullshit!" Fynn calls out, "She did that on purpose!"

"Did what?" Catalina looks up innocently, and I swear all I want to do is throw her over this table and fuck the shit out of her in front of all these people. I wonder if she would ever be that kinky. "Oh, did he take his shot without waiting for me to watch?" She juts her bottom lip out, "Well, darn... I missed it."

I can see the little grin she's trying to hold back, but it's all good, because I now know her game. I lift my foot up and pull off my trainer, tossing it aside. Since I missed, she gets to go again and now dunks it in the front cup.

I stand here waiting for her to give me her attention, and once I have it, I faze out everything and everyone around me, singing Cutthroat by Imagine Dragons in my head. This game shouldn't be taken so seriously, but when you have someone like Catalina Scott standing across from you, and you have a chance to get her naked, there is no time for fucking around.

The red solo cup is right there, unmoving and waiting to be conquered. It's like the woman standing behind it, waiting for me to miss once again. She will never admit it, but I've seen the look before; she wants to be conquered, and not by just anyone. She wants to sin badly; only she's not sure which sin she wants. Too bad for her that she will be sinning with more than one. The Lords of Sin do everything together, including their women.

The ball flies as though it's in slow motion, landing in the cup that it was meant for. It's a lovely sight watching the smile fade from Catalina's face. Instead of worrying about it too much, she smirks and tosses a heel. It's not what I was hoping for, but of course, she wouldn't go straight for her dress. It's all good because I will have her out of it in no time at all.

The game goes back and forth, and I lose my other shoe and jeans, whereas she's only lost her other heel. I'm now down to my boxers, but she's still got her dress on. It's her turn to go first. Making it in the far-left cup this time. When I toss mine, making it in the same one, she tries to hide her nervousness but instead, she straightens her back, stares right into my eyes, and pulls her bodycon dress over her head, handing it to her little friend.

I'm too busy staring at her banging body to realize she's waiting for me to take my turn. Her curves are in all the right places, and even though she's far from skin and bones, she is nowhere near being overweight. She's got the perfect amount of meat to her where I won't hurt myself as I slam into her from behind or when I have her straddling me while I have her ride my cock.

"Dude, take your turn." Oakley snickers, bringing me back to the game at hand.

I choose a cup on the side, the middle one to be exact, and I toss the ping pong. I stand with my thumbs in the front of my waistband, causing the material to dip and show off the deep V leading to my groin, but even that doesn't get her as her ball makes its mark. She throws her hands in the air, and all the women cheer.

She grabs her dress from her friend and goes to put it on, but I'm there in a heartbeat, snatching it from her hands, "Game isn't quite over, Lovely Lina."

"What do you mean?" She questions and then looks at the table.

Pushing her back so her ass is against the table, I grin, "I haven't lost my last article of clothing yet." I whip down my briefs and step out of them. Cheers go up around us, but Catalina doesn't dare look down.

"There, now it's over." She tries taking her dress back, but I toss it to Oakley, "Come on, give it back!"

"What's wrong, Lina? Are you afraid?" I step into her, ensuring my junk rubs against her front and her breath hitches. I glance down and stare at her breasts, now pressed against my chest, "I'm going to step away, and I want you to look at me. You need to see what you should be proud of. You're the first person to ever beat me at this game."

"Everybody, leave now!" Oakley calls out in his cold voice that makes everyone jump and disperse.

"I'm not going anywhere!" Catalina's little friend steps up stubbornly.

I don't spare her a glance, but I do cock my brow at my Lovely Lina, "It's okay, Dani. I'll be up at the house in a few minutes. They won't dare do anything with witnesses knowing they are the last ones out here with me."

She's good, and intelligent, which makes me smirk, "Leave us, Dani. I will make sure she makes it back to the house in one piece."

When the friend finally scurries away, I take a step back and wait for Catalina to follow orders. She's a firecracker, this one is, refusing to look down at my hardening cock. With a jerk of my head, Oakley and Fynn are on each side of her, forcing her to her knees.

"What are you doing? Let go of me!" she says heatedly.

"This would have been avoided had you listened like a good girl," I inform her and step forward again, "Do you see it now, Lovely Lina? Do you see what you have caused? How do you propose I take care of this?"

"Why the fuck are you asking me? There are plenty of females here," she spits.

"True, but you are the one that caused it, and I think it's only fair that you are the one to take care of it." My grin shows my thoughts' wickedness as I step a little closer to my Lovely Little Lina.

FOUR

Catalina

I won't lie; my palms sweat when I see his ball make it into the same cup. It's not, because I have to lose my dress. No, I have no issues with that, but I am nervous only because the Lords will see me in nothing but my bra and thong. I'm sure they see plenty of sexy naked girls. What will they think about my body?

Giving myself a little pep talk, I straighten up and then pull my dress over my head and hand it to Dani to hold onto. With a few extra unwanted pounds, it gives me the right curves, or so I thought. Now, I'm second-guessing myself, especially after seeing Jett's very fit physique.

I thank the good Lord that I win the next round, and Jett loses the rest. I don't want to stand around to see it, though, because I'm not sure how I will react after lusting over the three Lords since I saw them outside my window. Jett, however, has other plans as he stops me from putting my dress back on. In fact, he snatches it from my hands and tosses it to Oakley.

How I went from winning the game against one of the Lords of Sin to being held on my knees by two of them while Jett makes me look at his cock, I'm not so sure. I shiver at what he's insinuating that I need to do, but he's fucking crazy if he thinks I will suck his cock right here. You better believe that all the partygoers are staring out the windows to see what they will make me do.

I try struggling, but Oakley and Fynn only grip my arms harder, "This would have been avoided had you listened like a good girl. Do you see it now, Lovely Lina? Do you see what you have caused? How do you propose I take care of this?" He grins and steps closer as he holds onto his hard cock.

"Why the fuck are you asking me? There are plenty of females here." I practically spit my words out, acting like I'm disgusted, but really, I wish we were alone, because I would suck the shit out of his glorious cock. The girth of it alone is frightening, but I know I would manage.

"True, but you are the one that caused it, and I think it's only fair that you are the one to take care of it." His wicked grin tells me he's seriously going to shove himself in my mouth, but I close my lips and turn my head.

"Open that mouth, Kitty Cat; Jett's got some nice warm cream for you," Oakley tries turning my head back forward, but Jett stays him.

"It's all good, Oak, as long as I can fuck something." Jett states, and that's when I feel him push his cock into my cleavage, "Damn, Lovely Lina has got some nice tits for fucking.

I whimper, not from being assaulted, but because my core throbs from this treatment from them, and there isn't anything I can do about it. That's not the truth. I could, but I'm not giving in that easily.

"Oh, you like that do you, Lovely..." Jett's words are cut off by sirens blaring and red and blue lights flashing in front of the houses.

"Shit, let's go," Fynn says, "The last thing we need is our dads being up our asses for this!"

"One fucking minute... I'm almost there." Jett states, and I begin to struggle more.

I can yell if I want to, but I find myself being manhandled and titty fucked as the cops start charging in, hotter than hell. He's leaning over my head; the scent of his cologne is lulling me into hypnosis as he thrusts between my breasts.

"Oh yeah, here it comes. Hold her still so I can get all of it between these tits and down her belly." I can hear Jett talk to his friends, but I no longer listen. "Fuck!" He begins to jerk, and that's when I feel it, sticky warmth spurting on my belly and into my cleavage, "That's right, I'm marking you, and now you're mine, Lovely Lina."

When he's done, Oakley and Fynn quickly help me into my dress and sit me in one of the chairs. Jett yanks my head back and then dips his head; the feel of his tongue licking me all the way up my cheek is a bit disgusting, but it's Jett, so I don't mind so much.

"Until next time, Lovely Lina." He lets go, and all three are gone in the blink of an eye.

"What the fuck, Cat?" Dani comes running over, "We have to go before the cops haul us away!"

I'm finally able to come out of my stupor and stand up, but I let Dani hold my hand as she pulls me along behind her through all the backyards until we get to a few houses down from our Sorority. When she looks over at me, she makes a face.

"What the fuck is that?" she points to my chest.

"I look down to see that Jett's jizz has already started drying, "It's Jett's fucking cum, is what it is," I growl.

Dani's eyes widen, "Holy shit, did you guys fuck?"

"What? No! Fucking Oakley and Fynn held me down while Jett titty fucked me. Just because he had gotten a hard-on, he said that I needed to be the one to take care of it. Since I wouldn't blow him, he fucked my tits."

"Do we need to go to the cops and file a report?" My friend asks, concerned, but I wave her off.

"Of course not! The only thing that truly upset me is that I couldn't give him that blowjob, because we were in public, and now, I'm hornier than fuck and will have to take care of myself tonight!"

"Okay, that's TMI, Cat." She chuckles.

"Oh please, bitch, you've told me worse!" I then wrap my arm around her shoulders as we head back to the Sorority House.

It's been about two weeks since I've had any contact with the Sinners. I've seen them around, and all they do is smirk and make obscene gestures at me, so I'm surprised when I run into Fynn as I'm leaving the library this evening. I can't really say that I ran into him; it's more like him pulling me into the men's restroom, which smells like a combination of weed and urine.

"Fancy meeting you here, Little Saint." He pushes me against the wall and locks the door.

"Oh, is it? Something tells me that you don't really go to the library, so I can only assume that you are stalking me." I can't let him see me tremble at his touch, so I switch to bitch mode.

"Ah, you've got me there, but you didn't consider that there are meeting rooms in this building as well. My father is on the board, and they just happened to have met a little while ago, so I was here talking with him." He brushes my hair over my shoulder, "I usually like redheads, but I think I can make an exception for you, Little Saint."

"An exception for what?" I ask with a bit of attitude.

His mouth kicks up into a half grin, "What do you think? Tell me, Little Saint, did you shower right away after Jett blew his load between these gorgeous tits, or did you sleep with his dried cum between them?" He tries to pull my collar out with his finger, but I slap his hand away.

"Wouldn't you like to know?" I glare at his handsome face, but really, I yearn for him to grab me and crush his lips against mine.

"I just want to know so when it's time to give you mine, I know where it will be most effective." His salacious grin sends tingles right to my core.

I shove at him, but he doesn't budge, "You said it yourself; blondes aren't your thing, so why don't you leave me the fuck alone."

He chuckles, "You see, Little Saint, you have captured the eye of the Lords of Sin, and we do everything together. Even whores, and it's already been decided that you, Catalina Scott, will be our next one."

I gasp, "I'm no one's whore!"

His wicked grin shows through again, "Not yet you're not, but soon, Little Saint," he leans in close to my ear and rubs himself against me, "Really fucking soon!"

There's a sting on my earlobe as he bites it but then steps away. He winks at me before opening the door and leaving me standing here in the men's restroom, trying to figure out what the fuck just happened. More importantly, how the hell am I going to be able to stay away from the Lords after learning all of this?

FIVE

Fynn

God, I can still remember the metallic taste of her blood in my mouth. My little nip to the Saint's ear wasn't supposed to draw blood, but it did, and now, I can't get the taste of it off my mind. I'm like a fucking vampire or something. Catalina Scott has had some kind of hold on the three of us Lords ever since we saw her peeking through the curtains of her Sorority house. Now, with the taste of her blood in my senses, it seems worse; I must have her soon.

I walk into the Frat house after meeting my father, listening to him bitch at me once again. I was already in need of a good stress reliever, so when I see that Jett already has one of the groupies on his lap in a reverse cowgirl, I know exactly what I need to do. Oakley is sitting in the armchair with my choice of smoke as he watches some shit show on the big screen.

I take the roach, pinching it between my two fingers, and take a few hits before handing it back, "I just ran into our favorite Little Saint. God, I can't wait to tap that shit!"

"Yeah, well, it will be a little longer, so find someone to occupy your time for now." Oakley grins, "That's what Jett's doing."

"Hey!"

The one that Jett has his cock balls deep inside takes offense, "Awe, what the fuck are you complaining about? You're getting what you want, aren't you?" I pull myself out of my jeans, and the bitch licks her lips, "See, I could just be coming back from fucking another slut, and you would still be jonesing for this cock."

I take hold of each side of the little whore's head and direct her mouth onto my throbbing cock. I don't remember this one's name, and I'm not even sure if I've fucked her before, but she does a well enough job taking my girth deep. I tilt my head back and picture a blonde bombshell taking me instead of the bleach bottle blonde who is too willing to please any of the Sinners.

"What was our Lovely Lina doing when you ran into her?" Jett asks as he pounds into the slut from underneath.

Smirking, I say, "She was coming out of the library."

"Oh, gorgeous and smart? Now I really can't wait to stick her with this mighty sword of mine." My friend states with a wicked grin.

I pull out of the mouth I'm in and order her to open it nice and wide. I spit in it for the hell of it, showing her that we own her at the moment before thrusting back into it. I don't stop this time until I start to come, but I don't let her swallow it. I'm a bastard, so instead, I pull out and finish jacking off against her chest, painting her with my seed.

When I'm done, I step back and look at my handiwork, "Sluts don't deserve my cum," I tell her as I tuck myself away and let Jett finish his fuck.

I head to the third floor of the house where the three of us Lords share and go to my room. I throw myself on the bed and close my eyes. Now that I've fucked away my stress and had a few hits to clear my head, I can finally think about the chat that I had with my dad.

My father and Jett's father are on the board, whereas Oakley's father is the CEO. Hell, Catalina's father is the Provost, so I feel as though Little Saint is meant to be ours. That is for another discussion, though. I can't let her gorgeous blue eyes distract me from this.

I remember how my father looked at me when he said, "Watch your back, son. Someone is stirring some shit up, and until we figure out who it is, I want you and your friends to just watch your backs."

Yeah, it's all cryptic and shit, but he refused to tell me more about it. I should probably talk to the guys, but right now, I'm too relaxed to do anything but lay here. Unfortunately, the banging on my door is not affording me that luxury now.

"It better be fucking good!" I call out, letting whoever is on the other side know they can enter at their own risk.

Oak and Jett come through the door and take up their usual spots on the couch and chair I have in my room. Fuck, they both look like they want to have a serious conversation about something, so I roll my eyes and then roll off my bed. I can't deal with serious shit unless I'm in the right headspace.

Going to my dresser, I pull out my stash and light up before returning to my bed. Neither friend say anything until I've taken at least two hits of the joint. Once I feel I'm good to go, I offer some to the others, but they decline the offer.

"We need to devise a plan to get Kitty Cat into our clutches." Oakley starts the discussion.

I shrug, "It shouldn't be hard. Catalina is like every other bitch in heat here at Helshire; she wants in our pants."

"Maybe, but I really don't think she's like the others," Jett is the one to speak up this time, "She's got attitude, and she's got guts, that's for sure, and I don't think she will roll over and spread them like a good little slut."

"You don't think she's a virgin, do you?" I quiver at the thought. I fucking hate virgins; they don't know how to please you, and then they get way too clingy for my liking. Like I owe them for opening their legs for me and letting me fuck them... it's bullshit.

"Oh, hell no!" Jett laughs, "I'm pretty sure she will be a pro at sucking cock, and I'll put money down that she's had plenty of dick."

"I'm with Jett on this one," Oakley states, "I think Kitty Cat is going to be a wild cat once we let her have her way." He smirks.

I scoff, "Since when do you let any pussy have their way?"

Oak shrugs, "There's a first time for everything, isn't there?"

"Dude, the day I see you let a pussy take over in the bedroom is the day that I will kiss someone on the mouth," I tell my friend.

There is no way he can do it, just like there is no way these lips will touch any lips unless it's pussy lips.

"You're on, bro!"

The room goes quiet as we sit and contemplate, most likely about the blonde bombshell posing as a Saint. Thinking about the Little Saint reminds me of the meeting with my dad again. Sitting up straight, I stare at my two friends.

"My dad warned me about someone stirring up shit, but he wouldn't say more. He just told me the three of us should watch our backs."

"What the fuck?" Oakley is also now at full attention, "How is someone stirring up shit, and we don't know about it?"

"I don't know, dude, but my dad seemed a bit spooked by this one. Maybe we should do some digging."

"Actually, my dad wanted me to stop by as well, because he wanted to talk to me, but I figured he was going to lecture me, so I made up an excuse," Jett states, "I wonder if he was going to tell me the same thing."

I just chuckle, "Nah, you probably had it right the first time and are in trouble for something."

"No, fucking doubt," Jett grins.

"Oh, the invites are out for the Toga party in two weeks," Oakley informs me.

Every year the Sinners put on this big bash, mainly, because we "sacrifice" a virgin, and who better than to throw this type of party than the Sinners themselves? Of course, it's never an actual virgin that gets sacrificed because virgins at Helshire University are pretty much non-existent.

"So, who's the lucky slut getting sacrificed?" I take another hit, hold it, and let the smoke cloud filter through the air.

"Well, I have someone in mind, but she doesn't know it yet." My best friend's wicked smile tells me exactly who it is.

"Sweet! Two weeks will be plenty of time to have her on board." I snicker as I picture our Little Saint being sacrificed at the Toga party, "I wonder, though, will she go through with the sacrifice once she knows what it entails?"

"She won't have a fucking choice," Jett smirks as he adjusts himself at the thought.

"Well, this ought to be interesting. Catalina Scott is a little hellcat, and I can't see her playing the part of the sacrificial virgin." I snub out the roach I now have and place it in the ashtray by my bed, "A lot of sweet talking is going to be needed, and I'm sorry, dude, but you ain't got an ounce of sweetness in you...none of us do."

"Fuck you!" Oak picks up one of my shoes and whips it at me, "I can be fucking sweet. I've taken an acting class before; I've got this."

I roll my eyes and look over at Jett. As soon as our eyes meet, we burst out laughing, which only pisses Oakley off more. Just as he's about to get up and come at me, a knock on the door gets our attention.

"What the fuck do you want?" I call out.

The door opens, and my favorite redhead gets pushed inside. She stumbles forward, landing on her knees, because of the fuck-me heels she's wearing. She looks like a deer in headlights as she stares up at the three of us.

"Ah, your fuck-a-thon is tonight, isn't it?" Jett snickers as he continues staring at Lara.

Lara is a redheaded beauty that not only knows how to fuck and suck cock really well, but she's a freak and is game for anything. She's the only female whose name I can remember, but that's only because we have a standing fuck session each week.

"Yes, Lara is right on time. Boys, you will have to excuse us unless, of course, you want to join." I grin wickedly at the redheaded slut because I've never shared her with anyone before.

Oakley licks his lips, "Hell, I'm game."

"Thanks for the invite, but I'm all fucked out." Jett gets up and helps Lara to her feet, "Have fun, boys." He slaps my little fuck slut's ass, sending her forward onto Oakley's lap.

I grin and wave Jett off, "Oh, we definitely will..."

SIX

Catalina

"Dad, I'm going to be late for class!" I sigh as my father makes me sit in front of his desk.

"I'll make sure your professor knows you were with me; you're fine." My dad says, a bit annoyed.

My father and I have always had a good relationship, well, at least until my Senior year in high school when I started getting into trouble. It's not like I was a delinquent or anything; it was more like staying out past my curfew, sometimes drinking, messing with boys, you know, typical teenager stuff. I think he thought that by having me come here, he would be able to keep an eye on me better, but I've barely seen him since I've been here.

"So, what did you call me in here for?" I ask, frustrated that he's just staring at me but not saying anything.

"How have you been, Catty?" He asks, using the nickname I hate.

"Please don't call me that, Dad; not here anyway." I practically beg him, and when he holds his hands up in defeat, I continue, "I've been good. I'm doing well in my classes, and I've become good friends with Dani, the other Saint's Legacy."

My father actually makes a face, "How's that going? Living at the Sorority, I mean. You don't have to stay there, you know."

I roll my eyes, "Mom would freak if I quit the Saint's Sorority. She's been waiting for me to attend college just for this." I chuckle.

"Your mother doesn't realize how much has changed since she was a Saint."

"What do you mean?" I ask.

"Well, for one, there was no rule or ban on the whole Saints and Sinners not associating," my father chuckles, "I think that came about because of a bad break up between the Sorority President and one of the members at the Sinner's Frat house."

"How do you know this? I know you're Provost, but I didn't think you really got into the Sororities and Fraternities." I grab a piece of candy from his dish and pop it into my mouth.

"Your mother never told you about when we started dating?" he asks, surprised.

"I shrug, "Just that you guys met here."

He smiles, "Well, Catty... I mean, Cat," he holds his hand up in apology, "I met your mother my Junior year here. I lived in the Sinner's Frat house, and in my Senior year, I was one of The Lords while your mother was the President of the Saint's Sorority."

My eyes bulge at hearing this, "Wow, my father, a Lord of Sin. That's pretty cool...so what happened?"

"What do you mean what happened?"

"When did you lose your coolness?" I smirk, and he laughs after he catches on.

"I'll have you know that I'm still pretty cool amongst my friends." He leans back in his chair and stares at me again, "Has anything else happened since starting here?"

My brow furrows, "Like what?"

"Oh, I don't know. Has anyone harassed you or bullied you?"

I find it weird that he's asking me this. Has he heard anything about the present Lords, or is he asking in general? Should I tell him about my run-in with Fynn Morin or just leave it be? I decide to do the latter, and I shake my head.

"Nothing out of the ordinary. Why?"

He hesitates and then leans forward and opens a drawer. Pulling out a white envelope, he tosses it to me, "I found this on the floor. Someone had slipped it under my door yesterday morning."

I open it up and read the note on a folded-up piece of paper. My eyes widen, "Why would someone write this and give it to you?"

"I haven't the faintest idea, Cat. I'm not worried about myself, but I am worried about you."

"Why are they threatening us? I don't understand...have you pissed someone off?" I reread the letter and can't believe my eyes.

Mr. Scott

I know what you did, and you will pay, but you're not the only one...
You have a daughter, don't you?
Is she safe?
Make things right or else...

Of course, it isn't signed; what bad person would sign their name to a threatening letter? This has to be some kind of joke. I've never known my father to hurt anyone intentionally; they must have the wrong person.

"They have it wrong then. If you haven't pissed anybody off, they must have the wrong person. You should take this to the police." I say and hand it back to him. I then grab my bag and stand up to leave.

"Catalina, do me a favor. Be careful, and if you are ever in need of help and can't get a hold of me, I want you to go to the Lords."

My eyes bug out for the second time since being in my father's office, "You want me to break the rules and talk to the Sinners?"

He waves his hand, "You will not be punished. That rule is the Sorority rule and can be overturned, but no. I don't want you talking to just any of the Sinners. I want you to search out Oakley Harris, Jett Pelletier, and Fynn Morin. They are the only ones that would be able to help you. They have connections that nobody else has."

"How do you know this, Dad?"

Does he know everything about the Lords? I'm sure he doesn't; otherwise, he wouldn't be telling me to go to them. Instead, he'd be telling me to run far, far away.

"I went to school with their fathers, Cat. We were Lords together, and now their sons are as well. I was the lucky one to have a beautiful daughter." He smiles, but it looks a bit sad.

I move around the desk and give him a hug, "I know, secretly, you have always wanted a son, but you have never made me feel unloved, Daddy." I always call him that when I'm being sappy because I know it makes him feel better and reminds him that I will always be his little girl.

"I love you, Catalina."

I kiss his cheek and pull away, "I love you too, but I have to go now. I will be careful, I promise."

I leave his office with so many questions running through my mind. What could my father possibly have done to make a person threaten him and his daughter? I'm so lost in thought that I don't see the person rushing into the same building I'm leaving.

I had taken the back stairs because they were closer to the building that houses my next class, and when I go to open the door to outside, it slams open from the other side, and I'm knocked back onto my ass.

"Oh shit, I'm sorry!" A male's voice echoes through the stairwell.

I look up at the guy, but I've never seen him before. He takes hold of my arm and lifts me as though I weigh nothing, "Damn, are you a football player or something?"

He chuckles, "I'm the best lineman this University has ever had!"

"Wow, strong and conceited, I see. You seem to be in a hurry, so don't let me stop you." I step to the side to let him pass.

"Well, aren't you a bit of a bitch." He sneers, apparently not liking my 'conceited' comment.

"It is my middle name," I grab the door handle, but the guy slams his hand above my head, not allowing me to open it.

"Seriously, what's your problem? I said I was sorry for knocking you over."

"I thought you were in a hurry. If not, that's cool, but I'm already late for my next class."

He stares at me for a few seconds longer and then pushes away, "Whatever."

"Nice meeting you, Lineman!" I call out as I hurry through the door.

I make it to class just ahead of the professor, who gives me a dissatisfied look as I hurry to my seat. I have this class with Dani, and she's looking at me strangely. I look her over, pull my laptop out, and start it up. This is one of my favorite classes because I can make shit up and not get docked points for my creativity. Creative Writing has been my favorite since day one, and I'm always on time for it.

"Why are you panting so hard, and is that sweat on your forehead?" My friend wrinkles her nose as she examines my forehead.

I tell her about my little run-in leaving my father's office, "I mean, he was a total douche about it. 'I'm the best lineman that this University has ever had!' Who says shit like that?" I ask Dani.

"It sounds like Chris," she states, "Big guy, blonde hair? He can barely walk right because he's built like a house?"

"Yep, pretty much." I chuckle.

"He is a douche; stay away from him. He thinks he's God's gift to women because he's got a full ride here. If you ask me, I think he's on steroids."

"Oh, I don't *think* he is, he is. You cannot be that big and not be on steroids!"

"Oh! I almost forgot," Dani reaches into her bag and pulls out what looks like an invitation, "I was stopped on my way here and handed two of these, and they specifically told me to give the other one to you."

Whatever it is, my friend is very excited. Pulling the card from the envelope, the words TOGA PARTY stand out. It looks like I've been invited to some big bash. When I look at the location, my heart stops momentarily. I've been personally invited to the Sinner's Frat house for this party.

I look at my friend, "Shit! Where the fuck do you get a Toga costume?"

Dani chuckles, "All you need is a white bed sheet, silly!"

I stare at the card in my hand with just a little excitement, but then a thought comes to mind. What is it they want from me? Whatever it is, it doesn't matter because this may be a good time to get in their good graces in case I ever need them. Either way, if a bedsheet is all I need to wear to this party, then it's going to be the sexiest fucking bedsheet that anyone has ever seen!

"No fair! I wanted the last slice! I skipped breakfast this morning because I had to wait for the shower." I glare playfully at my friend and roommate.

We both had time to head to the local pizza joint for our lunch break and split a medium pizza. The hog, a.k.a. Dani, ate the last slice of my share. I don't really need it, and I'm plenty full, but I love giving her shit every chance I get.

"Didn't you say you were going to start a diet soon? I'm only being a good friend and helping you out." Dani winks as she pops the last bite to the last slice into her mouth.

"Are you calling me overweight?" I ask jokingly.

"Nope, just reminding you of what you told me only two days ago when we were trying to figure out a Toga style for you."

"Ugh, don't remind me!" I groan.

I really want to look as sexy as possible, but how does one look sexy in a bedsheet? I'm not freaking Susie Homemaker, and the only way to make my Toga sexy is by sewing certain areas. I need to be careful because if Felicia finds out I'm trying to make a Toga, she will immediately know what it's for, so I can't ask any of my sorority sisters, not that I really know any of them anyway.

"Oh!" Dani jumps in her seat excitedly, "The costume shop in town is now open! I forgot that it would be opening with Halloween coming up. We can stop after classes today and see if they have anything!"

"Thank God because everything we tried was horrible!" I don't know why it's such a big deal, but making a great impression at this party is my number one priority.

"Shit! Look at the time...we are going to be late for our next class!" Dani slides out of the booth as I look at the time on my phone.

"Fuck, I'm already late! How did this happen?" Throwing money down on the table, we take off in a hurry and run all the way back to campus, which is two blocks away.

I pant as I bend and place my hands on my knees while trying to catch my breath before entering the classroom. When I reach for the door handle, I notice the note on the door saying that class is canceled for today. I let out a long sigh and lean against the wall for a few minutes.

I should use this time to study before my next class, but instead of going to the library, I just duck into my American Lit classroom since nobody is here. I've just pulled out my laptop when I hear a noise behind me. Looking over my shoulder, I almost fall out of my chair when I see someone sitting right behind me. Not just anybody but Oakley, the Greek God himself.

"You fucking scared me, sheesh!" I have my hand over my chest for emphasis.

"My bad," his smirk makes my panties wet, and I have to squeeze my thighs together, "So, Kitty Cat, what are you doing in here, all by your lonesome?"

"I figured I'd get some studying done since my class was canceled; what's it to you?"

He shrugs, "I always make it my business to know everything."

"I see. Well, if you will excuse me, I want to get some study time in before my next class." I turn and give the Lord my back. I'm not trying to be a bitch, but I'm so fucking nervous; it's how I get whenever I'm around Oakley, or any of the Lords, for that matter.

"Did you get your invite to our party?" He asks; only now, he's right behind me, and I can feel his breath on my neck.

"Uh, yeah, I did." I turn my head to the side, just a hair, and then forward again when I see he's right there.

"Are you coming?"

I have to clear my throat before I answer him, and I don't want him to think I'm excited to be going, so I try to play it cool, "I have a previous engagement that night, but I'll try to make an appearance."

He caresses my shoulder and moves my hair back, "Try hard Kitty Cat. We want you as our special guest."

"Wait, what? What do you mean by a special guest? You won't have blood poured on me from overhead, will you?" I reference the movie Carrie, and all he does is chuckle.

"No, no blood or anything like that." Suddenly his hand comes around and wraps itself around my neck. Adding a little pressure, his mouth is now against my ear, "Say you will come, Kitty Cat. I won't take no for an answer."

My breathing is shallow the longer he holds my throat, but not in a bad way, "I will do my best, Oakley."

"That's not good enough, Kitty Cat..." I feel his mouth dragging across my skin, and I almost moan, "I expect to see you there...no excuses." He turns my head toward him, and I think he's going to kiss me, but he doesn't, "I bet you're fucking wet between those luscious thighs, aren't you?"

"W-What?" I stammer, his words bringing me back to reality.

"Come to the party, and I'll make you just as wet, only I'll take care of that achy need inside, just like the one you have right now, Kitty Cat."

"You wish!" I stare into his dark blue eyes, ones that remind me of a stormy sea.

He grins, "No, Kitty Cat...I know." Letting go of me abruptly, there is no sign of him at all when I look back to where he came from. It's almost as though I imagined him being here. Only, I can still smell his musky cologne, so I know I hadn't imagined it all.

"Cat, come on!" Dani whines outside the dressing room door as I try on at least eight styles of Toga costumes. I have three different styles picked out, and I'm now trying those three back on to make a final choice, "One of those costumes has got to work for you!"

"Keep your panties on, girl! I'm down to my final choices, and I'll show you each one."

"Ugh, hold that thought. My mom's calling me; be right back." My roommate calls out, so I take my time.

I've just put on my first of the final three when I hear rustling, "I like this one, but it may be too revealing in the front..."

I'm suddenly pushed against the wall and held there as a male voice, disguised, speaks low in my ear, "Tell Daddy that he better make things right, or else you will see the same fate as she did!"

"What? I think you have the wrong person! Leave us alone, or the cops will get involved!" I can barely speak, with my face shoved against the wall.

"You get the cops involved, and it's over for all four of them. Now, be a good girl, Catalina, and get your father to do the right thing!" He knocks my head into the wall and takes off.

"Son of a bitch!" I grab my head and run out of the dressing room, but I don't see anything unusual.

"What's wrong with you?" Dani comes up to my side, making me jump.

"Jesus, Dani!"

"Sorry! What did you do to your head?" Her eyes widen as she examines the goose egg I now sport by my temple.

"Did you see anybody run out? A man, perhaps?" I ask her as I go back to the dressing room.

"No, I was arguing with my mom because she wants me to come home the weekend of the Toga party. What guy are you talking about, Cat?"

"The fucking guy that came into my dressing room and threatened me, that's what guy!" I rip the curtain closed and change back into my street clothes.

Grabbing the last three choices, I bring them to the counter and buy all three; I'll decide which one later. My adrenaline is in overdrive right now, and my heart feels like it may pump right out of my chest. After the saleswoman hands me my receipt, I grab the bag and beeline straight for the door.

"Wait up, Cat! What about my costume?" Dani hurries to my side.

"You can stay and keep looking, or you can use one of the two I don't use, but I need to get back," I tell my roommate.

"You're scaring me, Cat!"

I stop short and turn to my friend, "I'm scaring you?" I point to my head, "You didn't just get your fucking head shoved into a wall and threatened! No, you were on the phone somewhere talking to your mommy."

Dani gasps, "That's not fair, Cat. How was I supposed to know that you would get attacked."

I take a few deep breaths, "You're right; I'm sorry. I'm just so jacked up right now; I need to get home and think."

"What do you need to think about? You should be calling the police! Did you get a look at the guy at all?"

"No," I look around at the people passing by, "I thought it was you coming in, and I started talking, and then bam, he shoves me into the wall and held me there by my head while he threatened me."

"Well, what did he threaten you for? Did he want something? Was he trying to mug you?"

I start walking as I begin telling Dani about the note that my father received, "He told me to watch myself and that if I needed help and he wasn't around, I'm to go to the Lords."

"He said what?" my friend exclaims.

"I know, right?" I chuckle, "He must not know how the Lords really are."

"Do what you want, but I think going to the Sinners may be a mistake." Dani's opinion is always welcome, and she's usually right, but I think she's wrong this time.

"No, not the Sinners. My father was specific, I'm to go to the Lords, and them alone."

"Well, like I said, I think it would be a mistake, but hey, you do you. I'm here for you either way."

I smile at my friend and then slip my arm through hers, "I'm so glad that they put the two of us together."

"Yeah, me too!" My roommate returns my smile with one of her own.

SEVEN

Oakley

My lips taste like vanilla now that they have been against her soft skin. I had snuck in through the back door when I saw my Kitty Cat slipping into the American Lit class after catching her breath. I'm not sure what she was running from, but you can be sure that I will find out soon enough.

I needed to know if she was accepting our invitation. First and foremost, I need to make sure she is coming to the party. My next step is convincing my Kitty Cat to be our sacrifice. Coming up with different ideas is the easy part. It's going to be the approach that is going to be the tricky part. These are my thoughts on the way home after leaving the school.

Walking into the frat house, I find a small party happening. It's nothing new here; it's what the Sinners do, except on Sundays when we give our time and volunteer within the town. Everybody knows that Sunday is a holy day, and it's no different for us Sinners. We don't go to church or any kind of shit like that, so we volunteer, and that is how we make up for the hell we let loose throughout the week.

"Yo, yo, yo, there he is! Oakley, my man!" I glance over and see Sean, a Sophomore carrying two solo cups, holding one out for me to take, "Where have you been, man? The party started two hours ago!"

I shrug, "I had shit I had to take care of," I look around the room, "Where are Fynn and Jett?"

Sean grins, "If you have to ask, are you really their best friend?" He slaps my shoulder and winks, "They went up…" He points to the ceiling.

I roll my eyes and point to him, "You are in charge of this party. If shit happens, it's on you!"

"Gotcha, bro. Just go…join the party with your boys; I've got this."

I take the stairs two at a time until I get to the door leading to our floor, and I have to unlock it before going up. This door always stays locked during parties; we don't trust anyone. We had some shit stolen once, and let me just say, those two fuck faces won't be stealing anything anytime soon.

"Where is Oakley? I was promised all three Lords." I hear a pouty female voice before being cut off, coming from Jett's room, so I head that way.

I lean against the door frame and watch my friends do their typical thing. There are always bitches wanting to take a ride with the Lords when we have these parties, but only a few select are allowed. We never do the same slut twice during our foursomes, so we make sure that we make it memorable for them.

The brunette is being spit roasted at the moment by my two best friends, and the way they are taking her, making her moan the way she is, has my cock throbbing already. Even though I have a particular blonde on my mind, I won't let it ruin my fun.

"Is there room for one more?" I grin and pull my shirt over my head.

"There's the man!" Fynn fist bumps me as he thrusts into the girl from behind, "See, I told you he'd be here." He slaps the slut's ass and then pulls out.

Jett pulls out of her mouth and gives her a little shove, "Get the fuck on the bed."

"Pick your poison, Oak," Fynn says, but Jett already knows and tosses me the bottle of lube and then a condom.

Catching each in one hand, I undo my pants and slide them down. The brunette's eyes widen when she sees my girth, "Y-You're fucking my ass?"

I grin wickedly, "You better believe it." I walk over to the bed and start lubing my cock up as Jett lies on his back and rolls a condom on.

"Maybe one of the other ones can take my ass instead." She's nervous, but they all are at first.

"It's either this way, or you can get the fuck out. There are others that are dying to take my cock up their ass." I stop stroking and just stare at the girl.

"O-Okay, just be gentle, please." Her request makes me laugh.

"Have you ever done anal?" I ask.

"Yes, a few times."

"Well, quit your bitching then and get that cunt on Jett."

I wait until she climbs up and impales herself on my friend before kneeling behind her and pushing her down against Jett, so I can work myself in. I spit down onto her pucker and smear it all over before adding a little more lube. Spreading her ass cheeks, I slowly work it in until my head is in.

"Oh, God... it's too much!" she moans, and I chuckle.

"It's just the tip. Just keep breathing, and you will be fine." I start moving, and once she really starts making noises, Fynn shoves his cock into her mouth.

I'm not one to hurt a girl anally, so I take my time, but once I'm in and she adjusts, it's balls to the wall, and tonight is no different. We take turns fucking each of the slut's holes, and then she begs for more. They always do, and so Fynn and Jett, the sick fucks that they are, really DP her, fucking her cunt simultaneously. I shove my cock into her mouth because she's getting too loud.

Finally, when we are truly all fucked out, me and my boys start to get dressed. There is a knock on the door, and since I at least have my pants on, I open it. The sight before me makes my cock grow all over again, especially when their eyes wander over my naked chest, all the way down to my jeans, which are still open, showing my treasure trail, and then even lower, at the ever-growing bulge just below.

"Well, well, well, I never expected to see you here, Kitty Cat." I nod at Brett, "Why don't you show this other one back downstairs."

"Will do." Jett walks the still-naked brunette to the door and throws her clothes at Brett.

"Make sure you dress her before you take her down this time." He smirks.

Brett is usually the one to bring the girls to us, and he made a mistake one time of not letting her dress before leaving our floor. He spent the next week walking around the house naked. Needless to say, he's learned his lesson. We don't disrespect women that way. They come to us, and everything is all consensual. They know that we use derogatory names for them, and they still come here, but I will not make someone leave us naked and be made to walk in front of others, not unless she deserves it, that is.

My eyes are on Catalina as she takes in the scene before her. Fynn and Jett are only in their boxers, but it's the girl who holds my Kitty Cat's interest, "Are you interested in a little girl-on-girl action?"

Catalina whips her head back to me, "You're disgusting! Did you guys just tag team that girl?"

Jett laughs behind me, "We don't tag team, Lovely Lina. We fucked her all at the same time."

I hear her intake of breath, and then she spins around, "This was a mistake coming here; Dani was so right."

"Hold up, who the fuck is Danny, and what was he right about?" I'm pissed that our girl is talking about some other guy. She may not know that she's ours yet, but she will.

"Dani is my roommate, she was at the party next door with me, in case you have forgotten, and she said it would be a mistake coming to you three for help." My Kitty Cat crosses her arms and glares at us, "Is this what you three do? Fuck women as a group?"

"Are you wanting to find out?" Fynn grins, "We usually only do one foursome a party, but I think we can fit you in."

There's that beautiful flush that I saw earlier. I smirk as I hook my thumbs into the waist of my undone jeans, causing them to go even lower. The deep V leading down under is very prominent, especially after the workout I just had.

"How about you come in and tell us what kind of help you're looking for, Kitty Cat?"

"No, I'm good right here." She's trying hard not to look down.

I shrug, "Fine, I guess we can't help then." I start to shut the door, but her hand slams into it, stopping it from closing.

"Fine, I'll come in, but don't you dare get any ideas!" She shoves the door open and walks right past me.

My Kitty Cat definitely has a bit of hellcat in her too. I love her little attitude, and I'm dying to put her in her place. Being the dick I am, I leave my pants open the whole time and make sure I stand right in front of her as she sits in the only chair in the room.

"So, Little Saint, are you going to tell us what you need help with?" Fynn asks.

"Oh, but most importantly, what are you going to do for us if we help you?" Jett gives our girl a salacious smile.

Catalina Scott isn't a pushover like the others and takes her time to answer the last question as her gaze sweeps over the three of us. I'm sure we make an intimidating trio, even if we are half-dressed. It's not a look of fear on her face, though. It's the look that we get from every woman who wants to fuck us, and she's now just given me the best idea on how to make her ours.

Placing my hands on each of the arms of the chair, I lean down, getting really close to her, and say, "So, what's it going to be, Kitty Cat?"

EIGHT

💀

Catalina

"Are you sure about this Cat?" Dani asks as we stand outside the Sinner's Fraternity house, staring at the big mansion.

It's the middle of the week, and there's a party going on inside. Not like the weekend parties, but there's still loud music and yelling coming through the open windows. The Sinner's Frat house is a big, stone three-story mansion with two peaks up top where there is a light on in one of the windows. Three archways showcase an outside porch where the front door is, and I head in that direction.

"You can wait here if you don't want to come in; it's fine," I tell my roommate.

"Um, excuse me, if there are hot guys in there, I'm going in!" She chuckles, "I was talking about you asking for help."

"I don't have much choice, Dani. My father would freak out if I told him I was attacked. No, this way is better."

I say this, but I'm nervous as fuck. What if they turn me down? Will they ask for something in return? None of them need money, so what would they want? 'Cat, do you really need to ask?' I ask myself. I can do this. So, what if they want a particular payment, it's not like I'm a virgin, and all three are hotter than fuck. I'm just not going to make it easy for them.

I take a deep breath and press the doorbell. When nobody comes to the door, I lift my hand to push it again, but the door swings open, "Well, look what we have here! What are a couple of Saints like you doing in our neighborhood? Are you looking to commit a sin?" The guy has really short red hair and piercing blue eyes.

"I'm actually looking for the Lords," I tell him, and he steps to the side, laughing.

"You and every other female here! I'm Sean..." He points to the kitchen, "Keg is in there." He eyes Dani as he talks, licking his lips when he's done.

"Yeah, nice to meet you, Sean, but I'm not here to drink. I need to talk to Oakley. Can you tell him Catalina Scott is here?" I'm annoyed that this guy is openly ogling my friend, but Dani doesn't seem to mind as she smiles back at him.

"Oh shit! You're Catalina? Here," he cups his mouth, "Hey Brett, get your ass over here!"

I turn to see another guy, with brown hair this time, coming our way, "Yo, what's up?" He looks back and forth between Dani and me.

"They need to see the Lords," Sean tells his Frat brother.

"But they are booked already..."

"Oh, Oak is going to want to see Catalina," Sean says my name carefully as though they know something I don't.

"Ah, gotcha!" this Brett guy eyes me up and down, "So you are Catalina, huh? Nice!" He turns towards the stairs, "Follow me, and I will take you to the Lords."

"Um, I think I will wait down here, Cat," Dani tells me as she follows behind Sean, walking deeper into the house.

I only nod and then quickly follow Brett up the stairs. He leads me down a long hallway to another door when we get to the second floor. Opening it up, I see it's another flight of stairs, and I'm hesitant to go up with this guy I've never met before.

I stare at the stairs and then at him because he's waiting for me to go first, "What the fuck is up there? Is that where you kill your victims and store the bodies until you can get rid of them?"

He chuckles, "That's not the stench of dead bodies, honey. You're smelling all different types of pussy that have come from up there," he laughs, "This is where the Lords live...on the third floor."

"God, do you have to be so vulgar?" I screw my face up at his use of words.

"Just stating the facts, honey," he sweeps his arm forward, "After you."

I cross my arms, "Nah, I think I'll let you go up first."

Brett stares at me weirdly and then shrugs, "Whatever, man."

I follow him up the stairs, and then we stop outside another door. There are noises on the other side of it, and I begin to get nervous once again. When Brett knocks on the door, it rattles under his fist, and I swear the whole door will bust down.

The door opens, and there stands the Greek God himself, Oakley. Only I'm looking at more than I bargained for because he's standing there with no shirt. His shoulders are broad and powerful, but his well-defined and immaculately sculpted chest and abs make my mouth water.

There's a sheen to his skin, like sweat glistening from a workout, but then my eyes roam lower, and I notice that he isn't wearing workout bottoms. Oh no, he's got jeans on, and they are undone, showing off the deep V and the patch of trimmed hair leading into his pants where there is evidence of a very nice size package.

Butterflies fill my stomach, and a heat ignites deep in my core, and I forget why I'm even standing here, "Well, well, well, I never expected to see you here, Kitty Cat."

Oakley's greeting only turns me on more, but then I hear his next words to his Frat brother, and the spark fizzles out. There is a naked girl in the room with him, and he's asking Brett to see her out. Scratch that; a naked girl is in the room with all three of the Lords.

I simply have no words for what I'm seeing right now. I know I should look away, but I can't as my eyes follow the naked girl out of the room. She's pretty and petite, the opposite of me. I'm curvy at a size eight, but it's not a fatty type of voluptuous. She still looks better than I do.

"Are you interested in a little girl-on-girl action?"

Oakley's question has my gut twisting, and then it really hits me, "You're disgusting! Did you guys just tag team that girl?"

It's Jett that answers my question, and it's as I thought, all three had sex with that little thing, and by the size of all their junk, I'm surprised she didn't break. Images run through my head of what they would do to me if they agreed to help. I'm far from a prude, but come on, all three at once?

I turn around and mumble about Dani being right about coming here, but then Oakley stops me demanding to know what I'm talking about and who Dani is. He almost seems jealous. Now that I think about it, this could work to my advantage somehow. I take my defensive stance and cross my arms.

"Dani is my roommate, she was at the party next door with me in case you have forgotten, and she said it would be a mistake coming to you three for help." I make a disgusted face, "Is this what you three do? Fuck women as a group?"

Fynn finally opens his mouth, but he's only saying perverted stuff, and I try to ignore him, but I feel my face heat anyway when he says something about one foursome at a party and that they could fit me in. Oh, dear God, now my Greek God is showing off more of his goods as he tucks his thumbs into his waist. Is that the base of his penis? I try acting normal, but I feel that I'm failing miserably.

After arguing back and forth about me entering their sex cave, when Oakley threatens not to help, I let him win and push past him, warning them not to try anything. Finding the only chair in the room because God knows my ass ain't getting on that bed, I pick up a crumpled shirt and toss it aside before sitting.

As I sit, I just happen to notice the trash can overflowing, and there are used condoms lying right on top. The good thing is that they at least use protection; the bad thing is... that's a hell of a lot of used condoms.

"So, Little Saint, are you going to tell us what you need help with?" Fynn asks, but Jett comes right in with a question of his own and one that I was expecting.

"Oh, but most importantly, what are you going to do for us if we help you?" His smile makes me tingle, and my eyes sweep down his tattooed body. Like Oakley, Jett and Fynn have great chiseled abs and trim waists. Jett is a bit shorter than his two friends but still stands over me.

I don't know why I'm thinking of these guys like I am. I feel like a guy checking out a hot chick. Oh, my God, am I just like them? No, I would never agree to a foursome! I glance around the room, gauging all three half-naked Lords...would I?

I jump as soon as Oakley leans down close, "So, what's it going to be, Kitty Cat?"

Calming my rapidly beating heart before trying to answer isn't working so well, especially with Oakley so close. Licking my lips, I stare into his eyes, "That depends on how much you help me."

Pushing away, Oakley chuckles as he walks around to stand behind me. I keep my eyes on Jett and Fynn, who are wearing identical smirks, "You know, Kitty Cat, you came to us first, and on top of that, there are three of us, so the payments may get a little steep at times."

"Are you even going to be able to handle some of those payments?" Fynn adjusts himself right in front of me, and I know it's a hint as to what they will be asking me for.

I lift my chin, trying to show a little defiance, "I can pay for your services in full; however you want payment."

"There will be a contract, you know. We don't work without one." Oakley informs me, and I actually sigh in relief; I'm glad there will be a contract, "But first, we need a little incentive to even think about this partnership."

"What is this incentive?" I ask.

I'm proud of myself for keeping my shit together this whole time. Maybe I can handle the Lords of Sin on my own. They are a bunch of pervs. I've handled their kind all through high school; what's a little longer?

"How about you get on your knees, and I'll show you?"

Complete and utter shock is what I feel at this moment just after he speaks those words. I stumble to find a response and figure out how to handle this. I'm no virgin to giving head, but I don't just drop to my knees either.

"I'm not sure what kind of woman you think I am, but I'm not one of your little groupie sluts." I cross my arms and lean back in the chair more.

I'm not going to beg these God-like assholes, but I need to figure out how to get them to be mature about this. Otherwise, I will have no choice but to go about it alone. I study each one briefly before my eyes finally stay on the one who propositioned me.

"I'm not saying anything of the sort, but you must know that everything comes at a price, Kitty Cat." He glances down at his opened jeans and tugs them just a little lower with his thumbs, "Are you going to sit there and tell me that you have never thought about how my cock would fit down your throat?"

I'm not about to admit anything to the Lords, least of all my sinful thoughts of all three of them. I lift my brow at him and then make it a point to glance down before rolling my eyes, "I came here for your help because my father told me that I could count on the three of you," I stand up, "What a fucking joke." I try to move, but Oakley pushes me back, causing me to lose my balance and fall back into the chair.

"Not so fast, Saint!"

I glare up at the one guy that could probably get me to do anything if he wasn't so cocky about it. I may not be a slut, but I'm a young woman with hormones, and these three are the hottest guys on campus. I sigh and then lean back once more, crossing not only my arms but also my legs. The throbbing that has begun in my nether regions is becoming too much.

"What the fuck more do you want, Oakley? I'm not sucking you off just for you to turn me down unless I suck your friends off too." Yeah, I'm onto his little game.

He gives me a knowing smirk; I fucking knew it, "You're definitely not like the rest, Kitty Cat," He leans back into me, only this time, he makes sure his package rubs against my knee, "That's why we are going to help you."

I'm afraid to tear my eyes away from his eyes because I know they will automatically look down, and I can now feel his full-blown member rubbing up and down on my knee. He's been doing it the whole time, and his jeans have worked their way down.

"Uncross your legs, Kitty Cat."

"What? No..."

"Do it, or I will do it for you," Oakley grins, "At least give me this..."

His voice has a pleading edge to it, and what can I say? I'm a sucker for these Sinners. So, very slowly, I uncross my legs, and he opens them just enough to push his shaft between my knees. I can't do it any longer, I look down, and now I wish I hadn't. He's thrusting himself, using my knees to jerk him off. It's the weirdest thing I've ever seen, and yet the hottest.

"Jett got to use those tits; it's only fair that I get to use something as well." He bites his lip and picks up the pace.

"Oh, my God..." It's all I can say in this situation.

I watch as Oakley Harris uses my knees to get himself off. I'm not thinking about the end result, like where he will shoot it off when the time comes. No, I'm just fascinated that he has the audacity to do something this perverse with someone he hardly knows.

"Admit it, Little Saint, you love watching him get off." Fynn's voice is close to my ear but doesn't faze me much.

"Are you feeling it yet, Lovely Lina?" Jett is in my other ear as his hand slides down my arm and then lower still, "Are you feeling the burn deep inside..." His hand stops just above my crotch.

I don't respond to either one as my heart pounds profusely. I'm too focused on their friend, not wanting to miss a thing. What is wrong with me? I should be running from these crude and cocky Sinners...but I can't.

"That's right, Kitty Cat; watch closely as I mark you as mine." Oakley groans, and then suddenly, it's there, shooting out all over my legs.

I can feel the warmth as it seeps through the fabric of my thin leggings. This is the second time I've sat here and let one of the Lords spew his shit all over my person. What the fuck is wrong with me?

"I-I have to go," I stutter a bit and try to get up, but I'm held down by Jett and Fynn.

"Not until you answer my friends, Kitty Cat," Oakley smirks as he tucks himself back into his pants, leaving the front undone like before.

"Excuse me? Answer what?" I wrack my brain, trying to remember what they were asking me, but I'm drawing a blank.

"I asked if you loved watching him get himself off." Fynn squats beside me so I can see his shit-eating grin.

"I'm not even going to dignify that with a response," I glare at the Lord, but he seems amused.

"What about my question, Lovely Lina? Did you feel the burn deep inside?" He slides his hand toward my crotch, and I slap it away this time.

"I plead the fifth," Being a smartass isn't going to help me with these Sinners, but it sure feels good.

"Well, since you won't answer, I guess there is only one other way that you can leave here," The grin on Oakley's face doesn't bode well for me, but I refuse to back down.

"I can sit here all night if I have to." I refuse to back down from these fuckers.

"Oh, sorry, Lovely Lina, I don't allow females to stay in my room unless they plan on putting out, and even then, I boot their ass out once I'm done with them," Jett runs his hand through my hair, "I could possibly make an exception for you, depending on what you have to offer." He bites his lower lip as his eyes sweep over me salaciously.

"You wish, Ink boy!" I say as I stare at all the tattoos littering his body. They are hot, to say the least, but again, I won't tell them what I think.

"Okay, that leaves us no choice," Oakley gazes down at me, "Are those your final answers, Kitty Cat?"

I recross my arms and raise an eyebrow at the Lord, challenging him, or daring him, however you want to look at it. My heart races when I see that grin again, and then he nods to his two friends. Suddenly, Fynn is holding me down while Jett stretches my mouth open. Oakley, the sick fuck he is, swipes his cum off my leggings and shoves his fingers into my mouth.

"Clean them, Kitty Cat."

I'm gagging because of how far he has them down my throat, but he orders me again when he pulls back a bit. I'm not planning on backing down, but just when I'm about to knee him in the balls, he gives me what I want as long as I do this one little thing.

"Clean my cum off, and I will draw up a contract. We will help you with whatever it is that you need help with all year long." He smiles as soon as I stop struggling.

Mustering everything I have, I figure that if I'm going to do this, I might as well make it look good, so I grab his hand and begin cleaning his fingers off in a very sensual way. Thrusting them in and out as I swirl my tongue, giving them a little show until I've licked every last finger clean.

"Jesus, fuck!"

"That a girl, Saint!"

His friends cheer me on as he stands there, gawking at my mouth, "Are we done now?"

He finally comes out of his stupor and backs up, "Yeah, you can go," He lets me stand up, and just as I get to the door, he calls out, "Oh, Kitty Cat, meet us in the library at three o'clock tomorrow. I will have the contract for you to sign."

"Fine, whatever." I don't stay another second.

Hurrying down the stairs, I try to open the door, but it's locked. Keys jangle behind me, and I see Fynn coming down the steps, "There's no getting away without these," He grins as he unlocks the door for me, "See you tomorrow, Little Saint."

I ignore him and quickly reach the first floor, where I find Dani doing a keg stand, "Really? I can't leave you alone for a few minutes, can I?" I chuckle, trying to act as normal as possible, "Ready to go?"

The two bulky guys holding my friend upside down bring her down and stand her on her feet, "Oh wow, yeah, let's go." She stumbles my way.

"Great, now I'm babysitting a little lush on the walk home." I'm teasing, but I'm finding it so hard to keep up the façade.

"Nah, I'm good; let's go."

Dani then marches right out of the room and out the front door without ever looking back, and I do the same. At least until we get outside and start walking down the sidewalk. I feel as though we are being watched, and as I look back and up, the Lords of Sin are standing in the tall window of the room I just left on the third floor. A chill runs through me at the intensity of all three of their stares. It's like they are looking into the depths of my very soul.

NINE

Jett

Fuck, watching Lovely Lina suck the jizz off Oak's hand was the hottest thing I've seen in a long time. I can't believe she did it; I thought for sure she would call it quits or call us out on it. Whatever it is she needs our help with, we would have happily done so. Of course, there would still have been some form of payment, hell, but this is way better.

"So, will the contract be like all the rest?" I glance over Oakley's shoulder as he types it up on his laptop.

"Is Catalina Scott like all the rest?" He asks without taking his eyes off the screen.

"Fuck no! Our girl is far above the rest." I grin.

"Exactly. A special contract for a special woman." My friend hits print and then leans back in his chair.

"Do you really think she will agree to all the terms?" Fynn asks as he sits in the chair, smoking his favorite greenery.

"Well, if she wants us to help, I think she will. Did you see how hot she was for us?" I ask incredulously, "I so wanted to slide my hand right into her pants and coat my hand in the wetness I know was there."

"Why didn't you?" Oakley asks, "She was so into watching me fuck her knees that I never saw her flinch when you got as low as you did. Hell, you probably could have finger fucked her, and she wouldn't have cared." He snickers.

I shrug, "I don't need any more shit from my father if another female complains. I will wait until the contract is signed. I pushed my luck when I titty fucked her at the party."

"Oh, but that was fucking classic, bro!" Fynn laughs from his chair.

"Well, once this contract is signed, Kitty Cat will belong to us to do with as we please. You can do what you want, but I get first dibs on fucking that sweet pussy cat of hers. Only then can you have her." Oakley's words are law around here, and even though there really isn't any leader when it comes to the three of us, he did see her first, so it's only fitting that he gets her first.

"Yeah, yeah, yeah, we know," I grin at my friend, "I wouldn't mind having her suck my cock the way she did your fingers."

"Holy fuck, that was hot!" Fynn leans forward, "I almost came watching her."

"I told you she would be good at sucking cock." I snicker as I adjust myself, "Fuck, now I'm all hard again. I'm going to hit the shower and head to bed." I fist-bump both Oakley and Fynn and head back to my room.

It's going to be a long night if I don't get this hard-on under control. Even thinking about grabbing one of the girls from downstairs doesn't sound all that appealing after seeing part of what my Lovely Lina can do with that fucking mouth of hers. So, grabbing my shit, I head for the bathroom, not really looking forward to a freezing shower.

The sound of the second hand on the clock ticks loudly on the wall. It mocks me, knowing I need it to move faster, but it only seems to slow down. I don't know why I have such a hard-on about seeing Lovely Lina at three o'clock, but I do, and this fucking clock won't tick any faster.

As soon as class ends, I head to the men's room to rub one off before meeting up with the guys. I've got another class, but it isn't for another hour or so, my last one before our meeting is to take place. So, finding the nearest restroom, I duck into it and lock myself in a stall.

I have never had to stop and jack off over a girl before. Usually, if I need to rub one off, I find a groupie to do it for me, only this time, no one will do except for a gorgeous blonde with blue eyes and a tight as fuck body. Just picturing her in my head, I struggle to pull myself out because I'm in such a hurry. Finally, I rest the back of my head against the wall as I stroke my girth vigorously, panting hard.

It doesn't take long when I picture her on her knees with my cock shoved down her throat, tears and mascara streaking her face as she gazes up at me. I make sure to point my shit toward the toilet as I come hard. I don't realize I'm making any noises as I finish jerking out the last drop.

Tucking myself into my pants, I flush and then step out, only to come to a stop. One of the jocks that I can't fucking stand, I think his name is Chris, smirks back at me through the mirror. I ignore him as I step up beside him to wash my hands.

"I had to do that the other day after running into a pretty little thing. She had a tongue like a viper, but I bet she would give the best head with it," he states, "How the fuck the Provost created something that smokin' hot is beyond me."

Red is all I see as it clouds my eyes after hearing his words, "You jerked off picturing Catalina Scott?"

"Damn right, I did. All I had to do was picture the bitch bent over, calling me Daddy..."

Those are the last words out of his mouth as I grip the back of his head and slam it into the mirror. Glass shatters everywhere, but I see no blood, so I slam him into it two more times. He's built like a fucking house, so it takes a few times. I then bring his head around to stare him in the eyes.

"Don't you ever fucking picture her like that again. In fact, don't picture her at all! Catalina Scott is off-limits to every fucking thing with a dick! Do you understand me?"

"What the fuck, man?" He shoves me away but doesn't dare try to come at me because of who I am. Sometimes I wish these guys would grow some fucking balls and try.

"Do whatever the fuck you want with every other female on this campus, but don't you even dare breathe Catalina Scott's name. Now, get the fuck out of my sight."

The big guy grabs some paper towels and stumbles out of the restroom. Broken mirror crunches under my feet as I finish washing my hands. When I head toward the door, it opens, and I curse out, "Fucking vandals," as I pass a couple of dudes walking in. They just look between me and the floor, not saying anything, but again, they know better.

Sliding onto the bench beside Fynn, I stretch out my legs as I lean back and watch all the poor saps rushing around, trying to get to class on time. Oakley is scrolling through his phone while Fynn just stares at me.

"What the fuck are you staring at, bro?"

"You just rubbed one off, didn't you?" He grins.

"What? Were you in the next stall or what, fucking creeper!" I shake my head and snicker.

"No, but I can tell after you have had a huge release. Your face seems more relaxed than any other time."

I scoff, "Whatever. Stop being fucking weird."

"It's true," Oakley chimes in, "He does it to me all the fucking time. It is creepy."

"Nah," I chuckle, "Everybody knows you rub one off almost every time you use the restroom. That's a no-brainer there."

My friend looks up from his phone, grinning, "This is very true."

"Damn, what the fuck happened to him?" Fynn questions, and we follow his stare. That Chris guy is walking with some friends while holding an ice pack to his forehead; blood still covers the front of his shirt.

I let out a growl, "The fucker had the audacity to tell me that he jerked off, picturing our Saint bent over, calling him Daddy."

Oak sneers, "He's lucky that it was you he said that to. I would have fucked up his knee, so he couldn't play football for the rest of the season."

"Damn, I didn't even think about that." I say, chuckling before leaning forward to look around Fynn to see Oakley better, "So, is the contract ready?"

"Yep, all I have to do is grab it and the dagger from the safe. I'll meet the two of you a little before three in the library."

"I may be late. Daddio wants to talk to me again. This is getting ridiculous, but he said that I should be out of there to make my three o'clock appointment." Fynn smirks.

"Yeah, I'm still avoiding mine," I grin at Fynn, "You should take notes from me on how to do it yourself."

"What the fuck ever, dude; my meetings with my dad aren't like yours. Nowhere near like them." He chuckles, and I shrug.

"Whatever, either way, have fun. I'll be there making sure the deed gets done without a hitch." I clap my hands and rub them together, "I can't wait to see her reaction to it."

Oakley stands, getting ready to go, "That's if she doesn't decide not to play with us. It all depends on what Kitty Cat is ready for. We aren't for the faint of heart, you know that."

Shrugging, I also stand, "I'm not worried. Something tells me that Saint wants to commit many sins, and we are the only ones who can give her what she wants."

"I hope you're right," Oak fist-bumps me, "I'm out of here; see you in a little bit."

"For sure!" I deliver the same fist-bump to Fynn as he continues to sit on the bench, "Later, bro."

"Yeah, see ya," He's too fascinated by something on his phone to even look at me.

Shaking my head, I walk to my last class, praying that the time flies this time around because I'm jonesing to know what her answer will be to our demands. She has to accept them because even though we do despicable and degrading things with females, it's always consensual, dubious consent, at the very least. Once more, I'm adjusting my junk because my Lovely Lina has me stirring. This is going to make for a long-ass class!

Oakley

I study my best friend to see his reaction as he reads through the contract. Jett isn't one to give anything away; always a poker face with him.

Most of the time, you only know what he's thinking once he's ready to tell. People always think no reaction is bad news, but I know my friend too well; it can go either way.

However, I'm not too worried about his reaction to this contract because I made it up with all three of us in mind. We are best friends for a reason; all three of us are sick fucks regarding women and sex. There is only one thing we don't do, which is anything non-consensual, and that is why I like drawing up contracts or video recording their consent. We may do some sick and depraved shit, but we don't want the backlash of anybody crying sexual abuse or the fucking R word all because we don't return their call the next day.

Plenty of females are willing to do whatever we want, but the moment they say stop, the game is over for good. It will be the same with Kitty Cat. Once she reads some of the things we may request of her at times, she will know just how fucked up we really are.

Her reaction from the other night, when I got off on her, also played a huge factor. I believe my little Kitty Cat has a kinky side that she still keeps tucked away in a closet, and I plan to bring it out.

"So, what do you think?" I raise a brow at Jett, "She will be here any minute."

His brown eyes meet mine, and slowly, a wicked grin forms, "It's fucking perfect."

"Did I leave anything out?"

"Are you fucking shitting me? You've listed every possible thing that we could ever want to do to her luscious body here! My only question is, will it be too much for the Saintly Scott?"

I scoff, "I guess there is only one way to find out." I nod as I look over his head at the person who is about to become our own little dirty possession.

Jett swivels around, and we watch Catalina Scott, the Provost's only daughter, saunter up to us to sign away her very soul. When she stops in front of us, she exudes a bitch vibe. She's trying to show us how tough she is, but we know her game, and we will call her out on it every fucking time.

"Before we start," she looks back and forth between Jett and me, "I will not be some kind of submissive. I will call none of you Master, Sir, or any other fucked up name, especially Daddy. Got it?"

Fuck, my dick just got fucking hard. Kitty Cat is damn hot when she lets her claws out. I give her my most wicked grin, "Good because I want to hear you screaming out my name when I have you coming like a freight train."

Blondie rolls her eyes, yet I can see the goosebumps littering her porcelain skin. "I will hold my own opinion until that time comes...IF that time comes."

"Oh, it will come, Kitty Cat; you can fucking count on it." I take the contract from Jett's hands and then pull out a chair, "Sit."

"I think I will stand, thank you very much." Our little hellcat crosses her arms as she smirks at me.

I'm not one for being forceful with women, but I need to get control of her attitude. Otherwise, it will run rampant, and she will think she can talk this way to us anytime. So, grabbing her arm, not quite in a bruising grip, but enough to warn her that I mean business, I pull her over and sit her in the fucking chair.

"There, much better." I smile at her, "Now, to answer your little demand, as fun as it sounds having you submit to us, it's not what we want. Although we can be sadistic at times, we don't want to control you like that. We actually like the fire you've got inside." I run my finger across her shoulder and then bend down close to her ear, "It turns us on like no other..."

"But," Jett finishes, "Make no mistake, the more you fight, the more we push."

I place the contract face down, leaving my hand over it, and lean on the table, "You will read through this contract and ask any question you want right now, but there is no negotiating on any of it. What you see inside this contract is what will stay and what you will be signing up for."

"You don't even know what I'm asking help with. How can you make up an agreement without knowing the details?" The Saint questions with less of a bitchy tone this time.

I only shrug, "We can help you with anything, so it really doesn't matter what our part is in this. We will be signing it as well."

"You should know, Lovely Lina," Jett chimes in, "Once you sign this, you are ours to do with as we please. The contract will state all the possible things we may request from you, but it doesn't matter. Do you know what a CNC is or dubious consent?"

I catch her rolling her eyes again and grab her chin firmly, "Roll those pretty blues again, and I will turn you over my knee right here and spank that gorgeous peach of yours!"

She nods slightly, and I let go, letting her answer Jett's question, "Of course, I know what they mean."

"Good," I run my fingers through her hair, "Because that is pretty much what this contract is about. You are giving us permission to do whatever we want to this body of yours," I hear her sharp inhale, "Don't you worry, though, because I promise you that you will like every twisted, depraved, and sadistic thing we do to you. You see, Kitty Cat, you are just like us. You were meant to be part of this group. It just so happens that you have a pussy instead of a cock, which puts you in a tough position."

"What is that?" she cocks a brow at me.

"Don't you understand? You were made to be ours, to be possessed by us alone, so" I bend down once more and run the tip of my tongue up the shell of her ear, "You can either join us by giving yourself to us, or you can walk away, never having the protection that only we can give you. You should know, though, we will probably make your life hell if you take the latter route."

"So, you're pretty much blackmailing me? I find it funny that my father told me to search the Lords of Sin out if I ever needed help, yet I have to sell my soul to the devil to get your help."

I chuckle, and Jett follows suit, "Oh, Kitty Cat, you're not signing your soul to the devil...the Lords of Sin are so much worse than the devil himself."

Pushing the contract closer to her, she glances up at me, and I nod, telling her that she can now read through it. I move so I stand directly behind her and reach around, flattening my hand over her sternum.

"May I?" I ask as I slide it down a little further, "I want to feel how many times your heart races as you read through everything."

She studies me for a moment and then gives a little nod. My cock jerks at her permission, and I slip my hand between her plump breasts.

The speed at which her heart races on and off is amusing. I've got some pretty sick shit listed in that contract, half of it is stuff that we will most likely never do, but I want her to know the depth of our depravity.

"Um, weekly enemas?" She asks, and I grin at Jett.

"Oh, Lovely Lina. You do realize that there are three of us, right? We share everything, so there will be times when all three holes will be full, fucked, and filled with our seed. That ass will need a good cleaning once a week."

I can't see her expression, but her heart is pounding profusely, and I can tell she likes the sound of that. With a few more questions, mainly on what a few terms mean, she finally places the contract down, and I come around to watch her reaction. I'm unsure what to think because she has closed her eyes. Is she getting ready to forget the whole thing? This contract is not for the faint of heart. I'm not sure why I made it as twisted as I did because anyone with a brain would turn it down, and our girl is a smart cookie unless she's just that desperate.

Catalina's eye snap open, and without looking at either of us, just keeping her eyes straight ahead, she says, "I'll do it."

We can't show her our surprise, so I stand and quickly pull the dagger out of my bag, "Be a good girl and give me your hand."

Looking between me and the dagger, hesitantly, she gives me her hand, and I swiftly stick the tip of her pointer finger, maybe going deeper than I needed to.

"Ouch!" she yanks her hand back, and I let her.

"Once you sign the contract, you will need to come to the Frat house at seven tonight for a small initiation," Jett informs her.

"Sign on the dotted line, Kitty Cat."

I watch as she stares at the blood dripping from her finger, and I would give anything to taste it. Finally, Catalina puts her finger on the paper and signs her name. It takes a few tries, and it's not all that legible, but Jett is recording it anyway.

I take the contract and blow on it to help it dry, "That's a good girl, Kitty Cat. Remember, come to the Frat house at seven o'clock on the dot. We wait for no one; never forget that."

"See you around, Lovely Lina," Jett smirks, dismissing her immediately.

Our newly acquired possession stands quickly, grabbing her bag and hurrying away while sucking on her finger. I watch her leave, already thinking about the ways we will make her bend. She turns one last time as I continue to stare, smiling wickedly.

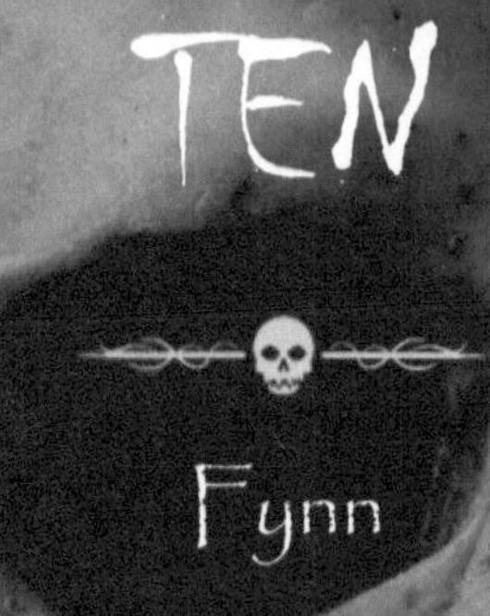

TEN

Fynn

"Do you want to tell me what's happening, Dad?" I ask my father since this is the second time, he's pulled me in to ensure we aren't having any trouble.

"All I know is that there have been some threats, and we are still looking into it at the moment." He answers vaguely.

"No, you don't get to do this. You keep pulling me in here to discuss something you are unwilling to talk about. Tell me," I stand with my hands on my hips, "Is this why Jett's dad keeps wanting to talk to him as well?"

"How the hell am I supposed to know? I only know of one other person so far that has been receiving threats, and that's Mr. Scott."

"Wait, the Provost?" I ask, furrowing my brows.

"Do you know another Mr. Scott here at Helshire?"

"Don't be a smartass, Dad..."

"Don't use that tone with me, Fynn!"

"So, what was this threat about? The one that Mr. Scott got."

"I'm not for sure," My Dad waves his hand in the air, "Something about him speaking up about something or other, or else they will hurt his daughter."

"Someone is threatening to hurt Catalina Scott?" I ask, surprised.

"You remember Catalina?" he asks as if I've met her before.

"We just met her a few weeks ago. Why?"

"No, Fynn. You three boys were young, but we used to have a lot of barbeques at the Scott home. Catty was only about two then, and you boys were four or five."

"Catty?" I grin.

"Yeah, that's what we all called her back then, but she hates it now." My father informs me.

So, not only do I know what our Little Saint wants help with, I now know that we used to play together as kids, and she hates the nickname, Catty...interesting. However, something else comes to mind, and I look back at my dad.

"How are you all friends with the Scotts?" I ask.

"Well, Devlin was a Lord with us. We have been friends since we all started college. Hell, Ashlee was the Saint's Sorority Prez back then." He grins as though he remembers a fond memory.

"What is it, Dad?"

"What? Oh, nothing. Just remembering a few good times with a Saint of our own back then. I wonder if she's still wild in the sack."

"Oh, that's gross, Dad," I tell him as I pretend to gag.

"Pfft, this was just before your mother, but let me tell you, Devlin was one lucky man marrying that Saint because she definitely sinned a lot."

"Okay, I'm out of here!" I jump up and head for the door.

My father laughs but calls out to me, "Hey, do me a favor and just kind of look out for Catty. Let me know if you see or hear anything."

"Yeah, sure, whatever." I raise my hand in a wave and hurry out, wanting nothing more than to get back and relay all this newfound information to the guys.

I wonder if Little Saint signed the contract or if she ran away as soon as she read it. I don't know anybody in their right mind who would sign it unless they are really desperate. Looking at my watch and seeing the time, I think I'm probably too late, but as I go to round the corner near the library, something, or I should say someone, slams into me.

When they step back, I grin, "If it isn't the sexy Little Saint. Is the deed done?"

"Deed?" She cocks a brow, and I smirk.

"The contract...did you sign it?" I question a bit impatiently.

She gets a slight attitude with me as she raises her finger, "What do you think?"

My cock hardens instantly with what this means for me, for all of us, "So, we own you now..."

"Nobody owns me!" She glares.

"The Lords do, and I can't believe you have the guts to stand here and talk to me like this, Little Saint." I bring my arms up on each side of her, caging her in against the wall. I can't help but take her finger and suck the droplet of blood still forming on the tip. Oak got her deep. When she yanks her hand away, I look her in the eye, "Oh, the fun we will have with our new little toy."

I can still taste a trace of her blood on my lip, so I lick it before biting down, but she has to open her mouth again, saying, "In your dreams, perv!"

"We will see about that..."

I push away from her but don't take my eyes off her curvaceous form. I still remember what she looks like without clothes on, and it does nothing to help with my raging boner at the moment. I have to walk away. I can't stay here; otherwise, I will drag her into the nearest bathroom, shove her to her knees and make her swallow my whole fucking cock just to watch her gag as it goes deep down.

I only take a few steps before I turn back and walk backward as I give her my farewell. Winking at her as she stands there, watching me, I smile and say, "I will see you real soon, Little Saint."

I meet the guys just as they are leaving the library, "I can't fucking believe she signed it!"

"How the fuck do you know already?" Jett raises a brow.

"Because I just ran into her in the hall, and she showed me her bleeding finger. Damn, her blood tastes so fucking sweet." I adjust myself.

"You're fucking gross, but whatever, man, you do you." Oakley chuckles.

"Did you have to stick her so deep?" I snicker.

"That's not as deep as I'm going to stick her with my cock as soon as I find the right time." My friend states, smirking.

"Just fucking do it so we can have our turn," I grunt.

Oakley stops walking and turns to me, "Kitty Cat isn't like the others. I usually don't like playing with my food, but this time is different; we will play until we have her out of her mind and begging for our cocks."

"Damn it, Oak! I was already picturing her sucking me off." I may be whining like a little bitch but fuck, I need that mouth on me.

He shrugs, "So have her suck you off. I'm only talking about the full deed and getting her off. We will tease the fuck out of her, and only when she begs nicely will she come for us."

"Dude, you are evil," Jett laughs and fist-bumps Oakley.

I have to admit that I'm looking forward to doing all of this and so much more. Our Little Saint isn't going to know what hit her by the time we are done with her.

I wait until we get back home to talk to them about my discussion with my father. Come to find out, Oakley already knew about Little Saint's mom being a Saint President herself but knew nothing of the rest. Maybe Mr. Harris didn't want him to know about the misdeeds he did in college. Both friends are surprised to learn that we used to play with our girl when we were children.

Hearing this from my father just confirms what we have said before. Catalina Scott is supposed to be ours; she was always meant to belong to the Lords of Sin, and we will fuck anyone up who says otherwise. Especially this piece of shit that's threatening our girl.

"Did Little Saint happen to mention what she needed our help with?" I ask as I inhale the good shit.

"Ha!" Jett chuckles, "She split as soon as we reminded her to be here at seven tonight."

"Well, I'm guessing it's because of this asshole threatening her father, but we still need her to confirm it." I pass the smoke to Oakley, "So, what's the plan for when she gets here tonight?"

"Well," he takes a hit and then blows it out before finishing, "We will tell her about her part at the party. Now that she's ours, there is no asking. Her costume should be in any day, and I can't wait to see her banging body in it. Oh, and Doc will be here for the exam as well."

"Dude, if she read that whole contract and still signed it, she's a shoo-in for our fake virgin sacrifice," something comes to me, though, "Do we really want people seeing who our virgin is? The last thing we need is for it to get back to her father."

"Yeah, he seems to have so much faith in us to keep his baby girl safe," Jett laughs and then coughs out his exhale from the smoke that Oak passed him.

"Oh, we will definitely watch out for her," I grin, "By the way, that package is over there on my dresser. You might as well take it to your room since it needs to be done in your bathroom." I tell Oakley.

"Awesome! You should have seen her reaction to the weekly enema clause," Oak shrugs, "But she still signed. I wonder just how freaky Kitty Cat really is? To answer your question, though, the answer is no. I've got it all figured out, so no one will know who it is we will sacrifice that night."

"Who knows how freaky she is, but I have a feeling that we will be finding out soon enough." I grin, and Jett fist-bumps me as he, too, agrees.

ELEVEN

Catalina

The clock says six fifteen, only forty-five minutes before I have to be at the Sinners Frat house. I look at my finger, where there is now a tiny scab from where I bled. I think he hit the fucking bone when he stuck me, but I wasn't going to cry like a baby in front of him or Jett. Had I known that he wanted it signed in my blood and would use an actual dagger, I would have done it myself.

"Are you sure you don't want me to accompany you?" Dani offers for the fourth time in less than an hour.

"Really, Dani? I think I can take care of myself. Besides, I have my mace with me; I've been dying to try it out on someone, so let them come get me." I dangle it from my keyring, "But seriously, I'll be fine; I won't be gone long."

"Famous last words before your body is found deep in the woods." My roommate goes back to doing her homework.

Rolling my eyes, I yank her head back by the hair, making her look up at me, "If it gets too late, I will call Uber."

Now she scoffs, "You're going to call an Uber when you're only two blocks away?"

"If it will make you feel better, then yes." I give her a cheesy grin.

"Fine. I'm going to hold you to it then."

I let her hair go and pat the top of her head, "Don't study too hard." We both chuckle because we know how little Dani actually studies.

Making sure I have my house key, I walk out the door, feeling a little confident that the guys will come through for me. I shouldn't because most people will tell me they only want a piece of ass, but I'm not so sure about that. They said I was one of them, or I was supposed to be, but I was born the wrong gender. Is it possible that they really do feel a kinship to me and will help me even if I don't do ninety percent of the things listed on that contract?

I think they would, but I also believe they are attracted to me and need to find a way into my pants. I'm playing this little game of theirs only in case there is a slight chance I'm wrong, but I don't think I am. I mean, what does knife play or gun play even mean in a contract like this?

If I am being honest, most things on that list turned me on; another reason to play their little game. They are more depraved than I thought, and although I'm into kinky shit, some of that contract scared me, but you better believe I will take every single thing they bring at me.

I ring the doorbell at exactly seven on the dot. Jett surprises me by being the one to open the door, "Lovely Lina, right on time." He steps aside, and I walk in.

The house is unusually quiet for this time of night, "Where is everyone."

"Oh, they're around somewhere," Jett grabs my hand and begins pulling me behind him toward the stairs.

"So, what sort of initiation do I have to go through?" I try to keep up with him, but it's a bit hard in the heeled ankle booties I wear, "Please, slow down!"

"Oh, sorry," he chuckles but never answers my question.

As we get to the closed door leading up to the Lord's floor, he opens it and waits for me to go, but I remain where I'm at, "I'm not going up first." I tell him.

He isn't having it, though, because he grabs my arm and shoves me ahead of him before shutting the door behind us, "Get your ass moving; I want to check out what I will be fucking soon enough."

I turn around as fast as I can, "I'm not having sex tonight!"

Jett grabs the back of my neck, not tightly, but enough to get my attention, "You forget that we own you, so if we want to fuck that sweet cunt of yours tonight, we will," he pauses as his eyes sweep down the length of me, "Lucky for you, that's not what we have planned for tonight, so be a good girl and get that cute little ass up those steps."

I study him, and once I believe what he says to be true, I turn and stomp up the stairs. Although I must say, my core now throbs a little at the thought of Jett taking me from behind. Just the thought of him gripping my hips, his glutes flexing with each thrust...

I hear voices coming from a different room than they were in last night, so I head in that direction. Jett is right on my heels and almost runs into me when I stop in front of the door. Reaching around to open it for me, his package rubs against my ass, and his cologne fucks with my senses. If there was a cologne that made women spread their legs, Jett's scent would be it.

"Ah, there's the woman of the hour! Come, Kitty Cat," Oakley grins as he makes a big production, "Make yourself at home."

Fynn is already inside, and another guy I've never seen before, "Oakley..." I cut myself off as I study the newcomer.

"You're probably wondering who this very handsome stranger is and what he's doing at your initiation. Well, Kitty Cat, this man," Oakley grips the guy's shoulder, "Has a vital role tonight. You see, this is Dr. Halsey, and he is here to give you your exam and to take samples. You know, make sure you're not crawling with STDs and whatnot."

"Excuse me? If anyone crawls with STDs, it'd be you three, as many groupie sluts you sleep with. This whole third floor smells like nothing but rotten pussy!" I back up, "I'm not letting one of your strange friends, who is not a Lord of Sin, come up in my shit."

Jett's hard body behind me stops me from going any further, "Lovely Lina, Doc may be a friend of the Lords, but he really is a doctor and works at the local hospital. Everything that takes place on this floor is confidential."

"Does anybody else take offense to Little Saint's description of what our floor smells like?" Fynn huffs, "I take great pride in fucking clean pussy!"

I roll my eyes, "That's not what I meant, but that's not even the point." Crossing my arms, I look around, and that's when I notice an actual exam table, "Seriously? You went all out for this?" I cock my brow at the Greek God standing there, grinning.

"We take this very seriously, Kitty Cat."

"How many other females have you done this to?" I walk over to the exam table and run my fingers across the edge.

"That's not something we disclose, Kitty Cat. Like with you, it's all confidential." Oakley smirks and I feel he's lying for some reason, but I don't press the issue. He says, "If you remember page two, section four B, it states that you will undergo a medical exam by a doctor of our choosing and allow them to not only examine you but to take samples for the lab, making sure you are clean."

Fuck, he's right, I do remember, but I also thought I would be going to an actual clinic. Do they not realize how unsterile it is in this room? Whatever, if they want to play dirty, I will too.

"Fine, but nowhere in the contract did it state that you three were allowed to be in the room. You know, doctor/patient confidentiality, and I have my rights, so although you have access to the test results, I'm not giving you access to be in the room while he examines me." I turn to the new guy, "And I will need to see your credentials before you know...I let you all up in my business."

All three Lords are grinning at me, but only Oakley responds, "You really did pay attention to the contract, didn't you?"

"Of course I did! What do you take me for? My father may trust you, but I don't; not yet." The guy pulls out his credentials, and I read through them before returning them and turning my attention to the Lords. I begin by unbuttoning and unzipping my skinny jeans but stop, "Excuse me. I'm sure the doctor doesn't have all night."

Fynn and Jett both frown while the last Sinner smirks before turning toward the door, "No fair, Doc gets to see her shit before we do!" Fynn grumbles as he leaves, and I can't help the mischievous grin I throw at the doctor.

"So, Doc, how do you want me?"

The guy is hot, I'll give him that, and the smile he gives me can make any girl's panties fall off, but he's not the Lords. What did they think they would accomplish doing the exam this way? Did they think I was that naïve as to not question this insanity? Is this part of their humiliation process? The contract talks of humiliation and degradation. The joke is on them because I'm not embarrassed to show my hoo-ha to a good-looking doctor.

I push my jeans down, along with my panties, and jump up onto the table. I even go as far as pulling out the stirrups and planting my legs on top of them, "Here you go, Doc. Have at it."

The hot doctor has been nothing short of professional as he does the exam and takes the needed samples. After learning that I am already on birth control, he gives me a clean bill of health. Of course, the lab results are still pending, but he will be rushing them through at Oakley's order.

Doc waits until I'm dressed before calling the guys into the room, "So, how's our girl doing?" Oakley asks.

"I don't think you will need to worry about her crawling with any STDs," Dr. Halsey winks at me, "She's got a pretty hot snatch, if I may say so myself."

Fynn takes offense to his friend's words, "Watch what you're saying about our Little Saint!"

"Hey," Halsey holds his hands up defensively, "You hired me to do a job, and I did it. Now I'm giving you my opinion. You forget I've got a girl, so calm the fuck down."

Jett slaps Fynn on the back, "Cool it, Halsey didn't mean anything by it."

Just before he leaves, the doctor looks over at me, "It was nice meeting you, Catalina. Don't let these three fuckers scare you, I think you will do well with them if you can learn how to handle them, and from the looks of what I've seen tonight, I think you will be okay."

"Thanks, Doc. It was nice having you all up in my business; it's been a while." I wink back at him, and he laughs as he walks out.

"Oh, it's been a while, huh?" Jett asks as he wiggles his brows.

I ignore his question like he did mine earlier and look at Oakley, "So, will that be all?"

"Try again, Kitty Cat. Two more things need to take place before you can leave."

"And please tell me, what are those two things?" I'm trying to act brave and put on a bitchy front, but inside I'm nervous to hear what they have in store for me.

"First of all, we need to see the goods we now own, so be a good girl and strip." The Greek God orders with a smile.

"Are you serious right now?"

"As serious as a heart attack, Kitty Cat."

I look between the three friends, and goosebumps break out all over my skin. They all take a seat and relax, waiting for me to get undressed. I'm not ashamed of my body, not really, but I know that they have been with a lot of women. From what I've seen, they are at least two sizes smaller than I am. My tummy is flat, but my curves are a bit much for some.

Fuck it. They have already seen me in just my bra and panties. What's the worst they will do? Decide that they aren't sexually attracted to me. But will they still help if that's the case?

As the Lords of Sin sit shoulder-to-shoulder before me on the couch, I grip the hem of my shirt and pull it up and over my head, staring intently at the trio as I do so. Next are my skinny jeans. Kicking off my booties again, I pull my jeans off and stand before them with my hands on my hips. I know what's coming, but I must try to be difficult, at least.

"You're not done yet, Little Saint." Fynn licks his lips as his eyes roam from my head down to my feet, "We have already seen this much of you; we need to see the rest."

Looking at the lust in their eyes, I'm slightly bigger than what they are used to. If they want a show, I will give them a show and hope that when Jett said they weren't planning on having sex tonight that it still holds true.

Reaching back, I unhook my bra, but before peeling it off, I turn and give them my back. I hear snickering as I pull it off, hold it to the side, and drop it. I then look over my shoulder to see that they are all enthralled by my little performance, so I hook my thumbs into my panties and rim the waist, prolonging the inevitable.

Taking a deep breath, I bend forward before pushing my lace panties down. Looking over my shoulder, I cover my breasts with one arm while my other hand goes down and covers my lady bits before I turn back and face the Lords of Sin.

Right away, Oakley is shaking his head, no, "Drop your arms, Kitty Cat."

"I've stripped just like you asked," I say sarcastically.

"Yes, but I also told you we wanted to see what we now own." Oakley stands and comes closer, circling me slowly as he checks me out.

When he comes to stand behind me, my heart thumps anxiously, not knowing what he will do. It's only when I feel his hands grip both my wrists that I realize what he's about to do and it actually has my core throbbing even more. It shouldn't surprise me that he is forcing me to show myself; it did state in the contract that they could have me strip and present myself to them whenever they wanted me to. I agreed to all of this and then some.

Oakley's voice is like silk floating through my ears after I feel his lips on my bare shoulder. I don't fight it when he pulls my arms away and holds them at my side, "Don't move Kitty Cat. Let them see...let us see what we now own."

"Oh, you are much lovelier than I thought, Lovely Lina. My name for you fits perfectly." Jett stands and comes closer.

I've changed my mind and am now hoping against hope that one of them or all of them will touch me. I need to feel their hands on me, caressing me. Jett dips his head and kisses my neck on the opposite side of where Oakley is. Moisture pools between my thighs, and a soft whimper slips from my lips.

"I think our Little Saint likes the attention," Fynn says as he joins the rest of us. Taking my hand, he places it firmly over the bulge in his pants, "I have someone who would like some attention too."

I try to yank my hand away, not because I'm appalled by the Lord's actions but because I'm craving even more from them. I need to play it cool and make it harder for them to get it. But how can I do that when every cell in my body screams at me to let them do what they will.

I clear my throat, "I have done what you asked. Now may I please get dressed?"

"What's the hurry, Kitty Cat?"

"I've given you what you wanted, Oakley."

"Yes, but there is still one more thing that must be done before you can get dressed and leave," Fynn states, running a finger from my belly button up the middle and through the valley between my breasts.

"What's that?" I try to keep my breathing even.

"Go to the bathroom and get into the shower stall. Be a good girl and get on all fours for us." Oakley's voice is close to my ear again.

I whip my head toward him, "Jett said there would be no sex tonight."

"Ah, I said we aren't planning on it, but this isn't about sex. Well, at least not yet." Jett looks like the devil himself as he gives me his wickedest grin.

I feel a hand slither down to my ass and squeeze my cheek, "We need to prepare you before we take you, remember." Oakley says as he squeezes my cheek a second time.

"Oh God, you are serious about the enema?" I close my eyes and sigh.

"Oh, yes, Little Saint, very serious." Fynn takes my hand and starts to pull me toward the bathroom.

I yank my hand away, "Wait a minute. What are you three going to do to help me? I've done some of the things you have asked, and now I'm about to get my ass fucked by a fucking bulb or some shit, so I need to know what you are going to do to hold up your end of the contract."

Oakley grabs my jaw roughly but not enough to bruise it, "We will do whatever it takes to keep you safe, Kitty Cat. Nobody threatens what belongs to us. Whether it's burning this whole campus to the ground, gutting a son of a bitch with a hunting knife, or putting a bullet right between their eyes, know that we will protect you at all costs."

The depth of emotion that this Lord has put behind his words, ensuring me that they will do whatever it takes, well, let's just say that I'm now looking forward to what they have in store for me. That is everything aside from these fucking enemas.

"Now, let's get this pretty little ass of yours cleaned out, shall we, Little Saint?" Fynn begins pulling again, and this time, I let him.

TWELVE

Oakley

I tilt my head as I watch Catalina's ass sway back and forth while Fynn pulls her into my bathroom. She's got all the right curves that a guy can grab hold of as he pounds away into that sweet pussy. I'm tired of fucking skin and bones, and that's pretty much what all the females are here. They are all on some fad diet or just not eating at all.

Not my Kitty Cat, though. Don't get me wrong, I'm not interested in just fucking her; none of us are. We were serious when we said that she belongs in our depraved little world, but since she doesn't have a dick, we might as well take advantage of it. Ultimately, she will be the Lords of Sin's Lady...the Lady of Sin. It has a nice ring to it. In your face, Felicia! Your little Saint will not belong in your joke of a sorority for too much longer.

"Easy now, Lovely Tina," I see Jett holding Kitty Cat's hand as she gets on her knees in the shower stall.

"Do we really have to do this?" she asks.

"Are we going to have to gag you and hold you down in order to get this done, Little Saint?"

"Oh, I'm sure Kitty Cat will be on her best behavior, won't you?" I squat down and caress her head as I grin at her.

"Oakley, please..."

I ignore her pleas and tap her bottom, "On your hands and knees, Catalina. Don't make me repeat it." I will use my authoritative voice if I have to. I don't make these contracts up for anything; I expect them to be obeyed, no questions asked, and Kitty Cat is no different. She may be one of us, but she's behind on the times and must learn her place with us.

She glares at me but moves to the position as instructed. Jett, being the perv that he is, kneels behind her and rubs himself against her as I grab the saline solution, enema bag, and tube. Fynn already has the lube in his hand, and I hand him the tube to lube up.

"Mm, I can't wait to have you just like this as I thrust into this cunt," Jett causes Kitty Cat to squeal, and I glance over at them, "Oh wow, seems like our girl is turned on just a little bit." Jett's hand is between her thighs, rubbing back and forth, "She's fucking soaked!"

"Fuck you, Ink boy!" My Kitty Cat hisses and tries pushing him away from her, but he holds steady.

"Shh, just let me do this for you, Lovely Lina. You are going to want to be relaxed anyway." Jett coaxes her in a soothing voice, and she stops fighting him as she hangs her head, "That's it...see. It feels good, doesn't it? Fuck, Lina, you are so tight."

I hear her moans, and after what Jett just said, I realize that the fucker is fingering her. Taking a moment to watch, I notice how her hips are now moving; she's enjoying my boy immensely.

"Yeah, I knew she would be a slut for us." Fynn chuckles, which makes my Kitty Cat stop humping Jett's hand.

Grinning, I now know that our girl doesn't like to be called that specific name, but she will by the time we are done with her, "Okay, I'm ready." I carry over the items and place them beside her, ensuring she can see what I'm using.

"Jesus..." is all that comes out of her mouth, but when Jett starts to spread her ass cheeks apart, she freaks out, "No! Can't I just do it on my own? This is all so personal!"

Jett holds her from behind, and Catalina now sits on his lap. She doesn't seem so concerned about her nudity now as she begs. He wrestles her back around until her head is shoved to the floor with her ass in the air.

"Now, Kitty Cat, are you forgetting that you signed the contract already? There is no need to be shy because we will know your body inside and out soon enough. There will be nothing to hide from us, so you might as well give up."

"Would you like something to help calm you down, Little Saint?" Fynn grins at me.

"Fuck you, I don't do drugs," she spits, and I must admit our girl is a little fighter.

"Well, calm the fuck down then, and let's get this over with!" I finally lose a bit of my temper.

Her body goes rigid, and then she gets back up to all fours as soon as Jett releases her head. Again, he opens her cheeks for me, and I feed the tube into her little pucker after lubing it well. I have to tell her to relax a few times by the time I have the tube in all the way, which is only about three inches. I begin pushing the saline through, and she groans.

"Your belly is going to feel bloated, but that's normal. You will need to keep it in for at least ten minutes, Kitty Cat."

"Oh God..."

"It will get easier over time." Fynn states as he kneels in front of our girl, "Want to take your mind off it, Little Saint?" He pulls himself out, and I think he must be crazy because she's in the position to bite it right off. He's being really gutsy at the moment.

"Yes, please," I hear her small voice, but then she notices what he's talking about when she looks up. Instead of cursing at him or even biting it off, she studies his cock in his hand like she's contemplating it, but then shakes her head.

I know she really wants it; I saw it in her eyes just a second ago, "Yes, Fynn, distract her."

He tries pushing his cock into her mouth, "You fucking bite me, and you will be in deep shit. Now be a good girl and open up, per the contract." He reminds her.

"If we must remind you of the contract every time, Kitty Cat, then we will have no choice but to terminate it. We will not put up with little brats." I warn her.

With her not being able to move much with the saline inside, I help Fynn out by taking her hair and pulling her head back, "Open nice and wide. Show us how much of a cock slut you really are."

She whimpers but opens for my friend, and he groans as he slides all the way in, making her gag, "Not too much! We can't have her pushing any saline out of her ass. If you gag her, she's liable to do just that."

"My bad," he smirks and starts fucking her mouth with small strokes, "Jesus, her mouth is fucking heaven!"

After a minute or so, Kitty Cat begins to struggle, and so I let her go, which allows her to pull herself off a frustrated Fynn, "You all are fucking assholes! If you want a piece of me, then I need to see some good faith from your end."

Jett and I chuckle, "We won't deny your claim, Lovely Lina, but we own you and this delectable little body of yours."

"Only under the stipulation that you help me," our smart cookie glares at my friend, "I've done more than enough so far; now it's your turn. Show me that you are serious about helping me, and you can do whatever you want, within limits, of course."

It's hard to take my Kitty Cat so seriously when she is on all fours and groaning due to having her belly full of saline. I look at Jett and shrug. She isn't wrong; I should have considered that Catalina Scott isn't as gullible as most of the other females on this campus.

Without saying anything, I dismiss Fynn with his scowling face, but another thought comes to mind. It may be a bit sadistic, but hey, that's our middle name. "Okay, Kitty Cat, let's get you up and emptied."

Because we have been friends for so long, I only need to make eye contact with my friends, and we know what each other is thinking. So, while Jett and I help our girl off the floor, I grin at both my friends, then place our girl on the toilet. Only Jett and I don't let go; we hold her in place.

"Since you teased my friend here by not letting him finish the blow job, Kitty Cat, it's only right that he gets to finish now."

"Wait, what?" She looks at me and then at Jett before her eyes land on Fynn and, finally, his mighty girth, which he's stroking leisurely.

"I'm going to mark you, Little Saint. Just like Jett did at the party that night and Oakley the other night. You will wear my seed, marking you as mine as well." Fynn grins wickedly as he picks up the pace, standing before our girl.

"You have got to be fucking kidding me!" She's yet to release the contents of her stomach as she's too engrossed in watching my friend jerk himself off.

I slip my hand onto her chest and cup her breast before rolling her nipple with my fingers. Jett follows suit with the other nipple, but all Kitty Cat does is moan and lick her lips. It's like she's in a trance, like she was the night I jerked myself off with her knees. Our saintly girl here has a sinner's streak inside of her, and we are going to bring it out of her.

Our ministrations must relax her enough that she suddenly empties her stomach. Fynn moves closer to where he straddles Catalina's legs and picks up speed. The sound of Fynn beating his meat bounces off the bathroom walls as his breathing becomes fast and shallow.

"Open that pretty little mouth of yours, Kitty Cat. Offer it to our friend here...take his cum like a good girl and swallow it." When she doesn't heed what I say, I grip her jaw and open her mouth just as Fynn starts jetting out his seed.

He's not trying to be careful as he throws his head back and grunts. Ropes of his cum shoot all over my Kitty Cat's chest, hair, and cheek. A little lands on my hand, but it bothers me none as I watch a few jets hit her mouth. It isn't until he's done that I let go of her.

"Now swallow it, Kitty Cat," I order.

"Mm..." she moans without realizing it.

I slide my hand down and rub a few circles around her clit, making her buck against it, "That's a good little slut."

Catalina's eyes come back into focus, and she begins to struggle once again. Jett and I let her go, grinning at our girl as we do, "You look absolutely stunning, Kitty Cat, you really do." I tell her as I admire the handiwork of my best friend.

Jett

"Finish up but don't clean Fynn off you. Once you are done, you may join us in the room," I inform our Lovely Lina before leaving her to clean her ass up.

"Fuck, you guys should have felt what I felt," Fynn exclaims as soon as we shut the bathroom door, "The Little Saint has a mouth of a sinner!"

"Or made for Sinners," I smirk.

"Regardless," Oakley adds, " she also has a brain, unlike the rest. Our girl will be so much fun to play with, but we have to use our brains if we are going to outsmart her."

"That, or we just use our muscles," I think back to when we held her down, and she didn't fight us. In fact, it's almost as if it aroused her, "I believe Lovely Lina likes being manhandled."

My friends stare at me like I'm crazy, "You seriously think Catalina wants to be handled roughly?" Oak questions.

I think about it for a moment, "What I think, and I could very well be wrong, but I doubt it, is that Cat is kinky as fuck but maybe a little shy about it. So, by letting us manhandle her, she justifies her kink by blaming us for 'making' her do it. Does that make sense at all?"

"Wait a minute," Fynn jumps in, "So you think we will be able to treat her like a little slut, and she will allow it?"

"Actually, I think Jett may be right," Oakley pipes in, "As long as we don't call her a slut, she's game for it."

"Calling her by that name must shame her for liking it too much," I say more to myself than the others.

"Yes," Oakley states, "But we will get her to embrace it all. There is nothing wrong with her being a slut as long as it's for her Lords only."

The bathroom door opens, and our girl walks out with her head held high even though she's still naked and covered in Fynn's jizz. She refuses to let us see any kind of embarrassment that she may be feeling, and it earns her a few extra points in my book. Lovely Lina is more gorgeous than I ever thought, now that I'm taking the time to really see her.

"Damn girl, come here." I crook my finger at her, and after looking at my two friends, she saunters over and stands before me, "I've been dying to do this, and I'm not going to be sorry..."

I grab the nape of her neck and roughly pull her to me, letting our mouths collide. My other hand grips her jaw, opening her for me, and I shove my tongue inside. In seconds, she's returning the kiss, and I grow way too fucking hard. Knowing it can't happen tonight, I pull away abruptly and shove her back. She stumbles into Oakley's arms, and he also ravages her mouth.

Fynn, not a huge fan of kissing on the mouth, stands behind the Saint and begins sucking on her neck while she is still in a make-out session with Oakley. I collect her clothes as I try and settle my guy down. When I hear a slight moan from my Lovely Lina, my friends pull away, leaving her in a dazed state.

"Let's get you dressed, Lina."

"My name is Catalina. Why won't any of you use it?" she asks, a bit grumpy.

"Would you like for us to call you Catty instead?" Fynn smirks.

She gasps, "How did you..."

"We know everything, Kitty Cat." Oakley winks at her and helps her balance herself as she steps into her jeans that I'm helping her with, "By the way, we will need you here an hour before the Toga party." He tells her.

"I already told you I have a previous engagement and will try to come." I stop what I'm doing to stare up at her after she says this.

"We all know that you have no other engagement that night." I snicker and then help her into her ankle boots.

"Besides, you are going to be our sacrificial virgin for the party." Fynn is the one that blurts this out.

I look at Oakley to see him rolling his eyes, and then he watches Catalina's expression, "What the fuck is that supposed to mean? What does it entail?"

"Well, Kitty Cat, we know you aren't an actual virgin, but you are our virgin. Our cocks have not been inside that cunt of yours...yet."

"Yeah, so..."

"So...you will be our sacrifice for the Toga party. We always have one, and this year, it's you." Oakley gives her a cheesy smile.

"What do I have to do?" Her voice is soft, almost like she already knows, deep down, what will be said.

I lick my lips and glance at Oak and Fynn, "Well, Lovely Lina, your job will be to remain where we place you while we officially make you ours."

I tell our lovely Saint that we are going to fuck her, and she runs away. There is no arguing, insults, or backlash; she just turns and runs. I never locked the door behind us when we came up earlier or after Doc Halsey left, so there is no slowing her down.

It's late, and I'm not keen on having her walk back on her own, especially in the state that she's in, "Fynn, come with me. I want to make sure she gets home safely."

"What the fuck do I look like, her damn bodyguard?" he asks, smirking.

"Really? You signed the contract, didn't you? That should answer your fucking question." I growl at my friend.

"Oh shit, my bad," he snickers, "It will take a while to get used to this. I'm not used to saving damsels in distress."

"Lina is no damsel in distress; I'm sure she would fuck up whoever it is that is threatening her father, but we've fucked with her head, and I can guarantee that it's all she's thinking about on her walk home." I tell him, "Anyone will be able to walk up to her, as distracted as she is."

"Okay, I get it; let's go before she gets too far ahead." Fynn is already heading for the door.

"Call me if you need any assistance. I'm going to clean all this shit up." Oakley glances around his room.

"Will do," I follow Fynn out the door, then jog to catch up to him.

We keep a safe distance behind our Saint, but I don't think she'd ever notice us even if we were right behind her. It's as I said, she's distracted. She seems to be talking to herself the whole walk back if all the curses leaving her mouth are any indication. Fynn and I glance at each other and smirk. We did this to her; she's all flustered because of us.

When I see movement in my peripheral view. I grab my friend's arm and stop him from moving forward. I nod at an area across the street just before we duck down. We watch as the hooded figure lurks in the shadows and then crosses the road, heading toward our girl.

Whoever it is, they're big, and I doubt our Saint would have any chance of defending herself against them. I decide to start moving again, and Fynn is beside me instantly. The stranger follows my Lovely Lina a few meters and then looks at their surroundings. Unable to duck in time, the person starts to flee as soon as they spot us.

"Keep following our girl!" I order Fynn in a loud whisper as I take off after the stranger.

I follow them through some bushes and then down multiple alleys. I lose sight of them a few times, but I find them again and again. I don't want to lose them, but they seem to know this part of the neighborhood better than I do, and after ten fucking minutes of chasing the motherfucker, I lose them. I kick a tall garbage bin, cursing.

I take the quickest route back to the Frat house and meet Fynn just outside. He's by his motorcycle, bent down, looking at something. A stream of curses comes from his mouth, sounding like I did just a bit ago.

"Hey, what's up?" I come up behind him.

"Some asshole fucked with my bike!" He barks out.

I examine his Harley, and my eyes bulge. They flattened his tires with sharp pieces of metal, which still stick out of one tire, gouged out his seat, and carved words into the gas tank.

'I warned them all, and now, it's time to play!'

"What the fuck is that supposed to mean?" I ask Fynn, who stands beside his bike, seething angrily.

"It's the motherfucker my father was trying to warn me about and who is threatening Little Saint! Maybe if you stop being a pussy and go talk to your dad, you may be able to find something out!"

"Whoa, buddy, don't be taking your anger out on me, bro!" I glare at my friend.

He sighs, "Sorry, but I'm serious. Go see what your dad wants. Maybe he can shed more light on this because Oak's dad hasn't said shit, even though I'm pretty sure he's received the same threat."

"What the fuck could all this be about?" I ask as I look over Fynn's poor bike.

"The fuck if I know," Fynn kicks the flat tire on his bike, "But we are going to find out and fuck that piece of shit up!"

THIRTEEN

Catalina

Oh, my God! What the fuck just happened, and what have I signed up for? I stare at myself in the mirror as I strip my clothes back off. Dried cum crusts my skin and pieces of my hair, and I feel a familiar stirring below. Thank God Dani is already asleep, so she didn't have to see the state I'm in. I didn't even take an Uber as promised; I just ran.

My tongue darts out and licks a little of the crust still by my bottom lip. My eyes close, so I can remember the moment I felt it land there. The Lords are sick, and I'm beginning to like sick, but I'm supposed to be good while here, I promised my mother. These Sinners are going to be my undoing if I'm not careful.

Remembering Jett's fingers being inside me, fucking in and out of me as his palm rubbed my clit; I was so close. Every time they got me close, they backed off. I know their game, they want me to beg them, but I won't. I will work them up until they are out of their mind with want and just take what they will.

I'm not too experienced with the whole pain and pleasure kink, but I'm no virgin when it comes to it, either. Is it wrong to want the Lords of Sin to hurt me until I come? I've never craved it until I met those three; Oakley, Fynn, and Jett, my favorite Sinners of all.

Sliding my hand down over Fynn's cum, I keep going until I feel the wetness between my legs. I've been on edge since Jett finger fucked me; now, I can finally give my body what it needs. Pushing two fingers into me, I fuck myself, rubbing the heel of my hand against my clit while I picture each Lord above me as they slam into my cunt repeatedly.

If what they say is true, in about a week, I won't need to imagine them fucking me because they told me they were going to. I'm not sold on them doing it in front of anybody, but the thought alone has me coming all over my fingers.

Banging on the bathroom door has me jumping back to reality. I grab my robe and quickly throw my hair in a messy bun so the dried cum isn't noticeable. Making sure no more is on my face, I open the door to a sleepy-looking Dani.

"It's after midnight, Cat! I hope you took an Uber like you promised." My roommate scowls.

"Yes, Mommy, and as you can see, I'm not lying dead in any woods," I smirk.

Flipping me off, she walks past me and goes straight to the toilet. Not caring that I'm standing right here, she pulls her bottoms down and plops herself on the toilet, "So," she stops to yawn, "What is it the Sinners wanted from you?"

I roll my eyes, "The Lords of Sin, Dani."

"They are still Sinners, Cat."

"Fine, but to answer your question, they wanted to go over everything I knew about this threat, and I told them about the costume shop." I lie through my teeth and pray that she can't see through me.

"So, what...they didn't ask for any sexual favors?" My friend cocks her brow.

I cross my arms, "Nope, so you see, you worried for nothing."

Dani wipes and then flushes before washing her hands, "Whatever, but I still think they want something from you."

I start pushing her out the door, "I need to shower, Mommy," I chuckle, "Besides, all three are hot; it may not be so bad."

She turns back to me, gawking, "You are such a slut!" she smirks.

"Not yet, I'm not," I wink and then close the door in her face.

The next few days are uneventful, as I don't see any of the Lords on campus. My thoughts are filled with what they could possibly be doing if not lurking through the halls of Helshire. Even as the weekend draws closer, one would think the top three Sinners of the Frat House would be out, hyping students up over the upcoming annual party, but maybe I'm wrong.

"Boo!"

I jump and almost punch my roommate in the face when she comes up to me like that, "Don't ever do that again, or else I won't be responsible for what my fist does to your face."

"Damn, girl...down!" Dani chuckles.

I roll my eyes and continue walking across campus toward the Sorority House, "Do you find it strange that none of the Lords have been around?"

"Why are you so obsessed with the Lords of Sin? They are sick and twisted, and they treat women like pieces of meat."

I glance at my friend, who is slightly frowning, "I can ask you the same thing almost. Why do you dislike them so much?"

"I don't dislike them. I mean, all the Sinners are hot, but I don't want to see you being another notch on all three of their bed posts." Dani smirks.

"Well, we are in college, you know..."

She gasps and shoves my arm, "So, you come to college to ho around?"

"Now, why do you have to put it that way? I like to think of it as experimenting before settling down, you know, like taking college classes, but you're not sure what you want to do with your life, so you take multiple classes until you decide." I grin.

"Oh, my God. Please tell me you did not compare college classes to men!" Dani stops and just stares at me.

I stop and face her, "So, you can have two guys to choose from at a party, but I can't have three to choose from?" I raise a brow, and when I turn back to continue on my way, I throw over my shoulder, "At least none of my three are into guys!"

My phone pings with an incoming text, and when I look at my phone, it's an unknown number, but the text itself tells me exactly who it's from.

'Meet me in the back hallway of the library, Kitty Cat.'

Tingles scatter across my nether regions, and my heart skips a beat. What does Oakley want to meet me for, and why behind the library? I need to think quickly since Dani is still walking close behind me. I stop short, letting her run right into me.

"Oh, sorry," I grab her and stop her from falling, "I forgot I needed to stop and grab a book from the library."

"Do you want me to come with?" She asks.

"Oh gosh, I'm only running there and coming back," I chuckle, "Hey, go into my closet and try on the two costumes. Figure out which one you're wearing to the party, and I'll be back in a few."

"Shit, I forgot all about that! Thanks for reminding me." Dani picks up the pace and hurries toward the Sorority House while I head in the other direction to meet with a Sinner.

I burst through the back door of the building that the library is housed in, and I'm instantly thrown into a nearby wall; not hard, but it's still a bit rough. My front is against the wall, and I feel a hard warm body lean into me from behind.

"Mm, I've missed you, Kitty Cat." My hair is pushed to the side, and his mouth is on my neck.

"Oakley..."

"Did you miss me?" His hand slides down and works its way to the front, and he cups my sex, "Oh, seems like somebody is getting a bit hot down below."

"What do you want, Oakley?" I try to keep my voice snarly, so he doesn't realize the state he already has me in.

"It's like I said, Kitty Cat, I've missed you." He yanks my hair with his other hand and devours my mouth with his.

I open for him instantly, letting him shove his tongue inside and tangle with mine. When he begins rubbing my clit through my pants, I make sure to grind against his very hard bulge that is sticking into my ass as he leans into me. He groans, letting me know he's totally into it, but I keep myself in check and don't make a peep.

Finally, I yank my mouth away from him, "What makes you think you can just take what you want, Harris?"

"Hm, your blood on the contract that I have tucked away in my safe." He pulls my back against him and grinds himself against my ass, "I'm dying to get inside of you, Kitty Cat. Are you going to be ready to take all three of us in just a few days?"

I have to take a moment to get my wits together to form a sentence, but I don't answer his question; I ask one of my own, "What is it you wanted to see me for, Oakley?"

He stops what he's doing and snickers before turning me to face him, "I wanted to remind you to come an hour early, and don't worry about a costume because I already have yours."

"I have one already."

He raises a brow, "Oh, so you were planning on coming."

I roll my eyes, "I have to go, Oakley."

He studies me and then takes my mouth again, but only briefly. When he pulls away, he smirks and lets me pass him, "Oh, Kitty Cat?" I turn back to look at him, and his eyes zone in on my crotch, "We like our women bare."

I feel myself blush and hurry back out the door, hearing Oakley Harris's laughter long after the door closes. I can't get home fast enough, and all the way back, I've got only one thing on my mind; how the Lords of Sin will be happy to learn that I like my pussy bare too.

FOURTEEN

Fynn

Someone's going to get their shit fucked up! Nobody touches my bike, and I know it's the same person threatening Little Saint. They must have missed the memo that you don't fuck with the Sinner's property, especially when it belongs to the Lords of Sin, and Catalina belongs to us now.

I had paid my father a visit at home the morning after my bike got fucked up. Closing ourselves into his home office, I go straight to my father's safe and use the combination to open the secret encased wall.

"What's going on, Fynn?" My father asks as he watches me study the weapons lining the wall.

Yeah, my father and Jett and Oakley's fathers may not be the kind of men you think they are. They love their weapons and will protect what is theirs at all costs; that is how we were raised. We aren't gangsters or mafia or some shit like that. We just like to be prepared, and I'm glad for it because someone is fucking with shit they have no business fucking with.

However, Catalina's father isn't in this mix, which is why it surprised me to learn that they are still great friends. It's understandable why the Provost would tell his daughter to come to us with any trouble because he knows that we can protect her.

"Someone fucked with my Harley, and Jett and I chased someone off who was following Catalina last night," I tell him how Little Saint came to us for help.

"Damn it, Fynn! You boys need to be careful with Devlin's daughter. She's not like your groupies..."

"Oh, we already know this." I grin.

"Please say you had her sign a contract." My father looks at me as if I'm an amateur.

"What do you take us for, Dad? Of course, she signed one; Oakley drew it up. Catalina Scott belongs to The Lords of Sin now."

My father sighs, "Jesus, I hope Devlin doesn't blow a gasket when he finds out."

"He's the one that told her to come to us in the first place!" I tell him as I return to the array of weapons my father keeps hidden away.

"That's because he knows you three will protect her. I doubt he meant for her to become the Lord's little sex toy." Glancing at my father, he runs his hand over his face as he sighs.

"Well, if it makes you feel better, Little Saint definitely has her own mind, and she's a smart little shit. I doubt she will let us get away with much. Besides, it seems like the Provost's daughter has a bit of a Sinner in her already. If not, she will soon enough." I wink at the older version of myself.

He chuckles as he shakes his head, "She must definitely get that from her mother. Just be careful with her, will you? Her parents are still our friends."

"Settle down, Dad. You know damn well that we protect what's ours, which is why I am here." I open the glass and pull one of the Glocks off the wall.

"Don't be dumb, Fynn. Take what you need but use your head. You can't go shooting up places, always bring the target to a secure location." I stare at my father briefly.

"I will do what it takes to take this fucker out." I grab a few more handguns and knives before closing the safe.

My father hands me a small duffle bag, "I want these back once you're done with them."

I smile, "Tell Uncle Tyler I said hi."

He snorts, "You're lucky that the Police Chief is your uncle and that you're his favorite nephew."

"I'm his only nephew," I grin and swing the bag up on my shoulder, "Oh, the body shop will be sending the bill to you for my bike."

"What the fuck, Fynn? That bike is your responsibility!" my father frowns at me.

"Yeah, well, it got fucked up because of you and your friends, so you can pay for it. I don't know what the hell you did to piss this person off, but they are becoming a pain in my ass!" I say, scowling.

"Just watch yourselves, and we will try and figure out what this little asshole wants because they still haven't clarified why they are pissed. We did a lot of stupid shit in college, which is why we are hard on you boys. Once we can pinpoint which fuck up it was, then we can try to rectify it."

Jakob Morin, Donavan Harris, Blake Pelletier, and Devlin Scott, all Lords of Sin back in their day, wreaking havoc, and now their offspring must deal with their fuck ups. How is that fair? It's not, and that is why I leave my family home with a bag full of weapons, so this little fucker will know that they chose the wrong ones to fuck with!

All has been quiet the last few days. The guys and I have made ourselves scarce, limiting the number of people who see us, including Little Saint. Oh, but we have been watching her closely. One of us guys always has her in our sight. Whoever it was that followed her the night she left our place hasn't tried to do so since, but we know it's only a matter of time.

"Fuck, I need inside her!" Oakley bursts into my room, "Her body, attitude, everything about her just screams at me to own every inch of her!" My friend paces back and forth, so I pass him the greenery I'm smoking to help calm him down.

"I take it guard duty didn't end well. What did you do, watch her masturbate or something?" I chuckle.

"God, I wish that's all it was. No, I needed to touch her, so I had her meet me in the hall behind the library. She fucking kissed me back, heatedly, I might add, and our little slut rubbed her ass against my already hard cock. I almost took her right there, damn it!"

"Why didn't you?" I shrug as I watch him take a long hit from my offering.

"You know why," he growls before blowing the smoke out, "Kitty Cat will be panting like a bitch in heat, begging us to take her before I actually do. We need her hornier than fuck for that to happen."

"I hate to break it to you, but she's probably fucking herself each time we leave her hanging; just saying, bro."

It's the truth. If she's anything like the rest of us, we are either rubbing one off or fucking a willing groupie since Little Saint has come into our lives. I grab my phone from beside me and type out a message. If my friend isn't going to help himself, then I'll do it for him.

Oakley has only been sitting in the chair in my room for a few minutes when there is a knock at my door. Instead of calling out to them, I walk over and open it up to see Brett standing on the other side of it with a blond that looks nothing like our Saint, but as long as he's tapping her from the back, he can pretend.

Lifting my phone, I go through the steps of recording her consent. I have a feeling that this little session may get a little wild. Once the chick has given me everything needed, I wink at our boy Brett and pull the girl inside. I don't worry about closing the door as I bring her to Oakley.

"A gift, my friend," I move behind the female and pull her top off; her bra comes off next. Cupping her breasts, I grin at my friend, "So, are you ready to take care of those frustrations?"

I can see the hesitation in Oak's eyes, so I spin her around and lift the skirt she's wearing, but he starts shaking his head, "It's not her; I don't know if it will work."

I scoff, "She's got the same hair color. Fucking her from the back; you can pretend it's whoever the fuck you want it to be." I feel the female tense, but she doesn't say a word.

He reaches up and begins massaging the female's ass before running his fingers through her slick folds. I know deep down my friend wants to bury himself inside of this cunt. When she moans, I know he's entered her with his fingers.

Taking the girl's chin in my fingers, I lift her head, "You want both of us?"

"Mm," her eyes are still closed as she enjoys what Oakley is doing to her.

"Look at me when I fucking talk to you," I chastise her, and her eyes snap open, "Now, do you want the two of us to fuck you?"

"Y-Yes, please."

I grin, "Good fucking girl."

After grabbing a couple of condoms, Oak and I take Emily, or whatever her name is, hard. I destroy her ass while my friend does the same with her pussy, but I bet anyone a million bucks that the same thing is running through his head that is running through mine; how we wish that this was Catalina Scott.

Oakley

Letting Kitty Cat go while sporting the hardest erection was the worst thing I've ever done. I should have had her take care of it before letting her go, but I have plans for the Saint, and I can't let my dick ruin it just yet. I should have known that Fynn would come in clutch and have my back. Even though it's hard to concentrate knowing that it isn't my Kitty Cat that I'm balls deep in, it's at least relieving the pent-up frustration I have going on.

"How are you doing on that end, Oak?" Fynn asks as he slams into the chick's ass.

"I'm good," I glance at the female with a goofy smile as she lets us use her, "What about you?"

"Oh, I'm good," Fynn pulls the girl's head back by her hair, "Here, suck those titties. They are screaming out for your mouth."

These tits aren't the ones I want, and there is a considerable difference between these and Kitty Cat's, but frustration takes hold once again, and I clamp down on Fynn's offering. I mark the slut with my teeth as I suck and bite her little mounds.

"Oh yes, Oakley...more!" Her voice is not the one I want to hear, and it starts to affect my hard-on.

"Shut the fuck up. I don't want to hear your voice right now." Yeah, I'm a dick, but she consented, so it's fair game. It's just not working out like I want it to, "Let's spit roast our little slut here."

My suggestion must piss off the female because she tenses and has the gall to speak again after being told not to, "I don't like being called a slut."

"Awe, you don't like having to face what you are, huh? Well, sweet cheeks, you consented. Say so now if you have changed your mind, and we will stop." I pull out of her as soon as Fynn pulls out of her ass.

"I don't want to stop the sex, just the name-calling; it's degrading." The female pouts.

"This is how we fuck, so either deal with it or get the fuck out." I scowl at the girl as Fynn chuckles behind her.

She looks back and forth between me and my best friend and then sighs, "Okay."

"Good girl, now get on the fucking bed," I tell her and wait until she gets on all fours.

Fynn climbs up and kneels in front of her, "Take this shit off me," he points to the used condom still wrapping his cock.

"But it was in my butt!" The chick exclaims while making a disgusted face.

"Yeah, and so was my dick, so take the fucking condom off so you can suck me off." Fynn can be such an ass, but I'd probably say something along those lines too.

Once the female slowly removes the used condom, Fynn wastes no time having her take him into her mouth. That's my cue to enter her again, and away we go. The fucking is hard and intense, especially from this back view. It really is almost like fucking our Saint.

Wrapping the girl's long hair around my hand, I grab her hip with my other hand and hammer into her like a fucking jackhammer. This will be the last one, the last groupie I fuck because once I have my Kitty Cat, I have a feeling that I won't want another cunt. At least not until we are through with our Saint.

Just thinking about Catalina has my balls pulling up, and I slam into the pussy I'm in one last time and let go. Fynn has the same idea, but he pulls out of her mouth because he never allows them to taste his cum; he's weird like that. Instead, he paints her face with it as he grunts out every last drop.

Tossing a rag to Emily or whatever her name is, we have her clean herself up before booting her out. I stare at my friend, having no words for what just happened. I almost feel guilty; for what? The fuck if I know. The contract doesn't say anything about being with others, but I know that anyone who tries getting with my Kitty Cat will get his dick cut off, and that's a fact. So, now I'm feeling guilty for doing what we will never allow her to do.

"Stop it. We aren't going to do this, Oak. You have to remember that Catalina is just another pussy to conquer. We have to drill that into our heads." Fynn starts putting on his boxers.

"Is she, though? I feel like it may be more; she's one of us, after all." I put my own clothes back on.

"That's just it, she is one of us, and once we are through with this threat and the contract runs out, she will remain beside us as she should be, but we will continue to fuck who we want."

"So, you will be fine with her fucking others then?" I ask him.

Fynn thinks about it, then sinks into the chair I occupied earlier, "Fuck, you're right. I knew this deep down, but I'm trying to keep some semblance of myself, so I don't lose my mind over one little pussy."

I grin at my friend because I know how much he must hate to come to this reality, "Chin up, buttercup; it's not all that bad."

"Fuck you, Oak. I'm not ready to give up my wild ways." He lights his special smoke.

"Please, there will be no giving any of that up. If anything, we are bringing her into our world, and I feel she may even like it a little." I head for the door, planning on going to my own room.

"I hope you're right," Fynn adjusts himself, "I'm going to have fun showing Little Saint just how fucked up we really are."

I scoff, "We aren't fucked up, my friend. The world around us is just too afraid to let go of the safety net. That's okay, though. We can't all be sick and depraved, and it may be a bit twisted, but it isn't fucked up, and don't let anyone tell you any different."

"Yeah, okay," Fynn's mouth kicks up into a half grin, "You can call it anything you want, but me, I don't mind being fucked up, especially where Little Saint is concerned."

I just shake my head and leave my friend in his own little world. I'm serious, though. People can think what they want, but they will never know what true freedom feels like until they are willing to let go and just be free about it all.

Putting the final touches on the party preparations, I go up to Fynn's room to grab the tappers for the kegs that are being delivered as we speak. Since he's on guard duty for the next few hours, I have to search for them myself. All he said was that they were in a bag in his closet.

The first bag I come to is not what I'm looking for, but I dig inside it anyway. Fynn said he brought some protection from his dad's office, but this is like an arsenal. I pull out a blade that looks to be for hunting. The grips on the handle fit perfectly in my hand like it was made for me. I'll have to get myself one of these, but for now, I will just borrow this one and let Fynn know I have it. I'm not much of a gun person, so the knife is perfect.

With the threat to my Kitty Cat, I've hired some outside security who will be dressed up as partygoers to blend in. Having a little extra protection on my person will keep me more relaxed, knowing that I can protect her myself if it comes down to it.

After the whole incident with Fynn's Harley, we realized that even though they are fucking with our shit, the perpetrator is going for Catalina first because they think she's the weakest between us all. If this person truly wants payback for something our fathers have done, they will be coming after all of us eventually. I don't plan on them getting very far.

Finding the tappers in the next bag I look through; I head back downstairs. Jett is working on the pulley system we are using to raise our virgin sacrifice above everyone while cuffed to a St. Andrew's Cross. Kitty Cat is going to look gorgeous as she suspends over the crowd. She will then be let down but only to be whisked away into a blocked-off area in the backyard already decorated for the themed party. That's where we will take her for the first time, not in front of everyone, but it will be live-streamed.

I'm dying to see our girl's reaction when we fuck her, only for the crowd to watch on a big screen. No one will know who she is as she wears a full-face mask and a wig. The last thing we need is for her father to find out. If it weren't for that alone, I'd fuck our girl for all the world to see so they all know that she belongs to the Lords of Sin.

I curse myself out for giving myself yet another hard-on. Walking toward the refreshment table, I drop the tappers on each of the kegs and then head to the bathroom to disappear for a while. Only a few more hours, and I will not have to rub one off anymore. Once we take our girl, she will be at our beck and call, but first, we need her to beg us to take her tonight. That shouldn't be too hard, right?

FIFTEEN

Catalina

I don't know whether to be excited or nervous. It's my very first Toga Party which should be exciting but knowing that the Lords of Sin are planning on sacrificing me has my nerves frayed. The thought of them taking me together, though? I've fantasized about having threesomes or, should I say, a foursome; it all means the same thing, I guess. Regardless, I never wanted to initiate one, and the guys at my high school were too lame; they probably wouldn't know what to do.

So, saying that I don't want it to happen would be a lie, but the part where it will be watched has me pacing my room with only thirty minutes left before leaving. I'm wearing the costume I had initially bought for it because I don't need Dani asking questions about why I'm not getting ready. She's already upset that I can't go with her because they requested me earlier.

"I don't know why you need to go so early. What are you not telling me?" My roommate questions as she starts on her own makeup.

"I can't answer that, Dani. All I know is I'm expected to be there an hour before the party starts. Don't worry, I'll be fine." At least, I hope I will be.

Do I feel like my life is in danger with the Lords? Of course not, but that doesn't mean it can't turn on a dime if I piss them off. I've heard stories, but whether they are rumors or not is different. Amongst the lust I see in their eyes whenever I'm around them, something more sinister lurks in their depths, and I haven't been around them enough to figure out what it is.

"Well, I will look for you once I get there." My roommate looks pointedly at me.

I shrug, "Okay, but like I said, I don't know what they want me to do yet, so I can't promise I will be able to hang with you much."

I really hate lying, especially to my only friend here at college, but as much as we are alike, I can still sense her disdain for me hanging around the Lords. It's not her family being threatened, so she won't understand, which gives me no choice but to lie.

I step behind her and take her hair in my hands, twisting it before putting the clips in to hold it in place. I smile at her through the mirror before she scrutinizes me closely. I try to act as normal as possible, and finally, she relaxes and lets me finish her hair for her.

"There! I love this hairstyle with the costume, and your makeup rocks the whole look!" Genuinely smiling at how gorgeous my friend looks, I glance at the time, "Oh shit! I better get going!" Grabbing my small handbag and dress coat on my way out, I wave at Dani and close the door behind me.

Quickly, I cover myself with my coat before making my way downstairs and thank God I did because Felicia just happens to be walking by. When she gives me a once-over, she stops and crosses her arms.

"Where are you going all dressed up?" Her eyebrow raises as she waits for my answer.

"Not that it's any of your business, but I'm going to dinner with my father. Would you like me to bring you back anything?" I ask and watch the Sorority President's whole demeanor change.

"Oh! Where are you going?" There is excitement in her voice now, thinking I'll bring her back food.

So, I quickly think of the one restaurant I know she doesn't like because she's gotten food poisoning from eating there, "Oh, Dad is taking me to the French place here in town. What's the name of it?"

"Pierre's?" She asks as her face turns a tinted green.

"Yes! That's the one. Would you like anything?" I smile on the outside but laugh my ass off on the inside.

Her hand goes to her stomach, "God no, and I hope you don't get sick from eating there like I did."

I give her a sympathetic look, "I'm sorry to hear that you got sick," I start for the front door but call out over my shoulder, "Call me if you change your mind!" Snickering once I'm standing outside, I quicken my steps and head for the forbidden Sinner's Frat House.

The front door is open when I get to the Frat house, so I call out from the doorway. Nobody is around to answer, but I see that the inside is decorated for the party and looks incredible. I step inside, and I look all around. The length they went through to decorate is impressive, and it is hard to believe that a bunch of Sinners did the work.

I hear voices toward the back of the house, so I make my way in that direction, stopping when I get to the back door. My mouth drops at the massive faux volcano that sits as the centerpiece in the backyard. Tiki torches line the pathways all around, and I notice a cable above my head running the yard's length, ending behind a fake wall on the other side.

A giant projector screen is set up in a far corner, and a few guys are setting up some tables and chairs. None of them are the Sinners I'm looking for, so I turn to head upstairs, only to run into a hard chest.

"You really need to watch where you walk, Little Saint." The deep rumble of Fynn's chuckle vibrates through my core, and I have to squeeze my thighs together.

His strong hands gripping my upper arms, keeping me from stumbling, don't help either. I look up and see the cocky grin he's sporting and take a step back. Fumbling with the tie on my coat, I'm trying to find the words I should be saying instead of gawking at the Gladiator-like man before me.

Fynn is already in costume, but it's not a Toga. Instead, he's wearing a leather loincloth, but it's more like a short skirt that covers both loin and ass with leather strips. His chest is bare, and the only other items he wears are the leather strips around his biceps and wrists and the leather sandals with leather strips wrapping his calves.

I'm not ready for any of this. I am way out of my depth here with these Sinners. If Fynn is dressed this way, I can only imagine what the other two are dressed like. My gawking is only amusing the Lord more, and he stirs me in the direction I need to go.

Something finally snaps, and I can form words again, "Where are you taking me?"

"Well, Little Saint, we need to get you into the proper attire and then explain what your role will be and what will be expected of you." His voice is close to my ear, and I can feel the heat from his breath as it tickles my neck.

I need to snap out of this state! I can't let them know how much they affect me. With that being said, I pull my arm away, causing Fynn to loosen his grip and let go altogether, "I don't see anything wrong with the costume I'm wearing."

The Lord plants his hard, mouth-watering body in front of me and tugs on my tie before I realize what he's doing. I try to snatch it, but he yanks it open before I get the chance, "Well, well, well, don't you look like the perfect little slut." He licks his lips as he looks me up and down.

"Fynn..." I say his name in warning.

He looks at me and smirks, "What? I have every right to look at what is mine." He stares at the deep V that reaches down to my waist with whisps of fabric barely covering my breasts, "I'll give it to you, Little Saint, you're sexy as hell in this get-up, but I think you will look even hotter in the one we have for you."

I cross my arms over my chest, blocking his view of the very thing he's staring at, "Oh, and why is that?"

Amusement dances in his eyes, "Because it's more fitting for a sacrificial virgin, that's why."

"I'm not a fucking virgin," I walk around him and head for the stairs.

He doesn't stop me but hurries to be at my side again, "No, not technically, but you are the Lords' virgin."

I stop and turn to him, throwing my hands up, "That makes no sense at all!"

"All I'm saying is that you're our virgin because you haven't had our cocks in that sweet little pussy of yours." He steps into me, grabbing my neck. Thinking he will kiss me, I close my eyes, but it's not my lips that I feel his mouth on; it's my neck. He gives a little bite and then a lick before stepping away, "That will all be rectified tonight."

It's my turn to hurry and catch up after he turns and walks away. I'm left panting with moisture pooling between my legs, but I ignore it. I continue to follow him until we reach Oakley's room, and the Greek God himself stands in front of his full-length mirror. It's just as I thought, the Lords of Sin are coming dressed as the sexiest gladiators that ever walked the face of this earth.

"Ah, Kitty Cat! I'm so glad you're here," Oakley states before looking me up and down, "As much as I love your costume, I'll need you to change into the one I bought for you. I picked it out myself, and I'm dying to see it on our lovely little virgin."

I roll my eyes at the whole 'virgin' spiel once again as Oakley goes to his closet and pulls what looks to be sheer curtains from the rack. He hands the hangar to me, and I can't help but drop my jaw once I realize what I'm looking at.

"You have got to be fucking kidding me!"

Both Lords grin wickedly as they usher me toward the bathroom, "You're going to look beautiful, Kitty Cat."

"I'm not wearing this, Oakley." No way in hell!

"I'm not asking, Kitty Cat. You will wear it and obey our every demand tonight," Oakley states.

"Yeah, especially after the damage to my Harley due to your little stalker," Fynn growls.

"Wait...what?" I snap my head toward Fynn.

"Oh, that's right, we never told you. Jett and I followed you home the night you were here to ensure you were safe. Lucky for you that we did because Jett ended up chasing after the perp when he got up right behind you, and you didn't even know. When we returned to the Frat house, I noticed my bike had been fucked with, so yeah, I think you owe us this one."

Well, shit. How can I deny them now that they have already protected me once? I doubt they would lie; Fynn seems too pissed about his bike to lie, so I do the only thing I can do. I take the sheer costume into the bathroom and turn myself into the Lords of Sin's sacrificial virgin.

Walking out of the bathroom, I can't help but keep my arms crossed over my chest. I'm not sure when Jett showed up, but he's now standing with his two best friends, looking just as yummy as they do in his own gladiator outfit. The Lords are dressed to conquer, and I'm the one they will be conquering later.

"Kitty Cat," Oakley says in warning, and I move my arms down to my sides but keep my head held high.

"Holy fuck!" Fynn and Jett say in unison as the three approach me and circle around like I'm their prey.

"I knew this was perfect for you, Kitty Cat." Oakley caresses my cheek before sliding his hand to the back of my neck and taking my mouth in a brief but heated kiss.

When he pulls away, Jett slides his hand into the top to cup my braless breast. I wasn't wearing one to begin with, but they were covered more with my costume than they are now. The top is the same style as my last costume with the deep V and strips covering my breasts, only this top is sheer, and you can faintly see my nipples through it.

The whole thing is sheer, but thankfully, they at least gave me a thong to wear under the sheer skirt. It's a long and flowy dress, and very pretty, but the nudity that comes with it I can do without.

I stand here while Jett gets his fondling in. When he tweaks my nipple, I glare at him, "Are you done yet?"

He pulls his hand out and winks at me, almost like he was only waiting for my reaction. Suddenly, my hair is pulled up and placed in a bun before a red wig gets pulled over my head.

"What the hell? Is my hair not good enough for you?" I ask with attitude, but I'm actually a little hurt.

"Do you want people to recognize you?" Oakley raises a brow, "We are doing this for you to help you out, but by all means, we can leave the wig and mask off."

Oh, wow. I didn't realize they thought about my feelings, to an extent, for this. Even though this is for them, they are still thinking of the outcome from my end. I turn my head back forward and let him finish putting the wig on.

"Thank you," I say softly.

"What was that?" Oakley asks, bringing his ear closer.

"Don't push it, Harris," I warn and get a chuckle from him.

He hands me a thin, golden, feminine mask to put on, and I look like an entirely different person when I do. My three Lords stand around me, and we stare at our reflection momentarily. I can't deny that we look beautiful together.

Oakley slips his hand around my midsection, pulling me against him, "Are you ready to fully belong to the Lords of Sin, Kitty Cat?"

I study each one who is staring back at me through the mirror. It should be illegal to be so good-looking. My core throbs from just looking at them. When Jett starts to smirk, I remember that Oakley asked me a question, and my eyes return to him in the reflection.

Nodding, I lick my lips, "Yes."

Fynn dips down and presses his lips to my bare shoulder, "I can hardly wait, Little Saint."

"Me, too," Jett comes around and yanks me to him, stealing my lips as he kisses me through the mask. It's more challenging, but he manages to slip me the tongue regardless, which only gets me giggling. Fucking giggling like a damn schoolgirl.

Oakley takes my hand and heads for the door, "Come, let's get you ready, shall we?"

They bring me to a room on the first floor with French doors opening to a patio. When they get me outside, there is a wooden structure shaped like a giant X with cuffs at all four points. My forehead crinkles; I've seen something like this before. I can't remember the name, but I know it's used for both torture and pleasure.

"What is this?" I ask as I continue to study the structure.

"This, Lovely Lina, is what we call a St. Andrew's Cross. In the old days, it was used in torture chambers, but this cross is a staple used in BDSM." Jett runs his hand along the dark, smooth wood as he smiles at me.

"What's it doing here now, though?"

"You see, Kitty Cat, we have it hooked up to this cable and pulley system, so once we secure this gorgeous body of yours to it, we will present you to the guests as our sacrificial virgin as you suspend from above. You will stay there until it's time to send you across the yard and behind that wall over there," Oakley points to the fake wall I noticed earlier.

"That's where we will make you officially ours, Little Saint," Fynn runs his fingers down my bare arm, now littered with goosebumps, "It's going to be fucking amazing."

Well, it certainly beats letting them take me in front of everyone. I guess it will be okay, but I'm still a little nervous about all three of them taking me. I know I need to get over it; I doubt they will be complete assholes about it.

"How long will I be in the air for?" I'm not afraid of heights but being suspended for a length of time isn't really my cup of tea.

"Only about ten, maybe fifteen minutes, tops. The sacrifice kicks off the start of the party, and besides, we are all dying to coat our cocks in Catalina cum." Fynn says vulgarly.

My eyes follow the cable up and across the expanse of the yard. I'll be moving over the faux volcano, the tables, and the pool with tiki torches all around it before ending on the other side of the wall. It's not too far, but it's far enough when I know the crowd will have a nice view under my dress. Thank God for thongs.

"So, nobody will actually see the deed being done behind the wall?" I turn back to Oakley, only to see the wicked grin painting his face.

"Oh, they will be watching, but it will be on the projector screen. Nobody will see behind the wall." He steps up to me and slips his hand inside a slit in the skirt, "Does that make you wet, Kitty Cat?" When his fingers slip into the thong, his eyes light up at what he finds.

Hardening my resolve, I look him dead in the eye, "It's not the fact that the crowd will be watching that has me in this state, Harris."

"Oh?" He pulls his hand back and holds it up to show Jett and Fynn before sucking my arousal from them, "Then what is it?"

"You will just have to find out," I move toward the cross and get in place.

Jett and Fynn are quick to fasten the cuffs on my wrists and then my ankles. Little wooden slats stick out for me to stand on, so it's not just the cuffs holding me in place. All the while, I keep my eyes focused on Oakley as he has his on mine. I can do this; it's what keeps running through my head. Nobody will know it's me, not while I'm in the wig and mask. Once it's all over, I'll change back into my other costume and join the rest of the party.

All three Lords check the restraints and the cables to ensure my safety before I'm lifted up. As I wait for them to finish, my heart pounds a mile a minute, but I'm not sure whether it's nerves or anticipation. It could be a little of both.

"Oh, we did leave out one small detail, Lovely Lina," my Ink Boy steps before me, "Once we've fucked your brains out, we will kill you."

"What!?" I cry out and start trying to bust out of the cuffs.

"Oh, stop it, you're freaking her out," Oakley chuckles, "He's kidding, Kitty Cat. Well, not really, we do need to sacrifice you, but it's all for show."

Oakley pulls out a dagger, which looks suspiciously like the one he used to prick my finger. I hold my breath as he slowly drags the point down between my breasts. I can see the drag mark as he goes down, then comes back up. He stops right over my heart, his stormy blue eyes dancing with amusement just before he plunges it in, only it doesn't puncture my flesh; it's a prop.

"Did you actually think I would end you here and now?" The Sinner chuckles, "The prop isn't made to take a life; however," he slides it down and rubs the handle over my clit, "it can be used to fuck a tight cunt like this pretty one."

My breathing quickens as desire flares inside, and I have to prevent myself from moaning. I keep my eyes on Oakley's the whole time. He knows precisely how his actions affect me, and when I think I can't hold back, he pulls the prop away.

"Naughty little Kitty Cat! You were going to come before it is time. No worries, we can give you what you want as soon as you reach the other side."

He winks at me before moving away. He then presses an earpiece that I never noticed, "Get ready. Wait until you hear me say the word before lifting the virgin." He grins at me the whole time he's talking to whoever is on the other side of that earpiece.

Suddenly, I find myself alone on the terrace, restrained to this cross. In just a few moments, everyone will see me high above their heads as the Lords of Sin present me. Will Dani know it's me? Will she judge me if she does? Thinking about this last question, I realize that I really don't care if she has a problem with it because, at the end of the day, I'm going to belong to the worst Sinners of all, and even though I shouldn't, I'm looking forward to seeing just how depraved the Lords of Sin can really be.

SIXTEEN

Jett

I can't take my eyes off her. She's like a fucking Goddess in the sheer white dress, an angel come to listen to us repent our sins. Only we will take her and make her our biggest sin of all. I want to do bad things to Catalina. I want to see just how far she will allow us to go. The things running through my head would even make the devil run the other way.

As Fynn and I stand on each side of Oakley, we let him take the lead for the start of the ceremony. I hate speaking in public, and Fynn likes to stand there with a pissed-off look, intimidating anyone who wants to talk to him.

"Ladies and gentlemen," Oak starts, "Thank you for coming to the Sinner's Fraternity Annual Toga Party! As always, every year, we kick off the party with a virgin sacrifice; this year is no different. So please, let's give a round of applause to our virgin Goddess!" He lifts his hand toward the terrace where we left our lovely Saint, and up she goes.

She indeed looks like a Greek Goddess as she rises above everyone. The crowd is chaotic as they get a look at our girl. There is no way of telling who it is behind the mask and wig. As she comes forward and stops just above our heads, I'm glad we had given her that thong; otherwise, these motherfuckers would see what now only belongs to us.

"Please, have a good long look at our virgin sacrifice because soon, the Lords of Sin will be claiming her before we sacrifice her for the angry Gods!" Oakley continues, "Unlike previous years, we will not be taking her in front of you," the crowd begins to boo, but Oakley holds his hand up, "You will, however, be able to watch from the big projector screen over in the far corner."

I look across the crowd, and something catches my attention. Tapping Fynn on the shoulder, I nod in the direction of the figure standing at the back of the crowd. Fynn follows my line of sight and tenses when he also notices the white hooded figure. My friend jumps down from the makeshift stage and slowly starts in the figure's direction.

While Oakley continues his speech, I keep an eye on Catalina. When the cross begins to move toward the wall, I glance in Fynn's direction, but I've lost sight of my friend and the mystery guest. Watching our girl, she's now over the volcano we brought in for the party. It's slow going, but she's soon moving over the tables and coming to the pool area.

Everyone watches in excitement. Once she reaches the pool, that is supposed to be our cue to head over to the wall, so we can be there to get her down. Oakley and I walk off the stage and head to the back as she passes over the first set of tiki torches before the pool.

My cock is hard as fuck, knowing that it's finally going to get inside its Lovely Lina. I take my eyes off our girl for two seconds, and a scream pierces through the area. Oak and I snap our heads in Catalina's direction, and I can see the fear in her eyes, even from this distance.

She looks straight at me and my friend as she calls for help; the cable is swinging wildly. Then, to my horror, I watch, as if in slow motion, as the cable breaks and the cross, along with our girl, plummets into the pool's deep end.

Of course, the crowd begins to freak out and moves toward the pool area, but nobody jumps in to help Catalina. Oakley and I fight the crowd to get to the pool. We dive in simultaneously and try to lift the cross to the surface, but it's useless. The cross is too heavy because of the metal frame that it's attached to.

I swim to the surface, "I need a knife!" Everybody just stands there, "Someone get me a fucking knife!"

I go back under and tap Oakley, indicating that he needs to go to the surface. I then press my mouth to Catalina's and give her air before returning to the top. When I break the surface, I see Fynn running our way. Oakley goes down to give our girl some air while I wait for Fynn.

"I've got the key!" He dives into the pool and goes straight to our girl.

I take another deep breath and go to the bottom. I see that Fynn already has one of her arms free just before I give her more air. Oakley and I take turns supplying Catalina with air while Fynn works on freeing her. When her last limb is free, I grab her and swim to the surface as fast as possible.

Catalina coughs and sputters as I swim to the edge of the pool, keeping her head above the water. Oakley pulls himself out as quick as he can and grabs our Saint. Surprisingly, the wig and mask are still on, and thank God, because if the dress was sheer before, it's entirely see-through now. Fynn and I follow close behind Oakley as he carries Catalina into the house.

I stop Sean and tell him he's in charge until we return, "Is she okay? I don't know what happened, man! All was good on our end; that cable shouldn't have busted."

The guy is freaking out, but I don't have time to soothe him, "We will talk later; just watch the guests." I catch up to the guys and follow them up to our floor.

As soon as we enter Oakley's room, we remove the mask and pull the pins from the wig to pull it off, "I s-saw t-them," Catalina's teeth chatter. It's the beginning of October, so the water in the pool is not warm at all.

"Saw who?" Oakley asks.

"The p-person in the w-white c-cloak. T-they cut t-the c-cable." She states.

"We must get these wet clothes off her and get her into the shower!" I tell the guys. I don't bother being nice about it as I tear the dress off her. It's flimsy enough that it rips easily. Oak hurries to the bathroom, turns the shower on, and all three of us join our Saint under the hot sprays. This isn't about anything sexual, and even though we do notice her banging body, none of us are sporting wood, but that could also be due to the cold pool.

I rub my hands up and down Catalina's arms from behind, and eventually, her teeth stop chattering, "Do you want to tell us again what you saw now that you're warmed up?" I turn her to face me.

"Someone in a white hooded robe was on the other side of the wall. They had some kind of wire cutters or something. It almost looked like those cutters that gardeners use to trim bushes. They were having difficulty cutting the cable; I first saw them as I was moving past the tables."

"That can't be right," Fynn chimes in, "I chased the hooded figure in the other direction. I lost them when I got to the front of the house."

"So there are at least two motherfuckers." Oakley growls.

"I-I think I'm good now, thank you."

I notice the look Lovely Lina gives the three of us; she can't look us in the eyes. Taking her chin in my hand, I tilt her head up, "Hey, there is nothing to be embarrassed about, Lina. We were eventually going to see you naked tonight anyway." I smirk.

Fynn crowds her in by coming up behind her, "It's your lucky night, Little Saint. Looks like there won't be an audience."

"What do you mean?"

It's so cute when she crinkles her forehead, "Now that you're good, we can finish the sacrifice. It just won't be watched on the big screen, and it won't be behind that wall." I cup her breast.

"Don't we need to find the perp who tried to kill me?" Catalina is a bit shocked by the turn of events.

"Oh, we will, Lina girl, don't you worry." I bend and put my shoulder to her mid-section, lifting her off her feet. I carry her over to the bed and toss her onto the mattress. I grab one of her arms while Fynn grabs the other, "It's time to finish this, Lovely Lina. Are you ready?"

"Wait! I just almost died! Are you seriously still going to fuck me?" She asks us, pretending to be stunned, but her body tells us differently.

"But you didn't die, did you?" I ask with a grin.

"But..."

I shut her up by kissing her. I feel the bed dip and pull away just as Oakley climbs between her legs. He's rolling on a condom as he stares at our girl. Even though her test results came back clean, he still uses the fucking things because you can never be too safe, he says. Fuck that; I'll be going bareback. It's been too long since I haven't used a condom. Now that I know we are both clean and Lovely Lina is on birth control, I will take full advantage of it.

"Be a good girl and open wide for him, Lovely Lina," I tell her.

There are no more questions, and she's stopped fighting it. Now, she just lays there watching Oakley as he lines his now-hardened cock up to her waiting cunt. I drew the big straw, so I get to go next, and I really can't wait to be inside the beautiful Saint.

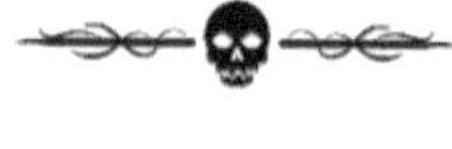

Catalina

My life had flashed before my eyes. I saw the hooded figure on the other side of the wall, but I thought they were just checking on things; I thought it was one of the other Sinners. When I realized that they were there to cut the cable holding me in the air, I freaked the fuck out. The next thing I knew, I was falling into the cold depths of the pool.

There were a few times I thought I was running out of air until Jett and Oakley fed me theirs. I will forever be indebted to them for saving my life. So, even though I'm nervous as fuck, and I think we should be finding the person who tried to kill me, I can't help but give in and allow them to finally claim me.

I quiver at the thought of being owned by the Lords of Sin, but it's what I've wanted ever since I saw them standing across the street from my Sorority House that day. Jett's kiss shuts me up, sending tingles throughout my body as he and Fynn hold me down.

I stop struggling when I feel the bed dip, and Jett pulls away. Oakley is there, gazing down at me, a wicked glint in his eye as he strokes himself and lines his cock up to my entrance. I give him a challenging look and refuse to make it easier on the Sinner by opening myself, as Jett suggests. I don't want to be a good fucking girl. I want to be the bad girl whom they want to punish and teach what happens to the naughty girls.

However, Oakley finds my challenge amusing, pushing my legs open further on his own, "You want to make it difficult, Kitty Cat? I can play this game with you. How long has it been since you've been fucked?"

"None of your fucking business," I state. There is no way I'm telling them that it's been almost a year since I've been sexually active with anyone.

"Hm, that mouth is going to get you in trouble, Kitty Cat," without any warning, Oakley's hips surge forward, sinking his thick cock as deep as it can go. He chuckles as I throw my head back, a silent scream forming on my lips from the impact, "Oops, my bad," he pulls back, "If it makes you feel any better, I wasn't expecting your snatch to be so tight." He thrusts in again, but he doesn't stop this time as he begins taking me like a starved man.

I try squirming away because he's so much bigger than I have had, "Oh, God...I can't! You're too big!"

"Help her relax, boys," I hear him say to his friends, and then their free hands are on me.

My body is on overload as I'm fucked hard and fast while hands play with my clit and my breasts. I want to scream for them to stop, but at the same time, I want to cry for more. I don't realize I'm moaning until Oakley snickers.

"See, I knew you would be such a slut for us. Look at you take my dick; you love it!" The way he states this with that cocky attitude pushes me over the edge, and I come hard. "That's right, give me what is mine, Kitty Cat. You'll give all three of us what we want because we own you now. Your body, your soul, your every fucking orgasm belongs to us now...remember that!" He jerks a few more times and grunts, releasing inside the condom.

"Flip her over," I vaguely hear someone say as I'm still trying to come down from my first orgasm, "Don't toss that out, Oak. We can use it as lube."

Suddenly, I'm flipped onto my stomach, and my hips are pulled back. Someone holds my head down on the mattress, and when I open my eyes again, I see Fynn smirking down at me, his cock in hand.

"Open that naughty little mouth Little Saint. I want you sinning all over my cock." He tries to push it through, but when I don't open it for him, he snarls like a freaking animal, then my hair is grabbed from the back, helping me to do so.

"Don't play shy now. You need to be showing us just how slutty you can be." Oakley says close to my ear.

So, as Fynn enters my mouth, Jett thrusts into me from behind. If that isn't bad enough, I feel my back door being poked and prodded. A sticky substance lands on my pucker, and that's when I realize that Jett is using Oakley's cum from the condom as lube.

One would think they would be disgusted at the thought of one guy using another guy's body fluids as lube, but I'm finding it a little hot. As if reading my mind, Jett chuckles, "This isn't the first time I've played around with my friend's cum, Lovely Lina."

"Oh, fuck..." A garbled moan erupts around Fynn's cock as Jett sinks his finger into my forbidden hole.

"That's it, relax, and maybe I will shove my cock in this hole instead of my finger." Jett says and then slaps my ass when I tense up, "I'm fucking with you. Tonight is only about claiming you. We will fuck your ass another night."

Fynn pulls his cock from my mouth, "You haven't earned it yet," Then proceeds to rub himself all over my face as he comes.

I can feel my drool smearing in with his seed as he rubs it all in, and that's when Jett stiffens and releases as well, "Damn it, Fynn! You know how that shit gets me off! You could have waited!"

"My bad," Fynn snickers, "You had her moaning all over my cock; what did you expect?"

Jett doesn't pull out as he fills me full. As soon as he pulls away, and I think it's over, I'm flipped again, and Fynn is now between my legs.

"What? You didn't think I'd be done already, did you? Fuck, I was just pregaming, baby!" His cock still stands at full mast, and he plunges into me. I now know what Tracy the Train from high school felt like when she would go into the bedroom at parties with multiple boys.

"You look fucking gorgeous, Kitty Cat!" Oakley leaves my side briefly and returns with a mirror.

As Jett grips my wrists above my head, Oakley shows me my reflection. Between my little swim, the shower, and now this, the little bit of makeup I was wearing is now smeared all over my face, accompanied by Fynn's drying cum. I glance at Oakley and see him wearing a lustful grin.

"You're fucking perfect, Kitty Cat."

Suddenly, he leans in and drags his tongue across my cheek, tasting the aftermath of his best friend. He then kisses me, sharing his friend's taste as that same friend takes me brutally. The Lords are not gentle by any means, as they twist, pull, squeeze, and pinch body parts that are way too sensitive. I've lost track of how many times I've come now.

If I didn't know any better, I'd say the more they dirty me with their release, the more animalistic they become. These Sinners like it dirty and are downright sick and twisted. Is it wrong of me to be turned on by all of it?

I open my eyes when I feel something odd rubbing against my clit and find Oakley rubbing the knife prop against it. I stare at him, challenging him, and he raises his brow. I know what he's thinking, and he's fucking crazy, but I find myself saying the complete opposite of what I want when I say, "I fucking dare you..."

There is no smile, grin, or smirk as he drags it down toward my entrance. Fynn pulls out but watches as his friend juices the handle by rubbing it through my cum-soaked folds before pushing the tip into me. I gasp and stay completely still. I don't know if he takes my reaction as a green light or just doesn't care because then his smile grows as he slowly pushes the handle in.

"Jesus, this slutty pussy is greedy for anything, isn't it?" Oakley chuckles.

"Please, take it out..." I pant.

"Oh, you don't like it? It's ribbed for your pleasure..." he pulls it out only to push it back in, "Come for me, and I will take it out."

At this moment is when I know that, without a doubt, the Lords of Sin have won because as Oakley fucks me with the ribbed handle of the knife meant to be used to "sacrifice" me, I begin humping it, meeting him thrust for thrust.

"Fuck me... that's so hot!" As he watches his friend get me off, Jett says, "Do it, Lina. Fucking come on that knife handle..."

I come so damn hard.

When I'm done, Oakley pulls it out, letting Fynn replace it with his cock again and finish himself, and I watch as the Greek God takes the handle into his mouth and sucks my arousal from it. His eyes are closed, and he groans while savoring my taste. I'm so enthralled in what Oakley is doing that another climax sneaks up on me, and I come once more as Fynn releases inside me.

"And that, Kitty Cat, is just the beginning of what we will do to you while you are ours." Oakley states, tossing the fake knife onto my chest, "Get dressed; we have a party to attend."

SEVENTEEN

Oakley

A slight pain streaks across the middle of my back as I walk away from the naked woman who just literally shook me to the core with how responsive she was while my friends and I claimed her as ours. The way she rode that knife handle after she dared me to fuck her with it...I almost came right then and there. I can't let her know she's already started digging under my skin; she will never have that kind of power over me.

I turn around and see the knife prop lying on the floor at my feet. Catalina is now sitting up in my bed, glaring at me as her naked chest heaves up and down. I want to laugh at how adorable she looks, but now isn't the time to let her see that side of me, she's still in training, so I need to act accordingly.

"I may be yours per the contract, but you don't have to treat me like a common whore, Harris!" She spits.

I'm at her side in seconds, gripping her jaw and squeezing enough to tell her that I mean business, "It's Oakley, Catalina. Do well to remember that, and as for the other...as long as that contract is in full effect, you, Catalina Scott, are the Lords of Sin's whore, slut, bitch...whatever we decide you be."

"Fuck you, Oakley!"

"I'm pretty sure I just did, Kitty Cat, along with my best friends. But hey, if you want to go for round two, I'm sure we can oblige." I smirk and shove her down onto her back.

"I'd rather be fucked by the knife handle again than have you fuck me." Her words don't match her body's reaction, but I don't mention that.

"I'm sure we will be fucking you with other things in the future; after all, we have a big box of props we can play with. Now, be a good girl and get ready to head back to the party." I let go of her face and turn to leave, only to see Jett and Fynn smirking, "What?"

"Are you sure you don't want to take care of that first?" Fynn's eyes slide down to my hard cock.

"It will go away. We have shit to do," I glance back at Catalina, who is finally climbing from the bed, "Stay close to us, just in case we do have an itch to scratch before the night is through."

"I think you had better find out who almost killed me first. I'll return the favor once you've scratched that itch of mine." Kitty Cat has a mouth on her, and I know we should be trying to squash it, but it turns me on like no other.

Fynn, on the other hand, isn't having it as he grips her hair and pulls our girl into him, "You had better watch that mouth of yours, Little Saint; otherwise, we will stuff it full every chance we get until you get it through that pretty little head of yours not to talk back to us."

"Awe, you think I'm pretty?" Kitty Cat asks sarcastically, and I have to hide my smile. Jett's in the same boat as he turns away, so she doesn't see his amusement.

Fynn stomps them both to the window that overlooks the backyard. The sheer curtain is closed, but again, it's sheer. He presses her against the window, "Keep running that naughty little mouth, and all those people down there will see just how filthy you are at the moment. I will march you through the crowd, still dripping with our cum. Is that what you want?"

I continue pulling my clothes on as I watch the scene play out. Catalina is stubborn; I will give her that, but she's picked the wrong guys to try and play brave with because we don't give a shit. We will break her down piece by beautiful piece until she begs us to put her back together again. Catalina Scott doesn't realize it yet, but now that she belongs to us, she will never be the same again.

I leave the room after witnessing our girl finally giving in. I can't stay any longer, or I will take her again. My head needs to be straight if I'm going to try and figure out who the hell tried killing my Kitty Cat. Just thinking about what happened has the rage inside me building back up. Nobody touches the Lord's property, and now it's not only one person but two we are looking for.

It's like a needle in a haystack. We don't even know if they are students at Helshire or not. The only thing we do know is that they know our fathers and that we are their kids. I will have to do some digging into the school records to see what I can come up with if my father refuses to tell me anything. I believe they all know what this is about but are refusing to say what it is that has this person threatening them, because it has got to be bad.

Guests swarm me when I step outside, but I refuse to answer any of their questions about the incident earlier. Keeping my expression blank, I make my way over to the three makeshift thrones that the Lords sit in every year. In past years we have tossed the sacrifice aside once we've claimed her, but this year is different. I want my Kitty Cat by my side the whole time.

Unfortunately, we don't want to make a scene and have guests begin to guess that Catalina was the sacrifice. However, now that I think about it, someone knew she was on the St. Andrew's cross. Either that, or they weren't after Catalina, but just giving us Lords a warning.

I'm constantly scanning the crowd to see if there's anyone here that shouldn't be. When I see my Kitty Cat emerge from the house, with Fynn following close behind, my cock stirs once again. Her original costume is just as sexy as the one I got, only it isn't sheer. Nothing about how she looks gives her away as the virgin sacrifice, at least not to the other guests. However, I have every one of her luscious curves seared into my memory.

As soon as Jett joins me and then Fynn, the females flock to us. My eyes wander to Kitty Cat, and I can see the fury in her eyes at the scene around us. She shakes a little as she fills her cup from the keg, so what do I do? I piss her off more by slipping my hand around the waist of the groupie trying to talk to me. Of course, I'm not paying any attention to this woman; I only nod to make it look good for Kitty Cat.

I lean into the female's ear, "You look pretty. I like your costume," I tell her, just so I can make sure she smiles. When I see that it's had the desired effect and Kitty Cat is now pissed the fuck off, I tap the female's hip, "Go join the party, and have fun."

"I was hoping to make you feel good, Oakley."

"Maybe another time..."

"Tina," she supplies.

"Yes, well, another time, Tina."

The girl walks away, pouting. Catalina is still watching, so I crook my finger at her, telling her to come over. The little vixen subtly shakes her head and turns her back on me. I glance at my two friends, and they both wear a look of disbelief. Nobody has ever given us the cold shoulder.

With strike one against her, I glance her way again only to see her chatting it up with some pretty boy; strike two. Sitting straight up on my throne, I watch our girl like a fucking hawk. She knows she's being watched, too. Her little over-the-shoulder glances tell me that she knows we are watching.

I lean back and try to relax to avoid creating any kind of scene, and I keep watch. My frown chases the other groupies away, and I'm okay with that; they aren't the ones I want anyway. The blonde bombshell with her tits practically falling out of her top is the only slut I want.

"Our Little Saint is looking for trouble, it seems like." Fynn leans over toward me.

"Oh, do you think so?" I ask sarcastically, my eyes never leaving her.

"Does she not realize that we were serious about her being ours? Why is she putting herself into the position to be punished?" Jett questions.

My grin grows at my friend's question, "Because, Jett, that is exactly what she wants from us. She's testing us, seeing how far she can go before we give in and do exactly what she wants." I give a low growl when I see my Kitty Cat and her pretty boy move over to the dance floor and begin dancing.

"So, what are you thinking? Paddling her, caging her, humiliating her..." Jett continues to list the depraved things we have doled out in past punishments.

When I see how Kitty Cat has just earned her third strike by allowing the guy to slide his hand down to her ass, I snicker, "None of the above. We are going to make sure that pretty boy knows that Catalina Scott is off limits, and she's going to watch us do it."

Fynn

My Little Saint is going to get herself into trouble with that naughty mouth of hers, and I am looking forward to doling out that punishment. I struggled to keep my face as blank as possible earlier because all I wanted to do was grin. Little Saint is definitely one of us and will fit in perfectly as soon as we break her.

Watching her now from our thrones on the stage, my fingers begin to drum on the arm of the chair as I watch her dig herself a grave. I should say dig the poor sap that she is dancing with a grave. Oakley is right, Catalina needs to learn a lesson, and the best way is to make her watch as we also teach the pretty boy that he can't touch what's ours.

I know what people will think, 'But he didn't know,' yadda, yadda, yadda. We don't fucking care. Little Saint should have known better; now, he must pay the price. She will know better before making this mistake again.

"How should we do this? What are your thoughts, Fynn?" Oak and Jett both stare at me, waiting for my input.

I return to studying our girl on the dance floor, witnessing her grinding on the pretty boy's leg. A mischievous grin slowly makes its way onto my face, and I bite my lower lip. The images running rampant inside my head are bringing me great joy.

"Let's wait until he goes inside, and then we will nab him. Let our Little Saint think that he left without a goodbye and then call her back tomorrow, so we can teach her just how much she belongs to us."

"So what? We have to sit here and watch her rub herself all over this guy?" Jett doesn't hide his displeasure.

"Chill, bro. It will be fine; we can handle this. Besides, we want to avoid causing suspicion with what we are going to do. We have to play it cool."

Jett isn't happy, but neither am I. What I really want to do is go down and pummel the pretty boy's face until he looks like a fucking crater. We are bigger than that, though. The Lords of Sin need to set an example in public. What we do behind closed doors is an entirely different story.

The rest of the party is spent watching our girl, and she knows it. She does keg stands, and plays flippy cup, winning every game as usual. Little Saint dances to almost every song you can grind to with her new little toy, neither of them leaving the backyard for hours.

Finally, when things begin to wind down, I notice the pretty boy lean in and whisper something into Catalina's ear. She nods and then watches him head into the house.

I turn to the guys, "Oakley, you go to your Kitty Cat while Jett and I meet her new toy."

My friend grins and nods before jumping from the makeshift stage. We watch as he walks up behind our Little Saint and wraps his arms around her waist. He whispers something into her ear, and whatever it is, she isn't happy if the glare she gives my boy says anything.

Jett and I head into the house in search of the pretty boy. We are about to give up when we hear noises coming from the bathroom toward the front of the house. The fucker didn't even lock the door, so when we open it and find our girl's pretty boy banging a skank against the vanity, both Jett and I laugh.

Mixed feelings hit me coming across this scene. Even though we are going to teach this fucker a lesson in not messing with what is ours, if that wasn't the case, he'd still be in trouble for taking up with another whore while trying to get with Catalina. He's dug himself a deep fucking grave and doesn't even know it.

"Oh, hey, guys! I'll be done in just a minute, and she's all yours if you want."

I glance at Jett, who has his phone out and is most likely recording the scene, "No worries, man, take your time. What about the hot blonde who you have been all over tonight?" I ask him as he continues to fuck.

"I'm not sure I'm getting anywhere with her, but I have a remedy for that." He smirks.

"Oh, and what's that?" Jett questions, giving the guy his fake ass smile.

The pretty boy nods to the fanny pack he took off before fucking the skank, "It works every time. You should try it sometime; I can hook you up with my supplier."

I look inside and find a small bag of white pills. The fucker is going to roofie our girl. I show Jett the baggy, making sure he gets it on video. Zipping it back into the fanny pack, I toss it on the floor and cross my arms.

"We don't have an issue with getting pussy," I look at the familiar skank that the pretty boy has bent over, "Do we Beer Bottle Betty?"

"I think Oakley would like to know you're back here after being told not to return." Jett grins.

"Fuck you, Jett!" The skank pants.

"Well, now, I don't think you are in a position to talk to us this way, Betty." I smirk, "I believe there is a particular video that we have of you that you don't want the whole campus to see."

"Betty? I thought you said your name was Jackie?" Pretty Boy snorts.

Before she can respond, I reply, "We call her Beer Bottle Betty because she let some guys fuck her with one, with a used condom over it. There's no telling what STDs Betty, here, has."

Pretty Boy pulls out immediately, "That's fucking gross! Get the fuck out of here!"

Jett and I step aside and watch the guy shove Betty out the door. He bends down to put on his boxers, and that's when I stop him, "Whoa, Pretty Boy! Stop right there. We never said you could finish dressing."

"Huh? What are you talking about?" He scratches his head and looks from me to Jett and finally notices that Jett is recording, "What the fuck, man?"

"Don't 'what the fuck' me!" Jett growls, "You better get yourself in check because you're already in hot water with us."

"W-What did I do to you guys?" Pretty Boy stutters a little.

My hand snakes out quickly, latching onto the guy's neck, "You see, Pretty Boy..."

"Rob, my name is Rob."

"Do I look like I give a rat's ass about what your fucking name is?" I squeeze his neck, making him wince.

"I'm sorry! Whatever I did...I'm sorry!" Catalina's toy stammers.

"You're going to be really sorry here in a bit." Jett grins.

"Nobody fucks with our property, Pretty Boy, and Catalina Scott, she belongs to us; she's our property."

His eyes widen, almost bulging out of his head, "I didn't know, I swear! I would never..."

"Quit your fucking whining!" I sneer, "You came to our party at our fucking house, and you didn't think to ask if she was off-limits?"

"I thought the virgin sacrifice was yours for the night!" He's practically pissing himself as he tries to escape this situation.

"Have you been to past parties, Pretty Boy?"

"Y-Yes..."

"So then you know that once we are done claiming the sacrifice, we move on," I explain.

"My bad...I didn't know! I'm sorry!"

I'm glad he chose this bathroom because it's closer to the basement door. Jett shoves his phone back into his waistband and pushes the fucker out the door. I pick up his fanny pack but leave his boxers on the floor. No way am I touching the pretty boy's underwear.

We manage to get him into the basement after a few tries of him trying to run off. He may have fallen down the last three steps but will be fine. His ego is what's going to be bruised the most...maybe.

"What the fuck?" Little Saint tries to hurry over to her toy, but Oakley grabs her arm and hauls her against him.

"Not so fast, Kitty Cat," Oakley slips his arm around her waist and nuzzles her neck, "It's our turn to play."

I look at Jett, and he shrugs, "I didn't want to wait until morning, so I texted Oak to bring her down."

I roll my eyes at my friend.

"Stop this! He has nothing to do with what's going on!" Our girl glares at each of us.

"Oh, but he does, Little Saint," I caress her cheek before gripping her jaw, "He dared touch what is ours. We have told you that you now belong to us..."

"Yeah, well, it should go both ways! I won't fuck any of you if you continue to fuck all those little skanks that hang around all the time."

Oh, Little Saint is too cute when she's jealous, and jealous she is, "You will obey us no matter what," I run my other hand through her hair until I reach her nape and then yank on it, "You are the property of the Lords of Sin." I then drag my tongue, licking from her jaw to her forehead briefly, "There, I licked you, so now you're mine. Is that better?" I grin before moving, getting a few curses thrown my way.

Because we use the basement to do unsavory things to some females who prefer that kind of kink, we already have the chains we need dangling from the ceiling. Jett and I quickly restrain the pretty boy while Catalina pleads with us to let him go.

"Punish me then! He had no idea...I only wanted to get back at you guys!" She pisses me off, pleading for this stranger's life. She doesn't even know what kind of a douche he really is.

"Shh, Kitty Cat," Oakley coos, "We can't punish you because you will enjoy it too much. This is the only way that you will learn your place. His pain will now be on your hands."

As soon as Jett and I are done securing the fucker, I return to Catalina and Oakley. I hand the fucker's fanny pack to my Little Saint, "Here, hold your little toy's pack." I peck her cheek and then take my place in front of the body dangling from the ceiling and say, "this may hurt a little bit."

EIGHTEEN

Catalina

I close my eyes as I see Fynn's fist come down, but it does nothing to keep me from hearing the impact of it. This is all my fault! Poor Rob is going to have the shit beat out of him all because I was using him to get back at the Lords.

"Let me go, Oakley!" I struggle as he holds me tight against him.

"Not a chance, Kitty Cat. Open your eyes and watch your punishment." The Lord tries ordering me.

"Like I want to watch them beat on a guy that can't defend himself!" I sneer.

"Oh, is that what's bothering you, Lovely Lina? Fine," I hear the chains and take a peek to see Jett releasing Rob, "There, now he's not defenseless." He then throws a punch, knocking the poor guy down on his ass.

"Jett! Stop this right now...I get it!" I scream at him.

"This isn't just about that, Catalina," he states, then yanks Rob's head back by his hair, "Are you going to tell her what you were going to do, or should we?"

I'm confused by what Jett is saying, and I look at Rob for his reaction. He looks at me and then back to Jett, "I don't know what you're talking about! Cat, don't listen to them! They're just jealous because you wanted me and not them!"

"What the hell are you guys talking about?" I ask, not paying attention to Rob's statement, but then Fynn sends his fist flying.

Blood pours from Rob's nose, and Fynn looks at his friend, "You may want to get a hit in, Oak."

"Oh, I'm having fun watching," he chuckles.

"Yeah, well, how about you watch this and then tell us you only want to watch us do the beat down." Jett hands Oakley his phone, then looks at me and points to the fanny pack, "How about you look at what Pretty Boy is carrying around with him."

I look over at the guy on the floor and then at his pack, "This is his stuff; I shouldn't..."

"Look inside, Catalina!" I jump as his voice echoes loudly down here. I faintly hear some of the audio from Jett's phone and glance at Oakley, "What is it?" I ask when I see his expression turning angry.

Oakley raises the phone, so we can both watch it, and my stomach turns right away. There is Rob in his toga, fucking some girl in the bathroom. He told me he would use the restroom and walk me back to the Sorority house.

The video is like a train wreck; I can't look away. When my name is mentioned, rage fills me, especially after seeing the pills Fynn pulls from the fanny pack. I tear open the pack, and there they are, a baggy full of little white pills.

Throwing the pack to the floor, I rush over and jump on top of the piece of shit. I slam my own fist down on Rob's face repeatedly, "You motherfucker! You were going to drug me? I was nothing but nice to you, asshole!"

When he starts swinging back at me and knocks me in the jaw, Oakley blows a gasket and pulls me from him, taking over on the beating. I'm trying to kick out at him, but Jett keeps pulling me further away as he laughs.

"Down Killer..."

"Let me go, Ink Boy! I'm going to fucking kill him!" I struggle, but he continues to hold on.

"Calm down, Lina, or else I will have to do something drastic." He tells me near my ear, his hand sliding over and cupping my breast.

"What the fuck, Jett?" I stop struggling, but I'm still panting really hard.

"If you can't be a good girl and listen to me, I'll fuck you right here, in front of that piece of shit." Jett's tongue snakes out and licks the shell of my ear, "Is that what you want, Lovely Lina?"

I refuse to answer him because I'm unsure what my answer would be. Of course, I shouldn't want him to make good on his threat, but at the same time, it would show Rob that he really isn't the one I want.

"Fine, just let me go."

He lifts his brow in a warning and then loosens his hold on me. I pick up the pack again and pull the bag of pills out. Opening the bag, I take out one of the tiny pills and glance at Fynn and Jett. Fynn smirks and gives me a subtle nod, and that's all it takes.

Moving over to the battered male on the floor, I place a hand on Oakley's shoulder, indicating for him to stop, "Open your fucking mouth, asshole!" I shove the pill into his mouth when it opens wide enough, "Now swallow it!"

He shakes his head, "No..." he croaks out.

"Swallow the fucking pill, and I will call them off. Don't swallow, and you will probably never leave this basement." I warn the motherfucker, and he swallows the pill immediately.

"Damn it, I wasn't done yet. I wanted to get a few more hits in!" Jett whines.

"That was so fucking hot, Little Saint. I hated to pull you off the bastard." Fynn grins.

Oakley is covered in the asshole's blood, but he doesn't care as he stalks over to me and wraps his hand around my neck. My costume is already full of blood, so what's a little on my neck?

He turns my head from side to side, "Did he hurt you?"

"What?"

"When he clipped you in the jaw...did it hurt?" He asks again.

"I barely felt it; I'm fine."

Suddenly, his mouth is on mine in a brutal kiss, and shockingly, I kiss him back. I'm not sure if it's the adrenaline still running through me or what, but I find myself climbing the Lord's body until my legs are wrapped around his waist. My nails dig into the muscle of his shoulders as he grips my ass with his large hands.

"See that? That's why she didn't seem interested, bro. You are not a Sinner and definitely not a Lord, so you had no chance in hell." I hear Fynn say, and when I pull away, I see him holding Rob up, making him look in our direction.

I'm too turned on to care. What is it with violence that turns a person on? My desire is through the roof, and as Jett approaches me, he pulls my head by my chin and kisses me. I feel a hand slither between Oakley and me, and then the Lord's manhood rubs against my covered entrance.

"Jett, move Kitty Cat's panties aside for me," I vaguely hear Oakley's words before he pushes into me, "Oh fuck, Kitty Cat..."

I moan because not only does he feel good inside of me, but Jett has one hand inside my top while the other rubs my clit. Our tongues still dance the tango as I get fucked by his friend.

"That's hot, isn't it?" I hear Fynn still talking to Rob, "I bet you wish you could be part of that, don't you?"

I open my eyes and meet Fynn's heated ones as he watches both his friends with me. I've noticed that Fynn has never kissed me before, so I pull my mouth away from Jett's and challenge Fynn.

"Come kiss me, Fynn," I bite my lip, "Let me see if you are just as good as these two."

"Sorry, Little Saint. I don't kiss on the lips, at least not those lips." He smirks.

"Fuck him, Lovely Lina; I will take these lips any time," Jett states and kisses me again.

"Fuck, come for me, Kitty Cat. It's been so long since I've fucked bareback. I want to feel you come around my cock as I fill you with mine." Oakley pounds into me as he watches me kiss his best friend.

When I let my eyes fall on Fynn again, he's standing much closer, stroking himself. This alone takes me over the edge, and Jett kisses me harder as I cry out with my orgasm.

"Fuck yes...that's it!" Oakley grunts, and I feel him release inside me, "Damn, your cunt clenches really well... it's got me in a vise, Kitty Cat."

Jett continues to muffle my screams with his mouth until I've got nothing left in me. When he pulls his mouth away, it's only to demand that Oakley keeps holding me up. I don't understand what's happening until I feel Jett enter me from behind while my legs are still wrapped around Oakley.

"I can't. I need to rest..." I lean against Oakley.

"Then rest, Lovely. I can still fuck you as you do."

And he does. He fucks me until he fills me and then moves, so Fynn can take his spot, "Jesus, Fynn," Oakley curses as his friend slams into me, "You knock me over, and I'll knock your ass out!"

"My bad," Fynn snickers and then cups my breasts with his hands and begins thrusting fast, "You feel too fucking good, Little Saint."

"Mm, I'm going to be so sore come morning," I chuckle. I'm not sure what's come over me; I'm not even drunk!

I look to the floor and see that Rob is passed out. Jett is dragging him over to a corner where there are more chains with cuffs. When he sees me watching, he winks at me. I bite my lip and then turn to Oakley, who is watching me like a hawk.

"Give me that mouth, Kitty Cat."

For once, I don't fight him or even question him when he gives me an order. I gladly lean forward and press my lips against his, letting him take them as he likes. Soon, Fynn comes and pulls out. I'm then carried to Oakley's room, barely hearing the Lord's conversation as we climb to the top floor. Sleep takes over as soon as I hit the mattress, and I'm out for the night.

Sunlight is a beast in the mornings. During that time when all you want to do is sleep longer, but you know your body is waking up, that's when the sun becomes cruel and shines right through the window, shining right on your face. You can toss and turn onto your stomach or throw the pillow over your face, but the damage has already been done.

"Argh!" I toss the covers aside and sit up on the edge of the bed.

This is when I notice two things. One, my lady bits are sore as hell, and two, this is not my room. I look around and recognize it as Oakley's, only he's nowhere to be found. I glance over my shoulder and can still see the indent in his pillow on the other side of the bed.

"Oh, fucking hell!" Looking toward his bathroom, I see it's empty, so at least he isn't here, witnessing me waking up.

I'm in an oversized T-shirt and my panties, but I know I can't sneak out in this. My blood-stained costume is balled up on the floor beside the bed. I don't bother grabbing it because it's ruined now, so instead, I hurry over to Oakley's dresser and search for anything that I can wear for my walk of shame as I go home.

Finding a pair of sweatpants, I quickly pull them on and grab my phone, which someone had set on the table beside the bed. Pulling up the Uber app, I send for a ride even though I'm only blocks away. I don't want anybody to see me in this state and then it getting back to my dad. I'm supposed to be a good girl while I'm here. Instead, I've already taken up sinning twice in one night now.

The Uber is only three minutes out, so after ensuring my hair is somewhat decent, I tiptoe out of Oakley's room and toward the stairs. I'm at the bottom of the stairs in no time, only the door doesn't open. I curse, remembering that they keep it locked. Movement behind me has me whipping around and finding Oakley standing at the top of the stairs, dangling the keys from his finger.

"Needing these?" He smirks, and I glare.

"Damn it, Oakley. I have to get home; I shouldn't have slept here." I watch as he descends the staircase.

"I could have found other things for you to do besides sleep." His cocky grin has me tingling when I shouldn't be.

"That's not what I meant, and you know it!" I try snatching the keys from his hand, but he yanks them away.

"Not so fast, Kitty Cat," his eyes sweep me from head to toe, "You look cute in my clothes, but I like you better without them."

"Just for once, can you be a decent person?" I cross my arms and stare at him with a raised eyebrow.

"How much fun would that be, Kitty Cat?" He takes the last step down, so we are now almost touching, and I have to tilt my head back a little to look him in the face, "You were going to sneak out on us." It isn't a question.

I roll my eyes, "I wasn't sneaking out. I just wasn't going to search for you to tell you I was leaving...there's a difference."

A sly grin forms on his lips, "You know, Kitty Cat, that venomous tongue of yours is going to get you into trouble one of these days."

He comes closer, causing me to drop my arms and back up into the door, "Not today; it's not, because I'm leaving. Now, open the door. I have an Uber waiting for me."

"Cancel it."

"What? No..."

"I said...cancel it." Oakley's stormy eyes burn into mine challengingly.

"I won't. I need to get home and shower."

"You can shower here...with me." He licks his lips.

"No, besides, my roommate is probably worried sick."

"Oh, you mean Dani? The same Dani that got her brains fucked out of her last night by my boy Sean...that Dani? Last I knew, she was still in his bed." His finger drags up my arm, "which is where you should be, because I didn't tell you that you could leave. I may have wanted a little 'pick-me-up' before taking you back."

I scoff at him, "I'm too sore to go another round. I will probably have to soak my vag for a week before it feels normal again."

"Why, we're just going to tear it up again. You might as well get used to it." Oakley grins proudly.

I sigh, rubbing my forehead, "Oakley, I really need to go, so unlock the fucking door!"

That was probably the wrong thing to say because his hand shoots up and grabs my throat, clenching his jaw, "Watch yourself, Kitty Cat."

I've just about had enough of their manhandling me every time I say something they don't like, so I do something I will probably catch hell for, but it makes me feel good. I reach down and grab his junk in my hand, giving it a tight squeeze. I can get a good handful with the basketball shorts he's wearing.

"I suggest you stop being a dick and let me the fuck out." I give him a sarcastic smile.

Oakley's eyes widen, but then a grin brightens his face, and he bites his lip, "Squeeze a little harder, and I may just come in my shorts."

"How about I give them a little twist, then?" Moving my hand counterclockwise, he moves in even closer.

"Do it, Kitty Cat. I'm not afraid of pain; it excites the shit out of me." His hand tightens around my neck, then he leans in, biting my earlobe before sucking on it, "Damn, Kitty Cat, I want to fuck you right here. Do you want that? Do you want me to lift you up and impale that sweet cunt on my hard cock, and just fuck the shit out of you against this door so all the Sinners can hear?"

It takes me a moment to respond, needing to calm my racing heart and clear all the images of us doing just that from my head, "Do you know what I really want...what I'm so desperate for?" My voice is low and seductive as I lick my lips, "I want you to stick your," I pause briefly and glance down at the package still in my grasp, "key in the keyhole and unlock this fucking door." I shove him away.

His laughter startles me because it sounds genuine, but then it abruptly stops, "You're going to pay for that, Kitty Cat. You're lucky that I don't have time to play around with you now. It's Sunday, and we Sinners need to repent, so cancel your Uber, and I'll have Fynn take you back. Or have you forgotten that someone tried to kill you last night?"

"I haven't forgotten, and I'd prefer to take the Uber..."

His hand slams against the door by my head, "Cancel the fucking Uber and get your cute little ass back upstairs and wait for Fynn."

The sound of his hand slamming against the wood by my head makes me jump, and I no longer argue. I push past him as I pull my phone from my pocket and cancel the damn Uber. Stomping up the stairs, I don't stop until I'm standing in front of the only room that I have yet to be in, Fynn's.

I follow the Lord out to the garage, where he hands me a helmet, and I realize he's a Harley guy. I run my hand over the gas tank and his leather seat as I admire the artwork on the bike. Skulls and flames. For some reason, I feel like it fits Fynn to a T.

"Gorgeous bike!"

"Don't tell me you're one of those girls that like to date bikers because she feels cool," he snickers.

"What?" I ask annoyed, "I would much rather be the one handling such a beauty. My father won't let me have one yet; says they are too dangerous."

Fynn straddles his bike and grins at me, "Maybe I'll let you take mine for a spin sometime," he jerks his head back, "For now, you have to ride bitch."

Scowling, I strap my helmet on and climb up behind him. I'm unsure where he wants me to put my hands, so I lightly hold onto his leather jacket. He smells so good, just like Jett, only it's a different scent, but one that still gets my panties wet.

He takes hold of my hands and wraps them around his waist, "Don't be afraid to rub those tits against me, Little Saint. This way, I know you won't fall off." Fynn revs the bike up, then takes off.

I have no choice but to hold tightly onto his midsection, which is nothing but a wall of hard muscle. All the Lords have bomb-ass bodies with muscle that goes on for days. I don't think they even have an ounce of fat to them.

Fynn takes a long way back to my Sorority House and then pulls up a block away, "I'd take you to the door, but I'm really not in the mood for the dragon lady to come out, yelling at me," he chuckles, "I don't know what her deal is."

"Yeah, my father said this stupid rule didn't exist back in their day," I tell him as I climb off.

"I'm glad it didn't because if so, you wouldn't be here in our clutches now, would you?" Fynn wiggles his brows at me.

I pull the helmet off and stare at him, "How do you know that?"

"We know everything, Little Saint, or should I call you Catty?" He smirks and holds his arm up when I threaten to punch him.

Fynn stops when he looks at my hand and then grabs it, "What are you doing?" I ask.

He examines the cuts on it from hitting that bastard last night, "Does your hand hurt?"

"It's a little sore, but I'll be fine," I pull my hand away quickly.

Fynn reaches behind me and grips the hair at my nape, "Don't ever pull away from me, especially when I'm checking an injury. Now, be a good girl and run home," I think he's going to finally kiss me as he leans in, but no, he nips my earlobe instead, "Stay out of trouble, Little Saint." He then sits back on his bike and watches me as I walk down the sidewalk and enter the Sorority House.

NINETEEN

Jett

It's Sunday. We are supposed to repent today by going to the soup kitchen, amongst other places, to help feed the line of people hoping to fill their stomachs just enough so it doesn't hurt anymore. Before we can leave, though, we have some unfinished business down in the basement.

Fynn is on Saint duty, leaving Oakley and me to clean up the mess. The unsavory sort of people would eliminate the puke altogether, but that's not how we work. No, instead, we will use blackmail on the fucker. This is just another reason why we like our videos. It's how we keep others in line and use them when needed.

"You can go to jail for a long time, Rob," I state as I pace back and forth in front of him, "You had quite a bit of date rape drugs on your person. Tie that with the video of you pretty much confessing of using them on women; you won't see graduation day."

"Aren't you here to be a lawyer or some shit?" Oakley stands back with his arms crossed, letting me take the lead. He still wants to pulverize the fucker for swinging at his Kitty Cat.

"Yeah..." Rob's a man of few words.

"You do know that we run this campus, right?" I squat down in front of him and wait for his next one-word response.

"Yes..."

"So, tell me, Rob, why did you not speak with one of us before approaching Catalina? You see how hot she is. Did it not cross your mind that she may belong to us on that merit alone?"

"S-She approached me..." He stutters a bit.

"I see," I stand to my full height, "Well, unfortunately, that doesn't help you out any. We may be assholes and use women who want to be used by us, but we never drug them to get laid. That's just for those assholes with no game, and you, my boy, must not have any game." I kick his thigh, making him howl in pain.

"Can we finish this?" Oakley asks, bored, "The Father is expecting us at the soup kitchen soon."

I nod and turn back to Rob. Man, we fucked him over good last night. I wonder how many of these bruises belong to my Lovely Lina. She was like a wild cat going at him, and it turned me on so fucking bad. Just thinking about it is getting me hard.

"Here's what we are going to do, Date Rape Rob," turning my attention back to the fucker, "We are going to release you, but know that we have this video that we will put out there for all to see, including the police, if we hear that you are going around telling people that we are the ones who beat the living shit out of you. We don't care what story you tell, as long as our names and Catalina's are left out. Do you understand?"

"Yes, I understand."

"Good," I tap his cheek, "You will be our little bitch for the time being, and you will never speak to Catalina Scott again. Do you understand that as well?"

"Yes..."

I study him for a few seconds before releasing him from the chains and helping him to stand up, "Damn, you look like shit. Go upstairs and clean yourself up before you leave." Rob wastes no time hobbling up the staircase as we watch him.

"Do you think that's wise," Oak questions, "Letting him go like that?"

I turn back to my friend, "What would you have done? We can't afford to have dead bodies in this house...never in the house, remember?"

"I know this, Jett, but still. That fucker deserved more than what he got, especially after the plans he had for Kitty Cat!"

"Hey, calm down. I know this, and if we didn't have this other fucker to catch, Date Rape Rob would have gotten more than he did. We need more eyes and ears, Oak. Hopefully, these fuckers will slip up soon because I'm telling you now, the people I've had on it haven't come up with anything."

I watch my friend sigh and then pinch the bridge of his nose, "I know, my guys too," he explodes, "How are they getting away from us?"

"I ask myself that time and again, man. I'm going to visit my father today," I tell him, and his head snaps up, "Yeah, I know. I'm desperate, bro. Maybe he can shed some more light on all of this."

"I doubt it, Jett. I think our fathers did something fucked up back in their day, and they don't want us to know about it." Oakley starts heading toward the stairs.

"What's worse than fucking people up, being the brawn behind every beating that happened at that time?" I ask him, causing him to stop.

"That's exactly what we need to find out." He turns and walks upstairs, leaving me here to think about his words.

Our fathers weren't bad people; they protected what needed protection and weren't afraid to use whatever force was necessary. It's how they still are and how we were raised. We show no fear because we have no fear, but there are still things you do not do; you don't cross certain lines. Rob crossed one of those lines by planning on drugging a female, and not just any female, but ours.

We repent because of all the sinning we do throughout the week, but seeing these people who don't have a warm bed or enough food and have to depend on others for help is exhausting. There is no shame with them; they do what needs to be done to survive another day. They leave me in awe each time they smile and thank me, but still, I'd rather just go to hell, knowing that we are only doing this to make us feel better. Not that the one good deed we do on Sundays will earn us a golden ticket through the heavenly gate, but it helps us deal with some of the fucked-up shit we do.

After the lunch shift at the soup kitchen, I head to my father's house. I know he's home because it's Sunday, and it's his day to sit at home and relax all day, but I'm about to fuck that all up. We always get into arguments when we come together; it's why I avoid him like the plague. It's been this way ever since my mother passed away five years ago due to cancer. It's been just the two of us ever since, and I can't figure out why our relationship is so sour because of it.

The big house is mostly quiet when I walk in; the man doesn't even have a fucking dog to keep him company. The only noise comes from a television in the distance, and I know he's most likely in the family room watching a football game.

Moving forward, I'm just about to the room when I stop abruptly. My father's voice booms over the television; he's on the phone talking to someone. I creep a little closer because whatever it is, it has my father in a state that I have never seen him in before.

"It can't be due to that situation, can it?" My father's voice is a little frantic, "We didn't do anything but what we were told to do, and that was to hold them. We were young, for fuck's sake!" I see his shadow as he passes by the door, "Besides, didn't they pass away?" There is a pause, then he says, "Suicide is still passing away! Dead is dead, so who the fuck is sending the letters, Jakob?"

I jerk back at his statement. He's talking to Fynn's father about the threats. So this does have to do with something that happened when they were in school. But why now? Why wait all these years to get payback? I only stay long enough to hear the rest of the conversation, which isn't much longer, and then I back away. I'm no longer interested in talking with my father as I leave the house quietly, then head back to the Frat House.

Oakley is in the living room watching a game, probably the same one my father was watching. I wasn't paying attention while I was there. He lifts his fist as I walk by, and I bump it with my own.

"So, how did it go with Daddio? You weren't there very long." Oakley says without taking his eyes off the television.

"That's because he didn't know I had stopped by," I sit in the spot beside my friend on the couch, and I'm swarmed with groupies. I have no clue where they even came from; it's like they lurk in the shadows, waiting for one of us to arrive. "Uh, excuse me? Do you mind getting the fuck out?" I growl at the five females that have made themselves at home around us.

Some scramble away instantly, but two of them are slow and move toward Oakley, "Are you fucking deaf? I believe he said to get the fuck out." My friend's glare at the remaining two has the desired effect, and they follow their three friends out.

"Anyway," I continue once I know we are alone, "I overheard my father on the phone with Fynn's father. I believe they know why they may be receiving the threats but not who is sending the letters."

"Well, that doesn't make sense," Oakley frowns and forgets all about the game, "If they know why, then how can they not know who?"

"My father mentioned something about the person, or persons, being deceased, something about suicide." I think back, trying to remember the whole conversation I heard, "Oh, and he said something, that they were made to hold them. That's all I got before he hung up. I left the house immediately and came home."

"Well, at least we know where to start then," Oak states as he turns his attention back to the game.

"Yeah, maybe if we find out who all died by suicide since our fathers were in college, then we can narrow it down." I nod.

Oakley glances at me once again, "Exactly."

Fynn

I probably should have driven Jett's Jeep or Oakley's Camaro. Having my bike kind of sucks ass when you're on a stakeout. Leaning against a nearby tree, I keep my shades on so passersby can't see me staring at the Sorority House. They'd think I was some kind of creeper. At least in a car, I can sit back and listen to some tunes, but no, I wanted to feel Little Saint's body pressed against mine as she held on for dear life. It's why I went so fast.

Not too long after our girl goes inside, I see her friend Dani walking up to the Sorority House. I remember vividly what I walked into when I went to see if Sean could take my place at the soup kitchen. A mass of dark hair was gripped in my Frat brother's hand as he held it against the bed. His hips were working vigorously as he pounded into the girl from behind.

I remember raising an eyebrow at Sean because I didn't know who it was, so he lifted her head up by her hair. Her eyes were closed, but her mouth hung open as a moan escaped. I chuckled silently, and once her head was back to being held down, I watched her body tense as I began speaking.

None of us Sinners give a fuck if our brothers see us fucking a girl. Well, it may be a little different now with Little Saint. I don't know what it is about her, but all three of us have become very protective of her, which isn't like us at all. The point is, I wasn't too surprised to see Little Saint's friend getting her brains fucked out of her; she was probably jealous of her friend hooking up with Sinners. Not that I know whether Catalina has told her friend, but girls tell each other everything, don't they?

Getting back to the present, though. I watch Dani go into the Sorority House, but something else also catches my attention. A silver Sedan drives by slowly as Dani walks up to the door. As soon as she is inside, the car speeds up and rounds the next corner.

Inside of an hour, the Sedan shows up, slowing down as it gets to the front of the Sorority House and then speeding back up. I can't text the guys because I know they are busy, and I can't leave my spot to chase down one perp when I know there are at least two. It's fucking frustrating as hell.

Luckily, just as the car disappears again, my Little Saint storms out of the house and starts in my direction. At first, I frown because it's too dangerous for her to be out, and she doesn't know that we have been keeping watch, but then I think, fuck it, and step out onto the sidewalk and into her path.

She's not even paying attention as she keeps her head down, so I reach out and stop her before she can walk into me again. She jerks at being touched until she sees it's me and brings her hands to her lips.

"Are you stalking me, Fynn?" The glare she gives me has no effect on me whatsoever.

I grin, "I have no need to stalk anyone. You all gravitate toward me, but I do need to keep watch. Make sure your real stalker doesn't make good on their threats."

"You have been standing out here this whole time?" she asks a little less angrily.

I nod once, "I have, and during this time, a silver Sedan has driven by slowly four different times, the first time when Dani came home."

"A silver Sedan? I don't know anyone who drives one," she states with her eyebrows furrowed.

I study her briefly and notice that she's a bit upset, "What's going on? You seem mad, Little Saint."

She waves her hand in front of her, trying to dismiss my question, "It's nothing that you need to be concerned about."

I step closer and look down my nose at the blonde beauty who has her hair in a messy bun and is wearing leggings and a Helshire hoodie, "Everything about you concerns me, Little Saint."

She goes to take a step back, but I grab hold of the front of her sweatshirt and just raise my brow at her. My Little Saint sighs and then looks over her shoulder to see if we are in view of the Sorority House.

"Let's go for a ride, Little Saint." I pull her toward my bike and plop the helmet back on her head before she can argue with me.

Surprisingly, she doesn't fight me on this, and she climbs on behind me once I've revved up my bike, "Where are we going?"

I grin at her in the little side mirror, "Somewhere, nobody else will be."

I hear her screech as I take off, and she grasps my waist. I pull one of her hands, and then the other, around, so I can feel her body against mine again. I don't bother removing my hand from covering both of hers. I feel possessive as fuck at this moment and don't want to let her go.

As my bike flies through back roads, the houses start to disappear until we leave the town behind us. I'm not sure how I found the spot that I'm taking my Little Saint to, but she will be the first to ever see where I go when I need time to myself. I remember finding it my Senior year of high school when I learned Mom was cheating on Dad. It was a rough time for me, and that's when I really started not giving a fuck about anything.

My father and I get along to an extent, we're not like Jett and his dad, but we aren't like the typical father-and-son duo either. Oakley is the only one who still has both his parents together, but it's not always roses with them either. We all have our family issues, and as I think about this, with Catalina on the back, I can't help but wonder what her home life is like.

I now know that her mother had belonged to the Lords back in their day, and she even married one of them. Is that what this is...the past repeating itself? If so, I wonder which of my friends will be the sap to marry her, because I've already decided that no woman is worth the hassle. I've seen firsthand what it can do when you invest too much into one person, and then they decide they no longer want you and move on to someone else. You find out that you have an open marriage, although you are the last to find out.

I turn when I see the narrow opening in the wooded area. The road is deserted, so no one witnesses my entrance. If I was indeed a sicko, Little Saint would be in a heap of trouble because no one is around for miles. I could be taking her to her death, and she wouldn't even know it because, for some reason, she's trusting me.

My bike climbs up the slight incline until we break through the trees, and I bring my bike to a stop on a cliff, overlooking not only a small valley but the town of Helshire as well. Cutting the engine, I let her climb off first before hopping off.

"Oh, my God, Fynn! It's beautiful up here!" She pulls off the helmet and steps a little closer to the edge.

I pull her back, "Not too close. I don't know how solid the ground is."

She doesn't argue as she looks out over the scenery once again, "How do you know of this place?"

I shrug, "I found it one day, my Senior year of high school." I'm not about to go on and have a fucking heart-to-heart with Saint. Looking at her, I lick my lips because she looks sexy as hell. Clearing my throat, I say, "So, are you going to tell me what you were upset about?"

She sighs, "It really is nothing, Fynn. You're making a bigger deal out of it than what it really is!" Seeing my stern look, she throws her hands up, "Fine! I got into an argument with Dani because she disapproves of me hanging with the Lords. When I mentioned how she stayed with a Sinner last night also, she got defensive, saying that Sean isn't as evil as the Lords of Sin and that she thinks it's disgusting that I slept with all three of you." She starts staring at the ground again.

"So, you told her about last night?" I question. Not that I'm mad, but I find it cute that she gossiped about us to her friend.

She only shrugs, "Not really, but I didn't deny it when she asked. She also asked if I was the virgin sacrifice, too."

I lift her chin up, "We don't care that you told her, Little Saint. We were only keeping it secret for your own benefit."

Her blue eyes study me, looking into the depths of my brown ones, and I have a hard time keeping a particular part of my anatomy from stirring. Being out here alone with this Little Saint makes me want to do very bad things to her, and with no one around, nothing is stopping me; well, nobody but her.

"So, that's all you were upset about when you left?" Her nod is the only answer I need, and I growl like a fucking wolf, "I think I'm going to fuck you now, Little Saint. Tell me to stop if you don't want it; otherwise, I will make you come as many times as it takes for you to forget the fight with your little friend."

I pull her against me, waiting for her to push away, but she raises her hands and fists my leather jacket. Her blue orbs stare innocently at me, but I know too well that this girl is far from innocent. When I remain silent, waiting for her answer, she finally finds her voice, and I'm so glad she does.

She smiles seductively at me, "Fuck me, Fynn. Do as you promised and make me forget."

TWENTY

Catalina

I've got to be fucked up in the head. I'm sore as shit, and here I am, asking Fynn to take me, but after the morning I had when Dani came back, I can seriously use the distraction. I thought Dani was my friend and that she was wild like me, and to an extent, she is. She's also a hypocrite. She tells me that I need to be careful and not trust the Sinners, yet she sleeps with one herself.

When she realized how contradicting her argument was, she changed tactics and tried making me feel like a whore for sleeping with all three of the guys. Do I feel like a whore? I sure don't. I hadn't had sex in so long; I had to dust out the Cooter Cave before letting anyone park inside!

Last night's excursion was a little awkward for me the first time, but the second round down in the basement, I felt it was hot as hell, and I enjoyed every minute of it. Now, I'm here with Fynn. He's the toughest one to crack because I know he's attracted to me, but I still can't get him to kiss me. It's good that I didn't need to depend on him to give me air in the pool because I would have most likely died.

"Fuck you, huh?" the Lord's voice brings me back to the present.

"That's what you promised, isn't it?" I raise a brow at him.

"Strip."

"What? It's chilly as fuck out here!" I tell him as I shake my head.

"I said...strip."

"You're out of your fucking mind..." I try walking around him, but he takes hold of my sleeve and spins me around, shoving me into a tree. His body presses against my back, and I can feel the hardness through his jeans as he rubs himself against me.

"You asked for it, and now, per the contract..." I cut him off.

"Fuck the contract, Fynn!"

"No, but I'm about to fuck you since you asked so nicely." Holding me against the tree, he pushes my leggings down my legs and then slides his hand between them, "Oh, seems like someone likes it a little rough." He chuckles as he makes slurping noises while cleaning his fingers off.

"You don't have to be an asshole," I tell him when I hear his zipper come down.

"This isn't me being an asshole, Little Saint. If you want Asshole, I can shove you to your knees and fuck that mouth of yours roughly." He wastes no time lining his cock up and then pushing in. It isn't too rough, but it's not gentle, either. In fact, it seems to be just right since a moan slips out, and I subconsciously push my ass back, so he has better access.

His hand fists my hair as my head is pressed against the tree bark. He grunts as he fucks me fast and hard while gripping my hip so hard that I know there will be a bruise come morning. Fynn is a furious fucker, making sure to get in nice and deep. I scrape my nails down the bark, trying to get some form of grip, but the only thing I get is bark and moss under my nails.

"Fynn..."

"What is it, Little Saint?"

"Turn me around..."

"Are you going to strip?" he asks with every thrust he gives me.

What is it with him wanting me to fucking strip? In truth, I am getting a little warm, so I let him think I'm giving in, "Fine."

He lets go of my head, "Then do it. Take your top off first."

It's a bit challenging, but I get the hoodie pulled over my head, and I feel him unclip my bra. He pulls out of me and steps back until my leggings are removed from my person, then he comes at me. Pinning my hands above my head, his mouth goes to my neck, where he starts sucking and biting.

Lifting my leg to his hip, he pulls back until his brown eyes burn into mine, "Beg me, Catalina," It's the first time I've heard him say my real name, "Beg me to fuck you until my name echoes through these woods. Beg me to own this fucking sweet cunt of yours until it's battered and bruised...fucking beg me!"

He already had me with the first 'Beg me' when he used my name. How can I possibly pass this up, "I fucking beg you, Fynn! Fuck me, own me, batter me...just fuck me already!"

Like a predator, he growls and plunges into me. The tree bark scrapes at my back, but I don't care. He's brutal with his thrusts as I remain pinned with my arms over my head. He bites my neck hard, possibly drawing blood, and then he sucks hard, and I know I'll be sporting a big-ass hickey on my neck by the time he's done.

He's marking me as his, claiming ownership like I begged him. This Lord does nothing half-ass as his hips slam into me repeatedly. I feel it building with his every thrust, and all it takes is Fynn taking my nipple into his mouth and biting down, and I'm thrown over the edge and climaxing.

"OH, MY FUCKING GOD...YES, FYNN!!" Like he wanted, his name floats on the breeze as it bounces from tree to tree.

"Fuck yes, cream my cock good, you saintly slut!" He lets go of my wrists and lifts me, making me wrap my legs around his waist.

"Oh God, oh God, oh God!" I continue to come as he hammers into me.

"I'm going to fill this slutty cunt up and then watch it drip down your leg once I'm done." He grunts, then jerks a few more times before releasing inside me, "Do you fucking feel that, Little Saint? This cunt isn't saintly anymore, now that it's filled with Sinners." He grunts several times before pulling out, "Don't fucking move."

Now that we are done, the cool breeze chills me, especially when I'm covered in sweat, "Fynn, I need to get dressed."

"No, you need to not fucking move until I tell you to." He then drops to his knees and spreads my legs, "Fucking gorgeous! Do you feel it dripping, Little Saint? Do you feel my cum running down your beautiful thighs?"

What is it about the sick way that the Lords treat me that turns me on so much? I gaze down at him as he watches his release drip from my used vag. Then, he does something that I have never seen done before. He sticks his tongue out and drags it up the inside of my thighs, where his seed coats me.

He stands up, and I'm so mesmerized at what I just witnessed that I can't take my eyes off him as he moves in closer and smears it across my lips with his tongue. It's the closest I've come to getting a kiss from this Lord. He waits, watching me, daring me with his eyes.

"Fucking lick it. Taste our cum mixed together; it's the best thing ever." He's cocky as he says this, but I don't care because I'm still so turned on that I do exactly what he wants.

I stick out my tongue and lick my lips, savoring our combined tastes. It's sick but sexy as hell, and as I finish the last of it, I look at him and grin, "More..."

His eyes light up, and he drops to his knees again. With another swipe of his tongue up and down my inner thighs and between my legs, Fynn then gives my lips one last swipe. I'm not sure if it's our taste or the fact that it's close to having Fynn kissing me, but I like it, and I'll let him feed me his cum this way anytime he wants.

After our little fuck fest up on the cliff, Fynn decides he's going to feed me and takes me to a nearby pizza joint. It feels natural being with Fynn, and that in itself is weird because Fynn is not a talker, but the silence is perfect, only talking when we feel like it, with no pressure from the other. It's nice, but it ends sooner than I'd like, and the next thing I know, we are headed back to the Sorority House.

"Can I trust you to stay inside unless you call one of us to go wherever you go?" The Lord asks as he pulls up to the curb down the street.

I sigh, "I can't always depend on you guys to escort me everywhere."

"Did you not read the contract thoroughly, Little Saint?" He gets annoyed, "It states that should any danger present itself; you are to inform us so we can take the proper precautions to keep you safe. The danger has presented itself, so now you have two options. You can either A, call us when you want to go anywhere because one of us is always out here watching, or B, you come and stay with us until the situation is handled."

"In your dreams, Morin! I barely know you guys; I'm not staying with you," I assure him of this.

"That's fine by me, but if we catch you sneaking out, you will not like the consequences. We take our contracts seriously." When I go to argue, he glances at his watch, "You better get back inside, Little Saint, or else dragon lady may come looking for you." He smirks and takes the helmet from my hands.

I gawk at him momentarily for dismissing me the way he just did before turning and hurrying down the street. I look his way as I turn onto the walkway leading to the front door, and he's still smirking. So, what do I do? I raise my hand and give him the bird before hurrying into the Sorority House.

"I'm sorry, Cat."

It's the first thing I hear when I walk into the room I share with Dani. She looks contrite as she apologizes to me, but I'm unsure if I'm ready to forgive her yet. So, I thank her for her apology, go into the bathroom, and turn the shower on.

"Cat, please! I said I was sorry!" she calls through the door.

I swing the door open, "I said thank you, Dani. I appreciate the apology, but you hurt me with what you said, and I'm not ready to forgive you just yet."

Dani bows her head as she picks at her cuticles, "I know, and I'm sorry. I don't think you are a whore at all, but I guess maybe I was a little jealous that you have three hot guys wanting you and I struggle to find one," she looks back up with hurt in her own eyes now, "You also hurt me by not telling me you were the virgin sacrifice for the Sinner's party."

"I didn't know I was going to be one either and what it all entailed, so it's not like I had anything to tell you. I did tell you they wanted me there early, did I not?"

She nods, "I'm sorry. How many times do I need to say it? Do I need to get on my knees and beg? Do I need to kiss your feet as I continue to repeat it?"

A small bubble of laughter bursts out, "That may help a little."

Dani chuckles too, "I really am sorry, Cat. I don't want to fight with you; you're my best friend."

"I'm your only friend here," I snicker.

"That's because everyone else is a pathetic asshole who doesn't deserve my attention," she smirks.

I study her, "Fine, but I swear, if you call me a whore again in a non-joking manner, I will knock your ass out."

A big smile breaks out across her face, and she slams into me, throwing her arms around my neck, "I promise not to call you a whore, or a slut, again, unless I'm joking around."

I pull back, "You never called me a slut," I frown.

She takes a step back and looks at me sheepishly, "I may have called you one after you stomped out of the room."

I punch her in the arm, "You're such a bitch," I chuckle, "But hey, I really need to shower now. We can talk more afterward." I close the door and take my much-needed shower.

About halfway through the week, I catch a glimpse of Rob sporting his new bruises. I like to think that some of them are from me, but I saw how hard the hits were that came from the Lords. I still can't believe he fucked some skank in the bathroom and planned on drugging me to get a piece from me as well.

Rolling my eyes, I turn to walk the other way, only to slam into something hard, "God damn it! Either stop working out so much or stop sneaking up on me like this!" I glare at Oakley, who's smirking, "Seriously, between you and Fynn, I'm surprised I don't have a permanent bruise on my forehead!"

"Suck it up, Buttercup. You love our physiques too much for us to stop working out." The Lord's cockiness has me stepping back.

"Oh really?" I cock my brow.

He shrugs, "How else would I be able to hold you up like I did the other night while my two best friends took turns fucking the shit out of you?"

I feel the heat creep into my face right away and look around to see if anyone close by had heard, "Will you shut the fuck up!"

"Fuck them! I don't care if people know I'm dipping my stick in this sweet cunt." He licks his lips as his eyes wander down the length of me.

"I can't have Felicia finding out, Oakley! She's a fucking beast regarding the 'No Sinning' rule."

Oakley scoffs, "She's nothing to worry about. In fact, all you have to do is say the word, and we will take care of her for you."

"What? No! I don't need you to take care of her for me. I only need to suffer one year because she graduates this year, and I doubt any other Sorority Saints feels as strongly about the rules as Felicia."

"That's true. Dragon lady was never this vocal until the end of last year when she was promoted to President. Maybe she needs a Sinner to show her what she's missing." He winks at me.

I poke the Lord in the chest, "If you dip your stick in her, I swear I will cut it off!"

Smirking, he looks at my finger still pressed against his chest, "Careful, Kitty Cat. Know your place. You don't get to tell us who we can and cannot fuck."

I step back and cross my arms, "Oh? Well, it doesn't say anywhere in the contract that I can't fuck others, and yet you all got crazy possessive about Rob showing me attention!"

"We are the Lords of Sin. This is our fucking world, Kitty Cat, and we live by our own rules, so you can either deal with it or not. Either way, you still belong to us until we are done with you."

Moisture pools between my legs as he continues talking about owning me. They don't know how badly I want them to do that, but I can never tell them this. I need to let them think they are always in charge. What I won't do, though, is cower in front of them, no matter what they dish out.

Ignoring his whole spiel, I go back to why he's even standing in my space to begin with, "Is there a reason why you stalked me here? I mean, usually, you Lords lurk in the background like fucking creepers, so why are you here now?"

I see that Oakley doesn't like my choice of words by the way his expression changes to one of hardness, "Creepers, really? We're trying to keep you alive, and you call us creepers? At least we are keeping our part of the bargain. We've been lenient with you and your venomous tongue, but that can all change. Keep it up, Kitty Cat, and you will see why everyone else fears us."

I continue to stare at his handsome face, waiting for him to answer my question and trying not to show the little tremble I've got going on. His threat has the opposite effect on me, making me want to pull him into the nearest building and let him take me. I've never been in a constant state of arousal until I met these three Sinners, and I'm worried that after knowing what they can all do to my body, I will never be the same again.

"Six o'clock on the dot, Kitty Cat. Don't be late!" Oakley turns and starts walking away.

Shit! What's at six o'clock?

"Oakley..." I call after him.

"I'm done talking to you, Kitty Cat. Remember, the library at six tonight," It's all he says before disappearing around a building.

Well, fuck. I guess I'll find out what we'll be doing once I get to the library. Why do I keep spacing off like that? More importantly, why do these guys have such a hold over me? It's distracting, is what it is. Maybe I should call my mother and have her come have lunch with me. I have a few questions about her time at Helshire with the Lords, but I should visit my dad first.

Since I have time between classes, I head for the building where the Provost's office is housed. My father is just finishing up a meeting, and I stand up when his door opens. I freeze as the CEO...a.k.a...Oakley's father, comes strolling out of my father's office. I can see where Oakley gets his looks from because his father is still hot as hell, even though he's in his forties.

Mr. Harris grins at me as his eyes drink me in from head to toe, "Hello, Catalina. I hope you are enjoying your time at Helshire."

Not wanting to be rude to the President of the University, I smile, "I am enjoying it, Sir."

"I take it our boys are treating you as...expected?" He smirks after his slight pause.

"If you're talking about the Lords of Sin, then yes. Thank you for asking." I'm beginning to feel slightly uncomfortable, but then Mr. Harris turns back to my father.

"Let's set up dinner plans. I'm sure our wives would love to visit with one another again. It's been so long."

My father shakes his boss's hand, "Sounds like a plan. I will talk with Ashlee tonight and get back to you."

The President nods at my father and then smiles at me, "Catalina..." He then walks out, leaving my father and I alone.

As soon as my father closes the door, I start in, "What was Mom to the Lords of Sin when the two of you were here?"

He looks at me sternly, "Take a seat, Catty."

"I'll stand, thank you very much," I state, annoyed that he's using his nickname for me.

My father frowns and circles his desk to sit back in his chair. After scrutinizing me, he sighs, "You are old enough now, and I think it's time that you know," he begins, "Your mother was the Lords of Sin's Lady."

"Did she have to sign a contract, too?" I ask with a cocked brow.

My father smiles, "No. Your mother willingly gave herself to the Lords. It just so happens that she and I fell in love by the time our reign ended here."

"Why did you direct me to seek out the Lords if you knew what they were like? Don't try to deny it!" I scold as I question this insanity.

His face hardens, "Because, Catalina, you are to be the Lord's next Lady. We all agreed to this when all of you kids were little, and you will do as you're told."

Disbelief takes hold as I listen to my father's words. I was sacrificed long before the Lord's Toga party and by my own parents! I was enjoying my time with the Lords, but now that I know this is how it will be, that little rebellious part of me is beginning to bubble up. I scoff to myself, 'Me, a fucking Lady to the Lords? Pfft, in their motherfucking dreams!'

TWENTY-ONE

Oakley

I crave her. It's been days since I was inside my Kitty Cat, and I'm beginning to go through withdrawals. Fynn bragged about having her all to himself the day Jett and I were repenting. I need time alone with the Saint. I need to remind her who she belongs to, so she doesn't get any ideas and try something stupid again.

Her running into me was no accident. Had she been paying attention, she would have known that I was here, standing behind her as she watches that Rob puke walk across the campus with some friends. She needs to be better aware of her surroundings; she must have a death wish or something. Kitty Cat isn't dying just yet because we are far from done with her.

When she spaced off while I was talking, I stopped and just waited. Smirking, I pretend I've been talking the whole time and remind her to meet me at the library. Now she will be wondering all afternoon why we are meeting there. It's easy enough; there is seldom anybody there at six o'clock, and even though there are a few things I do want to look into, it's mainly to get my Kitty Cat alone.

I watch her hurry to the building that her father's office is in, and then a few minutes later, I see my own father walk out, "Hey, Dad. Did you see Catalina in there?"

"Yeah," he smirks, "She's with Devlin right now."

"What's the smirk for?"

"Catty has become a hot little number, just like her mother. You boys are lucky." His words make me cringe because Kitty Cat is old enough to be his daughter, but I don't comment.

"Yeah, she is pretty hot, but she's got a mouth on her as well," I tell him.

He only shrugs, "Good, so she fits right in."

"Oh, that she does," I chuckle.

"Say, Devlin and I are going to plan a dinner together, and I want you to be there, along with Catalina, of course," my father states before walking toward the parking lot.

"Okay, just let me know," I say, then call out as he gets further away, "Where are you going?"

He turns and looks around, "Your mother called; she's bored." He gives me his knowing smirk, and all it does is make me want to puke. I hate when he refers to his sex life with my mother, but I guess I shouldn't have asked.

I wave to him to go, "Give her my love."

After watching my father leave, I return to waiting for my Kitty Cat. I pull my phone out and text the guys, letting them know I'm extending my Catalina watch. Jett is supposed to take over after my watch, but I need more time with her. If we don't catch these bastards soon, I'll have to hire security for her because we have more important things to do.

Suddenly, Kitty Cat comes storming out of the building, and instead of heading to her next class, she heads for the Sorority House. I follow casually behind and then take up a spot down the road where I can still see the front door. I wonder what she's doing back home and what has her so pissed off. I'll have to ask her later when we meet.

However, almost two hours later, I'm scrolling through social media and come across a picture of some acquaintances. They're celebrating something at a local bar, just off campus, but I don't pay attention to that.

My eyes are glued to the blonde bombshell who must have slipped out the back door, so I wouldn't see her.

"Son of a bitch!"

Instead of going straight to the bar, I return to campus and grab my Camaro. I waste no time getting to where I need to go and hurry inside. I've wasted time standing outside her fucking house, who knows if she's still here. I don't see her as I case the establishment, but I do see the guys from the photo.

"Hey, did you see where this chick went?" I show them a photo of my Kitty Cat.

They are already fucked up, and they start cheering when I step up to them, but with a stern look, they sober up and take a good look at the picture, "Oh yeah, she's right there..." They both point to the booth where she sat in the photo, "Sorry, bro. She must have slipped out after Joe, here, tried propositioning her." One guy slaps the other on the shoulder.

I growl, "She's fucking off limits!"

"Sorry, dude, we didn't know!" They both hold their hands up defensively.

"Are you looking for that hot blonde?" The bartender steps up and asks.

I nod, "Yeah."

He nods toward the back, "She asked for the restroom, and I sent her to the back."

"Thanks," I slap a hundred down on the bar, "For her drinks and a tip."

I head to the back and find the door with the restroom sign. I carefully check the doorknob, but it's locked, so I knock. Once I hear her voice call out that it will be a second, I grin and prepare myself for when she opens the door. She's in so much deep shit that it isn't funny, and she has no idea what she is in for.

As soon as the door opens, I push my way inside. She squeals, but my hand immediately comes up, muffling the sound. I lock the door as soon as I have her back against my chest and then push her against the dingy sink. My eyes glare into her pretty blue ones.

"Did you think you were being sneaky? That I wouldn't find out? How often must we tell you that we...know...everything!" I raise my brow at her through the mirror.

"Oakley..."

Yanking her jeans down, I ignore her as I take hold of the thong that she's wearing and tear it from her body. Balling it up, I shove it into her mouth and send her another glare, "This is your punishment, Kitty Cat. Do not spit those out!"

Using my hand, I give her five consecutive swats on her bare ass. She tries mumbling something as she glares at me, but I only grin, "Remember what the contract says about punishments. You agreed to take them like a good girl and signed off on it, Kitty Cat. Don't get mad at me for you disobeying us," I bring my hand down repeatedly as I talk, "We...are...trying...to...protect...you...and...keep...you...safe!"

I hear her moan on the last one, and her eyes are closed when I glance in the mirror. I massage her reddened cheeks before sliding my hand between her thighs. She's fucking soaked.

"Seems like someone loves her punishments," I say in a low voice by her ear as I undo my own pants, "Only one more thing before it's over, Kitty Cat."

I kick her legs apart as much as her jeans allow and thrust into her. Her cries are muffled as I fuck her against the small sink. She will have bruises from where her hips bang against the porcelain, but I don't give a fuck. They will be a reminder to her not to cross us again.

"This is what happens to bad girls, Kitty Cat. You get spanked, and then you get fucked. It doesn't matter where you are; remember that. We will dole out the punishment right then and there." I bite her earlobe when she closes her eyes, only to pop open again from the sharp pain of my bite. "You don't get to come, Kitty Cat. This isn't about your pleasure."

I shove her over further and take hold of her hips, slamming into her even harder until I feel my balls pulling up. I know it's going to be a full load, so I pull out and spin her around. Pulling the thong from her mouth, I shove her to her knees and order her, "Open wide, slut." When she refuses, I start shooting it onto her face, unable to hold it in any longer, "Open your fucking mouth!"

She opens, and I start fucking it until I'm spent, and the boys are entirely empty. I don't pull out yet as I glare down at our girl, "When I give an order, Kitty Cat, you do it. Do you understand?"

I pull out only when she nods and then wipe the excess from her cheek and chin, feeding it to her before helping her up off the floor. I pull her jeans up and reach around her to grab a paper towel. Wetting it, I clean the smeared mascara running down her face and any traces of cum that may be lingering.

Once I'm done, I grip her chin and make her look at me, "Don't ever run from us when we are trying to keep you safe."

She glares at me, so I lean in and press my lips to hers, only she refuses to open. I bite her lip until she gives in and kiss her brutally. When I feel her start to respond, I pull back and grin.

"So, are you going to tell me what has you all pissed off, or do I need to torture it out of you?"

"I'm allowed my secrets, Oakley," she sneers.

"You have no secrets from us, Kitty Cat. Now, you have two options. We can walk out hand in hand and go straight to my car, where I will then take you to get something to eat, so you can sober up, and you can tell me what has your panties all in a bunch...well, had your panties in a bunch," I smirk knowing she's no longer wearing any, "Or I can throw you over my shoulder, kicking and screaming, and I will then take you back to the Frat House, where you will be cuffed, gagged, and punished all over again. It's your choice, sweet cheeks."

I hold my hand out and wait. After staring at it momentarily, she finally makes the right choice and takes hold of it, "Good girl."

TWENTY-TWO

Catalina

Oakley is a dick! A smoking hot dick who knows how to turn me on, but a dick all the same. As annoyed as I am about him finding me, I enjoyed what he did to me in the public restroom at the bar. He took control and dominated the fuck out of me, but it still doesn't change my mind. I will not be their Lady of Sin on anyone's terms but my own. Although, I do love the sound of the title.

"You're spacing off again, Kitty Cat." Oakley glances over at me from the driver's seat, "I want to know what has you so pissed off and why you took off the way you did."

Pushing my head back into the headrest, I stare out the window, watching the buildings pass by. Other college kids are out walking around, having a great time with their friends; they don't have a care in the world. I'm sure they don't have parents who have promised them to three depraved males just because they can protect them.

Sighing, I finally answer the Greek God behind the wheel, "The first really isn't your business. As for the second question, I snuck away because I wanted to be alone."

"Kitty Cat..." the Lord says my name in warning, and I turn to look at him.

His stormy blue eyes burn into mine each time he looks my way. I ignore him, of course, but then he turns into the nearest parking lot and slams on the brakes. Note to self: always wear my seatbelt while riding with Oakley. His little tantrum doesn't have the desired effect that he was hoping for, though.

I glance around us, "Where's the restaurant?"

"Don't play cute with me, Catalina!"

"Who says I'm playing?" I give him a cheesy smile, unbuckle my belt, and try to get out.

He grabs my arm, "Where the fuck are you going?"

"I thought you were feeding me. Isn't that why we pulled in here?" I play coy.

Grimacing, he pulls me close, "You know damn well why I pulled in here. If you want our help, Catalina, we need to know everything!"

I glare back at him and get even closer, so our faces are only inches apart, "I will tell you everything, but my conversations with my father are none of your concern!"

The grin that appears makes the hot Lord look menacing, "That's where you are wrong, Kitty Cat. Every fucking facet of your life from now until we release you from the contract is our Goddamn business."

His tone causes chills to run down my spine, but I refuse to show weakness in front of him, "Fuck you, Oakley. You just keep me from dying and catch the bad guy, and I will keep being your fucking sex slave. Isn't that the main reason why you wanted the stupid contract to begin with? So, you can do your depraved shit to me?"

The little asshole smirks, "Is that what you think, Kitty Cat?"

I look him right in the eye, "Yeah, I do."

He reaches around and grabs my seatbelt, yanking it across my body before clicking it into place, "I guess I will just have to show you just how wrong you are, Kitty Cat," He puts the car in gear and takes off again, "Just remember that you asked for this."

I study him as he keeps his eyes on the road. There's a tick in his jaw, and now I'm beginning to feel that I may have opened Pandora's Box. Am I scared they will hurt me? No, not in a bad way, if at all, but I get the feeling that I won't like what he's about to show me. I'll take it, whatever it

is, only because it's as he said...I asked for it, and now I will deal with what comes my way by the time this is over.

Oakley brings me to the Frat House but doesn't take me upstairs. Instead, he takes me to the basement, which smells like bleach and other cleaning products. I'm guessing they came down and cleaned up after letting Rob go.

"What are we doing down here, Oakley?" I look around, thinking I'm going to find the others, but it's only the two of us down in the creepy dungeon basement.

"You'll see. Jett and Fynn are bringing what we need, so we must wait for them," he states, which tells me who it was he texted just as we were on our way here.

"You're not planning on torturing me, are you?" I cross my arms so he can't see the slight tremble my body makes.

"Torture you? I thought I was supposed to be proving you wrong as to why we have the contract with you. Why would I torture you?" My core throbs as he licks his lips at me, "Of course, if it's what you want afterward, we are always happy to oblige."

Suddenly, he's behind me, sliding a chair until it hits the back of my legs, making me sit in it. He's quick to secure one wrist, then the other, before I comprehend what he's doing. When he starts on my ankles, I finally come out of my muddled state.

"What the fuck, Harris?" I ask as I try thrashing and kicking out with my only free limb.

He takes hold of it, laughing, "Fight all you want, Kitty Cat, but I want you to watch the whole show and not try to leave when you get pissed off."

"What are you talking about? What show?" I ask, panting heavily.

"The show you asked for, Kitty Cat. The show that's going to prove to you that we didn't have you sign the contract just so we can do depraved shit to you," The basement door opens, and footsteps shuffle down the steps, "Because we have others that will allow us to do that." Duct tape stretches across my mouth just as I'm about to ask what he means.

"Ah, Lovely Lina," Jett hits the bottom step first, "I heard you have been very naughty today." He comes over and lifts my chin up, pressing his lips against the tape just over my lips.

When he moves away, Fynn is there, smirking before stepping aside to show me a fourth person. She's pretty and has long red hair, "Meet Lara, Little Saint. Lara, meet Catalina."

The redhead offers me a small smile, "Hi, Catalina. It's nice to meet you."

Jesus, what did they do, bring a virgin down here to play with? She looks to be my age and innocent as hell, but looking closely, I see she keeps stealing glances at Fynn...MY Fynn! I scrutinize all three Lords, letting my eyes land on Fynn last.

I start talking through the tape, but it doesn't work out so well. Oakley peels it away, letting me ask the question that's bothering me, "So, who is Lara to you, and why is she here?" I try to keep the jealousy out of my voice, but all three guys grin, so I'm pretty sure I did a terrible job of it.

Fynn steps up behind the girl named Lara and caresses the back of his hand down her arm, "Lara was my standing weekly fuck. She's the only one I had come back time and again." He states, "It's hard to tell by looking at her, but she's a freak in the sheets. She loves getting down and dirty."

Glaring at the cocky Lord, I sneer, "So what is she doing here now?"

Fynn nods to the redhead, and she comes over to me. One minute, she's all innocent, and the next, a grin spreads across her face as she becomes more seductive. Placing her hands on my arms, she leans close to my ear and answers my question.

"I'm here to show you that they don't need a contract to act sick and depraved because they have me, amongst many others who beg them to do bad things to us. So, don't think you're special, because you're not."

"That's enough, Lara!" Fynn glares at her, "That last part was uncalled for."

The bitch smirks and then drags her tongue up my face, but before she can get to the top, the back of her neck is grabbed by an angry Fynn. I watch in shock as he drags her to the nearest wall and slams her back against it. Lara laughs and licks her lips.

"She's tasty..."

"You did not have permission to touch her like that! She's the Lord's property," Fynn spits out, "I did not tell you that you could have her!"

Her eyes widen, and she grins, "Punish me, Fynn. Hurt me for touching your property."

This girl is fucking psychotic! I think to myself. Fynn used to fuck her? I watch as my Lord raises her off the floor by her neck, but it only seems to get her off more.

"Do you understand now, Kitty Cat? We didn't need your consent to use your body because there are plenty of whores like Lara that beg us to do messed up shit to them," Oakley snickers as he replaces the tape over my mouth.

Oakley and Jett go to a wall with a cabinet and open it up to display an array of whips and shit. My heart beats erratically as I watch them choose different objects. What the fuck? Are they actually going to do this and make me watch? I begin to struggle and scream through the tape. A few times, the chair almost tips as it topples on two legs.

Jet comes over and rips the tape from my face, "What is it, Lina?"

I glare at him and then over at his two friends, "If any of you touch that bitch, I'm done. I will fucking leave, and you will never see me again. I didn't sign that contract to sit here and watch you get your fucking freak on with one of your many whores!" My chest is heaving as I try to catch my breath from struggling.

"All you have to do is say it, Kitty Cat, and all this stops." Oakley walks over and caresses my cheek.

"Say what?"

"Admit that your business is our business," Oakley squats down in front of me and runs his hands up and down my thighs, "You see, Kitty Cat, it isn't the sex we want from you...well, at least it's not the only thing we want from you."

Jett comes from behind, sliding his hand over my shoulder and grabbing my breast as he leans into my ear, "We want your mind too, Lovely Lina," he bites my neck until I cry out, "We want to own your fucking soul."

I'm wet, and without my thong, the wet jean material now rubs against me, not helping the situation much. When I look over Oakley's shoulder and see Fynn standing behind him, I see that Lara is no longer here. It's just me and the Lords, and the three of them look like starving wolves.

"Wait!"

All three stop when I call out. The Sinners stand over me, ready to pounce with their feet spread shoulder-width apart and their hands fisted at their sides, waiting to hear what I will say next. The only problem is that I'm still trying to figure out what to say. I just need a moment to get my bearings.

"I..."

"You what, Kitty Cat?"

"I...need to get back to the Sorority House." I find the coward's way out, but it doesn't matter because they aren't having it.

Shaking their heads, Jett is the one to speak next, "You're not going anywhere, Lovely Little Lina. I think it's high time you find out what it means to be owned by the Lords."

"You said that's why you had me sign the contract," our conversation is coming back to me now, as well as the one I had with my father, "We all know that's a lie. This has been planned since we were kids."

When I look at all three, why do they look as though I'm crazy? They had to have known that I would find out eventually, right? I lick my dry lips while waiting for one of them to respond, but they remain quiet as well.

"Yes, I know all about the agreement between our fathers when we were younger," I state, but my voice cracks slightly at the end.

"What are you talking about, Lina?" Jett looks confused, "I know we used to play together, but I know nothing of an agreement." He looks over at his two friends, who look just as lost.

"Y-Yeah, right," I stutter a little because now I'm second-guessing myself. They seem to not know what I'm talking about, but that can't be. Why else would they target me?

"We really don't know what you're talking about, Kitty Cat," Oakley states, "Is that what you were upset about earlier? Did your dad tell you this?"

I was wrong, they really don't know, and now, I may have just given them something they can use against me. Well, it doesn't matter because they already own me, but at least the contract has an expiration date. If they follow what our fathers have planned, they have me indefinitely.

"Forget I said anything," I try changing my tactic, "I read you guys wrong, is all."

They all scrutinize me, then Fynn shakes his head, "No, you know something Little Saint. We just discovered that we all used to play together as toddlers, but we haven't been told anything else. There is something there because we are being pushed to keep you safe, and your father told you to come to us. So," he leans down and gets right in my face, "I'm going to ask you this one time, and if you lie to us, you're going to be in so much trouble."

Again, I wet my dry lips, nervously this time, "W-What is it?"

"Did the Provost tell you that it was agreed upon between our families that you are to be ours?" he asks slowly, making sure I hear every word.

"Does it really matter? You already had me sign the contract..."

"Fuck yes, it matters!" Fynn scowls in my face.

"Why?"

I need to know what difference it makes, whether I'm theirs because our families said so or because it's per the contract. The real question is, will it make my life easier with them, or worse if it's because of our families. I want to know, and yet, I don't... I'm nervous to hear the answer.

"I need to know the truth because something isn't making sense. If you are truly ours because our families deem it so, why did my father warn me to be careful with you? He said that your father was his friend and that he didn't want to piss him off."

Instead of answering Fynn's question and giving them the truth, I straighten up and ready myself to receive punishment because I'm not giving them anything more. If they think they can fuck it out of me, let them try. I'm not giving them anything that they can use against me.

"You will have to ask your father, Fynn. I don't know the answer to your question, and as I told Oakley earlier, my conversations with my father are private."

Fynn stands to his full height and looks down his nose at me, "Fine, I guess we will do it the hard way."

Jett uncuffs my arms but keeps my wrists in his grip as Fynn covers my mouth again with tape. Oakley uncuffs my ankles. Fynn goes to the cupboard, grabs a zip tie, and secures my hands behind my back. He then tosses me over his shoulder, and I kick out, trying to get him to drop me.

His hand comes down on my ass hard, "Keep still, or we will fuck you right in front of our Frat brothers! Is that what you want, Little Saint?"

Even though I feel a tingle at the thought of Fynn's threat, I stop struggling and let them carry me upstairs. I keep my head down as we make our way through the house, but snickers can be heard when we pass others.

I'm carried to Fynn's room, which smells of his cologne and his favorite grass that he smokes. It's not a bad mixture, but I can do without the greenery mixed into it.

He tosses me onto his bed, landing on my zip-tied arms and wincing, "I bet that was uncomfortable," he smirks before holding my legs.

Oakley undoes my jeans, and I'm then flipped to my stomach. Someone yanks my jeans off. "Oh, she's commando today," Jett chuckles.

"Nah," Oakley replies, "I stole them when I fucked her in the bar bathroom." I can hear the amusement in his words.

God, how can these assholes turn me on like they do? Why am I attracted to guys that get off on humiliating me? When I feel someone's fingers between my thighs, I squirm. It's not that I don't want them there, because God forgive me, I do, but I don't want them to know how their rough treatment turns me on like no other.

"Oh, Lovely, what do we have here?" Jett asks as his fingers slide back and forth. He then pushes two of them inside and gives them a few pumps.

I lay here, trying my best not to moan as his fingers fuck me. When he drags them up to the tight little pucker, I try moving away. Someone grabs my hips and holds me down, so Jett can slowly push a finger inside. I moan accidentally.

"In order to give you the full experience, Kitty Cat," Oakley comes into my view carrying two items, a bottle of lube and a butt plug, "We need to prepare your body to take all of us at once."

I close my eyes, not knowing if I should be scared or excited. I hear the cap to the bottle pop just before Jett pulls his finger out, and the cold drizzle of lube hits that exact spot. My breathing is heavy as I find it harder to breathe through my nose at this point.

As soon as I feel the pressure of the plug, I begin to squirm once again. My ass is slapped, "Relax, Lina, I'll have this snug as a bug inside this cute little hole in no time." Jett says as he slowly pushes the metal object into me.

When it gets to the thicker part, he thrusts it in tiny strokes, stretching my hole a little more before he finally pops it into place. I feel full already as the heavy plug sits in the most forbidden hole. When I feel the bed move as Jett leaves, I open my eyes.

Oakley is right there, grinning at me, "You look fucking hot like this, Kitty Cat."

I'm then rolled to my side, watching Fynn hold a sharp knife. I don't know what he sees in my eyes, but he smiles cockily, "No, Little Saint, this isn't for your cunt," he then cuts my shirt down the middle before doing the same with my bra, baring my breasts to them all, "But maybe if you're good, we'll let you ride the handle again once we're through with you." He tosses the knife onto the nightstand and proceeds to remove his clothing.

I love seeing them without clothes on. They are so fit and built that I can cream myself just by looking at them. They all have muscles for days, and I watch Fynn's abs ripple when he climbs onto the bed and rolls me to my back. It's uncomfortable with my hands tied behind me, but he doesn't care as he straddles me just below my breasts.

When he begins to titty fuck me, I unintentionally whimper because I want so badly to feel his cock in my pussy, "Don't worry, Kitty Cat. Jett's going to take care of you." Oakley says just before a girthy cock slams into me, making me feel so full with the plug also inside. I can't see behind Fynn's form, but I know Jett is taking me hard.

The tape then peels away from my mouth, "Open that slutty mouth, Kitty Cat."

I don't know why I do it, but I refuse. Maybe it's because I'm still upset with this Lord, but it doesn't matter because he pinches my nose until I open my mouth. He pushes his way inside and starts fucking it roughly. They are doing it; all three are fucking me simultaneously, but I know this isn't their idea of filling me. Soon, all my holes will be filled with cock; this is just them pregaming before the big game.

TWENTY-THREE

Jett

Fuck! I've had a lot of pussy in my day, but nothing ever prepared me for Catalina Scott's pussy. It's like she was meant for my cock, how her walls fit around me like a glove and squeeze me in all the right areas. Of course, Fynn and Oakley say the same thing, so maybe she was meant to be ours.

This will be the first time we take her simultaneously, and fuck if I'm harder than a damn rock because of it. I love dominating women with my best friends, and being able to take my Lovely Lina with them is going to be so fucking epic.

"How are those tits, Fynn?" I stare at my fellow Lord's back while his hips jerk back and forth.

"It's not her cunt or her mouth, but it's a great substitute as I wait for that ass." He begins to grunt, and I know he's coming. Lovely Lina will have a stunning pearl necklace by the time Fynn's done; how much do you want to bet?

My friend stands on his bed, his dick now losing its hardness as it hangs, "Fucking gorgeous! It may be my best one yet."

I look between his legs, and there it is, ropes of seed form beautifully across her neck and collarbone. Fynn jumps from the bed and goes to his dresser to light one up. He passes it to me, and I continue to pound into Lina as I take it.

Fynn then takes another one and passes it to Oak. The fucker bends down and blows it into Lina's face. I can hear her muffled curses as the smoke goes up her nose while her mouth is full. Oakley, like Fynn, acts like an ass and does the same thing. Poor Catalina will feel really good when she leaves us tonight. Even though she doesn't do it, we don't give a shit. She will take it regardless because it's what we want.

Not ready to spill yet, I pull out of our girl. Apparently, neither is Oakley because he follows suit. I nod at Fynn as I reach out and uncuff the object of our addiction, helping her to her knees. I begin massaging her shoulders and arms, getting the kinks out, not because I care if she's sore, but because we still have a ways to go, and I don't want her injured beyond repair.

Catalina moans with her eyes closed as I continue the massage, so she doesn't see Fynn attaching the ropes to the eyelets in the ceiling above his bed. When he's done, Oakley removes her torn top and bra, then takes one of her arms just as I bring my hand to her throat to hold her still. I know our little wild cat too well, and as soon as she realizes that her wrists are being restrained again, she tries fighting it.

"What the fuck?" She struggles, and I tighten my grip on her neck, so she can't talk but can still breathe.

"Shh, be a good girl and sit still. I promise you will get pleasure from this." I bite and suck on her neck, knowing I'm leaving my mark for all to see. I run my other hand through the sticky substance my friend left behind and rub it into her skin before bringing my fingers to her mouth and gagging her while I feed her Fynn's cum.

Once Fynn has both limbs secure, we stand back and take in the beauty of Catalina, in all her glory, waiting to be claimed by her Lords. She's up on her knees; her arms stretched wide open above her head. Her mascara runs once again as cum dries on her lips and chest. She a beautiful fucking mess; she looks perfect!

Lovely Lina will be filled to the brim with Sinners, and she will enjoy every minute of it. She tries turning her head to watch as Oakley moves behind her, but she can only move it so far with how her arms are restrained. The sounds coming from her mouth when Oakley plays with the plug in her ass, fucking it in and out before removing it, is music to my ears.

"Mm, this gape is perfect," Oakley states as he shoves two fingers into her without hurting her, "How about one more, Kitty Cat?" He slowly inserts the third, and we now know she's ready.

Lifting her up, I lay below her, having her straddle me, "Fuck, Lina. I can't get enough of this tight cunt." I thrust up into her hard, watching her tits bounce. I slap one and then the other before stopping all movement.

"You fucking liked that, didn't you, slut?" Fynn moves in behind her, coating his length with lube, "Deep down, you love being treated like a dirty little whore, but we all know you're not. You're a Saint, after all," he chuckles, and begins pushing into her ass.

I can feel him there, her cunt getting tighter the deeper he goes. She moans and hangs her head, but my friend grabs her hair and yanks it back up, "Look at Oakley as his two best friends take his precious Kitty Cat."

Oakley is already stoking his cock as he kneels beside us, watching the scene before him. Once we know she's adjusted to the two of us filling her, we begin moving, instantly forming momentum.

"Oh God...I'm too full!" she moans.

"That's the whole fucking point, Kitty Cat," Oakley says, "Now open wide and take me like a good girl."

When she doesn't do as she's told right away, Fynn yanks her head back more. Catalina cries out, and Oak pushes himself inside, "Now this is a perfect fucking picture," I state, and reach up to torture her gorgeous tits.

The room fills with moans and groans, grunts and curse words as we enjoy our girl, and she enjoys us. Believe me, if her little whimpers and moans tell us anything, it tells us that she's enjoying her Lords and has almost reached her climax.

"You will come for us, Lovely Lina," Fynn and I thrust harder, deeper, filling every crevice inside her.

She mumbles incoherently with her mouth full, so Oakley pulls out, letting her talk, "I can't, the feeling...it's too much!" She says it's too much, but I think it's the perfect amount.

"How about I help with that, then," I pinch her clit as Oakley thrusts back into her throat just in time as she screams and comes all over my cock, "Oh yeah, that's it..."

Three orgasms later for our girl, each of us releasing inside her, we all collapse on the bed. Lina hangs from the restraints as she remains impaled on my cock. When Fynn suddenly jumps up from the bed, he lights another smoke, blowing it in Catalina's face.

"Stop! I told you I don't do drugs!" she glares.

It's hard to take her seriously when she looks the way she does; restrained and dripping with cum. My cock hardens again, and I begin fucking her once more. If you have a warm pussy on your cock, why not?

"You're not doing it, Little Saint. We are doing it to you. If we smoke, you smoke." Fynn states, and this time, after taking a hit, he grabs her face and shotguns her, not quite touching her lips with his. She sputters and coughs afterward.

"You're a fucking dickhead!" she glares at my friend.

He only shrugs, "You say that now, but you will be begging me to fuck you when you're in a relaxed state, bet me."

"Fuck you!"

Fynn looks at me and grins, "As soon as Jett gets his fill, I will be happy to give you another load."

Lina's phone buzzes, and Oakley grabs it. Instead of giving it to her, he reads the text, and I see rage fill his features, "What is it?" I stop fucking and just stare at him.

"It's Dani."

"Why the fuck are you looking at my messages?" Lina scowls but can't do anything about it.

Oakley ignores her and looks at Fynn, "Uncuff her. We need to go check this out."

"Check what out?" Fynn asks as he moves to undo the cuffs.

"It seems like another hit was just put out on Kitty Cat. Apparently, the fucker didn't know that Catalina wasn't in her room," the tick in his jaw tells me that my friend is barely holding back his rage, "They threw a lit bottle of gasoline through Kitty Cat's window. A portion of the Sorority House is damaged." He looks back down when the phone buzzes again, "Dani is at the hospital for smoke inhalation."

"Let me go! I need to get to the hospital!" Catalina yanks on the restraint that Fynn has yet to get to.

"Calm the fuck down, Kitty Cat!" Oakley growls at her, "We will take you there and drop you off. One of us will stay with you while the other two go to the House and see what information we can find."

Fynn releases Lina's other arm, and she hops off as quickly as possible. Of course, my dick has already gone soft anyway, but it still annoys me that she can dismiss me that fast. When she goes to put on her clothes, I watch Oakley shove her toward the bathroom.

"Take a quick shower; you smell like a fucking whore house!" It earns him a glare, but she obeys his command anyway.

Once she's in the shower, I stare at my two best friends, "This is getting out of hand! We need to catch these fuckers!"

"They aren't going to get away with this, Jett. Nobody fucks with our property, and they sure as hell don't try taking it away from us. They are some dead motherfuckers!"

Catalina

Jett's black Jeep flies through town as he drives us to the hospital. I'm too freaked out over Dani getting hurt because of me that I don't pay too much attention to his speed. I want to get there as fast as possible, so it's good that the Lord has a lead foot. The small New Hampshire town we live in isn't all that small, but it's not a big city, either. Since it's on the other side of town from us, it takes almost ten minutes to get to the hospital with all the traffic and stop lights. So, Jett decided to take the less traveled roads, cutting our time in half.

"Stop biting your nails, Lina," Jett glances over at me and reaches out, taking my hand in his so I can't bite anymore.

"I can't help it! Why are they trying to kill me, Jett? What did my father do that was so bad?" I ask the Lord as I stare at him, expecting him to know the answer to my question.

His jaw clenches, "I don't know, Catalina, but we will find the fuckers, and they will pay for every wrong they have committed against you."

The Jeep takes another turn, and the hospital looms before us. Jett finds a spot and parks, but when I go to get out, he pulls me back in and raises his eyebrow.

"What?"

"Stay in the Jeep until I come around to get you. I want to make sure it's safe."

"You don't think they followed us, do you?" I ask as I start looking around at our surroundings. All I see are rows and rows of vehicles and a few people walking to and from their own.

"We can't be too sure, and I'm not willing to take the risk, Lina. Keep that cute tush inside until I open the door for you."

"Yeah, okay...but can you hurry? I really want to get inside and see Dani."

I'm impatient, but Jett doesn't seem to care as he takes his time looking all around. I get that he's trying to keep me safe, but my friend needs me now, and I don't give two shits about the fuckers trying to kill me. The glare he receives from me as he opens the door doesn't go unnoticed.

He firmly takes hold of my chin and leans in, "Your safety will always come first, Lina. Dani isn't going anywhere just yet, so calm the fuck down."

"She's in here because of me!" I push his hand away, "Don't ever dismiss my feelings like that again, Jett."

He keeps me from leaving the Jeep by blocking my way out with his hard, sculpted body, "We can stay here all night, or you can drop the attitude, so we can go in and see your friend."

I close my mouth for now, deciding to hold off on my few choice words for him. The moment he says, "Good girl," and takes my hand, I begin to relax. I don't know why the two little words have so much power, but they do.

I stay close to Jett on the little walk to the emergency room doors. I'm not sure why, but the hairs on the back of my neck stand up as if we are being watched. However, I don't see anything out of the ordinary when I look around, so I just ignore it.

Hurrying in through the door, we head straight for the nurse's station at the front, "Excuse me, but I am looking for Dani Richards. She came in with smoke inhalation or something."

"I'm sorry. Are you family?" The nurse asks.

I don't need them denying me access to my friend, so I lie, "Yes, she's my cousin and roommate."

"What's your name, dear?" The nurse asks, buying into my lie.

"Catalina Scott."

The nurse looks at her computer screen and smirks, "We have protocols, Miss Scott. Please remember that in the future, when you try lying to get in to see a patient. Lucky for you, even though your name isn't listed with the family, your name is on the list of visitors." The nurse winks at me, "Room 202. Take the elevator, located around the corner, then take a left once you get off on the second floor."

"Yes, ma'am. I'm sorry," I say sheepishly, then head for the elevator.

Jett chuckles behind me, but I don't acknowledge it until we reach the elevator. Once the doors close behind us, I turn on him, "What do you find so funny?"

"You," his grin is sexy, "You can't lie for shit."

I huff and turn away from him, "How was I to know they would be able to tell? It works in the movies..."

"Seriously?" The elevator stops, and the doors open, "You're taking tips from movies? You, Lovely Lina, are a smart cookie, but boy, your blonde moments are doozies!" he continues chuckling.

"Hey..."

He cuts me off as he shoves me toward Dani's door, "Shush, and go visit your friend. I'll be standing right outside," He crosses his arms, and with his feet shoulder-width apart, he takes the stance of a guard and gets into guard mode just outside the door.

"Cat! Thank God you're here!" Dani looks relieved as she looks me over.

Two others are in the room with her, and one just happens to be Felicia. I should be nervous about her being here with Jett standing right outside, but I don't give a shit anymore. Now that I know it's not a school rule and she can't kick me out of the Sorority for being with the Sinners, I couldn't care less about what she thinks.

"Where have you been?" The President asks, a little too snooty for my liking.

"Not that it's any of your business, but I was with friends," I turn to Dani, moving to sit on the edge of her bed, "How are you? Were you in the room when it came through the window?"

"I had just walked out of the room when I heard the crash," my friend explains, "I rushed back in and saw the flames. I tried putting it out before it did too much damage, but it was too much with the gasoline. That's how I took in too much smoke."

I lean in and hug my friend, "I am so sorry, Dani. Was the person caught? What about the security cameras?"

I look at Felicia, who now stands back, looking bored as hell. When she realizes I'm talking to her, she scoffs, "How do I know if anyone was caught yet? I've been here with poor Dani. I did give the police the camera feed before I left to come here."

I nod, "Good. Hopefully, they can catch this fucker."

"Catalina!" Felicia chastises, "Try to be a little more ladylike!"

A chuckle from outside the door is heard, and being the nosiest person I know, Felicia walks over to see who's chuckling. She gasps as she looks out into the hallway, and I grin at Dani. My friend immediately knows what the big deal is, and her eyes widen.

"You did not bring them here!" Dani mouths to me, and I shrug before looking over toward the doorway.

"Did you come with a Sinner?" Felicia looks as though she may faint, so I take it a bit further to really get her going.

Grinning, I wiggle my brows, "Actually, I came with a few of them...multiple times."

The Sorority President scrunches her face, not understanding my meaning, but it doesn't last long. There's a louder gasp once she catches on, "You didn't!"

"Don't ask if you don't want to know." I shrug. I feel Dani slap my leg, "What? She asked. I was recently told that I'm a lousy liar, so I told the truth."

The chuckling from outside has turned into full-blown laughter, which only fuels Felicia's temper, "You know the rules, Miss Scott! No fraternizing with the Sinners!"

"Uh, yeah, about that. You see, I recently learned that the rule was made up by a Sorority Sister not too long ago. My father, you know, the Provost...he was a Lord of Sin back in his day, and as you well know, my mother was the Saint's President. That rule didn't apply back then. Oh, and you should also know that I'm with the Lords per my father's order because they are helping me."

"W-Well," she stutters, "I can still give you a strike for not following the House Rules. After three strikes, then I can terminate your residency with the Saints."

I walk over to her, slowly, "You do know that to kick me out, it's got to go through certain channels, and they have to approve it."

"Yeah, so." Felicia now crosses her arms, looking all smug.

"It goes through eight people, and I can name at least four last names." Counting them off with my fingers, I give Felicia my own smug look, "Harris, Scott, Morin, and Pelletier. Oh, and all four were Lords back in their day."

Jett barges into the conversation, "Actually, all six board members were Lords back in their day."

"No, that can't be!" Felicia stomps her foot, "That's unfair!"

"What's unfair is for you to tell us who we can and cannot associate with," I glare at her, "I don't know who made up this rule, but it's ridiculous!"

Felicia throws her nose in the air, "My Aunt Charlotte's best friend was the Saint's Sorority President three years after my mother graduated, and she put the rule in place."

"Why?"

"The heck if I know, but it's a rule nonetheless, and rules must be followed!" she states.

"Yeah, well, rules are also meant to be broken..."

Felecia stares disbelievingly at me, then snaps her fingers, and our other Sorority Sister jumps up and follows her as Felicia starts walking down the hall toward the elevator. "Bye, Felicia!" I call out and snicker.

"You are so bad!" Dani laughs from the bed, causing her to go into a coughing fit.

I retake my seat on the edge of the bed, "Someone needed to put her in her place."

"You realize she will come at you with everything she's got. She will try her hardest to have you removed from the house," my friend says but grins about it.

"Let her try..."

"It doesn't matter because you will be coming to stay with us," Jett states from the doorway.

Dani and I both drop our jaws, "I'm what?!"

"You heard me, Lina," he holds his phone out to me, "Per Mr. Harris and Mr. Scott, Catalina Scott is to reside with the Lords of Sin until any and all threats are taken care of."

I'm at a loss for words at first, but then the anger starts to set in, and once again, my life is being dictated. I look Jett in the eye and glaringly state, "The hell I am!"

TWENTY-FOUR

Fynn

Being from prominent families in the area, our fathers have a lot of pull, and so, when Oakley and I pull up to the scene, the Fire Chief does not hesitate to talk to us. They have just finished going through the still-smoldering debris and are able to tell us their initial findings.

Even though there is still a lot to go through, the Chief is confident about one thing. The bottle used to set the fire is one that can only be found at a locally owned mom-and-pop shop here. The brownish-red tinted glass from the bottle holds chocolate-raspberry syrup for coffee and such. It's the first real lead we have received since this whole thing started.

As Oakley and I climb back into his Camaro after talking with the Fire Chief, our phones buzz. A message telling us that we are to have Little Saint move into the Frat House with us puts a huge smile on my face. I will love nothing more right now than to have our girl at our beck and call.

I glance over at my friend, and he's wearing a similar smile, "Little Saint is going to be pissed."

Oakley shrugs, "She has no choice if she wants to survive this. It's apparent that this stalker is serious and plans on following through with their threats."

I think about my friend's words, "It isn't just Saint that needs to be careful, Oak. They will turn to one of us if they feel they can't get to her. They are only targeting Saint because they think she's the easiest. We have to watch our backs, too."

"Yeah, well, that's not going to work for me, so I suggest we get this piece of shit as soon as possible," Oakley states as he revs the engine up. Putting the car in drive, my friend peels out and heads for the store that sells the specific bottle used in the arson.

Walking through the aisles, I sporadically knock shit off the shelves. I'm trying not to make too much of a mess, but the fucking owner is refusing to give us what we need. We've been here for twenty minutes, showing up just as they were closing the shop. We don't want to be the bad guys here, but we need this information; they are the only ones who can give it to us.

"My friend can do this until every item is on the floor, and you will have no choice but to replace everything," Oakley says to the owner.

"Please, go through the right channels, and I will gladly give this information to the police..."

Oakley slams his hand on the counter, making the owner jump, "Do you not know who the fuck we are?" His tone has now changed to one of anger; forget playing the nice guy, "We are the current Lords of Sin! Our fathers are Harris and Morin...sound familiar?"

Before we go any further, let me just say that our fathers are not Mafia or some shit like that, but they do have this town by the balls just because of all the money they put into it and what they donate. They don't threaten anybody if it isn't necessary, and they only hurt the bad guys, but they will do what it takes to get shit done, and that's precisely what we are doing right now.

"I-I understand w-who you are," the owner stutters.

"All we are asking for is a list of transactions of when this product was sold in the past six months and the camera footage. We don't want to hurt you, Mr. Tomlin, but we will if you refuse to work with us."

"I-I'm sorry, but I can't..."

Next, Oakley slams the owner's head down to the counter, holding it there as he leans in, "I know you are not going to refuse us again, Mr. Tomlin, are you?"

I walk over after sweeping a whole shelf of cereal onto the floor, "The sooner you give us what we want, the sooner we can send some help to clean this shit up, and you can go home to your wife. Otherwise, I will start smashing the jars, and there will be no help with clean up."

"Okay, okay, please..."

Oakley lets go of the guy's head, "Thank you. I truly appreciate it."

We both stand here and watch the middle-aged man type on his computer. He clicks a button, and I can hear a printer start running. It takes little time, which means that not too many were sold, making it easier for us. The owner grabs the two sheets and hands them to Oakley.

"If they paid with a credit or debit card, the customer's name will be listed. If they paid with cash, it wouldn't be," Mr. Tomlin informs us.

"How about you get us that footage now, so we can get out of your hair," I tell him.

The older man writes something on a slip of paper and hands it to me, "This is the company I use and the code to get into my feed. This is the easiest way to do it, or at least the easiest way I know of."

"Thanks," I say, pulling my phone out to send a message to Sean, telling him to send a few guys over to help clean this mess up.

Oakley and I head for the door, "What about my store?" the owner calls out.

I turn back, "A few Sinners will be here shortly to help clean up. Watch for them and let them in." It's all I say before we walk out the door.

Instead of taking this information to our fathers, we take it back to the Frat House. If our fathers don't want to be truthful with us, we will find the culprits on our own and take care of them. Truth be known, I think this may be a test to see if we are fit to take our rightful place once we graduate next year. Our fathers are very capable of taking care of this on their own, so having us in charge of Little Saint's well-being pretty much screams TEST.

We all play a part in our families; I'm still determining my role. Jett's and my father are deputy mayors, but my father is the first deputy mayor. He steps in when the mayor can't and has a lot of responsibility. The mayor himself is a well-known Lord. There is no secret society, or shit like that, but the Lords come with a lot of power because of what they can do. My uncle, another Lord of Sin, is the Police Chief, so even if the store owner didn't get us the information we needed, my Uncle Tyler would have, but it would have taken a little longer.

This test, if this is what it is, is the real deal. It's not a made-up prank like you do at initiations. Our fathers use real-life shit to test us. Seeing the message come through about Little Saint coming to stay with us confirms that this is serious because the opposite sex is not supposed to live at the Frat House. Them moving our girl in with us is huge.

"What do you think about all this, Oak?"

My friend sighs, "Honestly, I'm not really sure. Things are getting fucking serious. It's not the little piddly shit that we are used to. I don't think this will end with just sending the bastard to the hospital."

"I was thinking the same thing," I tell him, "I have a feeling this is going to be some 'last-man-standing' type of shit."

"Yeah, only there will be four of us standing in the end. We will not fall, Fynn. The Lords of Sin must always come out on top." The way Oakley says this would give anyone else chills, but I know all too well what he means and how true this is.

"Damn, I hope Little Saint doesn't give Jett any trouble when he brings her back here," I say excitedly, "I can use another release or two after all this shit."

My friend scoffs, "You are a fucking sex addict...you need help."

"Fuck man, you can't say you don't get hard just thinking about your Kitty Cat!" I scowl.

"I do, but I also know how much of a bitch in heat she is, even if she denies it. Giving it to her all the time is giving her exactly what she wants. Holding it from her is where the power lies. Keep that in mind."

I sit back and think about what Oakley just said, and it makes total fucking sense, but damn. It will suck holding back...unless I piss her off where she really doesn't want it, and then I take it anyway. Yeah, that's what I'll do. I guarantee she'll be screaming my name and telling me to give her more once I start fucking her; only I will hold her pleasure.

Little Saint is a slut for our cocks, whether she wants to admit it or not. Maybe it's time we start showing her who is really in charge here and just how much she likes us being in control. I know she can be a little hell cat, but deep down, she wants us just as much as we want her.

TWENTY-FIVE

Catalina

The message was made very clear. Oakley's father, and my father decided without even asking what I wanted. Moving in with the Sinners is a colossal mistake waiting to happen. It's not that I completely hate the idea, but I hate that the decision was made for me once again.

I can't be responsible for what occurs between me and the three Lords. I want all of them, twisted depravity, and all...and it scares the living shit out of me. I never thought I would love being treated the way I am, and I fight it because, to most, it's unnatural, but the Lords know me better than anyone. They have seen what their words and actions do to me and use it to their advantage. They are trying to break me; I know it. The question is...will I allow them to break me, or will I not have a choice? Some days I feel as though I can keep them at bay, and some...I turn into fucking jelly, not able to control my own body around them.

"Let's go, Lina," Jett says from Dani's hospital room doorway, "The guys are at home, and they have some information about the fire."

"I hope the fucker is caught," Dani states, "We lost everything, and I could have lost my life!"

"They will be found, make no mistake." Jett's statement makes me scoff, and he glares at me.

I turn back to my friend and hug her, "I will see you tomorrow after I talk with my father and get my living arrangements cleared up."

"Okay. Be careful out there, Cat." Dani hugs me back.

"I'll be fine, Dani. I'm sure my guard dogs won't let anything happen to me," I smirk back at Jett, who is still glaring, "I had better go," I wave and walk out the door.

Nothing is said as we ride the elevator down, but as soon as the door opens, Jett pulls me down the hall opposite where we need to be going. After turning down another corridor, he opens the door to a storage closet and shoves me inside, locking it as soon as it closes behind him.

"Do you have something you want to say, Lina?" He stalks me, making me back up into some shelves.

"What are you doing, Jett? I thought you said we needed to return to the Frat House?" I hold my hand out, hoping to stop him, but I should have known better.

He grabs my hand and lifts it over my head before grabbing the other one and bringing his face inches from mine, "Do you not have faith in your *guard dogs*?"

"Jett..." I lick my lips.

"What's the matter, Lovely Lina? Cat's got your tongue now that you're in the hot seat?" He dips his head and bites my neck hard.

"Ouch! Jett...that fucking hurt!"

"Good." He moves to the other side and does the same thing before he spins me around, "Do you know what else is going to hurt?"

"W-What...?" I stutter.

Taking both my wrists in one hand, he uses his other to reach down and pull my jeans down to my knees. Oh fuck, is he seriously going to take me right here in this closet? What if someone tries coming in? I struggle, but his grip is firm, almost bruising, as he holds me in place.

Suddenly, I feel a sting on my bare ass, and a slap rings out in the small room, "How about you count them, Lina."

"Jett, what are you..."

"I said to count them!" he growls in my ear just before another one makes contact.

"Two!"

"That's a good girl."

"Three!"

It continues until I reach twenty, and now my inner thighs are soaked. Hoping against hope that he will pull my jeans up without noticing, it's all lost as soon as I feel his hand squeeze my burning flesh and slide downward. I press my head against the shelf, knowing what he's going to find.

"Really, Lina?" His fingers glide back and forth through my arousal, "Do you honestly believe that we can leave this closet while this sweet cunt begs to be fucked?"

I hear rustling, and no more words are said. Pulling my hips out, he pushes into me until he's all the way in, "Mm, you are so fucking wet, Lina..."

He then begins fucking me as he holds my wrists above my head with one hand and grips my hip with the other. I can't move even if I want to. He slams into me repeatedly, grunting and groaning, not caring that I'm still sore from the three of them taking me earlier. Hell, I don't even care at this point, but I won't let him know that.

Letting go of my hip, he takes hold of my hair and pulls it back and to the side, making me look at him from this odd angle. He smirks, "How's that feel, Lovely? Is your greedy cunt happy now?"

I shoot him a glare, "Fuck you, Jett."

"You already are, Lina. I'm going to make this pussy come all over me, and you can't do a thing about it." He crashes his mouth against mine, our teeth scraping together in the brutal way he takes it. I bite his lip, and he yanks away, grinning, "You asked for it now. Keep your fucking hands right where they are."

He lets go of my wrists, and I have no choice but to grab hold of the shelf above my head to help keep me steady. Jett's hand comes to my neck, helping to hold me up, but I soon realize that little by little, his grip is tightening until I can barely breathe. His other hand goes to my clit where he begins playing and pinching it.

I'm becoming lightheaded from lack of oxygen, and just when I start seeing stars dancing in my line of vision, Jett gives a hard pinch to my clit as he lets go of my neck. Air rushes back into my lungs, only to be taken once more as I come hard. Jett's hand slaps over my mouth as he continues fucking me fast and deep.

"Here you go, Lina. Your fucking prize for being such a good girl." I feel him jerk, and warmth shoots deep inside me as he releases his load, "Fuck yes...it's all yours, little slut."

I'm trying to breathe through my nose as he keeps his hand over my mouth, jerking himself until he's empty. I do feel like his little slut the way I let him take me in here like he did. I could have said the one word I know will stop everything, but that's not what I want. I'm not ready for any of it to end.

I can barely stand up, never mind walk, so Jett picks me up and carries me out of the hospital. Nurses and patients stare, but I don't care. His scent, mixed with the state he's left my body in, is all too much, and I'm pretty sure I pass out by the time we get to his Jeep.

It's dark. I'm running through the woods, being chased by my Lords. If they catch me, I'm fucked...literally. I can hear them calling out my name one by one...Kitty Cat...Little Saint...Lovely Lina! Each of them wanting to make me submit in their own way. I giggle and continue to run. It's not like I'm trying very hard because, if I'm being honest, I want to be caught. I just don't know by which one...I can't choose.

"Gotcha!" Fynn is the first, but I'm able to slip away and disappear into the darkness once more.

I can hear them gaining on me as they laugh tauntingly. They are just playing with their food; we all know they can catch me if they want to. I'm okay with it, though. It's turning me on being chased by three hot Sinners, and I'm having way too much fun.

I'm pushed to the ground, lying flat on my stomach as a heaviness pins me down, "Did you honestly believe that you could run from us, Kitty Cat? You belong to us; we will never let you go."

"I'm only yours until the contract is up," I pant, finding it hard to breathe with Oakley's weight on me.

"That contract only allows us to do whatever the fuck we want to you, but you will always be ours."

"We own your body, mind, and soul," Jett's voice replaces Oakley's, "Always remember that."

"*Beg me, Saint...I love it when you beg me to batter this cunt... to own every piece of you,*" now Fynn's voice is in my ear, but none of my Lords are here when I'm spun onto my back.

A figure in a white cloak straddles my waist. Their face is a blur, so I can't tell who it is. Their body begins to shake with unheard laughter as they raise their hand. A gun appears, and it's pointed right at my head. Cocking it, their finger hovers over the trigger, and I squeeze my eyes shut just as a loud bang echoes through the woods.

I wake up screaming.

TWENTY-SIX

Oakley

"I just texted Jett, letting him know that we have some news about the fire and that he should bring Catalina home," Fynn informs me as he walks into my room.

I'm logging into the company with the video feed when he does, and I stop what I'm doing as soon as he says, "Bring Catalina home." Thinking about this makes my dick hard. I'm not sure what our fathers, hers specifically, thought when they made this decision. Mr. Scott has got to know that we will defile his little girl on a daily basis. After all, he was a Lord of Sin once himself.

"Has he said anything about how our girl took that news?" I smirk, continuing with what I was doing.

"No, just said that they would be home shortly, that they were leaving. That was almost forty-five minutes ago, though."

I glance up to see my friend frown, "Well, text him again..." I'm cut off by the footsteps in the hall outside my room.

Jett's signature knock sounds on my door before it opens, and the third Lord walks in carrying our future Lady. She's sound asleep as he walks over and lays her down in the middle of my bed. Raising a brow at him in question, he shrugs and drops into the chair beside me.

"What did you do, drug her?" I ask, still waiting for an explanation.

His smirk is knowing, "Nah, just gave her a good fucking in a storage room at the hospital, is all."

"That's all?" Fynn grins.

"Well, the fucking came after the twenty spankings," he states smugly, "Our saintly little slut called us her guard dogs, so I had to show her the error of her ways."

I chuckle and glance over at my little Kitty Cat, wanting nothing more than to fuck her myself, but we have bigger problems right now. Turning back to the matter at hand, I type in the password to the camera feed, and suddenly, it pops up.

"We're in!" I say.

"What exactly are we in?" Jett asks.

"The Fire Chief told us what bottle was thrown to start the fire, and that only one store in town has it. So, we paid Mr. Tomlin a little visit, and after a little bit of persuasion, he gave us the list of transactions on this product, along with the code to his camera feed." I tell him as I sit back and grin. I'm pretty proud of us for getting this far so soon.

"So, any names on the list pop out?" Jett questions looking at Fynn as he scans the two pages.

"Nothing with the credit cards, but most paid with cash, so I'm guessing we'll be watching a lot of camera feed," Fynn sighs.

"Hey, no biggie," I say, "I'm sure if all three of us each take two months' worth of footage, we can knock it out in no time."

"That's like seven hundred, twenty hours of footage!" Jett exclaims, and I just gawk at him for knowing that right off the top of his head.

"Yeah, well, we really don't have much of a choice, do we?" I scoff.

It's almost midnight, and so far, we've encountered three students who go to Helshire and bought this chocolate-raspberry syrup from this store. All of them are women, though. That's not to say we ignore them because we know that at least two people are working together. One of them can very well be a female.

I'm only about a quarter of the way through the feed when I notice movement over by my bed. Fynn and Jett returned to their rooms to watch their part of the footage, leaving my Kitty Cat with me. The three of us have decided that while she is here, Catalina will stay with each of us, rotating each night, so we can all have her to ourselves. She probably won't like that idea too much, but she doesn't get a choice.

She settles down, and I go back to watching the video footage, only to be startled two minutes later when a scream pierces through my room. Catalina sits straight up in my bed, her chest heaving up and down. I notice sweat glistening from her forehead, so I get up and go to her side.

"Bad dream?" I ask as I sit on the edge of the bed.

Surprising me, she throws her arms around my neck and literally crawls onto my lap, "Hey," I say softly, "It was just a dream..."

"It felt so real!" my Kitty Cat pants.

"It's okay. You're safe here, Kitty Cat. We won't let anyone hurt you."

She pulls back and gazes into my eyes, "What if they throw another fire bomb? Maybe I shouldn't be here; I wouldn't want your Frat House to burn down because of me."

I push some hair back behind her ear, "I think we're safe for tonight, and tomorrow my dad has a security company coming to put in a new alarm system."

"Why are they coming after me, Oakley? What did my dad do to make someone want to hurt me...to want to kill me?" her voice cracks, and just how she asks this simple question burrows deep down, affecting parts of me that I have had closed off for years.

"It isn't just you," I say with a sneer.

I don't want to be too soft with Catalina. She may be ours, but that doesn't mean I will ever have any feelings for her, not the kind most women want anyway. I've seen too many relationships go down the drain, and I swore I wouldn't let myself get into that position. My parents may still be together, but nobody knows that they both have side pieces...they can't remain faithful to each other any longer.

I feel Kitty Cat's body tense, and when I look back into her eyes, I see the confusion written on her face caused by my tone. Sighing because I know she hasn't been told yet, I tighten my grip on her, so she doesn't try to move away. I don't know if she will, but I'm unsure how she will react when she finds out we haven't told her what I'm about to tell her.

"What does that mean?" she asks before I can start.

"It means, Kitty Cat, that you aren't the only one being threatened. All our fathers received threatening letters; it wasn't just yours. We have concluded that they did something when they were Lords, and now it's coming back to haunt them, only they are still keeping us in the dark as to what it was."

"How long have you known?" She asks, squinting her eyes, "Did you know your fathers were being threatened before I came to you?"

"Of course, but we didn't find out that your father was also being threatened until right after you told us you needed our help." Just as I thought, she thrashes, trying to escape my hold.

"Let me go, Oakley...I mean it!" She's angry, but I don't care.

I toss her onto her back and take hold of her jaw, "What the fuck is your problem?"

"You and your stupid Lords of Sin status, thinking you can trick females into signing shit just so you can have your way with them! We are nothing but toys to you!" Her nails are embedded into my wrist, holding her jaw.

"I'm going to set you straight, and this will be the only time I do, so listen well! We may get consent from females, and yes, some sign an NDA, but you, Catalina Scott, you're special. We have never wanted to consume anyone like we want to consume you! You are our one and only contract signed in blood, and everything on those pages will be upheld...on both our ends."

"What if I say no...that I want out? I'll find help elsewhere..."

My chuckle may be a bit too sinister for her liking, but I don't give a flying fuck, "We are past that point, Kitty Cat. There is no going back now...the Lords are invested, and you," I lick my lips and let my eyes wander over her face and down to her still-heaving breasts, "You are too addicted to us. We are each others' drug of choice...none of us are able to get the same fix elsewhere."

"You're fucking delusional, Oakley. I can get the same thing from others...the Lords are nothing special!" Her eyes sparkle with defiance. She wants to go toe-to-toe with me.

"Tell me, Kitty Cat. What will I find if I shove my hand down your pants right now? Will you be as dry as the Sahara Desert or wetter than a fish in water?" I grin as I slowly undo her jeans.

She struggles against me, making me lay my entire length down on her, "Get the fuck off me, Oakley! You will never know the answer to that question."

"Oh really?" I crash my mouth against hers, so she can no longer deny me access to what is already mine. I finish undoing her jeans and push them down as far as possible while lying on her, "Ah, what do I feel?" I'm not even inside her panties, and I can already feel how soaked she is, "Tell me again how much you don't want this, Kitty Cat."

"Get off..." a moan cuts her words off as I push two fingers into her.

"You would like that, wouldn't you, Kitty Cat?" I pump vigorously, getting my fingers in deep, "Getting off..."

"Oakley..."

"Just shut the fuck up for two minutes and take what I'm willing to give you, Kitty Cat." I rub her clit with my thumb, and when she tries talking again, I grab her face and turn it away, so all that comes out is gibberish, "I'm going to have to teach this mouth when to shut the fuck up, aren't I?"

Catalina's hips begin to gyrate against my hand, and I grin knowingly. I knew she wouldn't be able to resist. I want to plunge into her so badly, but it will have to wait a little longer. I'm only taking a little break to teach our saintly little slut here a lesson.

"You like that?" I ask as I glance down and watch her fuck my hand, "You want to come all over my hand?"

I insert a third finger, and her body slowly tenses up. I fuck her harder, and as soon as she's about to come, I pull my hand away, wiping her wetness all over her face like a fucking jerk, but I don't give a fuck. She will learn her lesson eventually, even if I have to rub her face in a puddle of cum and make her lick it off the floor...I will do whatever it takes. We need her to trust in us completely and know that we know what is best for her.

I wasn't lying when I told her we are consumed by her, but that doesn't mean I will ever feel for her what other lovesick guys feel for women. She doesn't get that chance to hurt me, so she will have to deal with what I am willing to give, which is my sick and twisted tendencies, and she will learn to love every single one...guaranteed.

"Damn it, Oakley!" she's panting heavily as I move away.

"Patience, Kitty Cat. Be a good girl, and I will finish you off once I'm done with what I'm doing," I smirk as I turn away.

I feel a pillow hit the back of my head, and I stop but smile at her audacity. By the time I turn back around, my smile is gone, and I bring my hands to my waist, pulling off my belt. Catalina's eyes widen as she watches me remove the strip of leather from each hoop.

She tries to scramble off the bed as I take my first step, but she isn't fast enough. Grabbing her foot, I yank her back and capture her wrists. I quickly wrap the belt around her wrists and secure it to the headboard.

"Oakley," she growls, "Let me go, right fucking now!"

I raise an eyebrow, "I don't think you are in any position to make demands, Kitty Cat."

I pull her jeans all the way off and then reach under my bed for the rope already attached to the footboard. Once the first ankle is tied, I move on to the other, spreading her wide open. My dick jumps just looking at her, her cunt still glistening with arousal.

I leave her shirt on because what I need to do doesn't have anything to do with her tits, so moving over to my closet, I rummage around my trunk until I find what I'm looking for and bring it back to the bed.

"Whatever you're thinking about doing, Oakley, don't! I will tell my father everything that you do to me!"

I snicker at her words as I apply the strap to her upper thighs, "I highly doubt that Kitty Cat. After all, you wouldn't want Daddy to know just how much his baby girl is a slut for the depraved."

"I'm not..."

I slap her pussy hard, "Keep lying to yourself, Kitty Cat. In the end, I promise that you will accept what you are." I tell her.

"And what is that exactly?" The glare she's giving me has no effect on me whatsoever.

Next, I grab the wand and place it in its holder in the strap, right against her swollen clit. I give her my most charming, wicked grin, "Why the Lord's dirty little slut who loves every twisted and demoralizing thing we will do to you."

I don't miss her body's quiver at my words, and when I move to grab my phone, I point up at the corner of the room to where a red light appears on the camera. I use the app on my phone to turn the wand on, vibrating her clit on a low setting. After all, she will not be coming until I'm ready for her to do so.

"Oakley, turn the camera off!" she glares and moans simultaneously.

I tsk her, "Someone has already forgotten part of the contract, I see. I don't have time to remind you at the moment, but I promise I will make sure you memorize every word in it." I reach into the drawer on my nightstand and pull out the duct tape. Ripping a piece off, I lean down and place it over her mouth even as she tries to move away, "Be a good girl and keep quiet. I have to concentrate on my work." Bending over, I kiss her mouth over the tape and smile as I move away, her glare burning a hole in my back as I do.

Only ten minutes into watching more video feeds, I'm sending texts to Jett and Fynn, telling them to return to my room. I scrutinize the screen as I wait, trying to figure out whether they are a suspect or not. As soon as my friends walk in, their eyes go to my bed, and they smirk.

"I take it Lina is still being naughty," Jett states as he takes his chair.

"How the fuck can you work like this, knowing that there's a weeping pussy soaking your bed right now?" Fynn shakes his head and sits, not sparing another look at our girl.

I only shrug, "Because I know I'll be fucking her once I'm done here, but this takes precedence over my cock at the moment."

"Damn, bro, you have more willpower than the two of us put together!" Fynn exclaims.

"So, what is it that you found?" Jett asks, leaning forward with his elbows on his knees.

"I'm not sure yet. What do you make of this?" I ask and then turn my laptop around and show my friend the footage from about two weeks before classes started here at Helshire.

"Whoa! Is that..."

"Yeah," I cut Fynn off, "It is."

"Well, it can't be. There is no way it's her!"

All three of us glance over at the blond on the bed, panting and moaning, and then look back at the screen. Catalina stands at the counter, buying a bottle of chocolate-raspberry syrup and a bag of coffee. Of course, Jett is right; it's not her. Why would she do this to herself?

Taking my phone, I tap on the screen and turn up the vibration until she's just about to come, and then I turn it off completely. We hear her frustration and all snicker, but in all fairness, I did tell her that she could come once I allowed her to.

Turning back to my boys, I put my game face on, "We will find out if and what she knows about it because, honestly, I doubt she is part of it."

"Yeah, you didn't see how freaked out she was on the way to the hospital earlier," Jett states, "If she was part of it, then there is no way she would have reacted like she did."

"Do you want to know what I think?" I look at Kitty Cat, "I think that whoever these people are, I believe one of them may be closer to our girl than we think."

After discussing it further, we shut down for the night and all turn to our girl, "How sore do you think that cunt is after being used so much today?" Jett snickers.

"Does it matter?" I ask, "She has my dick so fucking hard that I don't care what hole I use as long as I get off. Maybe she will think twice about being naughty next time."

"God, I fucking hope not..." Fynn grins and follows me over to the bed.

My Kitty Cat's eyes pop open as we near, and she starts yelling something through the tape, most likely curse words. I unstrap the wand and holder while my friends release her ankles. I then pull the tape part of the way off so she can answer my next question.

"How sore are you, Kitty Cat?"

"Too sore," she growls back, and I laugh.

"Good, just how I like it." I put the tape back in place and pull out my cock as I climb between her kicking legs. All I have to do is look at the guys, and they each take a leg, opening her up even further for me, "Awe, poor little cunt is going to be so battered by the time we finish with it." I spread her lips apart and then spit down, watching it roll through her folds before pushing into her.

She moans as her greedy cunt sucks me in, "Yeah, she wants it," Fynn chuckles while holding her left leg up and bent by her chest.

"Get ready, Kitty Cat. It's looking to be a very long night." I sink into her hard and deep, not giving her an ounce of mercy.

TWENTY-SEVEN

💀

Catalina

Oakley Harris is one of the biggest assholes you will ever meet and one of the hottest. He's got everything: money, looks, attitude, self-confidence, and yes, a big head...in both areas if you know what I mean. His cockiness both infuriates me and turns me on like no other. All three of these Sinners do it to me. They take what they want, and I let them.

I put up a bitchy front but deep down, my body weeps for their touch, for their twisted perversions. I'm fucked up in the head, I know, but I can't stop wanting them, no matter how much they take from me. Until now, they have worn kid gloves with me; I genuinely believe that. I can sense them holding back, and I want them to stop; I want all of it. Every sick thought, perverse touch, and humiliating and degrading order they can give me is all I want from them.

The way Oakley held my head earlier when I tried to talk only made my pussy drip more, and then he left me alone. He can be cruel, bringing me to peak and then taking it all away, and as frustrating as it is at the time, I know that in the end, it will be earth-shattering.

I fight them because it's fun and gets them to restrain me. It's even better when all three are here because some torture my body while others pleasure it; pleasure and pain are lovely together.

I've been on the precipice of a climax for what seems like hours, and now, they are here, Oakley plunging into my sore vagina without care. It makes me feel alive as he pounds into me while his friends hold me still for him. I'm breathing heavily through my nose, feeling some snot leak out, but they don't care. I moan behind the tape, letting out a few curse words and making them think I'm pissed. It seems to be the only way to make them take me harder.

Suddenly, Fynn pulls out a switchblade and opens it as he grins down at me, "Seems like you are a little overdressed, Little Saint."

I hold my breath as he slices down the middle of my shirt. I glare at him because it's my only shirt now that my things were destroyed in the fire, but he doesn't give two shits. He flicks his wrist when my shirt falls open, taking my bra with it, and my breasts spring free of their cage.

"God, I love your tits, Lina!" Jett slaps the one closest to him, and Fynn follows suit to the one on his side.

They both take turns slapping and pinching my nipples as their friend uses me. Oakley's thrusts get harder and deeper as he watches his friends torture my breasts, "Look at me, Kitty Cat. I want your eyes on me as I fill you," he curls his lip as he picks up his speed, then grunts and jerks as he does exactly that; he fills me up full.

Fynn unties the belt from the headboard, then my wrists, but not for long. Yanking my arms behind my back, Oakley hands him a zip tie, and my wrists are once again secured. I try talking through the tape, but all they do is grin and go back to ignoring me.

With my arms behind my back, Jett and Oakley lift me as Fynn sits on the edge of the bed, and I'm lowered. Fynn lines himself up with my entrance, and I cry out as they impale me on his girthy cock. I'm sore as fuck, but I know I won't get any sympathy from these Sinners.

We are at the perfect height for Jett to slip in behind and take me. Thankfully, he lubes me up nicely, but it's still uncomfortable as he works his cock into my ass, "Relax, Lina. Let me in..." His voice is low and raspy in my ear.

I'm pressed into Fynn as they try to fill me, and he bites me on the shoulder, "Let him in, Saint, or he won't be nice about it."

I whimper, but it's not because I don't want them to hurt me; I want it with every fiber of my being, just not by ripping my ass apart. Maybe if Fynn were to pull out of me first, but that would be too easy for them. No, they like seeing me suffer, and they like challenges, so they continue the path they have taken.

"I've got something to help our girl relax," I hear Oakley as he comes closer, and that's when I smell it, seconds before it's blown up my nose. Taking another hit from the joint, Oakley rips the tape off and crashes his mouth to mine, giving me all of it, then sealing the tape back over my mouth, "There, that should help you out, Kitty Cat."

I glare at him because I've told them repeatedly that I don't do drugs, but they take it upon themselves to get me high whenever I'm around. After a few more hits of smoke up my nose, my body begins to relax, and soon enough, Jett is all the way in.

"Fuck, this is so tight!" he curses, and all I can do is chuckle because it's so much worse for me.

"Now we can get the party started..." Fynn grins, then he and Jett start rocking back and forth as they fuck me.

I can't move. All I can do is feel as they stretch me out, taking me however they want. One moment I'm pressed against Fynn with my head on his shoulder, and the next, I'm leaned back against Jett's chest, and my breasts and clit are abused. I'm not leaving this room without war wounds, that's for sure.

Jett has hold of my hair, ensuring his friend has plenty of access to my chest as his other hand tortures my clit. Fynn is too busy loving my breasts with his mouth and teeth to care what is happening around him. I'm stuck between the two, a doll for them to play with.

"Do you know why we record our sessions, Kitty Cat?" My eyes try and find Oakley's voice, but it's hard with the angle that Jett has my head in. When the Lord comes into view, he's holding his phone, recording, on top of the camera in the corner already recording. I growl and glare at him, but he ignores my reaction, "We do it not only to keep people in line but to watch it later, depending on how hot it is. I believe that I will be watching this one on repeat."

Fynn bites my nipple hard, making me cry out, and Oakley's smile widens, "Do the other one...make it hurt. She's so pretty when she cries."

Pain slices through my other nipple, and I cry out again, but I also come hard, "MMPH!"

"That's right, come all over my cock, Little Saint." Fynn looks me in the eye, "Are you our little pain slut?" Knowing it's a bald-faced lie, I shake my head, and Fynn frowns, "Don't lie to us, Little Saint. We may have to take drastic measures just to prove it."

Jett's breath is in my ear, "Do you want to come again or not?"

I don't answer him, so his hand comes up, and he pinches my nose. With the tape already over my mouth, I'm not getting any air, and I start to struggle. They all laugh at me, watching and waiting to see how far they can take this.

"Do...you...want...to...come...again?" Jett asks slowly.

As I start seeing stars dance across my vision, I nod, and my body begins to jerk, my life fading from lack of air.

"Holy fuck, that feels good how she's jerking on my cock!" Fynn groans and then gets off on me dying as he fucks me. He fills me up, and then I'm gasping for air as Jett rips his hand away, taking the tape with him.

I'm gulping in the air as both Lords fuck me hard, Fynn finishing up giving me his load as Jett is just starting his release. Surprisingly, I come, too, and I realize that I love what they just did to my body. It's a whole other kind of fucked up, but I like it all the same.

They have me lying on my stomach at the moment. As soon as Jett was done, he pulled out, and with Oakley's assistance, they lifted me and placed me face down on the bed. I feel like a bowl of Jell-O now as I try to catch my breath. Unfortunately, I'm feeling the effects of the greenery that Oakley blew into my nose and mouth, so I feel light and giggly even though I want to be pissed.

"How are you feeling, Lovely?" Jett asks softly.

I think out of all three of the Lords, Jett is the softest of the bunch, even though he did almost kill me but a few minutes ago. The tatted-up, meanest-looking Lord has turned out to be the nicest, to some extent. I smile at him, thanks to the effects of the weed.

"I feel great, so relaxed," I respond.

Feeling my legs spread as they all chuckle, I try looking back, but Jett places his hand on my head and holds it as he caresses it. He continues to look toward my legs, but I don't know what he's looking at, and I don't feel anything. That is, not until I feel a cool, damp cloth run up and down my inner thighs.

Someone is washing the mess made, and I sigh in contentment, but then Oakley climbs on the bed and shows me his phone. He replays our little fuck fest, and even I have to admit that we look hot, but then it jumps to a video of Fynn and Jett's cum seeping out of me, and I now know why Jett wouldn't let me look.

"What the fuck? Delete that shit!" I scowl, or at least I think I do, but it's hard to tell due to being high.

Oakley only chuckles and pulls it away when I try grabbing at his phone, "Not a chance, Kitty Cat!" I watch as he taps on his phone before looking at me again, "There, all stored away for safekeeping. We have to keep you in line somehow, don't we?"

As much as I find all this hot and wild, the last thing I need is videos getting out of me getting fucked by the Lords and then their gunk dripping out of me in a close-up. Somehow, some way, I will find those videos, as well as every other video they have ever taken of females, and I will destroy every single one of them.

"Wake up, Kitty Cat. Not everyone can sleep all day," a smirking voice wakes me from my peaceful slumber. I haven't slept well for a while, so it perturbs me that I'm being woken up now.

Groaning, I pull a pillow over my head as I turn to my stomach, "Leave me alone! I'm not ready to get up yet!"

The pillow is yanked from my hands just before the covers get pulled away from me. The air hits my skin, and I realize that I'm naked. Awareness slowly starts to creep in, and I turn to see a very annoyed-looking Lord. His eyes peruse my body, and a slow cocky grin appears.

"I bet I can think of a way to get you to wake up."

"No, my vag hurts too much," I growl.

"I never said anything about your used vag," Oakley takes hold of my hair with one hand and undoes his jeans with the other, "Be a good girl and open wide."

It's not long before I'm choking on his cock, but he never lets up until he's coming deep into my throat. He flings me away the second he's done, "Now get up; we have class this morning."

"What about me?" I may be sore, but like him, there is another way to get me off, and after his treatment of me just now, I'm throbbing.

"What about you?" He finishes tucking himself back into his jeans.

"You now have me horny. How about you return the favor!" I open my legs wide and run my fingers over myself like a wanton woman.

"You get off when we say you get off, Kitty Cat. Now, remove your fucking hand from *our* cunt, and don't let me catch it near it again unless we say it can be there."

I whimper, his words turning me on even more, "Oakley..."

He tilts his head, "Awe, is our little slut horny?"

"Fucking forget it..." I climb from the bed and try storming past him, but he grabs hold of my upper arm, swinging me around until I slam against his hard chest.

"Lose the fucking attitude, Kitty Cat," when all I do is glare at him, he wraps his hand around my neck and squeezes, "If you want to get off, I will happily fuck that cunt, but I'm trying to be nice because I know you are sore."

"You can always eat me," I say sarcastically.

"I could, but then again, it's much more fun knowing you will be horny all day. That way, when we fuck you tonight, you will come nice and hard. I want that pussy dripping for us all day long." He leans in and bites my lower lip, but not enough to draw blood.

"You put a lot of faith in thinking that you three have that kind of power over me. I fuck who I want, Oakley, and I have been letting you three fuck me because it passes the time, and I get your help finding the person threatening me. Unfortunately, the Lords are failing in the latter, so I may just start looking elsewhere for *help*."

I'm slammed against the wall, "Oh really? You seriously think we will let you go before we are ready?" Oakley grins deviously as his hand tightens, "Fucking think again, Kitty Cat." He grabs me by the hair and drags me from the room.

The other two Lords are exiting their rooms when they look up and see their friend dragging me toward the stairs, "Whoa, what's going on here?" Jett asks as he hurries up to follow.

"Seems Kitty Cat loves being a naughty girl. Her mouth keeps getting her into trouble," Oakley responds as he starts down the stairs. He slows, making sure I don't stumble.

"Uh-oh, Little Saint. What did you do now?" Fynn grins amusingly as he follows behind Jett.

When I go to respond, Oakley tugs my hair harder and answers his friend, "She's being a bitch because she wanted to get off by me eating her out. She's too sore to take a cock at the moment, but she had to keep going, and now, she's really going to be hurting by lunchtime."

"Oh shit, you're not..." Jett's words trail off.

"Yep, I sure am," he replies with a snicker.

"What are you going to do?" I try pulling back when he pulls me out the door at the bottom of the stairs. I'm completely nude, and most of the Frat brothers are still home.

"Oh no, Kitty Cat. I will parade you right through the house until we get to the basement," Oakley growls.

"No! What the fuck? Why can't you be normal for once?" I sneer, still trying to pry his fingers from my hair.

He stops, "How much fun would that be?" He takes my hands, grips them behind my back, and continues. His Frat brothers smirk as we pass them, some whistling, and some catcalling, not caring that Jett and Fynn are glaring at them when they do so.

"Did you have to let the whole house see her like this?" Jett asks his friend, annoyed.

"Maybe she should have dressed before getting mouthy with me," Oakley shrugs.

We reach the basement door, and Fynn hurries forward to open it. Once again, Oakley ensures that I don't stumble, and when we get to the bottom of the steps, he calls out, "Get the saddle and set it up."

Fynn, being another sadistic one, grins and does his friend's bidding. He pulls out a small machine which he places in the middle of the floor by restraints. He looks to Oakley for more instruction.

"I'll be nice. Let's use the medium size attachment, the one with the rabbit on the front," he grins at his friend.

"What the fuck is that?" I question suspiciously.

"That, my little saintly slut is called a Sybian. You are going to sit on it while we go to class." The Lord smirks when I wince.

"The hell if I am!" I try struggling once more.

"You will, Kitty Cat. You wanted to come, so now you can do it all you want. In fact, you'll come way more than you want to."

Fynn holds up a remote, "It even comes with a remote, so we can change the speed whenever we see that you're no longer coming."

"W-What do you mean when you see?"

Oakley sighs, "You don't listen well, do you?" He points to the corner, "We are always watching, and today, we will watch our little slut come repeatedly until lunch when we can return home."

"I need to go to class!" I try to argue, anything to get me out of this fucked up situation.

"No worries, I will take care of that for you," Oakley states as he pushes me toward the oversized saddle.

Thankfully, Fynn lubed it up well, but it's still tough going when they lower me onto it. My knees are bent with my feet behind me, where they are cuffed. My wrists? Cuffed behind me with restraints attached to the floor, so the dildo that they impaled me on hits just the right spot inside.

"You can't leave me here like this!" I scowl, but deep down, I'm already leaking.

Oakley snaps his fingers, "You're right! Of course, we can't leave you like this!" He walks over to one of the cupboards and returns with an open-mouthed gag, "We can't forget this, now can we?"

"No, please!" I hate open-mouthed gags. By the time they return, I will be a blubbering wet mess!

"Shh..." Oakley caresses my cheek, "You will be fine. Accept your punishment like a good girl, and we will reward you later."

"Wait!" Jett's voice echoes through the basement, "Before you put that on her, we should ask her."

"Ah, yes, you're right," Oakley responds, then turns to me, "Kitty Cat, how much do you like drinking coffee with chocolate-raspberry syrup in it?"

I'm confused, "Who says I like that stuff...gross!"

"Well then, why do you buy it?" Oakley cocks his head at me questioningly.

"I don't. Well, maybe once or twice when one of my Sorority sisters asked me to because I was already going to the store," I reply, still not sure where they are going with this.

"Who asks you to buy it?"

"What? You know what, no...I'm not answering that until you release me!" Why should I give them any answers if they are going to treat me like this?

"Fine. Now that we know it's one of the other Saints, we can start vetting them," Oakley and Fynn head toward the stairs.

Looking the most sympathetic toward me, Jett walks over and squats, caressing my cheek, "Be a good girl so you can get off this when we come back."

"Please, let me go now..."

He gently takes my chin and kisses me softly. When he pulls back, he gives me his puppy dog eyes and leans into my ear, "I hope you think of me as that slutty cunt weeps all over the saddle." He then licks me up the side of my face before pinching a nipple and chuckling, "Have fun, Lovely," he says as he straps the gag on me and follows his friends upstairs.

TWENTY-EIGHT

Jett

"So, what's the plan?" I ask the guys as we head for our first class. I have to take my mind off how Catalina looked restrained and fucked by that saddle. My dick is harder than a rock!

"Yeah," Fynn chimes in, "It's not like the dragon lady will let us in if we ring the doorbell."

"You're right, so this is where we bring our fathers in on it," Oakley states, "My father texted me this morning that we are doing this dinner with Kitty Cat's parents tomorrow night, so we will devise a plan then. Maybe we can have a letter from the Provost requesting the Saint's audience."

I nod, "Yeah, that's good. Get them all in one place, and we can vet them all simultaneously."

"Do you honestly believe that it's one of the Saints?" Fynn asks.

"I don't know who the fuck it is, but it's the only lead we have at the moment, so we will go with it."

I agree, then wave at both my friends as I veer off to go to my economics class, which I hate, but at least I can get a little nap in. I can feel that I'm being watched when the building comes into sight, and I look around. Searching my surroundings, I find nothing unusual, so I glance up at the building looming before me. A movement in one of the top windows catches my attention, but nothing is there when I home in on it.

Instead of just standing here, I haul ass into the building and take the stairs two at a time. If I'm right, that window leads to an empty classroom not being used until next semester. This building is the tallest on campus, and that window looks out over most of the grounds. Whoever I caught in the window was looking out for a reason.

By the time I get to the top floor, I'm breathing heavily but far from out of breath. I fling the door to the stairwell open and run to the classroom where the window is located. It's empty. I slam my fist down on a desk and curse as I walk over to the window.

Looking down at the campus, I can see why they come here. I knew you could see a lot from this view, but it spans further than I thought. I can see everyone coming and going from their classes, along with the parking lot off to the left. The Fraternity and Sorority Houses peek out in the distance, but those are too far to see more than the roofs.

Turning to leave, I notice something on the floor underneath one of the desks. I pick it up and see that it's a photo. My heart races as I stare at the two people in it. Flipping the picture over, the words *'I'm everywhere'* is scribbled on the back. I almost crumble it in my hands, but after thinking about it, I tuck it in my back pocket and take off.

After sending a text to the guys, I head back home. There is no fucking way I will be able to concentrate in my classes today while looking over my shoulder every two minutes. Opening the app that logs into our security cameras, I find the one for the basement. My Lovely Lina is still there, tears in her eyes and drool dripping onto her perfect tits.

I don't go to the basement right away. Instead, I head to my room, pull out a joint and turn my television on. I pull up the camera footage on the big screen and take out my cock. The sound is turned up this time, and I can hear her moans and cries as the dildo on the saddle fucks her while the little vibrating rabbit flicks vigorously over her clit.

"Hm, how many times have you come, I wonder?" I say out loud as my hand quickens its pace on my cock. Taking another hit from the joint, I hold it in before blowing it out.

After a few more puffs, I put it out and tuck myself back in. A gorgeous blond is down in our basement, getting off while wearing an open-mouthed gag. So, why in the hell am I jerking myself off?

I'm headed to the basement when my phone buzzes with an incoming text from Oak, telling me they will return once their class is over. I shrug and pocket my phone. It's not like I'll be bored as I wait. I open the basement door with that thought and jog down the steps.

"Oh, look how lovely you look, Lina!" I wipe away some of the drool that has slithered down to her nipples and twist a little before pulling them outward, "You're a fucking mess...I love it!" I slap both her nipples in quick succession.

"MMPH!" she mumbles through the gag.

"I'm sorry, Lina. I don't understand what you're saying," I lean in like I'm trying to hear what she's saying, and she makes the same mumbling sound. I pull away and grin, "How sweet of you, Lina! Of course, I can use your mouth for my pleasure. You don't need to ask me twice!"

I'm such a smartass, and as she glares at me, I pull my hard length out. She shakes her head, but I gaze down at her, caressing her head before gripping her hair, "Be a good girl and take care of your Lord, Lina, and I will free you of the restraints."

I don't try moving any closer just yet. Even though it's in the contract that we can do whatever the fuck we want with her without asking for her consent, I can't consciously fuck her mouth as she's shaking her head no...I'm not that much of a dick...well, I try not to be. So, I bribe her instead.

"Would you like me to help you off that saddle?" I ask pointedly.

She studies me momentarily before nodding her head. "That's a good girl," I see what those words do to her, and I smile inwardly. Now, I can fuck her face.

I take both sides of her head and guide it to my hardness. The moment I enter the warmth of her mouth, I want to spill, so I clench my jaw and stop. When I know it's safe again, I push until she's suffocating against my groin, "Fuck, Lina, your throat was made to take dick!" I pull out slowly, then slam back in. I do this a few times, knowing her throat will be sore as fuck later, but that isn't my problem as I begin owning this little piece of Heaven.

It doesn't take too long before I need to unleash my load, and since she can't swallow it with the gag on, as soon as I pull out of her mouth, saliva mixed with cum drips from her mouth. I pull my phone out and snap a picture, sending it to the guys so they can see the beautiful state our girl is in.

"I'll be right back, beautiful, and then I will take you off the saddle." I hurry up to my room, go into the little stash of pills we confiscated from Date Rape Rob, and head back to the basement, grabbing a bottle of water on the way. "Honey, I'm back!" I call out jokingly, and Catalina just cocks her eyebrow.

I examine her a moment, then grab a chair and place it in front of her so I can straddle it, "Now, I have a little something for you, Lina. Just know that you can say no, but it will help you to relax enough, okay?" I pull out the little pill, and she recognizes it right away.

Her head automatically shakes back and forth.

"Listen to me, Lina. I'm going to take you off the saddle as promised, but then I'm taking you upstairs, where Oakley and Fynn will also want a piece of you. Now, I know your cunt hurts, and now your throat; I made sure of the latter, so there is only one orifice left for them to use. Do you really want to be in the right state of mind while they take turns fucking your ass?"

I can tell by the way her breathing has picked up that the thought of my friends taking her like that turns her on, and so I work off that, "Do you know how hot it would be knowing that you are drugged and that your Lords are going to use this beautiful body of yours while you're incapacitated? We will record it all, so you can see exactly what we do to you.

When she doesn't say anything, I get up and squat down beside her, sliding my hand to the crack of her ass, "You know that the slut in you wants this. What if you take only half of the pill this first time, that way, you can be somewhat aware of what's happening?"

I know the gears are grinding in her head, and finally, her head moves in the direction that I want it to go in, and I'm instantly hard again. Pulling out my pocket knife, I cut the pill in half and return to her, "Stick out your tongue, Lina."

Her tongue slips out of the circle in the gag, and I place half the pill on it. She tips her head back, and I pour a trace of water into her mouth before pulling the gag off her completely and watching as she swallows everything.

"Such a good fucking girl..."

Fynn

Oakley and I walk into the Frat House to find some of the groupie sluts waiting for us. A brunette runs up to me, but I put my hand on her face, and with a little shove, I push her away from me, "Not interested."

"But Fynn..." she whines, and I spin on her.

"What the fuck did I say? I'm...not...interested!"

A blonde sidles up to Oakley and wraps her arms around him, "How about you, Oakley? Want to have some fun?"

My friend grins down at her, "What's your name?"

"Posey..."

"Well, *Posey*...how about you *mosey* the fuck away from me!" his grin turns into a look of anger, "Never touch me without my permission again!"

I snicker and head for the stairs until I hear one of the groupies mention my Little Saint, "Yeah, I heard Catalina Scott is the Lord's whore now. Give it a month, and they will be done using her stretched-out pussy."

I see red.

Stomping over to the female, I pin her against the wall by her neck, "If I ever hear you speak of Catalina like that again," I lean in closer, "They will *never* find your body. Do you understand me?"

Her head moves but just barely.

"As for us getting tired of Catalina Scott...know this...she is the Lord's Lady. She isn't *ever* going anywhere, and you will respect her like you do the Lords of Sin! Got it?"

Y-Yes…" she gasps as soon as I let her go.

I turn and look at every other female in the room, "We will not stop you from coming here, so you can keep letting our Frat brothers fuck you, but you will not approach any of the Lords again!"

Once they all acknowledge this, I head for the stairs again, where Oakley stands and grins at me. I shove him aside and head up. When I open the door to the third floor, I notice Jett sitting at the top of the stairs; something is in his hands that he can't seem to look away from.

"What is that?" I ask, and almost as if he hadn't noticed us, he jerks his head up and stands.

He takes a step back to let us through, "I found this on the floor of an empty classroom on the top floor of Foster Hall."

"What were you doing up there?" I question.

"Oh, I don't know, maybe going after the person who was watching us from the window up there." He's sarcastic, but I just let it slide off as I try to grab what looks to be a picture in his hand, only he pulls it away, so I can't.

He holds it up for me and Oakley to read the back, "*I'm everywhere,*" I say out loud, "Okay. What the fuck is that supposed to mean?"

"Oh, I don't know, Fynn. How about you tell me?" He turns the photo around, and I gasp, grabbing it from his hands.

"What the fuck?" I scowl as Oakley looks over my shoulder.

"Where was this taken?" Oak questions me.

I look back and forth between my two friends, "This was when I took Catalina to my special place up on the cliff. You know…when I told you about fucking her that day."

I glance back down at the picture, and even though I'm beyond livid that the bastard followed us there, I can't help but appreciate the angle. It's when I had my hand on her head, shoving it into the tree trunk as I fucked the shit out of her from behind. I made her beg me to fuck her that day and fuck her I did! They got her with an expression showing how much she was enjoying it. Her eyes are closed, but her mouth is open in a perfect O as her fingers claw at the bark.

"This son of a bitch followed you all the way up there, and you didn't know?" Oakley growls out.

"Well, it seems so, now, doesn't it?" I say a little on the defensive side because I know what he will say next, and he doesn't disappoint.

"How the fuck are we supposed to keep her safe if you can't even keep an eye out when she is with you?"

"Are you seriously going to fucking go there?" I step up to my friend, who I tower over by just an inch, "I was watching my fucking mirrors at all times and never saw another fucking soul!"

"Okay, let's not do this now!" Jett states as he pushes us apart.

Oakley sighs, "You're right, Jett," he then looks at me, "I'm sorry, I should have known better. It's just that it was a little too close for my liking."

"Oh, you think?" I can't help but be sarcastic. I turn and punch the wall, "I need to go see her..." I turn back toward the stairs, but Jett stops me.

"Wrong way, big guy." He's pointing toward my room, "You're the kinkiest out of all of us, so I stuck her in your room while I got her ready."

I cock a brow at my friend, "What do you mean got her ready? Ready for what?"

Jett slowly grins, "I got her permission to give her one of Rob's pills."

"You date raped, Kitty Cat?" Oakley growls.

"Calm the fuck down, Oak! With her cunt used and sore, and then me fucking her throat hard, I figured you two would be taking her ass, and so I offered her a half of a pill. You know, to help relax her a little."

"And she was okay with that?" I ask skeptically.

Jett rolls his eyes, "Watch the camera feed if you don't believe me."

I rush into my room and stop in my tracks. There's my Little Saint, bent over the foot of my bed. Her wrists are tied with the Shibari rope I keep in my stash, with her arms above her head and the rope tied to my headboard. Her feet are on the floor, but each ankle is tied to the bed, keeping her legs wide apart. My dick is so hard right now.

"I took the liberty of getting her ass ready by plugging it up until you got here," Jett chuckles.

I walk over to my bed and slowly run my hand from her ass to her head. Sliding my hands into her hair, I grip it and lift her head to see her face. Her eyes are glossy as fuck, but she's awake. I move my finger in front of her face, and she follows it with her eyes. At least she is somewhat with it. That makes me feel a little better. I don't know what the fuck Jett was thinking. I'm usually the one with fucked up ideas, but I never drug a girl to fuck her; I don't need to.

"Hey, Little Saint, how are you feeling?"

Her smile is goofy, but she answers, "I feel *really* good. Are you going to fuck my ass now?"

"Do you want me to fuck your ass?" I ask with a slight snicker.

"I think so," she responds, "Yeah, I like it when you fuck me. It feels so good."

I look at my two friends, who are trying hard not to laugh. I turn back to our girl, "Did you allow Jett to give you a pill?"

She nods, "Yes, he said it would relax me so you and Oakley can take turns fucking my ass, and it won't hurt."

I lean my head against hers, "Fuck, Little Saint...how can I say no to this?"

"Don't," she states, and I look into her glossy eyes, "I want you to."

If I didn't know any better, I'd say she knows exactly what she's talking about. It makes me wonder what strength the whole pill is if she is this observant with only half. Letting her hair go, I move behind her and drop to my knees. All she wanted was for Oakley to eat her out this morning, so that's what I'll do now.

Swiping my tongue up between her folds, I hear her moan. That's right, I will make her come before I pull the plug out and take her. Her taste is musky with a hint of sweetness; I don't know what is wrong with Oakley, why he wouldn't give her this one thing, but it doesn't matter now, because I'm going to give her what she wants.

Only a few minutes in, and she's crying out, "Oh God, FYNN!" she comes hard, and I pull out the plug waiting for her to finish coating my tongue.

I stand up, wiping my mouth. Jett stands beside me, holding the lube. He lubes her up while I open my pants, and as he holds her ass open, I push the tip of my cock into her.

"Mm, Fynn..."

"Yes, Little Saint?"

"Fuck me hard..."

That's all it takes. I push in as carefully as I can without stopping, and as soon as I know she is fully adjusted, I pull out and slam back in. Her tight ass feels like fucking home, and I never want to leave it. I give her exactly what she wants, fucking her hard and deep until she's coming once again. Her ass grips me, and I lose the battle I've been fighting since I slid in, painting the inside of her ass until my cum seeps out, and then I give her a little more.

TWENTY-NINE

Catalina

I hate that they just left me in the basement the way they did, yet I was so turned on by it. I don't know why I feel like I do, and they seem to know how much I like it. The Lords of Sin understand what their actions do to me, and I have the feeling that this is only the tip of the iceberg.

To say that I'm pissed about Jett manipulating me into taking that pill would be a lie. I don't do drugs, that isn't a lie, but that was before the Sinners. Do I want to become a drug addict? Of course not, but when Jett offered me Rob's little pill, my curiosity was piqued, but I was scared, so I said no.

His offering to cut the little pill in half, not giving me a full dose, had me rethinking my answer. I've had fucked up fantasies about being drunk and taken advantage of by the hottest guy in school; it turns me on. Of course, I would never want it in real life; who would? At least not knowing about it but *knowing* that the Lords will give me something before taking advantage of me, is entirely different, and I could hardly pass it up. Offering to record it so I can watch it later...even better.

Being judged for my sexual appetite by my peers isn't something I want, but these guys are different; I feel like I can trust the Lords. They are just as fucked up as I am, if not more so. The question is, do I really want them corrupting me more than I already am?

I'm lying here, bent over Fynn's bed. He's just finished with me, and I feel more relaxed than ever. I know we are far from done because Oakley still needs to get off, but as I lay here, the Lords fall into a conversation, completely ignoring the naked female bent over and restrained with cum seeping out of her ass.

I wouldn't put it past them to be doing it on purpose. They like trying to make me feel like a common whore, but they should know by now that I'm turned on by their treatment of me. Then again, maybe they are losing interest, and I should entice them a little more. Should I offer to let them give me the other half of the pill? Will Oakley be more inclined to fuck me, knowing that I'm completely passed out?

"I want the rest of it," I say before I change my mind, but it's too soft, and they all three glance my way, unsure whether I really did say something.

"What did you just say, Kitty Cat?" Oakley comes into my view.

"I said that I want the rest."

"The rest of what?" the Lord frowns.

"The pill. Give me the other half of the pill." I'm still feeling a bit hazy, but I know what I'm saying, and I know what they are saying and doing; I'm just feeling incredibly relaxed.

"I'm not giving you the rest of the fucking pill, Catalina!" For some reason, my request has made Oakley angry, and now I'm confused; I thought they would like this.

"Why not? I thought you would like doing me while I'm unconscious."

"Where the fuck would you get that idea from? It's one thing to fuck you when you're sleeping, knowing that you will wake up by my dick being inside you, but it's completely different to fuck you when you are passed out from being drugged, Kitty Cat!"

"Then why did Jett want to give me this drug?" I ask, confused.

"Lina, I only wanted you to be relaxed, but I won't lie; it's one of my fantasies to fuck you when you're drugged, but I would never do it without your consent, with or without the contract. As I said before, it's your choice. Maybe I was an ass on how I presented it but tell me the truth...did you like it?"

I suck on my bottom lip before finally nodding, "Yes, I liked it."

"See, Oak, our girl is just as freaky as I am. Stop being so pissy with me," Jett says to his friend.

"That's fine," Oakley states, "The two of you can be freaky like that together, but I like my pussy fully awake, and in the right frame of mind, so she knows exactly who's fucking her."

"Hey," Fynn chimes in, "I want to be in the freaky category too! I think it's hot fucking Little Saint drugged up, but only because I know it's what she wants or asked for. I'm up for anything as long as I get that sweet cunt of hers."

I grin to myself; they really do like me to an extent. They just have fucked up ways of showing it. It's too bad they don't know how badly I want to return the favor, though. What's good for the goose is good for the gander. I'll let them drug me because I find it hot for them to do so, as long as I know about it, but they better watch out because Mama has the same cravings as they do, and I'm willing to return the favor tenfold.

Oakley never took his turn with me. In fact, they let me fall asleep, and I don't wake up until hours after. I'm still bent over the bed in the same position. Still restrained by the silk ropes that Jett used to ready me for Fynn and Oakley, only I'm alone in Fynn's room. My bladder is full, so I have no choice but to call out to them and hope that someone is still here.

"Oakley, Fynn, Jett...can someone please help me?"

I don't hear anything at first, but then heavy footsteps sound on the wooden floor as someone comes my way, and Fynn opens the door, "Ah, you're awake. How are you feeling, Little Saint?"

"A bit groggy, but I have to piss like a racehorse!"

Fynn chuckles, "Always a lady..."

I scoff, "I've never referred to myself as being a lady, and I never will."

"You will be soon, Little Saint. You will be the Lady of Sin soon enough." Fynn releases my ankles first before starting on the rope at the headboard.

"I never agreed to that, Fynn," I wait for him to undo the rope at my wrists, but he doesn't, "What about this?" I hold my hands up.

He shakes his head, "We aren't done with you yet, Little Saint."

"Am I a prisoner here, Fynn?" I sigh because I'm beginning to feel like one a little.

"No, not a prisoner, just well-guarded, is all." He winks at me as he holds the rope and pulls me toward the bathroom.

"What if I don't want to be well-guarded?" I ask, "What if I want to go back home, say fuck school, and return to my mom?"

His amused expression changes to one of dismay, "I think we both know that isn't going to happen. We, as Legacies, have a duty, Little Saint, and you will do well to remember that. Just because you were born female doesn't change anything for you. You are still one of us."

I study him and think about everything he's saying. Since it seems like he's staying and not going to give me any privacy to relieve myself, I plop my ass on the toilet with a sigh as I empty my bladder, "If I'm one of you, then why do you treat me the way you do?"

"What way is that?" He tilts his head as he waits for me to answer.

"Like your personal whore," I huff.

His grin brightens his features, and his brown eyes twinkle, "I thought you liked it when we treat you like that. You come like a freight train every fucking time."

"That's beside the point! If I'm one of you, why do I not get to be included in your little meetings and such?" I sound a little whiny, but I don't care; I want to know why.

"You are still in training, Little Saint. You will be included more once we know that you can handle yourself well enough. But you must remember that you still serve your Lords in everything regardless of your place among us. It's what your Legacy is."

"Well, why doesn't Dani have to serve the Lords?" This puts a sour taste in my mouth because I don't want to share them, but I still want to know the answer, "Why is that rule about Saints fraternizing with the Sinners in place?"

"I'm not sure on the latter," Fynn responds as he shrugs, "As for Dani, her mother didn't serve our fathers when they were in school; your mother did, so Dani doesn't have to serve us."

I understand what he's saying, but it doesn't mean I like it. I want to be able to make my own decisions about my life, but it seems as though I will never have that. At least not how I want, anyway. I stare at the Lord before me. Would it be so bad to serve the three hottest guys on campus? It's only until I graduate, right? My mother married my father, though. Does that mean I will marry one of my Lords, and if so, which one would I choose? I laugh to myself because, come on, we all know that I won't have a choice in the matter.

I clean myself and stand, but Fynn yanks me to him immediately, grabbing my jaw firmly, "I'm going to tell you this only once, so listen well, Little Saint. You will always be our little whore behind closed doors, a slut for us to use and abuse because it's what you love, too, but you will always be our Lady outside of these walls, a Queen of sorts, amongst all the peasants here at Helshire. It's what you were born into, and I think it's time that you start playing your role as well."

His next actions stun me to the core as he grips my hair and presses his mouth to mine. Fynn Morin is fucking kissing me!

THIRTY

Oakley

Pulling up to the Scott family home, I have to chuckle because it's what all little girls dream of. A big Victorian-style house with a wrap-around porch and a fucking white picket fence. I glance at the blond sitting in the passenger seat and raise my brow.

"What?" she asks.

"I suppose you have a fucking dog, too, don't you?" I smirk.

Almost as if it knew I was talking about it, a little pure white rat comes out, barking like it's all big and bad.

Kitty Cat shrugs, "If that's what you want to call it. I call it the demon dog from hell."

I watch her get out and walk up the driveway before I get out myself, admiring her ass in the tight skinny jeans she decided to wear. Fynn and Jett stayed behind, wanting to try and watch more videos in case we are wrong, and it isn't one of the Saints. I don't want to be here myself, but I want to see what my Kitty Cat's mother is like.

Kitty Cat waits for me by the door, but before I can get to the top step, the little rat has hold of my pant leg, growling. I try shaking it off without hurting the damn thing, but it's like it has a locked jaw and can't let go.

Kitty Cat chuckles, "Fluffy, no! Let him go right now!"

The demon doesn't listen, though. Kitty Cat has to come over and pick the thing up before it lets go of my pants, "Jesus, don't you feed that thing? And what the fuck did you call it...Fluffy?"

She smirks, "My mom named him the exact opposite of what he is because she likes to be different."

I glance around at the house once again and say more to myself, "I wouldn't have guessed that."

Kitty Cat rolls her eyes at me, "Come on, they are probably all waiting on us."

Just as we get inside, I push her against the closed door and grip her jaw, "Roll those beautiful eyes at me again and see where that gets you!"

She glares at me, making my dick hard, but I don't let go until I hear a chuckle behind me. I slowly let her jaw go and turn to find my father standing in the doorway with his arms crossed, "A chip off the old block, I see."

"What do you want, Dad?" I scowl.

"Just wondering what was taking you two lovebirds so long. I saw you pull up, but you were taking too long to come in. I didn't mean to interrupt." He smirks at me, and I don't miss how he runs his eyes up and down my Kitty Cat.

"Oh, um, Fluffy here," Kitty Cat holds the rat up, "Thought that your son was a snack and wouldn't let go of his pant leg."

I can hear the nervousness in my girl's voice, so as soon as she puts the dog down, I grab her hand and pull her to me, "How about you show me around before we eat?"

"Sure," she tries pulling her hand away, but I grip it tighter.

"Don't be too long, kids. I wouldn't want to have to come look for you again." My father then turns and disappears into another room.

What the fuck is my father's problem? He's acting like a horny old man, and I don't like how he's staring at my Kitty Cat. I pull my girl upstairs and don't stop until I find a dark corner. I shove her against the wall and grab her hair, making her open her mouth for me. I kiss her hard, and when she lifts her leg up by my hip, I grab hold of it and grind my crotch against her.

"I'm going to fuck you before we leave here tonight," I growl and bite her lip.

"Fuck yes!"

"I'm going to gag that mouth and fuck this cunt so hard that your parents will still hear it. What do you think they will do?"

"They practically gave me to you Lords, so I don't give a fuck." Kitty Cat is panting so hard, and when I shove my hand down the front of her pants, I find her soaking wet.

"Fuck, Kitty Cat, is this all for me?" I ask as I work my mouth down her neck.

"Depends on if you follow through with your promise," she states as she tilts her head back, giving me better access.

"Oh, don't you worry, Kitty Cat. I'll make you my dirty little whore while our parents are eating their fucking dessert!" I'm not sure what's gotten into her, but I like this new version of my Kitty Cat.

Pulling my hand from her pants, I run a finger over her lips, coating them with her wetness, "Don't lick them," I smirk and suck on each of my fingers, "I want to save that for later." I grab her hand and pull her back toward the stairs just in time because my father is about to come up.

"Dinner is ready," he chuckles and watches as we descend the steps.

When we get to the bottom, he waits until we pass him, and I decide right then that I'm keeping my body behind Kitty Cat, so he can't stare at her ass. I'm going to have to have a little chat with my father. If he wants to fuck around on my mother, what the fuck ever, but it's not going to be with the Lord's Lady, not this time.

"So, Oakley, how are you liking being a Lord of Sin?" Ashlee asks me. The older woman is the spitting image of her daughter. No wonder my father is acting like a sicko.

I shrug, "It can be a bit boring at times, but Catalina makes it more interesting." I wink over at Kitty Cat, who is sitting right beside me.

"Well, I do hope she is doing her title justice. I know how stubborn she can be," Mrs. Scott scoffs.

"Ashlee..." her husband chastises her.

"Gee, Mom, what title are you speaking of?" Kitty Cat's silverware clanks onto her plate as she glares at her mother.

"Why, the Lord's Lady, of course!" her mother smiles broadly and looks around the table, "A Lady should always be available to her Lords, and she should know her place at all times."

I squeeze Kitty Cat's leg because I know she's about to explode on her mother, "Catalina knows her place and is turning out to be an amazing Lady, Mrs. Scott."

"Oh, that's a little hard to believe since she hasn't done what is expected of her since she was a sophomore in high school!" Ashlee titters, "When I was the Lord's Lady, I was at their every beck and call. You can't even imagine what all of them demanded of me..."

Kitty Cat's expression goes from anger to disbelief before her eyes sneak a peek at my mother. My mom knows all about the Lords and Lady of Sin, and it was never talked about. In fact, I don't think she even knew that Ashlee was the Lady back in the day, and if the glare that my mother gives my father is any indication, I'm right. My mother throws her napkin down, stands up, and thanks Mr. Scott for the invitation before leaving the dining room and the house. The next thing I hear is my father's Porcha revving and driving away.

"Well, I guess I will be calling an Uber when I'm ready to leave," my father chuckles.

"Mr. Scott," I start as we finish our meal, "I was wondering if you could send an email to the Saints requesting an audience. It's come to our attention that one of the Saints may be involved with the threats."

I hear a gasp beside me, "You never told me this!"

I look at her as if she's daft, "We were talking about it in my room the other night." I pinch her leg, knowing it's going to leave a mark. I'm going to have to remind her later which night it was.

"Oh yes, I'm sorry. I have a lot on my mind these days." Her fake smile is believed by our parents but not by me.

"I don't see why that would be an issue, but it will be up to you to keep that group there once Felicia realizes you want the audience." The Provost chuckles.

"Why would the Saints not want to be there with the Sinners?" Mrs. Scott inquires.

"Because, Mom, the Saints are forbidden to associate with the Sinners," Kitty Cat sneers.

"Oh, but what about you?" she asks her daughter, confused.

"I'm not going to get into that right now, Mother."

"Who is the President now?" Ashlee looks around the table, and I don't miss the strange looks coming from my father and Mr. Scott.

"Felicia Howard," I answer her, " a.k.a. the dragon lady."

"Howard? Why does that sound familiar?" she looks to her husband and then my own father.

"Her mother was the President your Junior year, dear." Mr. Scott replies, tight-lipped.

"Oh..." Mrs. Scott drags it out, and suddenly, the subject is changed, "Who wants dessert?" She gets up and starts clearing the dishes.

"Here, let me help with that," my father offers.

This is perfect timing as I hand my plate to my father and accidentally tip it, making the rest of the spaghetti fall down the front of my shirt, "Oh shit!"

"You are such a klutz sometimes," my father says in amusement, knowing very well that I'm not, "Cat, will you be a doll and show my son to the restroom and help him before that stain sets in?"

"Of course, she will!" Mrs. Scott eyeballs her daughter.

"Follow me, *my Lord*," Kitty Cat says sarcastically, glaring at her mother. Taking my hand, she pulls me from the room, but she can't see the wicked grin spread across my face.

I don't know what my father is up to now, but I don't care. It's time to play with my Kitty Cat and play with her, I will. I will have her screaming my name through the gag in her mouth as I take her in her parents' house.

Catalina

I cannot believe my mother. I've never seen her act this way before, especially around guests. Typically, she likes to put on a show, making it seem like we are the perfect family. If she's going to lecture me, she will wait until after our guests have left. What makes the Harrises different, or at least, Mr. Harris, since it seems like Oakley's mom knew nothing of my mother's role with the Lords back in the day.

Mom and I used to have a wonderful relationship; she seemed so loving. I never would have thought that she would pretty much give me away to a group of guys who will use me for their own needs and pleasures. Her insistence on me joining the Saint's Sorority now makes sense. Although it's clear that she knew nothing of the new rule, it's plain to see that my father never told her.

I'm two seconds away from screaming at my mother when I feel Oakley pinch my thigh, warning me to stay quiet. When he drops his food down the front of his shirt, I'm happy to get away from my mother, but not before getting a little jab in by calling Oakley *my Lord.*

Mr. Harris is finding this all quite a bit amusing, and I can't help but feel a bit uncomfortable around him. So, when I drag his son from the room and hear his laughter follow us, I get goosebumps. Of course, I know Oakley spilled his food on purpose, and honestly, I'm glad he did. He wants to get me alone as promised, and right now, I need what this Sinner can do for me, but it seems that his father knows exactly what's going to happen, and that creeps me out.

As soon as we enter the laundry room downstairs, Oakley locks the door and shoves me against the wall by gripping my neck, "You need to learn how to keep your cool, Kitty Cat. Never show when someone is getting to you because they will use it against you in the future." He nips at my bottom lip, "Now, I'm going to let you go, and you will take my shirt off and drop to your knees to take your penance."

I raise my eyebrow at him, "My penance?"

"Yes, Kitty Cat. You were a bad girl at dinner, giving your mother attitude. Now, you will be punished for it. I don't care if she deserved it; the Lady of Sin must always keep herself in check at all times."

"I'm not your Lady of Sin. I haven't agreed to it," I'm so turned on right now that my words come out breathlessly.

"We say you are, and even though you are still in training, you will soon see that you are, in fact, the Lady of the Lords, and you, Kitty Cat, will love every minute of it." His hand slithers down into my pants, and he chuckles, "That's what I fucking thought."

Stepping away, his fingers are slick as he pulls them from my pants. Instantly, I pull his shirt off him and drop to my knees. I will give him what he wants because I need him to give me what I want, and the sooner I let him fuck my mouth, the sooner he will drive his thick cock into me and get me off as promised.

My fingers fumble briefly as I hurry to open his jeans. His hardness is evident through his pants, and I feel a bit powerful knowing that I do this to him. It's one thing for a guy to want me; I'm used to that, but with these Lords, I get the feeling that they need me. They will never say so, but I can see it at certain times and how Fynn finally kissed me last night. That wasn't out of want...but out of need.

Oakley's cock springs forward once I release it, and I take a moment to gaze up at him. He reminds me of a God, with his ripped abs and well-defined chest, looking down on me and waiting to be served. He's breathing heavily, anticipating the feel of my mouth wrapped around him, and I'm more than happy to serve my Lord of Sin at this moment.

Reaching out, I wrap my hand around his girth and squeeze. His breath intake doesn't go unnoticed, so I do it once more before opening my mouth and swallowing him as much as possible. Of course, it's not good enough for him, and I know he will soon take my head and push himself in further until he's deep in my throat.

"Are you ready for your penance, Kitty Cat?" His jaw is clenched as he asks, and with a mouthful of his cock, I nod. "Good girl."

He does exactly as I thought, pushing his way in until I feel him deep. He waits until I struggle because I can't breathe before he pulls out. I only have a fraction of a second to take in a breath before he starts fucking my mouth hard.

I clasp my hands behind my back because I know it's how Oakley likes it when he uses my mouth this way. He says it will keep me from using my hands to try and play with my pussy, and he's right. Whenever they take me like this, I drip, and all I want is to touch myself.

Before he can spill in my throat, he pulls away and yanks me up, "I want to fill this cunt up with my seed, not your mouth. I want you dripping with my cum when we go back upstairs to our parents." He spins me around and bends me over the washing machine.

"Oakley..."

"Shut the fuck up, Kitty Cat. I know you want this. You are a slut for my cock, and me fucking you in your family home is turning you on, isn't it?" He's rough as he pulls my jeans down to my knees.

"Fuck yes!"

I hear him snicker, "You are such a bad girl, Kitty Cat. Are you going to scream for me?"

"Yes..."

"Well, I guess we had better gag you then," I feel him rip my panties from me, and shoving them into my mouth, he says, "Here, taste yourself as I fuck the shit out of you."

He lines his cock up to my entrance, and I moan as he slams into me. He repositions me so my feet no longer touch the floor, and he doesn't have to bend at the knees. Taking my arms, he brings them to my lower back and grips them tightly as he hammers into me. I can't move in this position and don't want to. I love when these Sinners take me the way they do when I can't do anything about it.

There is a pause, and I feel him pull my right leg from the confinement of my jeans, and he brings it upward, draping it over his arm. When he slams into me next, he gets so deep that I scream through the gag. He laughs.

"That's what I like to hear, Kitty Cat." He continues fucking me just like that until I'm coming all over his cock.

There is no way my parents aren't hearing this, and it brings me some joy knowing that their baby girl is being used in their own home by one of the men they gave me to. I do feel bad about my father, but he isn't innocent in delivering me to the Lords, either.

"Scream for me, Kitty Cat. Let your parents know who owns you now. Let them see what they signed their precious little girl up for...scream for me!" He growls through a clenched jaw as he pounds into me.

"FUCK, OAKLEY...YES!! I'M COMING...AGH!" I see stars this time and feel the slight pain of him fucking me so deep.

He continues taking me until I finally feel him start to swell and his body tense, "Milk me, slut. Take every last fucking drop."

I do exactly as he tells me to, and I clench myself around him, milking him as he releases his load deep inside. I moan, feeling his hot seed fill me up. It's already running down my legs; that's how much I've milked him. I feel a little pitter-patter in my chest, knowing I did precisely what he wanted me to do, and that's when he says those two little words.

"Good girl."

Oakley pulls my jeans back up and says, "Don't fucking clean yourself until I say." He then disappears while I go to the mirror above the sink in the laundry room and try to fix the makeup now smudged all over my face.

When I get to the top of the stairs, I see a shirtless Oakley approaching me with anger in his eyes. He grabs my arm and pulls me toward the door. He doesn't say anything, and I don't try to ask until we are tucked away inside his Camaro, and he's revving it up.

"Do you mind telling me why we just left like that?" I cock my brow as I click my seatbelt in place.

"Yeah, I do mind. All you need to know is that it was time for us to go."

"Oakley…" I start to argue, but he curses, cutting me off.

"Fucking hell, Catalina! Can you just trust me to know what is best for you at times and not question my actions?"

His using my real name tells me that I shouldn't argue, but fuck that, "I'll trust you more when you stop hiding shit from me! I'm sick and tired of being told I'm one of you, yet you won't let me in on anything, even when it has to do with me!"

He glares at me before an intimidating smirk appears, "Okay, Kitty Cat. You want to know everything that we do? You think you can handle everything? Fine, handle this… I went upstairs to say goodbye to our parents, and what did I find? I find that our parents have reverted back to their college days, Kitty Cat. Your father and mine were spit-roasting your fucking mother in the kitchen!"

THIRTY-ONE

Fynn

I need time. Time to figure out what the fuck I am doing where my Little Saint is concerned. I had no business kissing her like I did; I never meant for that to happen. I can't give her hope where she and I are concerned because I'm too fucked up, but deep down, I know that little by little, Catalina Scott is burrowing herself inside me. She's taken hold and has anchored herself to where I have her on my mind all the fucking time.

I stayed behind to work on video footage because even after having her stay with Oakley last night, in order to put distance between me and the blonde bombshell, I couldn't get that kiss out of my head. I never kiss a female on the mouth. It's my number one rule, so how could I have broken it with her?

The door to our third-floor slams, and I hear Oakley's angry voice, "Go straight to my room, Kitty Cat. We will talk about this attitude just as soon as I talk to the guys."

"Oh, I forgot, I'm not allowed to be angry about stuff! I need to be a perfect fucking Lady!" I hear my Saint growl back, and it makes me smile. I love it when our girl is feisty, but now I'm wondering what the fuck is going on.

I turn and glance at Jett, who sits beside me with a similar look to mine, "What do you suppose that's all about?" I ask him.

He shrugs, "I don't know, but they weren't at the Scott's for too long, so..."

Oakley stomps into my room and throws himself in the only available chair, "Kitty Cat is so frustrating sometimes!"

Smirking, I cock a brow, "What has her panties in a bunch?"

"Oh, they were in a bunch inside her mouth when I fucked her in her parent's laundry room. Now, she isn't wearing any," Oakley grins proudly.

I laugh, "You're such a dirty dawg, Oak."

He lifts his shoulders in a shrug, "Her mother was being a bitch, even chased my mother away."

"What?!" Jett exclaims.

"Yeah. I'm now wondering if Mrs. Scott intended to mention that she was the Lord's Lady back in the day just to piss my mother off."

"Why would you think that?" I put my laptop aside and go to my dresser to grab a smoke.

"Oh, well, when you walk in to say goodbye to the parents and find Mr. Scott sharing his wife with his friend, uh yeah. Mrs. Scott had this planned out. She wanted to live out her college days, and my mother was in the way."

"Oh, damn...that's harsh!" I say with wide eyes, "I can't believe Mr. Scott agreed to that!"

"Me either," Oak agrees, "It's one thing to share like we do, but none of us have a significant other. My father is a piece of shit! I also think he has his eye on Kitty Cat, so not only do we have to watch her stalker, but we have to watch my father as well."

"He wouldn't try anything with her, would he?" Jett questions with a disgusted look.

"Who the fuck knows," Oakley states, "After seeing what I saw tonight, I'm not putting anything past him."

"I'll go talk to her," I tell him, handing him the rest of the joint and starting for the door, but he stops me.

"She needs to be punished before she gets fucked, Fynn. We cannot allow her to be disrespectful like she was."

"Well, from what I heard coming from her mouth, she's not totally wrong. The Lady of Sin is held to higher standards than we are. Don't get me wrong, she is to serve her Lords at all times, but they should be able to lose their shit occasionally, especially over something like this." I truly believe everything I say to my friend.

Little Saint serves us, and yes, she has an attitude, but I find it hot as hell when she's being feisty, but I also agree with Oakley that she shouldn't take her shit out on us. She can lose her shit all she wants, but it should never be against her Lords.

"So, you're saying that she shouldn't be punished?" My friend scrutinizes me.

"Not at all. I only mean that you should consider her feelings and adjust the punishment to something more fitting. Punish her but then reward her and let her know that she can come to us to talk anytime as long as it's respectful." Sometimes I even amaze myself. Who would have thought that I, Fynn Morin, would take it easy on a female?

"Who the fuck are you, and where the hell is my best friend?" Oakley gawks at me as I walk out.

I don't knock as I open the door to Oakley's room, "I don't want to see your face right..." Little Saint stops talking as soon as she notices it's me that walked in and not Oakley.

"What did I ever do to you?" I grin.

"Oh, sorry. I thought you were Oakley. I swear he loves pissing me off!" She crosses her arms and goes to stare out the window.

"You know, if I am to take a guess as to why Oakley is being an asshole, I'd have to say it's because of that naughty little mouth of yours." I sneak up until I'm right behind her, breathing heavily on her neck.

"I know I have a mouth on me," her voice is low, and I sense that my close proximity is affecting her, "But if he would only treat me as an equal..."

I run my hands over her arms and uncross them before I slide them over her chest, stopping to cup her beautiful breasts, "You are only equal to an extent, Little Saint. We will protect you at all costs, and if that means not telling you something because we feel that we need to protect you from it, then we will." I nibble on her neck.

"No, I don't need to be protected that way," she's panting hard.

I move my hands to the hem of her shirt and lift it up and over her head so she stands in her bra, "You will be punished for the disrespect you showed your Lord. There is no getting out of that, but then, you are mine, Little Saint, and just like in the woods, I will expect you to beg me to give you what you want."

I don't think she ever noticed the eyelets on each side of the window frame or the cuffs dangling from them. So, while I have her distracted, Jett and Oakley come up to each side and grab a wrist, locking each one in place. I never stop nibbling her neck, even when she starts to struggle.

"What the fuck, let me go!" she curses.

I slap her ass hard, "Take your punishment like a good girl, Little Saint, so I can reward you afterward."

She whimpers, "You tricked me, Fynn!"

"No, I was enjoying myself as I tasted your skin. I had no idea they would come in and do this, but you must remember, you signed away all your rights to us, Little Saint. We are lenient in most places; we can take whatever we want, but we do consider your feelings...at times, more and more in the last few days. However, you must work with us to earn your rightful place with us.

Taking my knife, I cut her bra, exposing herself to all. If anyone were to walk by and look up, they would see her perfect tits bouncing once we start using her after her punishment, "Have you ever been into exhibitionism, Little Saint?"

"I-I've never really thought about it," she stutters a little.

"Tell me," I undo her jeans and slip my hand inside, "Does it turn you on that someone may see us fuck you right here?"

She moans as I begin running my finger back and forth, "Hm, I take it most of this is Oakley's jizz you have here, but tell me, Little Saint, how much of it is yours?" I push two fingers into her.

"Oh, God..." she moans.

"Don't make her come yet, Fynn," Oakley growls, "Punishment first, remember?"

"Take her fucking jeans off then, so we can get on with it!" I tell my friend as I fuck her cunt harder with my fingers, "You will get the paddle this time, Little Saint. You will get ten swats with it and take every single one like a good girl, won't you?"

"Mm, yes...Fynn...please don't stop!" Our girl is humping my hand right here in front of the window. We are on the third floor, and nobody is around at the moment, but it's just the thought for her that somebody can come by and see her in this state.

"Oh, yeah, fuck my hand, you greedy slut...that's so hot," I insert a third finger.

"OW!" she cries out when Oakley brings the paddle down on her ass.

"Come here, Jett," I summon my friend closer and pull my fingers from Little Saint's pussy, "Take over for a moment." I tell him, then shove my drenched fingers into Saint's mouth, "Now suck on them and don't make a sound."

Jett and I take turns finger fucking her and then gagging her with our fingers while Oakley delivers her punishment. We all pull away quickly on the ninth swat when she almost comes. She glares at us while we snicker, and we then return to the torture, adding three more spankings for making us stop.

By the end, her cunt is dripping and ready to be taken, so without giving her any rest, I pull my rock-hard cock out, kick her legs apart and thrust into her nice and deep. Jett's pinching and pulling on her nipples, and in seconds, we have her coming. I don't let up, though. I fuck her hard and fast, her tits bouncing once Jett lets go.

"I forgot to make you beg, Little Saint. How about you beg me to fill you with my cum." I grip her hips, so I can fuck her harder. Her cheek is pressed against the glass.

"Please, Fynn...fill me with your cum. Let me milk every last drop!"

"Will you scream for me, Saint? Scream nice and loud for your Lord."

"Yes!"

So, lifting her left leg, I shove her whole body against the glass on the window and pound into her with everything I've got. It's fast, hard, and the deepest I've ever been in this pussy. I want someone to see us. I want them to look up and see her nicely shaved pussy as it's being fucked by my cock. I want to see the envy on their faces as they wish they could have what I have.

Just the thought of it has me spending myself deep inside her, "Fucking come for me, Saint! Come on my fucking cock as...I...give...you...mine!" I roar, emptying myself completely. I feel her walls clench around me as she gives me exactly what I want.

Jett

I'm harder than fuck watching my best friend fuck our girl like he is. I've never seen him take a female like he's taking my Lovely Lina. By the time I finish with her, she will be well-used, precisely how our little Saintly slut likes it. I don't call her that in a bad way, either. I love how she can be open and slutty for the three of us, but she doesn't act like one in public, not like all the groupies do anyway.

Fynn roars with his release, making her come again, and as soon as he steps away from her, her cunt drips with all Fynn's seed. Yeah, I'm going to be a dirty motherfucker and just step right up and thrust my own cock into her.

"You don't need a break, do you, Lina?" I ask as I thrust into her fast.

"No," she pants.

"Good. Then let's see how much more cum this slutty cunt can take, shall we?" I love talking dirty to her. It makes her sweet pussy drip even more. Our girl loves being talked to like this, and we are *very* happy to oblige.

"Oh, God, Jett...please!"

"Please, what, Lina? Tell your Lord what you want, baby?" I slip my hand around her and play with her clit.

"Oh yes...that right there!"

"Do you want to be a good girl and come all over my cock, Lovely?"

"Yes, Jett...let me come."

At that moment, I see some of our Frat brothers leaving the house, but luckily for our girl, they never look up, but I still feel the need to mention it.

"Open your eyes, Lina. Look below and see our brothers out there."

She gasps when she sees them, and I grin when I feel her clench around me as she comes. She likes the thought of being caught. Too bad I will never take her in front of a group of people. This is different; we are still high enough that no one will see clearly. Catalina is ours. Her body...ours. Her orgasms...ours. Nobody will ever have any of the three things I just listed, not without a death wish.

I pull her back, and Oakley closes the blinds, "You didn't actually think I would let them see you being fucked, did you? It's one thing to be dragged to the basement by Oakley, naked, but another to let others watch me fuck you. I'm not into exhibitionism like Fynn is." I slam into her repeatedly, "But it's good to know that it's not completely off the table where you're concerned," I snicker and then come hard.

"Jett?" Her voice is shaky.

"Yes, Lina?" I respond as I pull out of her dripping pussy.

"Can I sleep with you tonight?"

"Of course, you can, but you may not get much sleep. If you sleep in my bed, you get used, hard. I'll take you without asking. Is that what you want, Lina?" I move some of her hair away from her face and grip it, so I can turn her head and look her in the eyes.

"Yes," she gasps, "It's what I need right now after the day I've had."

"You can be used by any of us, Lovely. All you have to do is say the word." I reach up and take her wrist out of one of the cuffs as Fynn works on the other. Once we have released her, I squeeze her red ass cheeks, "Go to my room, and I'll bring you something to eat."

"Can I have my clothes?" she asks, but I use my foot to shove them away further.

"No, there is no need for them up here right now. I prefer to watch our cum drip from you the rest of the night." I smirk, thinking she's going to argue, but then she swipes her finger across her thigh, gathering some of the drippage, and then sucks on her finger.

"Mm, okay, Jett. If that's what you want, I can do that." She then walks from the room, leaving the three of us gawking after her.

"So, something was said tonight at dinner that I've been thinking a lot about," Oakley states as the three of us stand in the kitchen making something to eat, "It was brought up how the Saints and Sinners aren't supposed to fraternize and when Felicia's name was brought up, and Ashlee Scott asked about her, she got the weirdest expression on her face. When her husband told her that Felicia's mother was the Saint's President when Ashlee was a Junior, something passed across her features, and the subject was changed."

"What do you suppose the reason is?" I ask as I finish with the turkey sub I'm making for our girl.

"I don't fucking know, but you better believe I will find out. That's what I plan on doing tonight, researching the alumni from that time." Oakley grabs an apple from the basket and his sandwich and starts for the door.

"So, is there anything you need us to do?" I ask.

My friend turns back, "Yeah, keep Kitty Cat well used and exhausted so she doesn't get in my way. I don't want to tell her anything until I know what's going on for sure."

"Are you sure you want to do that?" Fynn asks, "I mean, after earlier..."

"Catalina can throw all the fits she wants. It's our job to protect her, and that's what I plan on doing whether she agrees or not!"

Fynn holds his hands up defensively, "Hey, just asking."

"Yeah, well, I thought we had all agreed on doing it this way, but apparently, her golden pussy is starting to change you fuckers. One of us must always remain in control, even if it means having her hate me for a while." We watch Oakley storm from the room, and suddenly I feel like shit.

"He's right, you know," I say out loud, "I'll admit that my feelings have changed for her. I still want to protect her, but her pussy is too good, and that mouth of hers..." I bite my bottom lip, thinking about how hard I get when she sass's back.

"You don't have to explain it to me, motherfucker!" Fynn pauses and then stares intensely at me, "I fucking kissed her last night."

I choke on the sip of water I just took. Sputtering and slapping my chest, I finally say, "You what?"

"Yeah, exactly!"

"Well, shit! What do we do about this?" I ask him because I really don't know. I've never had strong feelings for any female.

Fynn shrugs, "We must never forget that her safety comes first. Abide the contract until we catch the fuckers, and then we decide what to do. Regardless, Catalina Scott is our Lady of Sin. How far we take it with her depends on getting rid of the threat."

I nod. I get what Fynn's saying, but why do I feel like it will be a lot harder than it should be? The Lords don't do relationships, yet we all want her. Yes, even Oakley, whether he wants to admit it or not.

Grabbing the subs and two cans of soda, I head back to my room. Lina sits on the edge of my bed as though she doesn't know what to do with herself, "I've brought you a sub. I hope you like turkey." I tell her and then open one of the sodas.

"Oh, is there any water? I don't drink soda," she states, looking apologetic.

"I think Oakley may have some in his mini fridge. I'll be right back." I find a few bottles and bring them back to my room because I know she will need to rehydrate later; I grin. .

She's still sitting in the same place when I return, only she's now eating the food I made for her, "Thank you for the sandwich. It's perfect."

I push some hair away from her face before sliding my hand to the back of her head and gripping her hair at the nape, "I'm glad you like it," I say, yanking a little harder, "Make sure to eat it all; you'll need the energy," pressing my lips to her forehead, I then let her go abruptly.

I pick up my soda and drink it down before setting it aside and picking up my sandwich. We eat in silence as I scroll through my phone, but then I glance over at our girl. Watching Catalina finish her sub has me ready to go again, "I hope you still have room for dessert."

"Oh? What's for dessert?" She smiles.

"Get on your knees, and you will soon see." I stand and open my jeans up. She watches me pull out my hard cock before she falls to her knees like a good fucking girl. Pulling my jeans down far enough, I sit on the edge of the bed, "Crawl over here like a good slut, and suck me off."

Licking her lips as she stares at my throbbing hard-on, she looks fucking hot as she crawls to me. Just like a needy whore, begging for cock. I take hold of the base and then grab her head, shoving my cock deep into her throat and holding it there for just a moment. I savor the feeling of being so deep before I let go and let her do her own thing.

THIRTY-TWO

Catalina

I stare up into Jett's eyes as I take him all the way into my throat and hum. His body tenses, and he grabs my head, holding it in place as he jerks, releasing his load down my throat, "You're such a fucking tease, Lina. I wasn't ready to come yet, but this slutty mouth couldn't help itself, could it?"

His words slur a little, and I wipe my mouth as I stand up. Clearing away the plates that are still on the bed, I move back over to where I was on my knees and start pulling Jett's shirt off him. I then take hold of the waist of his jeans and pull them the rest of the way off.

"Lay in the middle of the bed, Jett," I tell him.

"Are you trying to tell me what to do?" He asks as he scrutinizes me.

"Not at all, but I figured you would want to be lying down when it all kicks in," I tell him as he shakes his head, trying to clear it.

By now, it must be getting pretty fuzzy, and he may be experiencing a little relaxation all at the same time. He's bigger than I am, so I didn't stop at half of the pill but tossed the whole tablet in his soda can.

"When what kicks in? What the fuck is wrong with me?" he asks as he scoots back onto the bed a little more.

"Well, I thought you would want to be more relaxed. You know, maybe experience the same thing I experienced. I have to say, it was definitely a fun time." I grin as I take his cock in my hand. I stroke it until it's hard, which is surprising. I was worried I wouldn't be able to get him hard once it was in his system.

"What the fuck did you do, Lina?" he frowns.

I lean in and press my lips against his briefly before looking him in the eye, "I date raped you, Jett."

He tries to sit up as he curses, but I push him back down, "What's the matter? Don't you like the feeling? Are you not relaxed enough?"

Lifting my leg, I straddle the Lord and take hold of his cock to line it up, "You didn't have to drug me to fuck me, Lina." His hands go to my hips as I sink onto him.

"Mm, you feel so good, Jett," I grind against him as I pick up speed, "I didn't drug you to fuck you. I did it because I'm leaving, and I can't have you stopping me. I'm fucking you because...well, you're a great fuck, and I know I will miss it, so I'm taking one for the road."

He chuckles, "You dirty little bitch, we will find you. Wherever you go, it will not be far enough. You are ours now, Catalina, and we don't let what belongs to us go that easily."

"Okay, Jett. We'll see about that." I turn my body around and ride him in reverse cowgirl. Looking over my shoulder, I ask the Lord, "Have you ever been fucked in the ass, Jett?"

"Fuck no!"

"Hm, looks like it's your lucky night. It's a good thing for the drugs in your system. Now relax as much as you can." I instruct and suck on my finger before bringing it between his legs.

He wants to squirm and fuck me simultaneously, "Lina..." he warns.

I push my finger into his ass, cutting him off, but then he starts moaning, "See, it's not all that bad, is it?"

"Fuck you," he grunts as I ride him faster and fuck my finger into his ass.

"An eye for an eye, Jett. Always remember that." I'm almost at my peak, so I play with the taint between his balls and asshole, "Now, come for me, slut. Give me everything you've got!"

I give him back what he's given me, and he likes it just as much. I honestly didn't think my plan would work when I first thought of it, and if I'm being honest, I had planned on using the drug on Oakley because I was pissed at him, but then I remembered that he refused to fuck me when I was on this drug.

After returning from dinner at my parent's house, I stomp into Oakley's room. Oakley telling me how he walked in on both our fathers fucking my mother, well, let's just say that I didn't take it too well. I thought he was lying at first, but when I finally started believing him, I laid in on him about not wanting to tell me about that when it had to do with my parents as well.

I'm tired of being treated with kid gloves, but that's only outside the bedroom. However, I'm all woman when they get me into bed. I'm waiting for Oakley to come like he said he would, but I get bored and start looking through his drawers. That's when I see the familiar bag of pills.

The thought comes to me right away, and I find myself reaching in and grabbing a few of the little tablets. I think of a plan, and that's when I realize I can't do it to Oakley, but I am more than willing to return the favor to Jett. So, peeking out into the hallway to make sure the guys have yet to come up, I chance running to Jett's room, hoping he will take me up on his offer later.

I hide the pills in a shoe under his bed and hurry back to Oakley's room just as I hear the door opening. My heart beats erratically as I wait for Oakley to appear, but Fynn arrives first.

As I return to the present, Jett thrusts up into me, and he comes hard, "Fuck yes, Lina! Oh, my fucking God...what did you just do to me?"

I come, too, and ride it out until I'm depleted. The Lord below me sighs, and he's already fast asleep when I look over my shoulder. I may feel slightly bad, but I need to get away from here. I need to get away from all this bullshit and keep in mind that the Sinners will do whatever it takes to get what they want, too.

That said, and just for the hell of it, I cuff all of Jett's limbs to the posts. I guess the Lords having restraints on their beds comes in handy for me. I take a step back and bring my finger to my mouth as I think.

No...I shouldn't. It's just so mean. With a wicked smile, I rummage through Jett's drawers and closet, finding exactly what I'm looking for, amongst other things I didn't need to know about, and I walk back to the Lord.

I justify my actions by telling myself this will give me a little more time to get away. If Jett can't call out for help, the others won't know I'm gone until I have a good head start. So, opening his mouth, I stick the ball gag inside and then strap it around his head. Stepping back again, I take my phone and snap a picture...just in case.

I then hurry and find some clothes and a pair of flip-flops I can wear. Once I've concluded that I have everything I need, I grab my bag that Jett brought into the room earlier and shove the rest of the pills into the inside pocket. I grab the keys hanging up that lock the door at the bottom of the stairs, and quietly make my way out of the room.

I can hear music playing in Fynn's room, whereas I hear nothing coming from Oakley's, but I can see the light on under the door. A shadow moves close to the door, and I hold my breath, but he never comes out. I then hurry down the stairs and out to the second floor.

I don't want to cause alarm in case anyone is hanging around, so I try and act naturally. I take the back stairs because it will lead me straight to the back door, and nobody will be in the backyard at this time.

I swear I hold my breath the whole time, and it's not until I'm out of the house and skirting the bushes along the side that I can take a deep breath. I keep to the shadows until I'm on the next street over. I send Dani a text asking where she is staying.

My phone lights up, and I see she's given me an address to the dorms she's staying in until they can get back into the house. I haven't talked to her since the hospital, and I feel bad about it. I tell her I'm on my way, change direction, and head for the dorms.

I'm still a few blocks away and constantly looking over my shoulder when a set of headlights hit me. I stop breathing immediately, but as the car slows down and the driver rolls down the window, I can calm myself.

"A pretty thing like yourself shouldn't be walking the streets alone." Kaden's smile gleams in the darkness.

"What's Mr. Captain of the Lacrosse team doing slumming at this time?" I ask from the sidewalk.

"Oh, you know, just out trying to see if I can pick up beautiful women who may be out and about."

Kaden Miller is just as cute as he was at the party where I met him. It's too bad that he's one of the good guys, "So, you wouldn't happen to be heading toward the dorms, would you?"

"Actually, yes. I just ran an errand for a friend and need to drop something off. Would you like a ride?"

"That would be great! I will owe you one big time!" I grin and hurry around to the passenger side.

A faucet drips somewhere close by. My head throbs, and when I try to open my eyes, I open them to darkness. My arms are numb, and I realize they are behind my back, but I can't bring them forward. Neither can I move my legs. It feels like I'm sitting in a chair, my arms are restrained behind the back, and if I were to guess, my legs are tied to the legs of the chair.

I try remembering the last thing I did, but I'm coming up blank at the moment. It could just be due to the massive headache I've got right now. Either way, I'm fucked, and not in a good way. There is tape over my mouth, so I can't even call out for help, not that I expect any. I'm sure the only ones close by are the ones who tied me up.

Shutting my eyes, I try relieving some of the pain in my head, but it doesn't help much, so I say fuck it and start trying to move my body back and forth, hoping to knock the chair to its side. With any luck, it is wooden, and it will break. It's harder than you think, though. Either that or the chair is attached to the floor.

"Don't waste your time; you will never get it to move." I jump at the sound over an intercom.

I try cursing them out, but it only sounds like mumbling with the tape over my mouth. They laugh. Suddenly, my head is pulled back by my hair, and a whispered voice next to my ear says, "Try all you want, bitch. Even without the tape, nobody will hear you!"

Whoever it is uses a voice changer, so I can't figure out who they are. Very carefully, I ask, "Why?"

"What was that? Why?" I can sense them circling me, "What? Are you that stupid that you have forgotten about the threat? I warned you all, time and time again, but no one tried to right the wrong that was done!"

They are angry, and I really wish I knew why. Maybe then I would be able to help more. I keep trying to talk, hoping they will remove the tape, but it only gets me a hand across my face.

"Shut the fuck up already! Jesus, are you always like this?" They ask, annoyed.

My face tingles and throbs now. I may not be able to tell by the voice, but I doubt a female can hit like they just did. I'm fucking pissed that this person has the audacity to kidnap me and then hide themselves from me like a fucking coward!

"It's all good because you are going to take a little nap before we call your friends," they scoff, "To think that they thought they would actually keep you safe. You all have it coming to you. You were just the easiest target. The longer your fathers go without confessing, the longer you will be tortured."

I feel the tape peel away from my mouth, but before I can say anything, something is shoved into the back of my throat, and my mouth is again covered. They keep my head tilted back and plug my nose. I struggle for air, and in the process, I swallow whatever it is they gave me.

"There we go," they tap my cheek, "Even if you didn't swallow it, it will dissolve, and you will be sleeping like a baby in no time."

I try thrashing once again, screaming behind the tape. All they do is laugh as I struggle. When I start feeling sluggish, I curse some more. I'm not going to lie; now I'm getting scared. It's one thing to be awake, so I can try fighting my way out, but once I'm passed out, there is no telling what will happen, and that alone scares the shit out of me.

I groan as once again I hear the drip of a faucet. I thought maybe I was just having a bad dream, but as I wake up once again, I'm in the same predicament. Something feels off, though. A cool breeze is coming through the room, and I realize I don't have all my clothes on. I'm not entirely naked, but I'm not fully dressed, either. What the fuck happened?

I hear a door open, its hinges giving off a horrible squeak as it does. I hear what sounds like a cart being rolled in, and suddenly I hear that voice again, "Seems as though someone dressed in haste before leaving the safety of the Sinner's place. Tell me, Catalina, were you running from them, or do you make it a habit of wearing men's underwear and dressing in their clothes?"

That's when it hits me. I escaped from the Sinner's Frat House by drugging Jett and putting his clothing on because I didn't have any in his room. I remember I was headed to the dorms. I was going to see Dani, and then he was there, Kaden. He offered me a ride...well, I asked him, I guess, but that's not important. Is that who has me, Kaden Miller?

"I guess it really doesn't matter at the moment," they say, "How about we get ready for our big debut?"

Suddenly, the blindfold is ripped away from my face. I blink at the bright light coming from a ring light directly in front of me. Once my eyes adjust, I see myself on a television screen tied to a metal chair. My arms are still behind my back, and my legs are duct taped to the chair legs. I look a mess, but that's not what has me freaking out.

I am no longer in Jett's clothing. That may be why they drugged me, so they could untie me to remove my clothes. As I said before, I'm not naked. I'm now wearing what looks to be boy shorts and a sports bra, so I at least have some coverage. I close my eyes and thank God for this, but then I think about how I came to be dressed this way. Did this person change me? If so, did they do anything else while I was passed out?

A chuckle comes from my right side, and I turn my head. A tall figure, too big to be female, stands next to a cart, "What, did you think I was, a pervert like the Lords of Sin? Don't get me wrong, I love a beautiful woman when I see one, but I don't take what isn't given to me freely." They remove the towel covering the tray, but it's too high for me to see what it contains.

I don't take my eyes off who I know now is a male as he walks over to the video camera pointed at me. He presses a button, and I see a light come on. I'm now being recorded, and for some reason, my stomach drops because this can't mean anything good.

The guy comes back over to me and squats so he's eye level with me, "Let's see if your little boyfriends can light a fire under their father's asses after this. You better hope they care enough about you to do something because I may not be into raping women, but I'm not above physically hurting them." He chucks me under my chin and winks through his black ski mask before moving away.

I hear metal scrape against metal before I feel him move behind me. You can only see from his chest down on the screen, so I'm the main focal point. With the voice changer still on, he begins talking.

"Good morning, Sinners. I'm sure by now you are aware that you are missing your Saintly whore," the guy snickers, "You shouldn't let your property wander around at night, especially when there's a crazy stalker on the loose."

He brings his hand around to my front, and that's when I see the scalpel in his hand. My eyes widen, and I keep them on his every movement. My heart races as he slides the flat part against my chest bone and whistles.

"I'm tired of waiting for your fathers to do the right thing, so let's just say I'm lighting a little fire under their asses. I'm sure your fathers won't care about her life, but I think the Provost does, and I wonder," he pauses, turning the little knife around and cutting into me just below my collarbone, making me scream, "Just how far are you three willing to go to save your whore?"

He moves to the other side and does the same thing, making about a two-inch incision on each side. I can't help the tears that fall. I want to be strong, but this fucking hurts. This asshole means business, and now I wish I took them more seriously.

"Each day that goes by without any results," he continues his little fucked up speech, "Two more cuts will be added, and they will be deeper and longer than the day before. Oh, and that will be after I reopen the older ones."

Using his hand, he pushes my sweaty hair back from my wet face, but I shake my head, trying to remove his touch. He grips my jaw, making it feel like he's about to crush it, "Be a good fucking bitch; otherwise, you will get more than two cuts each day!" He then makes it, so I have to look into the camera, "Look at her! She's a pathetic fucking mess," he addresses the camera, "I look forward to wrecking her, so if I were you, I'd get my ass in gear. Tick tock...time is being wasted."

Shoving my face away, he walks over and turns the camera off. The television screen goes black, and that's when I vaguely see a silhouette walk up behind me. Excruciating pain streaks across the back of my head, and everything goes dark once again.

THIRTY-THREE

Oakley

I wake up to my phone beeping, telling me I have a message. I glance at the time and see that it's just after seven. My first class isn't until nine, but I might as well get up now since I'm already up. So, reaching over, I grab my phone and start going through my messages, leaving a video message that I received for last.

Finally, clicking on the video, I have to adjust my eyes because I think I'm seeing things. Sitting up, I zoom in on the video, and the whole world disappears as I watch the female tied to a chair being sliced open by some psycho. The female looks an awful lot like my Kitty Cat.

I turn the volume up and can hardly believe what I see and hear. It's got to be some fucking sick joke, right? Kitty Cat is with Jett; it's where she stayed last night. That has to be someone who just looks like our Saint.

"I look forward to wrecking her..."

Those words continue running through my head as I jump from my bed and run for my door. Fynn meets me in the hall with his phone in his hand also. We both hurry to Jett's room, and I turn the knob only to find it locked.

I pound on his door, "Open the fucking door, Jett!"

"Wait a minute," Fynn moves his ear to the door, "Do you hear that?"

I understand what Fynn is talking about when I place my own ear against the door. I hear what sounds like a muffled call for help coming from the other side of the door, and I don't waste any more time. Using my shoulder, I ram it into the door, which slams open, breaking the entire frame.

"Whoa, dude...what the fuck?" Fynn stops in his tracks and cracks a small smile, but then realization dawns on him, and his eyes widen before coming over to the bed. I came straight over and started working on taking the ball gag off.

"What the fuck happened, Jett?" I growl, "Did you seriously think that letting her cuff you was a good idea?"

"Fuck you, man! The little vixen gave me Date Rape Rob's pills...she fucking drugged me!"

I stop what I'm doing and stare at him, "Are you fucking serious?"

"Fuck yes, I'm serious!"

It's my turn to crack a smile, "Maybe she does have what it takes to be our Lady."

Jett cracks a small one of his own, "Yeah, I thought the same thing right after she told me she had given it to me. Then she fucked me, saying she would miss it and was taking one for the road."

"Oh man, her ass is in so much trouble..."

"You're telling me! I'm going to..."

I cut him off, "No, seriously. The stalker has her now, and she's in trouble. He's already sent the first video."

Jett looks from me to Fynn, grabs his phone, and watches the same video that was also sent to him. I take this time to study Fynn because he's been pretty quiet, and I can sense the rage building inside him. I believe our fucked-up friend has finally found a female he likes enough to keep around for a while, and now she's been taken from him. This is not going to end well with the fucker who took her from us.

"FUCK!" Jett whips his phone across the room, and I watch it break into pieces.

"Calm the fuck down, man! We will get her back; we just have to trace her steps," I say.

"Oh, because that's going to be fucking easy when we don't know when she left or how!" Fynn glares.

"Come on, guys. Use your fucking heads; don't fall apart on me now," I scold them both. They are known to act first, and I always have to bring them back a few steps.

"Jett, you go back and watch the security footage to find out when exactly Catalina left, what she was wearing, and which direction she went in," I wait for his nod before turning to Fynn, "Call her friend Dani and see if she's heard from her at all and then call your father and let him know what's going on. I'll call mine and Mr. Scott. They better fucking come clean! The sooner we know what this piece of shit wants, the sooner we will get her back.

"What if we don't?" Jett says, his voice dangerously low.

"We will tear this fucking town apart until we find her," Fynn growls, "And then I'm going to torture that motherfucker for days before giving him an agonizing death!" He pulls his phone from his pocket and leaves the room to make his calls.

"They have her," those are the first three words that come out of my mouth when my father answers his phone.

"Well, hello to you too, kid," he fucking chuckles.

"This isn't the time for fucking jokes! Get your dick out of Ashlee Scott and listen to what I say!" I yell through the phone.

"Watch your tone, Oakley, and mind your fucking business where my sex life is concerned."

"Well, your only sex life should be with Mom, but I guess that's not happening." I don't care how disrespectful I'm being. I need to get Kitty Cat back, and our fathers are the ones who know how to do it.

"What the hell is your problem?" my father sneers over the phone.

"Whoever the fuck you pissed off is our fucking problem! They have Catalina! Now, are you going to tell me what the fuck you guys did to warrant these threats?"

"We didn't do anything that wasn't expected of us. I don't know who this is that is sending the letters, so I can't help you."

I stand here, stunned momentarily, at hearing what is coming from my father's mouth, "You piece of shit! They are cutting her up, Dad! Each day we don't give them what they want, they will cut her more!"

"Well, then, I suggest you figure it out. This is a good test to see if you can hack it in life, Son," my father sounds unaffected by this.

"THIS ISN'T A FUCKING GAME! Un-fucking-believable..." I end the call, still trying to grasp my father's words.

My phone rings, and I see my father's name pop up, so I ignore it and instead call Mr. Scott. Unfortunately, it goes to voicemail, and I leave him a message to call me back, that it's about Catalina. I walk out of Jett's room and run into Fynn.

"Dani said that Little Saint texted her last night asking where she was staying and that she was heading over there, but she never showed up. Dani has been trying to call her since but keeps getting her voicemail."

"Did you talk to your dad?" I ask.

He shakes his head, "His phone transferred to his office phone, and his receptionist said that he had an early morning meeting that will probably take all morning."

"What the fuck? I doubt Jett will call his dad, so it looks like we are on our own," I tell him.

"Did you find anything while researching last night?" he asks.

"Actually, I think I may have. However, it was so late, I was going to take another look at it today in case I was imagining some of it."

"Well, there is no time like the present," Fynn states, "I won't be going to class until we have our Little Saint back here where she belongs."

I jerk my head toward my room, "Let's get to it then."

I pull out all the information I found as soon as we get in my room, "Jesus, that's a lot of shit!" Fynn exclaims as he shuffles through the stacks of yearbooks I had delivered from the library and all the newspaper clippings I had delivered to me as well. The one good thing about being in a powerful family is that you have so many people at your beck and call.

"So, I didn't find much about the years that our fathers went to school here, aside from them being Lords and such, except there is this one incident. A woman who graduated the year before our fathers graduated committed suicide two years after graduating."

"Huh. Who was this woman, and does it say why? Was there a note left?" Fynn asks as he takes the newspaper clipping I hand to him and reads the article, "Are you fucking serious? Howard, as in Felicia Howard's mother?"

"Yeah..."

"That may explain why Mrs. Scott acted weird, but how would this fit in with the threatening letters?" Fynn hands me back the clipping and shuffles through more stuff.

"I'm not sure," I drop the piece of paper and watch as it floats downward, landing on the stack of others, "But I feel like this means something, and I'm not going to stop until I figure it out."

"Well, we had better get to figuring it out then," my friend grabs a stack of other newspaper clippings, "I really don't think I can watch them cut up our girl again. We are the only ones allowed to do that, and this motherfucker should know that."

I stare at Fynn, knowing that he's fucked in the head at times, and yes, we have made women bleed together, but other than signing the contract, I never thought about making Kitty Cat bleed much. My cock stirs at the thought, but then I chastise myself for it. First and foremost, we need to bring her home, and then we will see about taking our play dates to another level.

Fynn

I storm through my father's office door uptown and find him sitting behind his desk. The fact that he is no longer in his meeting and has yet to call me back has me livid as fuck. It's well after lunchtime, so I'm taking it upon myself to come see him in person.

"What the fuck, Dad? Do you need to hire a new receptionist for not doing her job? I've called twice, leaving messages for you to call me back!"

My father looks at me, annoyed for barging in the way I did, but I don't give a flying fuck, "You need to learn to have patience, Fynn. I can't always drop everything just because my kid calls needing something." Jakob Morin sits back in his chair and crosses his hands over his chest. My father thinks he is a big deal, and maybe he is, but right now, he's being a dick!

"They took her, Dad! Whoever wrote the threatening letters took Catalina!"

"Yes, I know. Donavan called and informed me of the situation," he responds.

I stare at my father blankly. He knew, and he still hadn't called me back. He must have known what I was calling for once he talked to Oakley's father. I lose my shit and swipe everything off his desk as I roar with rage. My father may be nice and fit, but I can beat his ass with one hand tied behind my back, and he knows it. Even knowing this, he remains sitting in his chair with a raised eyebrow.

"Are you done throwing your little fit yet?" he asks me, bored.

"Fuck you, Dad! You knew why I was calling and couldn't pick up the goddamn phone and call me back? Does all this mean so little to you that you couldn't care less about what happens to us?"

"I warned you about the threats, did I not? I came to you and told you to watch your backs, didn't I?" My father glares at me as if this is on us, not them.

"Whatever the fuck you guys did back in your day is why this is happening, and you all are just going to sit back and watch as though it's a fucking show? They are cutting her up, Dad!"

"What the fuck do you want us to do, Fynn?"

"We want you all to come clean and fess up to whatever you did to piss this person off!" I yell at him. My hands are fisted at my sides, and I'm trying really hard not to reach over and rip his fucking head off.

"We aren't one hundred percent sure of what they are talking about, and even so, keeping quiet is the best thing to do for our families," my father states and then sighs, losing some of his steam.

"So what, we let them cut Catalina up piece by fucking piece until she's dead? No, that's not going to happen! If you know something, you need to tell us!"

"We have faith in you boys. It will be easier to clean up after you than if we do it ourselves. Because of the positions we hold, our hands are tied. That is why we are relying on you three."

Again, I stare at my father in disbelief as I take in everything he says. I reach into my back pocket and pull out the clipping on Felicia's mom's suicide, "Then at least tell me what this is about, and if it could have anything to do with what's going on," I slam it down on the empty desk and stand back.

My father picks up the thin paper and studies it. A moment later, he sighs and shakes his head, "I'm sorry, but I can't help you. It could have something to do with it, but I really can't say. There was no note left. I remember when she took her life, but nothing much was said about it."

"Unbelievable! Fine," I snatch the clipping back and tuck it away again, "If you won't tell us anything, I'm sure Mr. Scott will. I doubt he will keep information to himself when his daughter is being tortured!" I turn and head for the door, but my father's words stop me.

"Don't count on it, Fynn. If this does have something to do with what happened back when we were Lords, we are sworn to secrecy. You can look into it all you like, but we cannot say a word about anything that happened."

"Oh, I see. You are all a bunch of fucking pussies!" I scowl.

"Guys have been found dead after spilling a secret from when they were Lords," my father states.

"Again, fucking pussies!" I yank the door open.

"No pussy is worth dying over, Son. Even if she is the Lady of Sin!" his voice rings out as I keep walking, not daring to look back because I can't promise to control what I'll do if I look at his face after this last comment.

By the time I get back, Oakley and Jett have already rallied all the Sinners together in the living room. I called Oak as soon as I left my father's office. If he says we have to do this on our own, so be it. We are going to fuck shit up just to get our girl back, proving to our fathers that they are no longer needed.

"Hey, is everyone here?" I ask as I look around the large room.

"Everyone except for a few that are in taking a test and can't get out of it. I also sent Brett and Drew to go watch Felicia. We can catch them up later," Oakley states.

"Yeah, okay." We are not entirely sure if she is the stalker, but we aren't taking any more chances.

Jett starts the meeting off, "I'm just going to get right to it," he says loudly, "Catalina has been taken from us. Our future Lady of Sin is in trouble, and we must find her ASAP! Now, we only know that she snuck out a little after ten last night wearing a pair of my white basketball shorts and a light blue Nike t-shirt. She was also wearing my black Nike flip-flops."

A few of our Frat brothers snicker, and I growl, "It may seem funny at the moment but make no mistake, this situation is far from humorous!"

Jett waits for me to finish before continuing, "We received information that she was headed to see her friend Dani at the dorms but never arrived. So, with that said, we now know the vicinity in which she was taken."

"Why was she taken, and who took her? Is there a ransom demand?" Sean is the one to ask.

I glance at my two best friends and clench my jaw, "Yeah, there's a reason. Something that happened when our fathers were attending Helshire, and were Sinners themselves, caused this person to threaten their offspring, and they went after Cat first."

"So why not go to the police? Isn't your uncle the Chief?" Another Sinner asks.

"Because my Uncle Tyler may help cover shit up, but he won't willingly do anything leading up to the mess. We don't plan on letting these motherfuckers live." I stare at the room full of Sinners waiting to see if there are any objections. Now is not the time to be weak. It's time to step up and show what they are each made of.

"All they want is for our fathers to come clean for what they have done, but as you all know, we take our shit to the grave, or so that's what they want us to do. We are a new generation of Sinners, and with that, we make our own rules, and as of right now, we are going to do what it takes to get our Lady back." Oakley starts passing out papers with a schedule and map on it, "This will list where we want each of you until Cat is brought home. We will not leave anything unturned in this town, but we still need to be smart about it and not hurt the innocent. You will work around them, checking their homes and businesses when they are not around or at night when they sleep."

"If you are caught," Jett chimes in, "That's when we will bring Tyler into it if necessary. If anyone gives you beef, you'll know what to do."

"We don't want dead bodies all around town, so let's try and keep this on the down low," I state, "Besides, we don't want them to know how close we are getting to them. If you happen to find them, do not move in. You wait and call us, and we will deal with the motherfuckers."

"So, there is more than one?" Sean asks.

"We believe there are at least two of them working together, one male for sure," I inform them, "The clock is ticking, Sinners! Every day that goes by, they hurt her more. We want Cat back like yesterday!"

"You all have your schedule, so get the fuck out of here and find her!" Oakley growls, and they all disperse instantly.

I turn to my two best friends, "I think it's time we pay the Provost a little visit, don't you think? If he won't come to us, then we will go to him."

THIRTY-FOUR

Jett

Am I pissed for what my Lovely Lina did to me? Damn right, I am, but it's because she put herself into a situation where we now have to save her. The fact that she drugged me and then fucked me, well, I'm a little proud about that. I'm not saying that I like being drugged, but she showed me that she can give it just as good as we can.

After finding out the information we needed from the security feed, I called an acquaintance and I have them looking into the town's street cam footage. It will take a little while, so we are on our own in the meantime.

We are on our way over to the Provost's office to chat about his daughter, and I'm hoping he doesn't pull the same as what Oak and Fynn's fathers are pulling. My own father...fuck, that would just be a waste of time, and time is not something we have an abundance of at the moment.

My phone rings. Speak of the devil, and he shall appear. I ignore my father's call, "You know, you can't ignore him forever," Fynn says as he sits in the backseat of Oak's Camaro.

"No, but I can wait until we have our girl back. I don't need my father pissing me off to the point where I can't think straight. I need all of my attention on finding Lina." I tuck my phone away and stare out the passenger window.

"How do you know he doesn't have information concerning Little Saint?" Fynn continues, "I mean, it wouldn't hurt...every bit helps."

I scoff, "We are talking about Blake Pelletier. My father will help us just as much as your own fathers. They are best friends; what's the point in wasting my time?"

Fynn shrugs when I glance back at him, "It was just a question. Who knows, maybe he has something that will help."

"Oh, he knows something. All three of our fathers know something but refuse to tell us what that something is," Oakley states disgustedly.

"Yeah, well, let's hope Mr. Scott loves his daughter enough to give us something that will help." I'm not really holding my breath, though.

We arrive at the Provost's office on campus and walk straight to his office. Ms. Davis, his receptionist, tries to stop us, "Mr. Scott is unavailable at the moment, boys!" she calls out, but she should know better.

Mr. Scott's office door is unlocked, so we walk right in, only to find the room empty, "I told you he was unavailable!" the receptionist huffs from the doorway.

I roll my eyes and slam the door in her face, locking it before moving over to the desk, "There has to be something here that can help us."

I start by searching the drawers, but when I get to the bottom one, I find it locked. I look around the top of the desk, searching for something to pick the lock with. I see that my two friends are searching the bookcase and the file cabinet, so I continue with my own search.

Finding a letter opener, I try to jimmy the lock until it clicks, and I can open the drawer. There are a few files of little importance to us on the top, but as I dig deeper, I pull out a manilla envelope. It's a bit bulky, so I reach in and pull the contents out, finding multiple letter envelopes addressed to Mr. Scott with no return address.

Pulling the folded paper from the first envelope, I realize I've found his stash of threatening letters. The one I have in my hands must be the first one, so I read it out loud to Oak and Fynn.

Mr. Scott

I know what you did, and you will pay, but you're not the only one...
You have a daughter, don't you?
Is she safe?
Make things right, or else...

"What the fuck is that supposed to mean?" Fynn growls.

I ignore my friend and open the next one, reading it to myself before I read it out loud to the others. If I'm to understand this one correctly, it sounds like whatever they did, it wasn't so much Mr. Scott, but he witnessed it.

Mr. Scott

This is warning #2! It makes no difference whether you were involved in the incident or not. You were there, so you are just as guilty as the others. Come clean, and this will all go away...

"What the fuck did they do?" Oakley asks incredulously, "Whatever it was, it was some serious shit!"

"No kidding! To think about how hard our fathers have been on us for some of the shit we have pulled; I don't think we did anything that would warrant being threatened in the future."

"Yeah," I say as I stare at this letter, "We are dicks, but it sounds like our fathers may have really fucked up at some point."

I open the third envelope addressed to the Provost and begin to read it, realizing that he must have just received it, which means, the stalker is close because this one wasn't mailed...there is no postage stamp on it. That means it had to have been delivered personally somehow.

Mr. Scott,

I've warned you what would happen if you didn't come clean. Now we have your daughter, and the fun can really begin! I have sent you a video, the first of many, if my demands are not met.

Come clean, or your lovely daughter won't be so lovely anymore...

"They are close," I tell my friends, "How else would they have been able to deliver this letter so soon after what they did to her?"

"They can still be anywhere in town, though," Oakley states.

"I'm not so sure," Fynn says, "I have a gut feeling that they are close to the University."

I nod, "I think you may be right. They always seem to be coming and going on foot. Unless they stash a car somewhere, I believe they may be students here at Helshire."

"Now that you mention it," Oakley pauses momentarily, "I find it odd that these threats didn't start until all four of us offspring were here. But that still doesn't mean they are students; it's just an observation."

I pick up the last envelope. There is no writing on it, so I pull out the folded paper. There is a small note written on the front of it.

Do not read out loud...they are always listening.

Oakley and Fynn are reading over my shoulder, and when I glance at them, they nod their understanding. My attention returns to the paper, unfolding it, my eyes skim the small paragraph scribbled on the unlined paper.

Lords of Sin,

Remember to keep ANY and ALL evidence in the safe tucked away in the basement wall of the Fraternity House. These secrets are ours to keep. We take everything to our graves.

"What the actual fuck?" Fynn steps back.

A grin slowly appears, "I think we are done here, guys. There isn't anything here that's going to help us find our girl." I put three of the four letters back into the manilla envelope and place it back in the drawer.

Tucking the fourth one into the back pocket of my jeans, I make sure my shirt covers it as I head to the door. Mr. Scott will know that we were here, so he will know that we got his message. I'm not sure what we will find in that safe because I've yet to use it, but whatever is there will help find my Lovely Lina; it has to.

Oakley is just pulling up to the Frat House when my phone pings. It's a text from the guy I had work on the street cameras. He's giving me a heads-up that he has sent me a file with his findings and that he could only track her so far, but then she just disappears. He tells me to just watch the videos, and I will understand.

Before heading to the basement, we head to my room to open the email with the videos. The first one is when Catalina leaves the Frat House and hugs the shadows so as not to be seen. He then captures her on the next street over, where she uses her phone to text someone. It must be Dani because she turns toward the dorms when her phone lights up and reads it.

My heart races when we see a car pull up next to her. I zoom in on the video and see her smiling. Catalina knows the person in the car, but we can't see the person clearly enough. When our girl gets into the car, and it drives away, we get a clear view of the car and license plate.

My friend keeps track of the car heading toward the dorms but stops at the convenience store on the way. A video outside the store still has no clear view of the driver, even as they get out because their head is down as they type away on their phone. The only thing we do know is that it's a guy who picked her up and that alone pisses me the fuck off. The fact that she would willingly get into another guy's car when she belongs to us is inexcusable.

Finally, the last video shows the car pulling up to the dorms and our girl getting out of the vehicle. She smiles and waves before turning and walking up the walkway. It's not very bright, with one of the streetlamps burnt out, so she doesn't see the shadowy figure stepping out from behind the bushes. We see them, though. It's just too bad they are wearing a mask and are dressed in all black.

We watch the stranger sneak up behind Lina and grab her, lifting a white cloth to her face before she goes limp. This person is male and is much bigger than our girl, so when he tosses her over his shoulder, it's as if she weighs nothing. Looking around, the stranger heads to the side of the brick building, disappearing into the shadows and taking Catalina with him.

THIRTY-FIVE

Catalina

I wake up to a splitting headache and remember getting hit over the head right after that motherfucker recorded himself cutting me. I glance down at my chest and see someone glued the two cuts. How fucking nice of them. Looking around the room, I notice the tray is still sitting close by, and I wonder how long I've been out. There are no windows to tell me whether it's daytime or nighttime, so I have to sit here and wait.

My stomach rumbles, and I realize I haven't eaten anything since I've been here; I've been tied up the whole time. Well, except for when I was changed while I was passed out. I'm still in the boy shorts and sports bra from earlier, so that's a plus. It tells me that my clothes remained on this time.

It's about an hour after I've woken up when I hear the door open, and the big guy comes back in carrying a tray this time. I watch as he walks over to the cart and places the tray on top of it, metal clattering once again as it's moved around.

I'm taking in everything, so the first chance I get, I can get the fuck out of here. I will not die here, no matter what I have to do. I'm so busy being inside my head, trying to figure shit out, that I don't notice the fucker standing beside me. The tape is ripped from my mouth, and I can't help but cry out.

"Fuck! Seriously? You couldn't warn me first?" I scowl.

The guy gives me a creepy laugh using the voice changer, "My bad." He then shoves a piece of bread in my mouth, "Just on the off chance that your father comes clean and we release you, we won't starve you entirely." He then holds a bottle of water to my lips.

Once I swallow, I glare at the masked guy, "Well, aren't you a good fucking Samaritan!"

"Has anyone ever told you that you swear like a sailor?" Mr. Mask questions.

I shrug, "Maybe a time or two, but does it look like I give a fuck?" I cock my brow.

"I thought you were supposed to be a Lady?"

I scoff, "I've never claimed to be one, so I don't know where you're getting your information."

"Yeah, well, you need to shut the fuck up and finish your bread. I'm already tired of hearing your mouth." My abductor states as he holds another piece to my mouth.

"How about a bathroom? If I don't go soon, I will piss all over, and you will have a mess to clean." I tell him as I chew the dry bread. It's not a lie; I have to go, but I also need to see what's beyond this room.

"You think I'm stupid, Cat?" He sets the bread down and picks up the scalpel from the cart, "Sit really still unless you want that slutty cunt all cut up."

"What? No! Don't come near me with that thing!" I try moving, but it's no use.

He slaps another piece of tape over my mouth before squatting and feeling under the chair. I jerk when I feel his hand touch my crotch, not realizing that there is a hole in the bottom of this chair. He pulls on the material and cuts through it, causing me to feel a draft once he's done. A five-gallon bucket is then slid under the chair.

"There is your throne, Your Royal Highness." The fucker laughs and walks out, leaving me alone once again.

I glare at his back, but honestly, I don't care because my bladder hurts so much. At least he's given me some privacy, so as soon as the door closes, I sigh as I release myself in the bucket below. I close my eyes at that feeling of satisfaction, you know the one I'm talking about.

I feel my eyelids become heavy. The asshole has drugged me again. Was it the bread or the water, I wonder? I didn't take much of either, so hopefully, I won't be out long. Those are my last thoughts before darkness takes hold again.

I hear a grinding noise and jerk awake. The heavy door slams closed as my eyes adjust to the room's low lighting, but then the ring light is turned on once again, and dread fills me. Seeing movement beside me, my head snaps in that direction to find my kidnapper wiping down the items on the cart; a strong alcohol scent burns my nose.

I try begging through the tape, but all he does is turn and wink at me through his mask. The guy is big, and I know I could never take him physically, but if I could only get my hands on one of those scalpels, I'd stab him in the fucking eyes so he can never wink again. When he begins to whistle, I try pulling on the tape around my legs even though it's no use. This guy is psycho, enjoying my torture too much, and I have to try anything to escape.

It's one thing to enjoy cutting if it's being done sexually. I've never done blood play. I'm sure others who do, enjoy it, but this is a different kind of fucked up. He's making me bleed for shits and giggles, making it all the more dangerous because he won't care if I bleed out.

He walks over and turns the television on, then the video camera, grinning at me the whole time. Stalking around to where I'm sitting, he caresses my cheek with the back of his leather-gloved fingers, "Let's play."

I stare into the camera, trying to convey something to the Lords. I'm unsure what that is, but I want them to know I'm trying to be strong. I'm sure they're pissed at me for getting into this mess...I'm pissed at myself; I should have known better. I've always said that I wouldn't be that ditzy blonde who walks into danger and look where I'm at.

"Good morning, Sinners!" The fucker's robotic voice cuts into my thoughts, "I see that some are not taking my threats seriously. Either that or this slut means nothing to all of you."

I growl behind the tape and try to move away from him when his hand comes up and pulls my hair back behind my shoulders as he stands behind me again. I can see him on the screen, but his head is cut off again.

When his hands slide over my shoulders and stop over the two wounds he made last time, my heart stops, "As I said yesterday, every day that goes by, your little whore will receive another cut...after I reopen her old ones."

Before I realize what he's doing, pain streaks through my chest where he had cut me, "MMPH!!" I scream through the tape, but he isn't finished as he does the same to the other cut. He's ripped open the first cuts he glued.

"She bleeds so pretty, don't you think?" He uses his hand and smears my blood all over my upper chest. "Now, let's see how well your whore really takes pain, shall we?"

I watch on the television as the asshole wraps a strap around my forehead and ties it to the back of the chair. I can no longer look down, but I can still see the screen. Once he's done, he moves to stand before me, then squats; his hand caressing the bare skin on my midsection.

"This is going to hurt like a bitch, but I suggest you sit still; otherwise, I may go too deep," he fucking chuckles and begins.

It starts as a burning pain and quickly escalates the longer he keeps going. There are times when he retraces over whatever it is he's doing until I feel wetness drip. If it doesn't bleed right the first time, he retraces it. I hold as still as possible, but I can't help the scream that comes out at each new cut he gives me. My face is soaked with tears, and I can feel my nose begin to run.

He chuckles and stands up, stepping back to admire his handiwork, "Fucking gorgeous! You are such a mess but look how hard I am, Cat." He grabs his package, but I close my eyes, "Awe, do you think I'm going to fuck you? Ha! I don't want the Lord's sloppy seconds, and I already told you that I don't take women against their will, sexually," another chuckle comes out, "Besides, you're marked as the Lord's whore, and I wouldn't dare fuck what is theirs." He finally moves away, and I open my eyes to see the words '*Whore of Sin, Property of the Lords*' carved into my mid-section. "Well, what do you think?" he whispers in my ear.

Tears and snot streak my face as he grips my jaw and turns back to the camera, "The next time, I will carve up this pretty little face! Time is ticking, boys..."

He goes and turns the television and camera off. I'm expecting another blow to my head like last time, but nothing comes; he must be on his own today. When he rips the tape from my mouth and shoves a pill into it, he glares at me in a warning. He then brings a bottle of water to my lips, and I take a drink. I sputter and cough, but eventually, I get the water down.

"That's a good girl," he then releases my head, "I will be right back with the glue to close those chest wounds."

I wait until he closes the door behind him, pretending to stretch my neck in case someone watches the camera. When I turn my head opposite the camera, I spit out the pill and watch it roll into the room's shadows.

My head is slumped over when I hear him return. Making sure my breathing is slow and steady, I pretend to be passed out from the drug he gave me. I've only got one chance to get this right, or he will probably kill me. I'm not even sure if anyone else is here, but it doesn't matter; I have to try.

"Stupid bitch," I hear him say before there is a sting to my cheek, "Out like a light."

Thank God I'm able to remain still when he slaps me in the face. I just let my head flop around as if I were passed out. I want to smile when I feel him cutting the tape from around my leg. He knicks me with the knife, but again, I don't react.

"What's one more cut?" he says amusedly before going around to remove the tape from my wrists behind the chair.

I have to wait before doing anything because my limbs are so numb that if I try anything, I will fail. So, I suffer through the fact that this fucker lays me on the cold cement floor and strips me down. Surprisingly, he really doesn't touch me inappropriately. He washes the blood from my body and cleans my face before redressing me. He's smarter this time as I feel the draft in my crotch, knowing he's already cut it out for bathroom use.

He doesn't move me right away, but I don't dare try to open my eyes yet. It's not until I hear him moving the bucket from under the chair and hear his footsteps recede that I crack one eye open. The guy doesn't leave the room but does walk over to the door and sets the bucket outside as he grabs another one.

During this time, I notice how close I am to the cart, and hope soars as I start thinking of my next move. I wait until he's cleaned the chair of my blood and then comes to stand over me. Even with my eyes closed, I feel his stare on me, and I wonder what he's thinking about.

"It's a shame. All they have to do is come clean. Tell the truth about what they did, and all of this can be over." I want him to keep talking to see if he reveals anything more, but then his hands lift me under my armpits.

This is my chance. I take a deep breath and then put my weight on my feet. I'm still a bit weak, but I can stand. Startling him, I bring my knee up and slam it into his groin, causing him to let go of me, and when he bends over enough, I head butt him in the nose. The fucker drops like a rock.

"YOU FUCKING LITTLE BITCH!" He grabs both his groin and his nose at the same time as he lies on the floor.

Stumbling over to the tray, I fall into it, knocking it and all its contents onto the floor. I curse and go to crawl over to one of the scalpels when his hand reaches out, gripping my ankle. I struggle to get him to remove his hand, and when he brings his other hand up, I kick out hard, hitting him in the face again.

"I'M GOING TO FUCKING KILL YOU FOR THIS!" he screams.

A sharp pain slices through my hand as it finds one of the scalpels, but I don't care. My adrenaline is on overdrive as I grip the small blade and swing it at my kidnapper. I feel it make contact, and he curses. It's not enough. I lift my hand and bring it down again and again. I am fueled by rage, and I can't stop.

His hand finally grabs my wrist and squeezes, making me drop the scalpel. He backhands me, and I fly backward, hitting the turned-over cart. I crawl further away and see a hunting knife close by. Snatching that up, I return to him and straddle him as he lays on his back.

He bucks his hips, knocking me off, and my head slams into the floor. We both lay there panting, trying to catch our breaths, but he will win if I lay here any longer. I can't let him win.

I kick out once more, getting him in the side of the head, and he grunts, "You're a feisty little bitch! I'm going to have fun killing you now."

"Fuck you! The only one doing any killing will be me!" I swing my hand, embedding the knife into his upper thigh.

"FUCK!!"

I yank my hand back and bring it down again, hitting his gut. I get up onto my knees, and his eyes widen as he watches me grip the handle with both hands and plunge it into his chest.

"You motherfucker! How does it fucking feel? Huh? Who's the little bitch now?" Over and over, I bring the knife down, stabbing him in the chest and stomach. It's overkill, but I can't help it...I can't stop.

It isn't until my adrenaline starts to waver, or maybe it's the blood loss, that I begin to feel a bit woozy. There is a burning in my side, and when I toss the knife aside, I realize that at some point, the fucker stabbed me with the scalpel I was using on him. It protrudes from my side, so I take hold of the handle and yank it out.

"ARGH!" I clench my jaw and then climb off the dead asshole.

Finding some bandages inside the door of the tipped cart, I wrap my side up and then stare at the guy I stabbed to death. I drop to my knees and search his pockets, finding his cell phone tucked away in the front pocket of his jeans. I pull it out and dial the one number that I know will answer my call.

As I wait for them to answer, I close my eyes to the lightheadedness I'm feeling but reopen them when I hear his voice, "Who the fuck is this?" Oakley's growl sounds like heaven.

"Oakley...help..." I've lost too much blood and can't stop myself from slumping over my kidnapper as the phone slips from my hand. I can hear Oakley calling out to me, but I can do nothing as I slip into total darkness.

I'm not sure how long I was out, but I wake up still sprawled across my dead kidnapper. I jerk away and then curse as pain streaks up my side and through my midsection, where the fucker carved me.

I kick the dead asshole, trying to take my anger out on him for carving me up the way he did. I'm grunting and groaning with each kick because it hurts like a bitch. It isn't until I give up and I'm panting that I hear the voice calling my name.

I look around and see that the phone is still lit up. I must not have been out very long. I lunge for the cell phone, "Oakley...is that you? Are you there?"

"I'm here, Kitty Cat! We are on our way!" Oakley says calmly.

"I don't know where I am, though."

"Don't worry about it. Just stay on the line with me, and we will find you. We are in the Jeep now and almost there."

"But how do you know?"

"I'll explain later, baby. Listen to me, Kitty Cat," Oakley pauses briefly, "Can you tell me how many people are there with you?"

"I-I don't k-know. It's just the d-dead guy and me right n-now," I stutter.

"Dead guy?" he questions.

"I k-killed him O-Oakley...I k-killed a man!" It's starting to sink in, and I don't know how to feel about it.

"Good girl...you did good, baby. Don't worry; he can't hurt you anymore." I nod, forgetting that he can't see me over the phone. "So, you don't know if anyone else is there with you?"

"I think he may have been here alone today. There were two yesterday, but he's the only one who came here to make the video," I tell him.

"Video? HE CUT YOU UP AGAIN?" He shouts through the phone so loud that I have to yank it away from my ear.

"Y-Yes. It's okay...it will heal," I tell him.

"Why haven't we received it yet?" he asks.

"He probably wanted to clean me up and glue my cuts first, but then I k-killed him." I can't say the word without stuttering.

"Where did he cut you, and how deep?" he growls.

"He c-carved me this time..." I hear a bunch of expletives and then a brief silence, "Oakley?"

"I'm here," he sighs, "We are two minutes away, Kitty Cat. Stay right where you are, and don't hang up."

"O-Okay...please hurry." I glance at the dead guy and shiver.

"Kitty Cat?"

"Yeah?"

"Who is it that you killed?"

"I don't know. I haven't lifted the mask up," I tell him and inch my way back toward the dead body.

"Can you look? If not, I understand. We can do it when we get there," Oakley says soothingly.

"No, I can do it. Hold on a sec..." I stop and kneel by the kidnapper's head. Taking in a deep breath, I exhale and then lift the mask, "Oh, my fucking God!" I gasp.

THIRTY-SIX

Oakley

It's early morning, and the sun isn't even up when my phone starts ringing. We spent most of the night going through the items in the safe. There are at least a hundred and some years of secrets in that safe, and none of them are dated, so we have to look at every single letter, document, picture, and like sixty-seven years of video to find what we are looking for.

We had barely made a dent when we had to call it quits. So, when my phone begins to ring, I almost toss it across my room, but for some reason, I answer it. When I hear her voice, my body becomes wide awake, and I jump from the bed.

"Kitty Cat?" I don't get an answer, but she hasn't hung up either, so I remain with it to my ear, hoping to hear something.

Fuck! I quickly grab my discarded clothes from the floor and put my cell on speakerphone before tossing it on the bed so I can dress. As soon as I throw my shirt over my head, I pick up the phone and open the app I downloaded a while ago, right after we learned of the threats. As long as she remains on the line, I can track the phone that she is using.

I run from my room, burst through Jett's room first, and wake him up, "We have to go!"

"What the fuck, man?" he moans and throws the pillow over his head.

"Get the fuck up! I've got a location on Catalina!" I bark out.

I've never seen Jett move so fast, and now that I know he's up, I hurry from his room and go through the same thing with Fynn. We are outside and in Jett's Jeep within seven minutes of Kitty Cat calling. I connect my phone to his Jeep's GPS so he can also see the location, and we are off. She's about halfway across town.

"Catalina, are you there? Come on, Kitty Cat, answer me!" I keep calling out to her, and finally, I hear some movement, and I call out again, "CATALINA!"

"Oakley...is that you? Are you there?" Her voice sounds rough, but it's music to my ears.

I tell her that I'm here and that we are only a few minutes out and to stay on the line so we can find her. She seems to be in an old warehouse district that was condemned almost twenty years ago. I don't know why they picked this place because it is one of the most dangerous places in town. The buildings have been known to collapse with the slightest noise.

She does not understand how we can be on our way, but that can all wait. When she tells me about killing a guy, overwhelming pride consumes me, and I feel the need to praise her, "Good girl...you did good, baby. Don't worry; he can't hurt you anymore."

She tells me that she doesn't think anyone else is there, which is good and bad because as much as I want to grab her and get her the fuck out of there, I want this to all be over. I want to end any and all people involved in this shit, especially after her telling me how they carved into her this time.

I wish she hadn't killed the fucker because I would take great pleasure in torturing the person who marred up my Kitty Cat. She belongs to us, and we are the only ones allowed to do shit like that!

She tells me to hurry, but we can't get there any faster, so I try a distraction and ask her to find out who the guy is. I don't want her to if it will traumatize her, but she steps up and does it anyway.

"Oh, my fucking God!"

"What is it? Do you recognize him?"

"Uh, how long before you get here?" she asks.

"We are pulling in now. Why?" I ask, getting worried all over again.

"Just please hurry. You need to see this for yourself."

As we climb from the Jeep, the decrepit warehouse looming before us is dark. It's still early; the sun is just rising as we walk to the front entrance. My eyes roam our surroundings, but I get no indication of being watched, so I continue.

A ping sounds, and Fynn pulls his phone out of his pocket, reading the text that has come through. He stops, "It's Drew," my friend's brow furrows, "Felica is missing."

"What the fuck does he mean, she's missing? Haven't he and Brett been watching her at all times?" I frown, irritated that our own brothers are irresponsible and can't follow simple instructions. It's not how we are trained.

Fynn shrugs, "Who the fuck knows. He said that they took shifts, so they could each get some sleep and that he should be relieved soon. He hasn't seen anyone come and go all night. We will deal with that later; Saint is the one who needs us now." He pockets his phone and puts his game face back on.

Fynn can be a scary motherfucker if you don't know him. Hell, there are times he still scares me, and the same goes for Jett. I'm more of the preppy-looking Lord but make no mistake, I will fuck you up if you deserve it. You could say I have been known as being the dangerous one because of the way I look. No one expects someone like me to make anyone disappear or even beat someone to a pulp like I have, all because of my pretty boy looks.

We reach the door and pull it open, the screech echoing through the early morning. I let Fynn and Jett go in first as I keep watch before entering myself and closing the door. It's dark. The high windows are too dingy with dirt and scum to let in much light, so we pull our phones out to use the flashlights.

"Jesus. Are you sure Lina is here?" Jett questions as he looks around at all the old boxes and crates lying around.

I look at the red dot blinking on my phone and notice that Kitty Cat should be right where we are standing, "There must be a basement because, according to this, she's right here. Kitty Cat is just below us. Let's find the staircase."

We spread out and start opening doors. It doesn't take long before Jett calls out from across the room, "Here!"

Fynn and I take off across the space. Jett waits until we are close before disappearing through the door. The sound of my friend's feet pounding down a metal stairwell echoes through the building. We follow close behind, calling out to our girl. I try not to yell too loud because, as I said, this structure is far from stable, and the slightest sound could cause it to come tumbling down. Being in the basement is not an ideal place to be if that were to occur.

A muffled "Here!" comes from a room down the dark hallway. I can hear water dripping somewhere in the distance, and the pungent odor of a wet, moldy basement consumes my sense of smell. God, I can only imagine the kind of room they have my Kitty Cat in.

We stop in front of a door with a dirty five-gallon bucket just outside. Looking inside the bucket, I immediately realized that this was what Kitty Cat was made to use if she needed the bathroom. The bastards couldn't even take her to an actual toilet! Scowling, I rip the door open and rush in, only to come to a dead stop when I see our girl rocking back and forth with her arms wrapped around her knees.

"Kitty Cat?" I say softly, not wanting to startle her.

Her tearful eyes move from the dead body to mine, "I'm sorry...I'm so sorry!"

Holding my hands out in front of me, I continue to talk softly, "It's okay, Kitty Cat. You have nothing to be sorry for."

"I didn't know...I swear!" Her eyes are wide; she's scared.

"What didn't you know, Little Saint?" Fynn asks from my left side. When I glance at him, I can see his concern, a look I have never seen on my friend's face before.

"Please, don't be mad at me!" she pleads, confusing us as to why she would think we would be, "You can punish me for drugging Jett and leaving, but I swear, I didn't know who they were!"

My heart begins to beat a little faster as my eyes land on the still form lying on the floor beside my Kitty Cat, "Come here, baby." I motion her with my hand, but she doesn't move. She's in some form of shock.

I can't make out who the body belongs to from this angle. All I see is the top of the guy's brown hair, but something in my gut starts to churn, and the three of us step closer. Our movement is slow, so as not to freak Catalina out any more than she is.

Her head snaps back to us, "I swear, I didn't know!" she repeats herself.

Moving around, so we are now standing over the bloody, cut-up body, I'm in total shock. I stare down at the guy, and now I know why my Kitty Cat is freaking out. My brain is in overdrive trying to figure out why I'm looking at what I'm looking at.

"What the fuck?" Fynn growls, making Kitty Cat jump.

I quickly step over the body and pull my Kitty Cat into my arms, "Shh, it's okay. You did good; we're not mad, I promise."

"B-But..."

"No, Lina," Jett scowls, "If you hadn't killed him, we would have." Fynn and I both nod in agreement.

"I don't understand, though. Why was he part of this? It makes no sense." Catalina states.

"I don't know, but you better believe we will find out." I kiss her temple and then stare down at the bloody remains of our very own Frat brother, Brett.

Catalina

They all assure me that they aren't mad at me for killing one of their Frat brothers, so I begin to calm myself. Oakley is holding me tightly, and as soon as I start to relax, the pain in my side begins to burn, and I hiss. I try pulling away, but the Lord refuses to let me go.

"Please, Oakley. You're hurting me..." I pant.

He jerks away from me quickly, and I show him my wounded side. The carving is covered by the bandage I have wrapped around my midsection, but his eyes widen regardless, "What's wrong? How are you hurt?"

"He stabbed me in the side with a scalpel."

"Jesus, Cat! Why didn't you say something sooner?" Oakley's use of my real name tells me that I fucked up.

"I'm sorry. I forgot all about it once I saw his face," I stare back at Brett's body.

"Come on," Oakley helps me to stand, "We need to get you back to the Frat House and have Dr. Halsey come and look at you."

"What about him?" I ask and try to look back, but Oakley doesn't allow it. When I cry out from trying to walk, I hear a curse.

"Fuck this!" I'm scooped up into Fynn's arms and carried from the room.

"I can walk. It will just have to be slow," I say, but they all ignore me.

"I'll call my Uncle Tyler and have him take care of this," Fynn states, "He may want to talk to Little Saint if he wants to call it self-defense. He will only do that if there is no other way of covering it up." He isn't talking to me directly, so I don't say anything more.

I can feel Fynn's body shake as he carries me. Whether it's out of anger or adrenaline, I don't know, so I rest my head in the crook of his neck while wrapping my arms around it, "Thank you for coming for me," I whisper, thinking it's what he needs right now to help calm him.

"Why wouldn't we come for you? We will come every time," he pauses briefly, "It's in the contract, is it not?"

I stiffen in his arms at his words. They sting. Here I thought the Lords were beginning to feel something for me, but that may not be the case at all. They may only be fulfilling the contract we have.

"I can walk now. Please put me down," I tell Fynn, but he again ignores my request. "If all I am is a stupid contract, then fine, you have fulfilled it by coming for me. There is no need to carry me," I growl.

Nobody says anything as we approach Jett's Jeep, and Fynn gets in, keeping me in his arms. In fact, I swear he's holding me against him even tighter. Some of the anguish subsides when I realize something. These bad boys are too prideful to admit their feelings to anyone. I may be wrong, but I genuinely believe that the Lords of Sin like me, even if it's just a little. Smiling smugly, I rest my head on Fynn's shoulder and finally relax; they've got me.

I must have fallen asleep at some point because I wake up in Fynn's bed feeling groggy as hell. When I try to get up, a slight pain stretches across my side, and I yank the covers off to examine my side. My brows furrow when I find myself without a stitch of clothes and a fresh bandage.

My breath hitches when I realize I also have a new one on my midsection. They've seen the carving. Laying back, I close my eyes and swallow hard. I can only imagine what their reaction was. Peeking under the side bandage, I notice the stitches and know Dr. Halsey has already been here. How in the fuck did they stitch me up without me knowing?

Then it hits me. The fuckers drugged me...knocked me out, so they could patch me up. They knew I would fight them, so they wouldn't see the carving, and that's why they did it...assholes. I guess there isn't much I can do about it now.

I climb from the bed and go to Fynn's closet to find something to wear. Grabbing the first shirt hanging up, I throw the dark gray AC/DC T-shirt over my head and let it drop to the middle of my thighs. I love that it smells like him.

Next, I go into his bathroom and put my hair into a messy bun. I need a nice hot shower, but the guys must have cleaned me up while I was out because I don't see a trace of blood on me, and I don't feel as dingy as I did earlier. I search the cabinets for a new toothbrush, and once I find one, I brush mine hastily before spitting and rinsing. My stomach rumbles, crying out to be fed just as I finish. Heading for the door to go down and rummage through the kitchen for something to eat, I come up short when I find the door locked.

"What the fuck?"

I start pounding on the door, yelling to be let out. Once I hear a key being pushed through the lock, I step back. Fynn's face appears when the door opens, and even though my heart skips a beat at seeing his gorgeous face, I glare at him. All he does is stand there and smirk at me.

"Why am I locked in here?" I bark out at the Lord.

He crosses his arms and leans against the door frame, "Well, for starters, you can't leave if the door is locked..."

"This is bullshit Fynn, and you know it! I won't leave again, not until this is all settled!" I go to shove past him, but the smirk leaves his face and is replaced with irritation as he grabs me by my throat and pushes me back into the room. Slamming the door closed, he continues to walk forward until my back is against the bathroom door.

"I'm only going to say this once, Little Saint, so listen well," his fingers tighten a little more around my neck, but it's not cutting off my air. The only thing it's doing is making me wet, "We will keep you locked up here for as long as we want. You belong to us, and since you cannot be trusted, the doors will remain locked."

"You can't keep me prisoner, Fynn," I croak, even though I know they can. It's in the stupid contract. They can do whatever they want in order to keep me safe...I signed off on it.

A grin appears on his face once again, but it's not one I like, "Wanna bet, Little Saint?" He steps in closer, "We can do whatever the fuck we want," he glances down toward my stomach, "You're the Whore of Sin and the property of the Lords, or have you forgotten?"

I deflate at his words. How dare he use the carving against me! "I never asked for this, Fynn," I say barely above a whisper, "I didn't ask him to carve me up..."

"Didn't you, though?" He raises his brow, "The moment you drugged Jett and snuck off, you asked for it, Little Saint. We have been too lenient with you. We take our Lord of Sin status and our contract seriously, but we let a nice fuckable pussy distract us from what we were supposed to be doing."

"So, what now? You won't touch me anymore?" I ask, hoping that isn't the case because I'm addicted to all their cocks, the sex is phenomenal, and it would be a shame never to have it again.

Fynn's smile turns wicked, "I don't think you understand what it means to be the Lord's property, Saint." He leans in until his whole body is against mine, "We will keep you...we will restrain you...we will degrade and humiliate you...we may even make you bleed for us...and yes, we will fuck the ever-loving shit out of this beautiful cunt of yours. Your pleasure depends on how good you can be for us, but make no mistake," he runs his other hand up my thigh, not stopping until he's cupping my pussy, his wicked smile broadening because he can feel how wet his words have made me, "We will always take our pleasure from you."

The moment I whimper at his touch and thrust my hips into his hand, he drops both hands and steps away. I close my eyes and just breathe, trying to get my body under control. I don't know what I was thinking. I'm in no condition to have sex right now, and it's evident that Fynn isn't going to give it to me. They may be happy to have me back, but they are still pissed that I left. I can see that my actions have pushed us back to the beginning, to where the Lords were real assholes.

I squeeze my thighs together at that thought. What is it about the Lords of Sin taking what they want that has my body in constant arousal? I never thought I'd like it if my rights were taken away, but then again, I had never known anyone like the Sinners of Helshire.

THIRTY-SEVEN

Fynn

"What the fuck is Brett's motive in all of this?" I ask Oak and Jett as we sit around in Oakey's room.

As soon as we returned to the Frat House, Halsey showed up shortly afterward and gave Little Saint a shot to knock her out for a bit before stitching her up. Seeing the carving on her stomach sent all three of us into a rage. That son of a bitch is lucky his ass is already dead because he wouldn't like what we would do to him.

"I think he may have been the bitch behind it all because he definitely wasn't the brains," Jett states, "Now that they've lost their partner, they will have two options…"

Oakley finishes what our friend is thinking, "Either give up their plan for revenge or get pissed and get careless."

"Exactly," Jett nods.

"Let's hope it's the latter. There has got to be some kind of connection between Brett and his partner, though." I stare at my two best friends, "I'll say one thing, it now makes sense how the stalker knew that Saint was the sacrifice. He also knew she was here the night of the fire at the Sorority House, so that was just a warning."

"But what about the rest?" Jett asks, "That first night we followed her when your bike was vandalized?"

I shrug, "He knew when she left but didn't realize we would be following her. He made it back before we did and fucked my Harley up. Also," I point out, "he was already watching the dorms the night Saint was taken because Oakley put him on that watch with Drew, so he saw her being dropped off and nabbed her."

"At this point, it's all circumstantial because we don't know exactly what happened," Oakley states, "How did he have chloroform on him? I can only assume from the video feed that he covered her mouth with a cloth doused with it."

"Wait a minute! The text that I got from Drew earlier," I forgot all about it, "Felicia is missing! So, either that chloroform was meant for her before Saint presented herself, or we still don't know why Brett had it, and Felicia has disappeared because her partner is dead."

Banging down the hall catches our attention, and I grin, "The little hell cat has woken." I get up and head for the door, "Keep brainstorming while I quiet her down."

"Don't fuck her; she needs to rest," Oakley calls out.

I turn and glare at my friend, "I may be a dick, but I know when not to fuck an injured female."

I unlock the door to my room where Little Saint has been resting and open it only to meet a pissed-off Saint. Smiling, I wait to see what she wants. You see, my fellow Lords and I have concluded that we have been too lenient on our girl. We need her safe, and we need her to trust us. When we shirk our duties all because we all are starting to fall for the one that's supposed to be forbidden to us, she sees it as if she can do whatever the fuck she wants.

We cannot have that.

Yeah, I tell her how it will be from here on out and that we will fulfill our part of the contract without any distractions. Someone out there still wants to hurt Little Saint, well, all of us, but they have their eye on her first and foremost, so we will protect her no matter the cost.

After getting her some food and giving her the pain pills Halsey left, I return to Oakley's room. The pills should knock her out again once they kick in. I know she doesn't like drugs, but she needs to heal, and that won't happen if she doesn't allow herself to rest. If she won't take care of herself, then we will.

"Damn, took you long enough," Jett chuckles, looking up when I walk back into the room.

"She was pissed but also hungry. Once I explained to her that we will be following the rules of the contract and reminded her just how much she belongs to us, I fed her," I stop what Jett is about to say, "I fed her real food, perv!" I roll my eyes and smirk, "I gave her the pain pills, so she should be out for a few hours at least."

"Well, while you were fucking around," Oakley says jokingly, "I think we are close to finding the secrets of our father's time here."

"Why do you say that?" I pick up an old letter that looks older than dirt. Our father's graduated in ninety-nine...that's twenty-four years ago.

"I figured if we start looking through the newer-looking stuff, we will find it faster," Oakley states.

"I thought that's what we were doing last night?" I ask, confused.

"Uh, yeah, well, there was another compartment to the safe, and I found a bunch of the newer stuff in there," Jett says sheepishly.

"I thought you got everything out the first time?" I growl. We wasted so much time last night going through shit as old as my grandfather's time. Hell, we even found shit from our great-grandfather's time here!

"Yeah, that's my bad," he snickers, and my hand comes up to slap him on the back side of his head, "Hey, fucker! I'm sorry!"

"Just shut the fuck up and start looking," I smirk.

Thirty minutes in, we are interrupted once again by yelling coming from downstairs, "What the fuck?" I say and jump to my feet; Oakley and Jett follow suit.

We jog down the steps, and as we approach the second landing, a very pissed-off Dani comes at us, "WHERE IS SHE? WHAT HAVE YOU DONE WITH MY BEST FRIEND?" Her face is red, and it's quite amusing seeing such a small girl come at three very fit guys.

I cross my arms and take a stance in front of the door to the third floor. I put on my blank face even though all I want to do is laugh. Oakley approaches the petite hell cat while Jett leans against a nearby wall looking bored.

"Calm the fuck down, woman!" Oakley growls at her, "You don't come up in our House and start demanding shit!"

"Where is Cat? That's all I want to know! I haven't been able to get a hold of her in days, and her father won't tell me shit! Now, either you assholes are going to tell me what's going on and where my friend is, or I will go to the police and file a missing person report. I will make sure to name you three as suspects!"

Oakley steps into Dani's space and glares down at her, "Who do you think you are, coming in here and threatening us? We are doing what we can to protect your friend, so she will not leave here until we say so!"

"Whoa, what's going on here?" Sean asks as he tops the steps.

"Control your fucking toy, Sean, or else I will!" I watch my friend take another step toward the female, making her have to step back.

"I'm not afraid of you, Harris, or any of you Lords for that matter!" The little spitfire turns her attention to me, and I step forward, bringing myself to my full height while Sean tries pulling Dani back.

"You better stop while you're ahead, little girl. Just because you're Cat's friend does not mean you are untouchable." I stand beside Oakley, and I see Jett stand on his other side, "Threaten us again, and you will see why nobody fucks with us." I grit my teeth.

"I will go to the police!" She huffs and crosses her arms.

I chuckle and bend down, so I'm face to face with the little one, "My uncle *is* the police, so go right ahead. You've forgotten that we run this fucking town. It's not just Helshire's campus. Our families make this town, so how about you go back to your dorm and shut the fuck up. Catalina will call you when WE say she can call you."

"So, she is here! Why can't I see her now?" The female just won't stop.

I grab her upper arm and drag her toward the stairs, "For Christ's sake! If it will shut you the fuck up and get you to leave, I will show you your fucking BFF!" I yank her upstairs and drag her to my room. Unlocking the door, I open it and find my Little Saint passed out, just like

I knew I would, "She is on painkillers right now, so as soon as she's better, I'm sure she will call you." I pull her back downstairs and shove her toward Sean, "Get her the fuck out of our sight!"

"Wait!" She calls out, and I roll my eyes, "Why is she on painkillers? Was she hurt?"

"That's usually what happens when stalkers get a hold of their victims," Jett states snidely.

She gasps, "Her stalker finally got to her? What did they do?"

"He stabbed her with a fucking scalpel...that's what he did!" I scowl.

"He? Did you see him then? Who is it?" What the fuck is up with all the questions, sheesh?

"Don't fucking worry about it. Our girl took care of him on her own," Oakley states proudly, "Now, leave before we call the police on you for trespassing!" I grunt in agreement before we all three turn and head back upstairs, making sure to lock the door behind us.

THIRTY-EIGHT

Catalina

When I next wake up, I find myself cocooned in warmth from the shelter of large arms. I'm lying on my uninjured side as, who I presume to be Fynn, spoons me from behind. My mouth is parched, but Fynn's arms tighten automatically when I try to free myself.

I stretch my arm toward the bedside table where a water bottle sits, but it's just out of my reach. Again, I attempt to remove the large arms, but I'm pulled backward this time. Finally, I've had enough, and I have no choice but to wake Fynn up because I now have to use the bathroom.

"Fynn, let me go." When there is no response from him, I say it louder, "Fynn, let me up!" I shove at him at the same time, and he jerks awake.

"What's wrong?" He nuzzles my neck, and as much as I would love to stay like this with him, I need up.

"I need to use the bathroom, and I'm thirsty as fuck," I tell him.

I don't think he realizes our position right away because the moment I'm done talking, he jolts and sits up, "Uh, do you need any help with anything?"

"No. I just needed you to let me go." I get up and hurry into the bathroom to relieve myself.

My side is throbbing, but I don't want more pain pills, so I search the medicine cabinet until I find some ibuprofen. Taking a few from the bottle, I head back to the bedroom. Fynn is now sitting on the edge of the bed staring at what; I'm not sure because his back is to me.

I keep my eyes on him as I take the medicine. Our conversation from earlier runs through my head, and I get a little perturbed. His words made me wet earlier, or maybe it was how he delivered them, but now that I'm thinking over everything he said to me, I feel like I have to say something.

"I know that I fucked up by leaving, Fynn, but I didn't ask for Brett to carve me up or cut me. I could place blame with you three if you really want to place blame because had you not treated me like your whore, he probably wouldn't have carved these words into me. We both know that none of us is to blame, though. The only blame would be against our fathers for putting us in this position to begin with."

When he doesn't say anything, it fuels the anger that is only simmering at the moment, and I walk over to the other side of the bed to stand in front of him. He's just staring at the wall, a blank look on his face. His brows furrow before looking at me.

"I shouldn't have said it the way I did; it's not what I meant, but the rest of it...about being our property? I meant every word. You belong to us now, Little Saint. We won't give you up until we are ready, if we ever are ready." The last part comes out a bit softer than the rest.

"I'm getting used to that idea, Fynn, but..."

"No, you still don't get it. When I said that we may make you bleed for us, I meant it. We can and will make you bleed, but we will also bleed for you. We may be demanding assholes and push you past your limits, but you must know you aren't just some warm pussy for us."

I cock my brow and skeptically ask, "Really?"

He yanks me until I stand between his spread legs, saying, "This is hard for me, Saint. I've never been one to express my feelings to a female, they were only warm cunts to use for my own gratification, but you're not. You have drawn the three of us in from the get-go. We knew you were special; you're one of us and meant to be ours."

"What about the contract then?" I question, not understanding why it's in place if they believe all that Fynn is telling me.

A slow smirk grows on his lips, "That was to get you in our grasp. To show you what we can do for you, show how much you would love being owned by us. Make no mistake, Little Saint, the contract still stands because, in the end, we are still dicks, and we will continue to show you just how much you love being our little slut."

Fuck me. Why is it these Lords get me so worked up all the time? I should be pissed at Fynn still, not forgiving him for what he said earlier, but instead, I drop to my knees and stare up into his brown orbs.

"Are you sure you want to be down there, Little Saint?" I can hear the want behind his growly voice, solidifying my decision.

My only answer for him is to pull his semi-hard cock from his boxer briefs and stroke him. As soon as I feel him grow until he's completely hard and see the bead of precum form at the tip, I run my lips over him, coating them with it.

Fynn's hand comes up and entangles itself in my hair, then yanks my head back. His mouth crashes against mine for another earth-shattering kiss. For someone who doesn't like to kiss, I'd say he's the best out of them all, even though they all have their own talents.

He devours my mouth and his essence from my lips, moaning as he does so. This alone turns me on, and I continue to stroke him. I want so badly to impale myself on him, but I know I'm in no condition for that, so I will just have to be happy with pleasing him instead.

He breaks away, "Open that dirty little mouth, Saint."

I do so and stick my tongue out as well, bringing a smile to the Lord's face before he lowers my head to make me take him deep into my mouth. He doesn't care that he's choking me or that I'm drooling all over him as he holds me down. He's showing me his dominance, telling me I'm his to do with as he pleases, and I'm all for it.

My hands grip just above his knees as he gives little thrusts deep into my throat, "Reach down and finger fuck yourself if you want to come, Little Saint. We won't be touching you for another few days, not until Doc clears you, so you will have to do it yourself. Don't think you can do it whenever either. You play with that cunt when we tell you, understand?"

I try to nod.

"Good girl." He pulls out, letting me take a few more breaths before going back and fucking my throat again. We do this for a few minutes, and when I feel him getting a little rougher, he says, "You better come, Saint, because I'm about to feed you a heaping load, and once I'm done, so are you."

I whimper and begin rubbing my clit harder and faster. I wish I had a toy; they always get me off faster than my hand does. Thankfully, Fynn reaches down and tweaks my nipple, which helps send me over the edge. The moment I feel the pain he inflicts as he squeezes my nipple hard, I come, and so does he as I scream around his cock.

I'm alone in Fynn's bed when I wake again. It's morning now, a new day to be thankful I'm still alive. I wonder if the guys will let me out of the room today, or will they keep me prisoner. I meant what I said, I will not leave again without one of them.

I take my time using the bathroom and getting dressed before I even try opening the door. When I can no longer procrastinate, I stand before the door and slowly place my hand on the knob. Taking a deep breath, I twist my wrist, and surprisingly, the knob turns with it.

Opening the door slowly, I pray that it doesn't squeak. Why? I don't want them knowing I'm awake yet. When it opens enough for me to slip through without making a noise, I do. I creep across the hall toward Oakley's room because they usually gather in his room for some reason.

I can smell the burning of their favorite smoke as I get closer and see that the door is cracked open. I flatten myself against the wall, just wanting to know what they are discussing before I make myself known. I'm not above eavesdropping when it comes to these Sinners. Maybe I wouldn't have to stoop so low if they were more open with me.

"Why haven't we fucking found it yet?" I hear Oakley curse.

"Calm down; we still have a few more to go through yet," Jett's voice carries over to me, "You know how it goes; it's probably going to be the last one we look at."

"We have her back, so we have time to find it, Oak. Relax a little," Fynn says to his friend, "I doubt our Little Saint will make the mistake of leaving again."

There is a scoff, and Oakley speaks once again, "Hopefully, she listens to everything you told her because I will tie Kitty Cat to my fucking bed if I have to in order to keep her safe."

I should be pissed, but instead, my body floods with warmth at the emotion I hear behind his words. The Lords of Sin are not weak and don't put themselves out there, either. If, by what I've gathered about their home lives, love is pretty much non-existent, why would they feel the need to want it themselves? Deep down, they are afraid of getting hurt, I bet.

"Lovely Lina needs to be shown her place with us," Jett starts in, "I don't like keeping her in the dark, and I won't, not about everything, but until she figures out what we need her to be for us, we don't have any other options."

"Yeah, well, let's hope it doesn't take Kitty Cat that long to figure it out," Oakley sighs.

"After how she took care of Brett, I think she is well on her way to getting where we need her to be." This comes from Fynn as he exhales.

Now is as good a time as any to show myself. I push the door open and cross my arms, "You know, I will learn much faster if you just tell me what you want. What do I need to be for the Lords of Sin?"

"Kitty Cat..."

"No, I never wanted to be the Lady of Sin, but it's apparent that it's what my future is regardless. So, how about you tell me what is expected of me, and we can stop dancing around until I figure it out on my own!"

"It's not nice to eavesdrop, Little Saint."

"So fucking punish me. It's not like you really need a reason to do just that anyway." I glance around the room, looking at each Lord, "So, what will it be?"

"Lina, you don't understand..."

"You're right...I don't understand because you assholes won't explain it to me!" I walk over to Fynn and snatch the joint from his fingers, "You want to get me high," I take a drag, "So be it," I hand it back to the Lord as I exhale. "You want me to strip," I pull the shirt over my head and yank my shorts down, "Fine! You want me on my knees...I can do that too!" I drop to my knees and glare at each one of them. "I will do whatever it is you want me to do...what you need me to do. Just stop keeping me in the fucking dark about everything!"

All three Lords remain silent, staring at me as if I've gone crazy. Maybe I have. I'm crazy about each of them, but I will keep that to myself a little longer. I know their feelings for me are changing, and they don't want to admit it, so I won't admit mine just yet. It's what they want, me falling for them, and that is one thing that I'm not willing to give them until it's the right time.

"Now that," Oakley grins, "is the way the Lady of Sin is supposed to act."

THIRTY-NINE

Jett

My Lovely Lina looks like a fucking Goddess, naked and on her knees before us. The only thing ruining the moment are the bandages covering her wounds. The three of us have already talked about it and will be paying to have the *Whore of Sin* removed. As for the rest, it's yet to be decided. We like what it says but hate how it was put there, so we will discuss it further with Lina.

"Get up, Lina," I tell her as I rest back on the loveseat I've taken over.

She only glares at me, challenging me. I set aside the letter that I'm holding in my hand and stand. Slowly, I walk over to where she kneels on the floor and gently caress her cheek. My thumb grazes her bottom lip softly before I move my hand to the back of her head and grab hold of her hair. I don't yank on it, not yet anyway.

"Is this what you really want, Lovely? To kneel before us whenever you are in the same room as us? That can be arranged, but we decide when you are to kneel." I let my eyes wander down to her bare chest and lick my lips, "Now is not the time to kneel before us because when we have you kneel, you will know that we are about to use that filthy mouth of yours, and then some."

"Oh, her mouth works perfectly fine," Fynn chuckles, "Go ahead and test it out." I cock my brow at my friend in askance, and he shrugs, "She was a slut for my cock in the wee morning hours. Little Saint devoured my cock like it was her last meal, didn't you?"

A whimper comes from our girl, but I don't know if it's from my friend's words or the fact that my hand has tightened in her hair, "As much as I would love to watch you choke on my cock right now, we have work to do." I pull up on her hair, so she stands up, and I grip her jaw firmly, "Put your clothes back on and join me on the loveseat if you want to participate in what we are doing." Her eyes light up, and I can't help but lower my lips to hers.

She opens her mouth willingly, and what I had planned to be a simple kiss turns into a heated make-out session. Her hands come up and fist my shirt as our tongues dance together. Finally, once my dick is harder than a fucking rock, I pull free and stare into her lust-filled eyes.

"Be a good girl and get dressed," I let her hair go abruptly and sit back down as I watch her pick up her clothing and get dressed.

"I'd rather watch her walk around naked..." Fynn grins.

Oakley is sitting back, just watching the whole interaction. His jaw is tight, and I know that, more than anything, he wants his Kitty Cat. We are all in the same boat, wanting something more than anything but not being able to have it, at least not until she is healed. Yeah, Lina can suck us off, but that is never enough with her. We need to be inside her in order to feel truly satisfied.

"Can we stop fucking around, now?" Oakley asks and then turns to Lina, "This was a bold step, coming in here like you did. A Lady needs to command the room when she enters it, and you definitely did Kitty Cat. You don't need us to teach you how to be our Lady because you are learning quickly all on your own."

Lina smiles smugly, but before she can get too cocky, I feel I need to remind her of one thing, "Even though we are proud of you for coming in here the way you did, in the future, if you come in like that and talk to us that way again, you will be punished. Always show your Lords respect, Lovely. Trust me, you will always be rewarded for doing so." I wink at her, then hold my arm out for her to join me as soon as she's dressed.

"So these are all the secrets of the past Lords?" Lina asks astonishingly, "Should I be looking at them since I'm not a Lord?"

The fact that she even asks this question tells me just how much she's learned so far, and I smirk, "Probably not, but we won't tell if you don't tell," I say and kiss her shoulder.

She still sits on my lap as we read through the letters and look at the pictures. We laugh at the funny ones, and she tears up at some of the sad ones, but I straighten up when I come to one that is a bit suspicious. A Polaroid picture is hidden inside the letter.

"What the fuck is this? I may have found something, guys." I skim the contents of the letter and then examine the photo.

The woman in it is a dark-haired beauty with a bit of familiarity. If it wasn't for the gag over her mouth and the red, swollen eyes from crying, we might be able to figure out who she was. It's a close-up, showing off her breasts as well. Her arms are out to the sides, and what looks like part of a hand is wrapped around one of her upper arms, and another grips her neck.

"Jesus, is this what I think it is?" I pass the Polaroid to Oakley as I begin to read the letter.

It wasn't supposed to happen that way. No crime was supposed to be committed during our initiation last year...it's in the rules. The Lords were not ones for following rules, though. Not the last ones, anyway. We all took oaths beforehand, making it hard to be able to say anything to anyone. If the four of us were to be the next Lords of Sin, we had to partake in the initiation.

We were told she was a willing participant, playing the role of a victim. I was the luckier one that night, being instructed to record the initiation and take photos. My three best friends were made to partake in it physically.

We knew the Saint very well since she came over often with the other Saints. She wasn't like the others, though. She was indeed a Saint among Saints. That's why it was hard to believe when we were told she was willing. You never question the Lords of Sin, though.

From the start, I knew it was wrong, and I did nothing to stop it, so I am just as guilty as the rest. I thought I was going to be sick that night; just writing this letter is causing my stomach to churn. The things that took place in the basement last year should never have happened, but they did, and now we all must live with it, especially after today's news.

The senior Saint brought to the basement by her friend that fateful night a year ago has taken her own life. I always wondered what happened to her after graduation; she seemed to have disappeared. But then again, wouldn't you if you were held down and gang raped by the Lords of Sin? Nothing about it was consensual; the fear in her eyes told me as much.

I will live with this sin for the rest of my life because, as a Lord myself now, I am bound to the rules of the Lords. All secrets must remain just that, secret.

God forgive us...

D.S.

"Is that my father's letter?" Lina asks as she takes the paper from my hands and skims it once again.

"Yeah, I think so," I tell her as I glance at Oak and Fynn to see their reactions.

"My father partook in a rape?" My Lovely Lina's voice is just above a whisper.

"He didn't know, Lina. Not at first, anyway, and you should know by now that you don't say no to a Lord. It's frowned upon if a Sinner is chosen to be initiated to be a Lord of Sin and turns it down," I explain to her.

"We need to find this video that he recorded," Oakley states, turning my attention to him.

"Yeah, we do," I look at the pile of tapes and see that there are only four left, "It's got to be on one of those tapes. Let's get to it."

A friend of mine loaned us his converter, so we could transfer all the old stuff to digital. If any of the past Lords knew what we were doing, we would be in deep shit. Thankfully, none of the rooms up on the third floor have cameras that weren't put in by us. It's mandatory for the rest of the house, but as the Lords, we get to have our privacy.

"Why don't you grab something to eat downstairs, Kitty Cat," Oakley states casually. I know what he's doing, and so does Lina.

"Like hell, I'm leaving!" She glares at my friend.

I sigh, "Lina, watch your tone," I warn, "You cannot see what's on these other videos because you are not a Lord. You're not supposed to see any of this, so be thankful. Once we find the video your father recorded, we will share it with you, but only that one video."

Studying me for a moment, she then rolls her eyes, "Fine..."

I slap her ass as she stands, making sure I don't jar her side too badly, "That's a good girl. We will call you back in when we find it." She doesn't argue anymore as she walks to the door. Turning, she stares back at all three of us one last time before walking out.

Oakley

"It's not here!" I throw the last video across the room, watching it smash into pieces when it hits the wall. It's not that it was anything important, and we already transferred it to digital, "Where the fuck is it?"

"Mr. Scott's note said that the evidence was here, and the letter said it was recorded..." Jett's irritation is just as strong as my own.

"Someone got to it first," Fynn concludes, "But how did they know which one it was?"

"They didn't," I state, "Because it was never put into the safe. That's the only explanation that I can come up with."

"But everything was put into that safe," Jett is still in disbelief as he shakes his head.

"Maybe not. Remember what the letter said, it was against the rules to commit a crime during initiation, so I think whoever the Lords were at that time didn't want the evidence to be found...ever."

"You think they destroyed it?" Jett asks me.

"No," Fynn scoffs, "If they were sick enough to rape a female for an initiation, they were sick enough to keep that video for their spank bank."

"One of those Lords has the video..." my voice trails off.

"Do you think our fathers will tell us who the Lords were?" Jett asks but already knows the answer.

"We don't have to ask. Their pictures are in the Lord's Chamber, remember?" I remind him.

"Fuck," Fynn stands up, "I've forgotten all about that room. I haven't been there since I was shown it my Freshman year."

"Me neither," Jett chuckles.

"Well, what are we waiting for?" I stand as well, and it's almost like the house is on fire as we race down to the first floor and enter the room.

We already know where our father's group plaque is located on the wall, and since they go in order by the year, the plaque we need hangs just beside theirs. Stopping in front of the only plaque that matters, we study the three Lords of that year. Kevin Douglas, Bradley Simmons, and Travis Gifford.

What we never noticed the first time we were in this room two years ago is that the Lord's Lady is also in the picture with them. I glance over at our father's plaque, and Ashlee Scott stands right between Mr. Scott and my father; go figure.

Looking back at the one of importance now, the Lady of Sin looks very familiar, and I don't need to look at the name below it to know that it's Julia Howard, Felicia's mother. She seems cozy with Kevin Douglas, as though they are an item.

"Is that my mom and dad?"

All three of us whip around at Kitty Cat's voice. She's holding a bowl with Ramen Noodles in it as she stares at the plaques hanging on the wall. I take a few steps and stand before her.

"You shouldn't be in here, Kitty Cat." I'm not mad that she's in here; more like worried. I take her arm and pull her toward the door, "There are cameras in this room, and nobody but Sinners is allowed in here."

"I'm sorry. I was walking by and saw the door open. When I peeked inside and saw you three inside, I came in." She explains, but she doesn't sound all that sorry. If anything, she sounds irritated, and I grin inwardly.

I stop outside the door and turn toward her, brushing a straggling strand of her hair behind her ear, "Why don't you take your food up to my room, and we will be there in a minute."

"Oakley..."

"Kitty Cat," I say her name in warning, "There are some things that we cannot tell you and some places where you cannot go, "Rules are rules.""

Her lips kick up in a devilish grin, "Rules are made to be broken. I thought we established that when we started fucking."

I laugh, "As true as that may be, past Lords have made it hard to break some rules, so be a good girl and go to my room." I tip her chin and kiss her lips firmly before letting her go and stepping away.

"Fine, but you're going to owe me later...stab wound or not...I want a reward." She looks over her shoulder at me and grins.

Readjusting myself, I join my friends in the Lord's Chamber again, "Damn woman..."

Fynn chuckles, "You too, huh?"

"I don't know what you're talking about," I scowl.

"Just fucking admit it, Oak. You are falling for her just as much as we are." He grins, and I roll my eyes.

"Whatever. It doesn't mean we have to have a fucking pajama party and talk all about our crushes." I study Kevin's face on the plaque, but my mind is on Catalina Scott.

"We are well past the crush phase, my friend," Jett snickers and slaps me on the back.

"Can we just get back to why we are here?" The last thing I need is to admit to feelings I don't know how to deal with.

"Fine, but we will need to discuss it at some point, Oak," Jett states, and I sigh because I know that my friends are right. We need to talk this shit out, but I'm not ready for that talk yet.

"What were you guys doing in that room? I thought you were watching the videos," my Kitty Cat starts in as soon as we walk back into the room.

"The video we were looking for isn't among all these others. It's missing," I tell her.

"So, what now?" she scoops a mouthful of noodles into her mouth.

"We went down to see who the Lords were the year before our fathers..." I say, but then Jett cuts me off.

"Wait a minute...those names on the plaque..." I watch his eyes focus on a nearby wall as he thinks, "I've seen them before."

"Where at? Are you sure they were the same names?" I ask.

"Yes! When we were in Mr. Scott's office, I found the envelope with the note about the Lord's safe under some files that I thought were insignificant at the time."

"Which files were those?" Fynn asks this time.

"Douglas, Simmons, and Gifford. Those were the files of the Lords from the year before...damn it! Why didn't I think to look through them?" my friend curses.

"Calm down! How were you to know that we would need them?" I question.

"They were sitting on top of the envelope meant for us!" Jett's not going to go easy on himself over this. He gets so pissed when he fucks up, even if it's not his fault.

"I can get them," Kitty Cat states as she sets aside her food.

"Kitty Cat, you don't..."

"No, let me do this! After all, it's my father's office, so it's no big deal," she shrugs.

I'm sitting in the chair at my desk, and I swivel it around to face her, "Come here, Kitty Cat."

The way she licks her fucking lips before standing and walking over to me has my cock stirring. Opening my legs, she stands between them and gazes down at me. I don't say anything as I lift her shirt past the bandages and pull off the one over her stab wound, so I can examine it.

"Does it still hurt?" I ask.

"Oakley, what does this have to do with me getting the files? You're changing the subject," her gaze turns into a glare, and I raise my brow.

"My concern for your wound is not me changing the subject, Kitty Cat. I'm considering your suggestion and trying to determine if it will be too dangerous for you." I cover the wound and pull off the other bandage. The carving is scabbed over, and I lightly trace the second part of it with my finger. I probably shouldn't, but we will disinfect it when we clean it and change the bandage, "You keep forgetting who you belong to, Kitty Cat."

I hear her intake of breath at my words, and when I look up at her, she stares back at me with eyes full of want. When I reach the end of the word *property*, I keep going, dipping my hand into her shorts. I never take my eyes off hers as I slide my hand further down until I feel the wetness that pools between her thighs.

"Why so wet, Kitty Cat?"

"Oakley..." she moans.

"Tell me..."

"Mm..." her hips thrust against my hand as I rub my middle finger back and forth between her slippery folds.

Her whimper when I pull my hand away makes me grin, and I yank down her shorts, "Sit your ass on the edge of my desk, Kitty Cat."

She doesn't move but just stares at me.

"Now..." I say in a stern voice that has no room for argument.

Lifting herself up to sit on the edge, I scoot my chair in, and she automatically places each foot on an arm of the chair, so she's spread open for me to feast my eyes on her gorgeous cunt.

"Jett, Fynn..."

There is no need to tell them what I want them to do. They just do it, going to the other side of the desk and clearing items away before pulling Kitty Cat down to lie on her back. They hold her down as I begin kissing up her thighs.

"You are being rewarded, Kitty Cat, just like you wanted, but I want you to tell us if it gets to be too much or if we are hurting your wounds in any way."

"Yes, Oakley..." she says breathlessly.

"This is a reward, but you should know that we are going to use your dirty little mouth pretty well," I inform her, so she has no expectations of this being all about her because it's not.

"I understand..."

"Good girl."

I know we shouldn't, but it's been too long, and I need to touch her... to taste her. I'm sure the others feel the same way, even if Fynn got his rocks off already. Catalina is our stress inducer; more importantly, she's our stress reliever. There's so much to do if we are to keep her safe, but we need this, and deep down, Kitty Cat does too.

FORTY

Catalina

Good God, the things these Sinners do to me...the way they make me *feel* every time they touch me. I may be going to hell from just my thoughts on what I want them to do to my body, but at least I won't be going alone...they will be right there beside me.

Oakley's head is buried between my thighs as his tongue does things that would even make the devil shy away. He's got the tongue of a serpent, nice and long, flicking up and down viciously. He holds my hips down when I try to grind against his mouth, making me take everything he does to me.

Jett and Fynn are pinning me down by my arms, not allowing me to move at all. I'm so turned on, but every time I feel as though I'm about to come all over the Lord's face, he pulls away until my body comes down from the high, and then he picks back up.

I look into Jett's eyes as he gazes down at me, and I bite my lip. My eyes wander to his crotch, licking my lips as if I'm staring at my next meal, "Does that slutty little mouth want to be filled?" he asks.

I nod, "Yes," I pant.

Oakley has pulled away once again, and I hear clinking before coldness rubs against my clit. I try to look down, but Fynn holds my head in place with one hand while Jett unzips his pants with his own free hand. My mouth is then filled with Ink Boy's girth just as the icy coldness gets pushed into my pussy. That's when I realize that Oakley is using the ice cubes from the glass of water I brought in with me.

"Damn, your cunt is so hot, it's melting these cubes instantly, Kitty Cat," Oakley chuckles and pushes another inside me before using his mouth again.

Fynn pulls my shirt up, exposing my bare breasts before his mouth covers a nipple, and I moan. My three Lords are here, worshipping my body, and all I can do is crave more of it. With all three touching me in some sexual way, I can't hold it in any longer, and before Oakley can stop it, I come, crying out around Jett's cock.

"Fuck, Kitty Cat...you taste so good!" Oakley groans as he laps up the cum that now drips with the water from the melted cubes.

Jett grips my hair, "Get ready to take mine, Lina. I have a feeling it's going to be a big load," he jerks a couple of times before shoving all the way into my throat and releasing his seed, "Oh fuck..."

Meanwhile, Fynn devours my breasts, waiting patiently for Jett to finish. No sooner does Jett pull out than he turns my head toward his best friend, whose cock is already out and waiting, "Suck it, Saint. Remind me how filthy that fucking mouth is."

Jett takes Fynn's place and starts playing with my breasts while Oakley still uses his mouth, but it's not enough. I pull off Fynn's cock, earning me an annoyed grunt, and I look down between my thighs, "Fuck me..."

Oakley stops and stares at me, "Kitty Cat, I don't know if that's a good idea, with your wound and all..."

"I'm fine, but I'll be better when I have your cock pounding into me," I grit my teeth because I need him so badly...I want to be filled by Oakley's cock.

"I always knew that mouth of yours would get you into trouble one day, Kitty Cat. Remember that you asked for this..." Oakley stands and unzips his pants. Lining his cock up to my entrance, he gazes into my eyes as he pushes into me, "Fuck...you feel so good, Kitty Cat."

"Oakley..." I start to tell him how I want it, but he has other plans.

"Shut her the fuck up, Fynn," Oakley grins at me and winks.

"My pleasure," Fynn states as he thrusts back into my mouth.

Oakley doesn't fuck me hard and fast but slow and deep... making me realize that it feels just as good as being pounded into. I know he's trying to be careful of my wound, something I should be doing myself, but I lose all rationality when I'm with these Sinners.

The Lords of Sin are my Kryptonite and my choice of drug. Fynn always wants me to smoke with them, but if he only knew how high I am every time I'm around them, I'm sure he wouldn't push me so much. I'm weak around them, unable to say no, but only because I want it just as bad as they do.

"I'm going to come inside you, Kitty Cat," I look at him the best I can while Fynn's cock is jammed down my throat and see him sucking his thumb before bringing it to my clit, "My cum is going to paint a gorgeous masterpiece inside this beautiful cunt of yours. Tell me no if you don't want it," he smirks, knowing the predicament I'm in.

I wouldn't say no even if I didn't have a dick shoved down my throat, stopping me from saying anything. They all three chuckle as I grind my hips against him. They know I want it...I want everything they have to give me.

"Such a perfect little slut," Jett pinches my nipple, "Fill her nice and full, Oak."

Between Jett's words, his pinching, and Oakley's torture, I come hard, clenching around Oakley and vibrating Fynn's cock, "Jesus, fuck!" Fynn pulls out and slams back into my mouth just as he releases his seed.

Oakley grips my thighs and begins slamming into me repeatedly before thrusting once more and painting me just as he said he would. The jarring bothers my wound, but I don't care; the pain is so worth the pleasure. They like to think they use me, but little do they know I'm using them just as much.

"Jesus, Kitty Cat..."

I wait for Oakley to finish what he's going to say, but he doesn't. He tilts his head back as he tries catching his breath with his cock still buried deep inside. Unlike his friend, Fynn pulls out and caresses my cheek, "Thank you for that, Little Saint," Bending down, his lips graze mine before he steps away and tucks himself back into his pants.

"Fuck!" Oakley curses and pulls out of me, his seed dripping from my pussy as he does, "Get some new bandages, Jett."

I look down and see that I'm bleeding through the bandage covering my stab wound, "It's fine..."

"No, it's not! This is why we should have waited!' Oakley scowls as he pulls the bloody gauze away.

"It doesn't look too bad," Fynn states as he leans over to examine the damage, "The stitches look like they are all intact."

"It doesn't fucking matter; she's still bleeding," Oakley glares at his friend, but Fynn winks at me.

"I told you we would make you bleed," he chuckles, and I can't help but giggle.

"I'm glad the two of you think this is funny..." Oakley stomps away and disappears into his bathroom.

Fynn grips my hair but not in a harsh way, "You bleed so pretty, Saint."

He takes my lips again, and I lose my breath momentarily. It's what happens every time Fynn Morin kisses me. You wouldn't guess him to be the type to kiss anyone, so it was no surprise when I learned this initially. Fynn's kiss, though...there are just no words, and I will say it every damn time. I lift my hand and grip his short hair, making him grunt into my mouth.

The kiss is over all too soon as his friends come back, "Pull the other bandage off too," Oakley instructs Fynn, "We might as well change it all."

Surprisingly, Oakley is gentle as he cares for my wound, and I smile the whole time I watch him work. There is a concern as he cleans and examines the stab wound, but it turns to relief once he realizes it's not all that bad. Patching me up takes no time, and before I know it, they're helping me sit up.

"No more sex, Kitty Cat. Not until it's healed completely," his lips are soft as they press against my forehead, and I frown at his gentle treatment of me.

Oakley Harris makes no sense to me. Yes, I knew they were all starting to fall for me, but I never thought about them being gentle. It's out of character for them, and I'm not quite sure if I like it or not.

I slide off the edge of the desk, "I'm going to change and head to my father's office."

"Like hell, you will!" All three Lords say it in unison.

I put my hands on my hips, "What the fuck do you mean? I thought we agreed that I would go and get the files?"

"No, you offered, and we never agreed to that. Do you honestly believe it's safe for you to be out and about, Kitty Cat?" Oakley sits back in his desk chair.

Swallowing the words I want to say, not wanting to ruin what just happened between us all, I change tactics and straddle his lap. I bring my hands up to cup both sides of his neck, "No, I don't believe it's safe yet, which is why one of you will come with me." I seductively press my chest against his as I brush my lips over his mouth.

He grips my hair and tilts my head back, "You, Miss Scott, are playing with fire." The Lord's eyes move to my mouth when I lick them before tucking in my bottom lip and biting it.

"So, does that mean you will go with me?" I ask and give him a sensual smile.

He growls, "You're fucking trouble, Kitty Cat," he pauses briefly, "Fine, but you better listen to me and do everything I tell you to."

"Mm, yes, Sir...whatever you say."

Before going to my father's office, Oakley makes a pit stop at the dorms. When I look at him in question, he sighs, "Dani has been upset, not knowing how you are doing. We told her you would call when you were doing better, but I figured since we are out and about, we might as well stop."

I smirk at him, "Awe, look at you. Your concern for my friend's feelings is so out of character for you, Harris."

He frowns as we pull up to the curb in front of the building, "Actually, I just don't want her coming over and demanding things from us again because I can't promise I won't shut her up myself."

I snicker and go to get out, but Oakley grabs my arm, "Call her and tell her to come out. I don't want you going in there."

Rolling my eyes, I pull my phone out and call her, "Oh, my God...Cat! Is that really you?" my friend squeals from the other end, causing me to yank the phone away from my ear.

"Yeah," I chuckle, "I'm outside the dorms. Can you come out?"

"Well, just come in," Dani tells me.

"No, I have Oakley with me," I inform her.

She scoffs, "It figures..."

"Dani, someone is after me, so I will always have someone with me." I'm a little annoyed that my friend doesn't care much for my well-being.

"I didn't mean it like that, Cat. All I'm saying is that they can leave you with me to hang in my room." She's seriously delusional if she thinks the Lords of Sin will trust anybody to keep me safe.

"Don't take offense, Dani. I doubt they would even trust my own parents to keep me safe. They are taking their duty seriously and have already failed once...they won't let it happen again."

"Fine, whatever," I see her walk out of the building and walk my way before hanging up her phone, "So, why did you even come over?" She glares at Oakley through the Camaro window.

Being the asshole that he is, he winks at my friend and goes back to scrolling through his phone. "He said that you were worried about me, and since I need to go see my dad, he figured we would stop on the way, so you can see that I'm okay in person."

"Well, that was thoughtful of him," she says snidely.

I cross my arms and glare at my friend, "Actually, it was thoughtful of him, because he didn't have to drive over here just so I could see my friend, but now I'm beginning to think it was a waste of time." I go to open the car door, but she stops me.

"Wait!" She grabs my arm, "You're right. I'm sorry. It's just that I've been so worried, and I've missed my friend, Cat. I feel like I've lost you as a friend now that you have the Lords."

"Dani, you haven't lost me as a friend, but you will lose me altogether if I don't keep myself safe until this fucker is caught," I tell her because I've come to realize this myself.

The guys may act like douchebags and say all the wrong things, but they mean well, and I'm going to listen to them from now on. I worry about them just as much, though. If this person threatening us can't reach me, which Lord will they go after first?"

After saying goodbye to Dani and promising to have a girl's night over at the Frat House soon, Oakley drives us to my father's office. I've already texted him and found out he's in a meeting most of the afternoon, so now is the perfect time. I don't know if my father will be mad about me going into his office, but at this point, I don't give a fuck. He's yet to call me to ensure I'm okay after my ordeal. Not once has he tried to see me; deep down, that hurts.

Oakley argues with me once we get there, insisting that he's coming in with me, "You will not go anywhere without one of us, Kitty Cat, not even your father's office, or home for that matter."

I roll my eyes at him, "Fine, but at least let me do the talking to his receptionist; she likes me."

He holds his hands up, "The floor is all yours. I'll just be your arm candy," he winks at me, and I burst out laughing and shake my head.

He follows me into the building and up the stairs, grabbing my ass every chance he gets. When we reach the door just outside the office, Oakley shoves me against it, pressing his body to mine. His warm breath tickles my ear and neck.

"Thank you for earlier, Kitty Cat. Your cunt felt so good wrapped around my cock, but I meant what I said. There will be no more sex until you're healed. However," he pauses and forces two fingers into my mouth, gagging me, "this mouth is going to work overtime until then."

I haven't the slightest idea why he is bringing this up now when we are about to walk into my father's office, but I nod, letting him know that I understand. I also whimper with need because, as always, his words and treatment have turned me on. His little snicker tells me he knows exactly what he's done to me, and he rubs himself against my ass.

"God, you're such a slut for our cocks, aren't you?" When I don't respond, he yanks my head back by my hair, "I asked you a question, Kitty Cat. Are you a slut for our cocks?" I nod, and he chuckles, "That's what I thought. Let's get what we came here for, so we can get the fuck out of here." He pulls his fingers from my mouth, and drool follows, but before I can wipe it off, Oakley smears it across my face, "Leave it."

Like a good girl, I do.

Ms. Davis isn't at her desk, and her computer is shut down. Looking at the clock, I see it's a little after noon, so she must be at lunch...perfect. I go straight to my father's office door only to find it locked. Oakley doesn't let that stop us, though. He walks over to the receptionist's desk and finds what he's looking for before coming over and jimmying the lock until it unlocks.

We walk straight to my father's desk, and once again, Oakley uses the tools and opens the locked drawer. He pulls out a few files and briefly looks through them, making sure they are the ones we are looking for. I ensure everything remains in place, so it doesn't look like we were here, but my accomplice has other ideas.

"On your knees, Kitty Cat."

"What? You can't be serious!"

"I am dead serious. Get on your fucking knees and open that beautiful mouth." His hands go to the button and zipper on his jeans, and he opens them up, pulling his stiff cock out. It throbs in his hand as he waits for me to obey.

I drop to my knees, my heart racing, afraid we will be caught, and yet, turned on by the thought of being seen in this position, and he doesn't seem bothered by it, so I go with it. I open my mouth and automatically put my hands behind my back as I wait for him to use me like he wants to. It doesn't take him long once he slides his girth into my mouth and fucks it fast and hard before he makes me swallow every drop.

I'm before him, still kneeling, as I gaze up at him. Caressing my cheek, his grin tells me all I need to know; he's proud. Using his thumb, he swipes at something at the corner of my mouth, "Tuck me back in, Kitty Cat."

I do so quickly before he takes my arm and helps me to stand. However, when I go to move away, he spins me around, "Oakley! What are..."

"Shh..." He bends me over my father's desk, "You didn't think I would leave you hanging after being such a good girl for me, did you?"

"What are you doing? We can't..."

He cuts me off, "Oh, but we can..."

FORTY-ONE

☠

Oakley

She's so fucking wet! I can't get enough of Catalina Scott, and I'm not just talking about fucking her. No, if I'm being totally honest with myself, I want every fucking piece of this woman. Every broken, fucked up piece, and I will do whatever it takes to get what I want. I want her pleasure, and I want her pain...the latter has yet to come to fruition, but it will, and I already know that my Kitty Cat will love every minute of it.

"Oakley, what if my dad comes back or Ms. Davis?" she asks as I push a finger into her.

"Then I will tell them to get the fuck out until I'm done pleasuring you," I tell her, "Now, arms above your head and hold onto the edge of the desk. Don't let go until I say."

I push a second finger into her as I press down on her lower back so she can't move. Once I have them soaking wet, I remove them and shove them into her mouth, "Suck them, Kitty Cat. Taste how addicting you are."

The way she sucks her essence from my fingers reminds me of a fucking porn star, and I have to stop because I'm getting hard all over again. I've already had mine, this is about her now, and I want to see just how far I can push her. I want to see the different ways that I can make her come.

I grab her hair and pull her head back, "Tell me what you want, Kitty Cat."

Her eyes burn into mine, challenging me, "I want you to fuck me, Oakley. Fuck me like you did earlier when you made me bleed."

I chuckle, "You know I can't do that, naughty girl."

"But I want to be fucked...please, Oakley."

"What, are my fingers not enough to get you off?" I thrust my two fingers back into her, fucking her hard, "Is this not enough, slut?"

"No, I need more..."

A wicked thought comes to me, and I grin. Picking up the letter opener that has a thick resin handle with the Lords of Sin's signature dagger and skull inside it, I bring it to her face, "If my fingers don't do it for this slutty cunt, maybe I need to get creative, huh?" I scape the tip of the opener down her cheek, leaving a red line, "What will your father do when he goes to open his mail only to find his opener covered in his daughter's cum? Then again, maybe he won't even notice."

I push her face down onto the desk, "I want to hear you scream my name, Kitty Cat." I watch as I run the handle through her wet folds before pressing it into her opening. Once I know it's in the right place, I lean over her once again, "How is that my beautiful little slut?"

"Oh God, Oakley..."

"What is it, Kitty Cat? What do you want? Do you want me to stop?" I stop fucking the opener into her, leaving it embedded inside her cunt while I grab her face and kiss her brutally. She is so fucking perfect for me, for us...we couldn't have asked for a better Lady to serve us.

"Please...don't stop."

"Tell me, Kitty Cat, who the fuck are you?"

"I'm your Lady..."

"Yes, you are, but most importantly, what are you?"

She whimpers, "I'm the Lord's slut," she pants heavily.

"Fuck yes, you are," I pull her up, "Stand up." I wait for her to stand, the opener hanging between her legs, "Sit in your father's chair and spread those gorgeous legs."

She turns and sits, moaning because she can feel the handle embedded inside her, "You now have a choice, Kitty Cat. You can either get yourself off using your new little toy or by my hand. What's it going to be?" I cross my arms and wait for her to reply.

Her hand shakes as she takes hold of the sharp end of the opener and slowly starts to move it in and out of her, "Fuck..."

I smile as I lick my bottom lip, "Now, be a good slut and come all over that handle."

Watching her enjoy herself as she gets off is a win for me. This was part of a test. Yeah, it's a degrading test but one that tells me a lot about who Catalina Scott really is. The fact that she can do the same depraved shit to herself that I would love to do to her tells me just how perfect she is.

Her breathing is getting heavier, "That's it, you love it, don't you, Kitty Cat?"

"Fuck yes..."

"Faster, baby...come for me. Rub that slutty clit and come." I want to jerk off and come again myself, but I won't. I can wait until later when I'm showering and picturing all the dirty and crude things I want to do to our girl. And she is precisely that, *ours*.

I'm too busy helping Kitty Cat straighten her clothes to notice the smoke coming from under the door, "What is that smell?" she asks with her nose in the air.

I sniff as I turn around, and that's when I see it, "Fuck! Someone set a fucking fire in the outer office!" I run over and feel the door, only to be met with warmth, "God fucking damn it! Call the fire department while I call the guys!"

I watch her pick up the office phone while I wait for Fynn to pick up, "Yo, what's up?"

"Get to the Provost's building now! Someone set the outer office on fire. Catalina and I are trapped in her father's office!"

"Shit! We are on our way!" Fynn hangs up just as Kitty Cat is hanging up.

"Go to the window, now!" I reach for her hand.

"We are on the third floor, Oakley! How are we supposed to get out?" I can see the fear in her eyes, and I pull her to me.

Grabbing her face in both hands, I make her look at me, "Hey, we are going to be fine. Now is not the time to lose your shit, okay? I need you, Kitty Cat; I need my Lady, so we can figure this out. Can you do this for me?"

She stares blankly at me but then nods, "Yeah, I'm good. Let's do this."

"That's my girl." I kiss her forehead and then pull her toward the window.

Kitty Cat is correct. There is no way out, not even a ledge, to climb out on. I tell her to stay by the window, so she has fresh air, and I go in search of anything that we can use. I come up empty-handed everywhere I check until I open the small closet and find a rope, oddly enough. Hoping it's long enough, I go back to the window and tie it around Kitty Cat's waist.

"Do you know how to rappel?" I ask her as I test the knot.

"I've done it once in high school, but I'm not very good at it," she responds.

"That's okay," I tie the other end around my own waist, "I will be the anchor while you rappel down. Once you get to the bottom, untie the rope so I can bring it back up, tie it off here, and come down."

"What? No, we go together!" she argues, and I grab her face once again.

"Listen! We are too heavy together; the rope won't hold us both. We are wasting time arguing, now get that cute butt up on that sill and climb out!" I crash my lips against hers, "Hurry!"

Kitty Cat does as she's told and dangles her legs out the window before turning onto her stomach. She looks me in the eye, "Don't let go," she holds my stare for a moment.

"Never!" I tell her and then lift my arms to brace myself against the frame in order to hold her body weight. She doesn't weigh much, so it shouldn't be an issue.

After what seems like forever, I feel the weight disappear, and I lean out the window to see that Kitty Cat is untying the rope. I quickly pull it up and search for a place to tie it off. There is an older heat register close to the window, and I tie the other end to it, ensuring it will hold my 215-pound body weight. The room is filled with smoke, and I cough and choke as I go back to the desk and grab the files we came here for in the first place. Tucking them away in the back of my pants, I head back to the window.

I already know it won't take me to the ground, but it will be close enough. Pulling my pocketknife out, so I can have it ready to cut the rope when needed, I climb out the window. I can hear the fire trucks getting closer as a crowd gathers and watches the old building go up in flames.

I start descending. I begin to breathe easier as I come to the second floor, but then I'm not sure what happens. I hear a loud explosion, and I start falling. Catalina's scream is the last thing I hear before I hit the ground and darkness takes me.

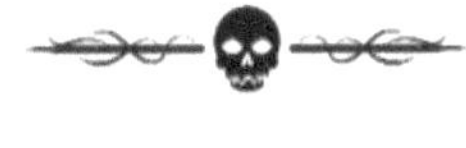

Fynn

Jett and I are sitting in my room, enjoying the aftermath of what Little Saint's mouth did for us. I pass him the rolled-up smoke as I stare at the ceiling. So many things are running through my head right now, most of them confusing.

"Dude, have you ever thought about what you will do after graduation?" I ask my friend.

Jett waits until he exhales, "I try not to. One of the reasons why I ignore Blake."

I turn my head toward him, "Is it that bad that you can't even call him Dad?" I chuckle, but it's nothing to really laugh at. I know it hurts my friend to not only have lost his mother but to lose a father who is still living and breathing but doesn't acknowledge the relationship with his son.

"When he starts acting like a father, I'll start calling him Dad again." Jett passes the smoke back to me.

"Well, let me rephrase my question then, have you ever thought about meeting someone and settling down?" I take another long drag and hold it in.

I can feel my friend's eyes scrutinizing me, "Where the fuck is this coming from?"

I just shrug, "Nowhere, just making small talk is all."

The room is silent as we sit here, both of us lost in our thoughts. I wonder if his are on a particular blonde bombshell like mine. I can't get Little Saint out of my head. Somehow, she's dug her claws into me and refuses to retract them. I'm unsure how I feel about my feelings for her.

This was supposed to be fun. Taking a Lady to get our dicks wet until graduation, but somehow, things got fucked up, and now we all feel something for Catalina Scott. We are supposed to go our separate ways after all is said and done, but I doubt we will be able to do that when the time comes. I can't speak for my two best friends, but if the way they are around her is any indication, then I'm not the only one thinking these thoughts.

My phone rings, and I reach across the loveseat to grab it. Oakley's name pops up, "Yo, what's up?"

Oakley's voice comes over loud and a bit panicked as he tells me that the Provost's building is on fire and that we need to get there now. The two of them are now stuck inside a burning building. What the fuck? They were only going for the files; how did they get trapped? Better yet, how did the perpetrator have time to start a fire in the little time it should have taken for them to grab the files?

"Shit! We are on our way!" I hang up and slap Jett's leg, "Oak and Saint are in trouble; let's go!"

"What the fuck is going on? What kind of trouble?" my friend asks as he jumps to his feet and follows me.

"Someone set fire to Mr. Scott's office while they were getting the files. They're both trapped inside!"

"Damn it," Jett curses, "That office is on the third floor! How are they going to get out?"

"I don't know," I start down the stairs at a fast pace, "Let's hope that the fire department gets there quickly."

Jett is hot on my tail, pulling his Jeep keys from his pocket. It takes no time to get to the school, and although the parking lot is a distance away from the building that Mr. Scott's office is in, Jett doesn't let it bother him as he drives up onto the grass. He does slow down for students now jumping out of his way, but he's a man on a mission.

When the building comes into view, we can see the smoke and some flames flickering out of a few windows on the third floor. We also see Little Saint trying to rappel down from the window. It's not very graceful, but she makes it to the ground, and I sigh in relief.

Jett slams on the breaks as we reach the outskirts of the growing crowd, and we jump out just as the rope goes back up. We reach Little Saint, wrapping our arms around her while staring at the third-floor window. She turns her head into my chest but doesn't cry like I thought she would. Concern dances in the depths of her eyes when she lifts her head, and they meet mine. We both turn back to the window.

Oakley starts lowering himself, and I begin to breathe easier again. He makes it to the second floor, and just when I think both my people are going to be okay, an explosion erupts above us, and suddenly my best friend is falling. The woman in my arms screams, and then we are moving toward the body, now lying on the ground, unmoving.

"Oakley!" Catalina calls out his name, her tears finally making an appearance and streaming down her face.

"Don't touch him. Moving him could worsen his injuries, especially if his neck is broken," I tell Jett, who is about to shake our friend.

The sirens are getting louder, and I know help will be here momentarily. Oakley lays still, his shirt hiked up to show off his six-pack, but that's not what I'm looking at. I can see a manilla file folder peeking out from underneath him. Shit! We can't let the emergency crew see these, but we can't move them either.

I look over at Jett, who has also noticed the files, and nod at him. While holding Oakley as still as possible, Jett takes hold of the files while Little Saint blocks the crowd's view. My friend pulls as gently as possible and finally works the files out from inside the back of Oak's jeans.

"I really hope those files were worth all this," a stern voice comes from behind us, and I see my Uncle Tyler standing just a couple of feet away.

"Uncle Tyler, help him!" I plead, ignoring his remark about the files.

"The EMTs are just getting here. They will take care of Oakley," he eyes Little Saint up and down, "Were you up there with him too?"

Catalina nods but refrains from saying a word. Taking Oakley's hand, she's careful not to jar him as she gives him all her attention. She doesn't want to look at the Police Chief standing behind her, grimacing. I can tell she hopes he will go away, but she doesn't know my uncle very well.

"Miss Scott, I'm going to ask that you come with me so I can ask you a few questions." My uncle steps toward her, but I move to stand between my uncle and our girl.

"Can't you come to the hospital and ask the questions, Uncle Tyler? She also needs to be checked out for smoke inhalation, and I'm sure she wants to be close to Oakley, just like Jett and I."

My uncle leans in, "I will take her to the hospital, but I can't show favoritism in front of so many witnesses, Fynn. For Christ's sake, I need it to look like I'm actually doing my job!" His jaw is tight, and knowing my uncle, I know he's telling me the truth.

"Okay, but can you wait until the EMTs load him into the ambulance? Let her comfort him until then," I plead with my uncle, and he finally nods, giving in.

"Fine, but then I'm going to walk her to the back seat of my car and help her into it. When we get to the hospital, you will also tell me what the fuck is so important in those files that your friends had to cause all this commotion to get them."

I sigh and then agree, "Okay, I'll tell you, but just so you know, all of this could have been avoided had your fucking brother, and his friends come clean with us about everything. We wouldn't have had to take such drastic measures."

"No worries, Fynn. I will be talking to your father as well. Between the last incident and now this, I feel it's time that he comes clean with me also." I can tell my Uncle Tyler is pissed, as he should be. Being left in the dark and yet expected to clean up mess after mess would put anyone in a pissy mood.

I turn my attention back on Oakley just as the EMTs arrive on the scene. Pulling Little Saint away, I hold her so her back is against my chest as we watch them work on our friend. They put a neck brace around his neck and slide a long board underneath his prone body. They then lift my best friend onto the gurney and load him into the back of the ambulance. I see them place an oxygen mask over Oakley's face just before the doors start to close.

"Wait!" "Jett calls out, "I'm riding with!" He tosses me the keys to his Jeep and hops in the back.

I planned to ride with Saint in the back of my uncle's car, but it looks like I'll be driving the Jeep instead. I hug Little Saint to me, "Will you be okay?"

She glances at my uncle, then back at me, and nods, "Yeah, I'll be fine."

"Okay, I'll be right behind you." I kiss her forehead before letting her go.

I turn and look at my uncle, giving him a warning look, but all he does is roll his eyes and start for his car parked right beside the Jeep. Turning Little Saint, we follow my Uncle Tyler, not even looking back at the blazing inferno as the fire department hoses it down.

FORTY-TWO

☠

Jett

I hold my best friend's hand on the way to the hospital. The EMT sets up an IV drip and attaches a blood pressure cuff around Oakley's arm. I don't take my eyes off him the whole ride. I'll be damned if he dies on the way because I missed something vital that could have saved him.

As soon as the back door opens, I jump out, the files now tucked away and hidden in the back of my pants. Nobody will get their hands on them until we have had the chance to look them over. They almost got my best friend and girl killed. The question is, did the stalker start the fire because it was their only chance to take out both Lady and Lord, or did they know that Oakley and Lina were after evidence?

I pull at my hair in frustration as I pace the waiting room. The hospital staff wouldn't let me go back with them when they pushed Oakley through the set of double doors; a sign saying 'Authorized Personnel Only' hung from the door.

About five minutes later, Chief Morin, my Lovely Lina, and Fynn burst into the room. Lina throws herself into my arms, and I hold her tightly. Burying my face into her neck, I can smell the acrid scent of smoke as it lingers on her skin and clothing. I pull away and examine her.

"Are you sure you're okay? You should be looked over, Lina. You took in a lot of smoke."

"I'm fine..."

"No," I shake my head and then turn to Fynn, "Will you get a nurse to come in and look her over?"

"Yeah, of course," Fynn states before walking out.

"Jett, I'm fine," Lina whines, "I stood by the window most of the time after the smoke started rolling in under the door."

I make her sit in a chair and take the seat beside her. Chief Morin stands guard by the door as though we will take off. Taking her hand, I kiss her knuckles, "Tell me, Lina, how did they have time to start the fire? Were the files not in the drawer? Did you have to go looking for them?"

The pink flush that rises on my Lovely Lina's face should speak for itself, but I insist she tells me. She looks over at the Police Chief and then leans closer to me, "Oakley and I, we sort of...you know."

I don't want to assume anything, and I don't give a fuck if Fynn's uncle is standing a few feet away; I need clarification. When Lina tries turning her head again, I take her chin and hold it firmly, "What about you and Oakley, Lina? Don't make me guess."

Lina glares at me as she straightens in the chair, and with a bit of attitude, she spills it all out, "We got each other off, okay! Is that what you wanted to hear? We christened my father's office, and while doing so, it gave the fucker time to set the reception area on fire. There now you and the Police Chief know. Your little slut was too busy getting off for one of her Lords to notice anything amiss!"

She tries getting up, but I yank her back down, "You will not talk to me in that tone, Lovely. I'm only trying to understand how this happened. There is nothing shameful about getting off or where you're getting off, but we need to know everything if we are going to find the person who did this."

"He's right," Tyler states and walks over to us, "I had my fun back in the day and probably would have done the same thing as the two of you horn balls," he chuckles, "But the fact remains that someone is trying to hurt you, and we can't catch them without all the facts."

Lina nods, "Nobody was there when we showed up," she begins, "I had texted my father, and he said he would be in a meeting, but Ms. Davis wasn't there either. She must have been at lunch. We were supposed to be in and out, but apparently, we were still worked up from earlier."

She looks at me, and I understand exactly what she means. I grin, "So, you went in and..?"

Lina sighs, "Oakley went straight to my father's desk and retrieved the files. I was then instructed to get on my knees."

I'm starting to get hard just listening to her retell how my best friend made her suck his cock, "Go on..."

"I don't think I need to repeat every action. Suffice it to say, I blew Oakley, and then it was my turn to be pleasured. When we were done, I was the first to smell the smoke. Oakley went to the door and felt that it was warm, so we knew we couldn't leave the way we came."

"Catalina," Tyler jumps in, "Was there anything else that may have stood out to you while in your father's office?"

Her forehead crinkles, "No, why do you ask?"

The Chief shrugs, "No reason, just wondering if anything else was out of place."

"Not that I was aware of. The only thing I found strange was that Ms. Davis wasn't at her desk. She never leaves the office while my father is in meetings."

"Hm, are you sure?" Tyler asks.

"Yes, I'm sure. She's supposed to be there in case a student needs something, and my father isn't there to help." A phone buzzes with an incoming call, and I watch as Lina pulls her phone out, "Speak of the devil; it's my dad."

"Answer it," I tell her.

"Hey, Dad..." she puts the call on speakerphone.

"What in the hell happened, Catalina? My office burns down, and I'm told that you were seen climbing out the window and that Oakley was taken to the hospital from falling! You better start explaining, young lady!"

"Oh, you can't call me after the guys saved me when I was kidnapped and stabbed, but you can call me when your precious office burns up? Go to hell, Dad. I don't have to tell you anything."

"Catalina! You will not talk to me so disrespectfully! First off, I knew you were in good hands with the Lords. I've been doing my investigative work on my end. We are trying to figure out who is doing this; there are cameras all over campus and the town, so we have been watching the footage to see what we can find out."

"Who the fuck is we?" my girl growls out her question.

"Who do you think? Your little boyfriends' fathers and myself!" Mr. Scott yells through the phone.

"If you know why this is being done, why are you not just coming clean? It's all they want, for Christ's sake, Dad! Fess up to the rape, and this will all be over."

Nothing but momentary silence comes from the other end before her father sighs, "You don't understand everything, Catty."

I see Lina cringe at her father's nickname for her, "You're absolutely right because you and their fathers are too much of pussies to tell us what happened. You're so afraid of the alums coming after you that you would rather see your children get hurt. Well, don't worry, Dad, we'll figure it all out on our own. Don't waste your time investigating... we've got this!"

My girl hangs up on her father and pockets her phone. She stands up, and I let her. She's frustrated and hurt by her father's actions and words, and I can't blame her one bit. I'm glad she has us; we're her family now, and we will always have her back.

Fynn finally returns with a nurse who looks bedraggled as she approaches Lina, "Please, sit so I can check you out, Miss Scott." The nurse side-eyes my best friend as he stands with his arms crossed and an annoyed look on his face.

I don't say anything until the nurse has cleared Lina and hurries from the room, "Okay, spill. What did you do to that poor woman?"

Fynn shrugs, "She didn't want to come to check Little Saint out because she didn't come by ambulance and wasn't told about her. She was too busy texting on her phone. It took me a bit because I hacked into her social media account and found a few interesting things about Nurse Deedee. It seems she likes to party a little too hard and loves her *candy*, so I had to blackmail her to come check our girl out." He caresses Lina's head as he explains all this to us.

"Fynn, you do know that I'm standing right here, right?" His Uncle Tyler chuckles.

"What did you hear?" Fynn asks his uncle.

"Oh, did you say something?" Tyler grins.

"Exactly..." Fynn smirks, "Now, what's going on here?"

I go on to tell him everything we have discussed as we've waited. By the time I finish, Fynn's full stature is tense. There is a tick in his jaw that wasn't there when I started, and he sits down, pulling Lina onto his lap.

"You better fucking believe that we have this," Fynn scowls, "If our fathers didn't want to help in the first place, then we don't need them now. Fuck any kind of test to see if we have what it takes. Our lives are being threatened, and they're worried about their fucking reputations!"

"Fynn, I'm sorry," Tyler places his hand on his nephew's shoulder. I hadn't realized how much of a dick my brother was being. Please, anything you need, just ask."

My friend looks at his uncle and nods, "Thanks, Uncle Ty."

The door opens, and a doctor walks in, "Are any of you Mr. Harris's family?"

I growl at his question, "We are his brothers."

The doctor stares at us in question, and Chief Morin speaks up, "You can tell us, Dr. Logan. Oakley would want them to know before any other family member. As you can see, his parents aren't even here, and they have been informed."

"If you say so, Chief Morin," the doctor clears his throat, "Your *brother* is a fortunate man. I was worried he might have broken his back in the fall. Falling from two stories up is likely to do that, but someone was definitely watching over him today. He has a concussion, so we will keep him overnight for that alone, but I also want to ensure nothing else occurs after the fact."

"Can we see him?" I ask hopefully.

"Yes. The nurse can take you to his room, but he is still out of it a bit from the painkillers. We want him to stay awake as much as possible for now. So, if you can keep him from going to sleep, that would be helpful. Just don't let him do anything too stressful."

"We won't," the three of us say while Tyler remains quiet in the background.

When we go to walk out, Tyler grabs our attention, "I'm going to head out for now, but I will be back later to talk to Oakley. I'll need to verify stuff for my report."

"Thanks, Uncle Ty. We appreciate all your help." Fynn says, and I nod in agreement, "If you get the chance, can you check the security feed for the office? Maybe the person fucked up and is caught on camera."

"Will do. You kids stay safe, and I will send an officer to stand outside Oakley's door. The last thing we need is for this person to return and finish their job."

The Chief's last words before he walks out leave chills racing down my spine. It's all becoming surreal now that the stalker has upped their game. We are getting hurt, and I have a feeling that it's only the beginning. Whoever this fucker is, they are really good. We can usually find out everything that happens on campus, but we're stumped over this one. One thing is for sure; we will not stop until we bring this motherfucker down for good.

FORTY-THREE

Oakley

I feel like I've been hit by an eighteen-wheeler multiple times as I try to open my eyes. I'm being rolled down a bright hallway, and the scent of disinfectant immediately tells me that I'm in the hospital. I think back to try and figure out why I would be here, but my head throbs too much.

"The medication should kick in soon, Mr. Harris," an unfamiliar voice of a woman reaches my ears, "You had a nasty fall, so your body is going to be hurting for a while."

"What happened?" my throat feels like sandpaper as I try to get the words out.

"You don't remember?" We stop moving, and the face of an older, concerned woman appears over me.

"My head hurts to think right now." I'm annoyed that this woman keeps making me talk when it hurts like hell to do so.

"Oh, that's understandable," we start moving again, "There was a fire, and you used a rope to climb from the window, but the rope broke, and you fell two stories. It's a miracle that you didn't break anything, but you do have a concussion and a nasty bump on the head."

"Yeah, that would do it alright," I say dryly, as the events start coming back to me, "Is Catalina..."

"Oh, the pretty blonde?" the nurse cuts me off, "She's perfectly fine. Aside from worrying about you, that is," she chuckles softly.

Is my Kitty Cat really worried about me? I find it hard to believe when my parents don't even worry about me. Ever since the dinner at the Scott residence, I've barely talked to my mother, and she still isn't talking to my father, but it doesn't seem to bother him. My mother would be the one to come here to see if I'm okay, but not at the expense of possibly seeing my father.

I still can't believe they were married all these years, and Mom never knew that Ashlee Scott was the Lady of Sin back in college. I don't know how often my mother had mentioned her friend Ashlee while I was growing up, but I never saw the woman. I guess I did when we were young, but I don't remember her.

Returning to the present when the bed slows down again, I watch as they maneuver the rolling bed to fit it through the doorway. The older nurse and a young guy, maybe an orderly, lock the bed in place, and the woman starts moving around the room while the guy leaves.

"When can I leave?" I ask and try to sit up, but the pain that slashes through my skull tells me to lay the fuck back down.

"Dr. Logan wants to keep you overnight for observation since you have a concussion." The nurse gives me that grandmotherly smile, "I'm Tabitha, and I'll be your nurse until the next shift comes on. Then you will have Katie overnight."

This news is not welcome. I'd rather be in my own bed while feeling like shit, "What if I don't want to stay?"

Tabitha stops what she's doing, "Oh, well, the doctor won't sign off on your discharge papers until he feels that you are ready to go home."

"You can't keep me here if I don't want to be here," I scowl.

"Already harassing the staff, I see," a familiar and welcoming voice comes from the doorway, "Stop being a dick to the nice nurse, Oak. She's only trying to help."

"Fuck you, Jett!" I grin when I see my best friend, along with my other best friend and my Kitty Cat standing there smirking, "Come here, Kitty Cat."

I hold my hand out to our girl, and she rushes over to take it, "How do you feel?" Her eyes wander down my form.

"Like I let you beat the shit out of me while I took what I wanted from this gorgeous body of yours," I bite my lip as I remember watching her fuck herself with the letter opener.

Her face turns bright red, and she glances at the nurse, who is humming as she writes on a whiteboard, "Do you have to be a douche all the time? Here I am, concerned for your well-being, and all you can think about is fucking!"

I grin, "No, all I think about is fucking *you*. There's a big difference."

She tries to pull away, but I don't allow it. Instead, I make her look at me as I gaze into her pretty blue eyes, "How are you? Are you hurt at all?"

Her face softens, and she gives me a small smile, "I'm good. The guys had a nurse look me over, and I was cleared."

"Good, now get that cute ass up here and lay beside me." I wince as I try moving over; my head really fucking up my game.

"No. You need to take it easy. Maybe later, once we know you're in the clear."

I growl at her response even though I know she's right, "Fine, but you will sit here on the edge."

My Kitty Cat obeys like a good girl, and I finally turn my attention back to my friends, "Please say that all this wasn't for nothing. Where are the files?"

Jett grins, "You're lucky we spotted them when your lazy ass was sprawled on the ground taking a nap." I watch him pull the files out from behind his back.

I scoff, "Believe me, I wish that's all I was doing. I fucking hurt all over."

"Yeah, well, be lucky that you will be walking out of here come morning instead of being in a wheelchair." Fynn's jaw is clenched, "Watching your best friend fall two stories isn't a pretty sight."

"Awe, you do care!" I tease.

"Of course, I fucking care, dickhead! You're like a brother to me." Fynn glares, "I'd feel the same way if it was Jett."

My grin falters when I see how serious Fynn is being, "I know, man. I'm only trying to make light of the situation."

Suddenly, the big fucker leans in and gives me a hug, "Don't ever fucking scare us like that, bro!"

"Hey, tell that to the fucker who set the fire," I roll my eyes, "Speaking of that, have you heard anything?"

"Unless you count my father calling to yell at me for us burning down his office..." Kitty Cat starts in dryly.

"No, not yet," Jett adds.

"My uncle will be back later to talk to you. He knows you two didn't start the fire."

I furrow my brows, "How does he know that?"

Jett grins, "Because our girl here told us what happened while the two of you were in the office."

I glance at my Kitty Cat, "Did she now? Did she tell you every detail?"

Catalina shakes her head vigorously, "They didn't need to know every detail."

I reach up and tuck her hair behind her ear, "Oh, but I think the guys should know just how slutty this pussy is, don't you?"

Kitty Cat looks around the room, and I can see the relief on her face when she realizes the nurse is gone, "Oakley, please stop."

"Oh, do tell!" Jett rubs his hands together.

I study my Kitty Cat, and for some odd reason, I can't make myself reveal our filthy little secret...even to my two best friends, "Nah. If you want to hear about it, Kitty Cat will have to be the one to tell you."

I keep my chuckle to myself when she whips her head toward me, surprise written all over her face. Winking at her open-mouthed expression, I feel something thump inside my chest. It's been a long time since I've felt that organ beat, so it's a total surprise to feel it over such a minor thing now.

"What?" Jett whines, "You're seriously not going to tell us?"

Grinning, I shake my head, "Nope. Technically it's not my story to tell since I'm not the one that did anything."

My girl gasps, "That is a bald-faced lie, Harris! You started it all..."

"Yeah, but you didn't have to finish it like you did. You had a choice," I remind her, and Kitty Cat's face colors again, but she remains silent.

"So," I look over at Jett, changing the subject, "Let's see what's in these folders that Kitty Cat and I risked our lives for."

Fynn rolls his eyes, "A bit dramatic, don't you think?"

"What? Am I not in a hospital right now?" I ask.

"Had you gone in, grabbed the folders, and left, you wouldn't be here now. Would you?" Fynn cocks an eyebrow at me.

"What the fuck ever," I scowl, knowing he's right but not wanting to admit it, "Just open the damn folders, will you?"

Jett passes us each a folder, and when I open the one he gives me, Kitty Cat gasps at the photo of the man inside. I look at the name on the folder and see that it's Bradley Simmons. I skim through the information inside but come back to the photo. The guy looks familiar to me, and by the way, Kitty Cat is gawking at it; she must also recognize him.

"What's wrong, Kitty cat?"

Her eyes meet mine briefly and then return to the photo, "You don't recognize him?"

"He looks familiar, but it's probably because his picture hangs on the wall at the Frat House," I reply.

She shakes her head, "No, he's familiar because his son goes to school here, only he's not a Sinner."

I study the photo again, but nothing comes to me, "I'm not sure I know who you're talking about."

"Bradley's son is the Captain of Helshire's Lacrosse team..."

Catalina

He's wearing clothing of a different decade, but I would know that good-looking face anywhere. I dismissed him after our first meeting because I thought he was too good for me, and then I accepted a ride from him, where he was the perfect gentleman. There is no denying it, though. It's like I'm looking right at the face of Kaden Miller, Captain of Helshire University's Lacrosse team.

Does he know what's going on? Is he being threatened too? If so, has he gone to the police? No. If he had gone to the police, then Chief Morin would have told us.

"Son of a bitch! You're right, Kitty Cat. It's that goody-two-shoes Miller that everyone goes gaga over." Oakley's voice hints at a bit of jealousy, and I smirk.

"Who goes gaga over him?" I cock my brow.

"All the girls. Hell, you were all cozy with him when you were at the jock's party," he scowls.

I lean back to get a better view of my handsome Lord, "Were you jealous?"

"Fuck no!" he says a little too quickly.

I glance at Jett and Fynn and see their smirks, "Hm, I see," I figure I'll be nice, but only because he's lying in a hospital bed, "Well, I had already deemed the guy a no-go, even if he was the nicest guy I had met at the time."

"Oh yeah," Oakley looks at me skeptically, "Why is that?"

I grin, "Because I'd eat him alive. I needed someone," I pause and look at the other two, "Multiple someones, that would put me in my place and give me exactly what I need."

I lean down and take Oakley's lips. I never initiate the kisses with the Lords; there is no need to because they are always doing it themselves. Oakley's lips just look so kissable, especially after he had licked them seconds ago as he listened to what I was saying while staring at my mouth.

"Fuck, Little Saint, you have me harder than a rock," Fynn groans.

I pull away from Oakley, smiling.

He grins, "So, tell me, are your Lords meeting your expectations?"

I shrug, "They are doing okay. I expected more...I don't know, depravity, humiliation...you know...the things bad boys like you do to their victims. You're actually pretty tame, but it's working for me, I guess."

I never see them move, but suddenly Fynn and Jett surround me as I sit on the edge of Oakley's bed, "We have been a little preoccupied trying to keep you safe, but we can't have you thinking that we are less than your expectations," Jett states.

"Fuck, Little Saint, if you only knew half the things that we've been wanting to do to you...and with you. You may want to run," Fynn's eyes are dark and full of want as he clenches his jaw. He grabs the hair at the back of my head, "If you want depravity and humiliation, then we are at your fucking service. No more stopping when we embarrass you in public.

If we want to talk about your slutty pussy or how much of a slut you are for our cocks, and others are around to hear it, so be it."

"Fynn..." I whimper.

"What's wrong, Saint? Are you rethinking your wants?" He runs his tongue over his lips, "That's too bad because now that we know what they are, we will give you everything you need. Believe me, Little Saint; you will never want for anything again."

His mouth crashes against mine brutally. Biting and sucking. Taking what he wants and not caring if it's hurting me is precisely what I need them all to do. My core throbs from his attack, but he pulls away, leaving me needy and desperate.

"How's that cunt, Kitty Cat? Is it wanting to be filled again already?" Oakley asks me, and I know I should be ashamed, but there is no room for it when it's the four of us.

"Yes..." I reply while staring into Fynn's eyes.

"Lock the door, Jett," Oakley orders his friend.

"No!" I cry out as Fynn's hand tightens in my hair, "You need to take it easy, Oakley."

Even in my state, I try to do the right thing to make sure Oakley is okay, but he has other plans. Ones that are about to give me a lesson in exhibitionism while letting him enjoy being the voyeur. It won't really count, watching his friends fuck me, but it's a start, and it still turns me on.

"Bend her over the bed and spit roast our little slut, boys. Take turns at each end and leave her dripping with cum," Oakley's tone is thick with lust as he instructs his friends on what to do to me.

Fynn gives me his sinister smile as he uses my hair and lifts me from where I sit. Placing a light kiss on my lips, he stares into my eyes, "Here we go, Little Saint," he waits for just a brief second as if he's giving me a chance to change my mind, but all I do is wet my lips and give a slight nod, ready for whatever they are going to do me.

I'm thrown over the end of the bed, and my bottoms are yanked down, "Ah, traces from your little tryst earlier are still evident," Fynn chuckles.

"I know I said we weren't going to fuck you, Kitty Cat, not until you're cleared, but fuck that," Oakley's grin is a devilish one, "If you bleed, you bleed. No more mister nice Lords."

"We have been too lenient with you, my Lovely Little Lina. It's time we go back to taking whatever we want, and you giving us permission to do so...well, let's just say... game on," Jett unzips his jeans, "I would love nothing more than to hear you scream, but I want that filthy mouth around my cock more."

I'm expecting to feel Fynn's cock thrust into me, so I'm surprised when it's his tongue I feel first. I moan as he pulls my opening apart and shoves his tongue deep inside. The tip of his nose tickles my ass hole the deeper he goes.

"Oh fuck..." I moan.

"Why don't you tell them what you did earlier, Kitty Cat?" I turn my head and see Oakley staring at his best friend while he tongue fucks me, "I bet it will only make them fuck you harder."

I whimper at the thought. I am worried about my wound during this little fuck session. I didn't want to tell them because I knew how they would react, but the rope rappelling down the building irritated it. Luckily, it didn't break any stitches, and it didn't bleed again, but it is a bit sore. However, what they are doing to me, or what they are going to do to me, is very much welcomed, and the fact that they don't care if I bleed only makes the thrill of it better. Call me twisted, but I'll bleed for these men any day.

Oakley said I didn't have to tell them, and I believe him that he won't say anything, but it's like he said, it will only make them hornier, which will only make them take me harder. When I feel Fynn push the tip of a finger into my tight pucker, I moan and fuck myself back onto it.

"Such a greedy little slut aren't you?" Oakley grins, "Just like earlier..."

Biting my lip, I take a deep breath and just let go, "Like when you watched me fuck myself with my father's letter opener?"

Fynn freezes in his ministrations and growls, "Fuck, Little Saint! You got off with a letter opener?"

"Not just any," Oakley never takes his eyes off me, "It was one of the thick-handled ones with the Lord's dagger and skull inside the resin handle. She fucked the Lords of Sin's crest into her."

"I think I've tasted enough of this dirty snatch," Fynn grunts, and that's when I feel it; his cock lining up to my pussy. I wait in aching anticipation. He grabs my hands and holds them at my lower back, "Take this, my filthy little slut."

He slams into me and doesn't stop. He fucks me hard and fast, the bed wheels scraping as they get pushed across the floor. He stops momentarily and lifts one leg and then the other, so my knees rest on the edge of the bed, opening me up nice and wide.

"What the fuck are you waiting for, Jett?" Oakley scowls at his friend, "Fuck that dirty mouth; make her take your whole length until she cries."

There's my cruel Lord, the one I've been waiting for. Yes, he's been a douchebag, but this is the one I've been waiting for. I want them to take what they want. Maybe we needed time to form a certain bond before they let loose and showed me their true nature because these Lords here...are the ones I expected from the beginning.

Jett yanks my head back, and I automatically open my mouth and stick my tongue out for him. He doesn't say anything as he guides his cock into my mouth, not stopping once. I gag when he gets to the back of my throat, and both he and Oakley laugh but still, he doesn't stop. He pushes through until my nose is against him, and I feel his length inside my throat.

"Fucking gorgeous, Kitty Cat."

Fynn continues to fuck me hard, and I realize he has even worked two digits into my ass. My holes are stuffed full at Oakley's request, and I can no longer look at him to see his reaction to his friends taking me the way he orders them to. All I know is that I feel like I have died and gone to heaven. I've been waiting for this. I've been waiting for the real Lords to show themselves. I know this is nothing right now, but I can tell this is only the beginning and the start of a beautifully twisted relationship.

FORTY-FOUR

Catalina

Oakley has been home for a day, and I've been staying in his room in case he needs anything. He still hurts, but falling two stories will do that to you. Fynn and Jett are in and out, not telling me where they are going, but I worry about them. If the stalker tried to kill Oakley and me, they will try and get to them, too.

"Stop staring out the window, Kitty Cat. Come sit with me and watch a movie." Oakley pats the area beside him on the couch.

He wanted out of bed, so I helped him to the couch. Now he keeps trying to get me to sit with him, only to molest me. "Are you going to behave if I do?"

He gives me his most innocent smirk, "I'll try."

I roll my eyes and go back to watching out the window. The other two left about an hour ago, and I've been waiting for them to return. I'm usually not like this, but when a psycho is on the loose, I can't help it.

Hearing Oakley moving around and a drawer closing, I see him moving to sit back against the couch. My eyes go to the table beside the sofa, and I scrutinize the Lord. He's trying to hide something as I watch him lift his leg and slip whatever it is underneath it.

He crooks his finger at me and says, "Come here, Kitty Cat," leaving no room for arguing, but I still shake my head, "Now..."

My eyes drop to his leg once more before I sigh and slowly walk over to him, "Oakley..."

"Shut up and turn around," he's not harsh, but he does mean business, so I do as he says, "Now, give me your hands."

I move both hands to rest on my lower back, and he grabs them. I hear what sounds like a zipper, then something tightens around my wrists; he's zip tied my hands together. My heart thuds inside my chest, not knowing what he is up to, but I think I can guess.

He doesn't say anything as I feel him scoot up to the edge of the couch, his hands coming to my bare thighs. Oakley leans his head against my back while his hands slowly move up the sides of my thighs.

"Fuck, Kitty Cat. I need inside this tight cunt so badly," his hands reach the top and slide into my booty shorts, working their way to the front.

"You can't yet, doctor's orders..." I say just above a whisper, his touch turning me on as usual.

"I know we can't fuck, but you're going to suck my cock like a good girl, right?" He thrusts two fingers into me and scissors them back and forth as he fucks me.

It doesn't take long for him to get me to the brink, "Oh, God, Oakley..."

He pulls away, making me whimper, "Me first, Kitty Cat," he sits back, "Turn and get on your knees."

Getting on my knees with my hands secured behind my back is harder than hell. Oakley sits there, smirking, as he watches me struggle. I'm not graceful as I come down hard on both knees, glaring at him.

"Don't give me that look, Kitty Cat. I could have made it worse for you," He pulls his cock out and gives it a few strokes, "Tell me what you want me to do."

I lick my lips. Excitement fills me, thinking about what he will force me to do. Yes, I'm willing, even though he will force my head down, shoving his girth deep into my throat, and there won't be a damn thing that I can do about it. For that alone, I'm getting wet.

When I don't say anything, Oakley says, "Seriously? My little slut isn't going to beg for my cock? Maybe you aren't as slutty as we thought," he taunts.

My head snaps up, and I look him in the eye, "Please, my Lord. I want your cock. Use my mouth for your pleasure..."

"I don't know, Kitty Cat..."

"Please!" I beg, "I will be your good little slut; just please use me!"

I'm not ashamed to beg anymore now that I know it's what turns them on. It's all part of the humiliation, too, and sickly enough, it turns me on just as much. I open my mouth for him, but he continues to stare at me.

"Lean in closer to my cock, slut."

I lean forward, and he grabs hold of the messy bun I threw up earlier. He then proceeds to slap me in the face with his cock. I keep my eyes on him as he does so because I know that's what he wants. Precum beads at the tip, and he smears it around my cheek before slapping me more.

"Whose slut are you?"

"My Lords'..."

"Whose cocks fuck you?"

"My Lords'..."

"Who gets to hurt you?"

"My Lords..."

"Who belongs to you?"

My heart pounds, and I swallow hard, loving this question and the answer I'm about to give, "My Lords..."

His grin is wicked, "Remember that Kitty Cat. Every single piece of you belongs to the Lords of Sin, as we belong to you. You will not be free of us until we decide to set you free. Do you understand that?"

"Yes, my Lord."

"Good. Now, open wide and choke on my cock." He wastes no time thrusting into my mouth, not stopping until he's all the way in. I can't breathe, and I'm doing exactly as he instructed; I'm choking on his cock. My eyes are on his as they take on a sinister look. Biting his lip, he brings my head up just to slam it down again.

"Take my cock slut. Choke on it and cry for me. Only then will I give you your reward."

I let him use me. I gag, choke, and even cry, giving him exactly what he wants. When I first saw the Lords of Sin outside my window, I never thought I would give this Greek God a blow job, never mind belong to all three of them. I feel wanted for once in my life. My father used to make me feel that way, but now, I'm not so sure. Now I have the Sinners, and at this moment, it's all I need.

"Get ready, Kitty Cat," Oakley grunts, and that's when I feel it, ropes of seed shooting into the back of my throat, "Don't swallow it yet," he instructs me.

My mouth is full of the warm salty substance, and I want nothing more than to swallow and feel it as it slides down my throat. Oakley pulls his cock from my mouth and grins down at me. I'm sure I look a mess and will have to fix the little makeup I put on this morning, but they all love this look on me and strive to give it to me every time they fuck my face.

"Fucking beautiful..." Oakley caresses my face, "Open and let me see the reward I gave you."

Tilting my head back, I open my mouth and let him look inside. I don't expect him to stick two fingers in and scoop some out, "You wanted depravity, Kitty Cat..." his grin is wicked as he opens the front of my shorts and shoves his hand down, thrusting his cum-soaked fingers inside me, fucking his seed into me. He pulls them out and scoops more of his cum out, only this time, he pulls me forward and slides his hand in the back of my shorts before rimming my asshole. He works it for a moment, then I feel the stretch as he pushes his finger into me, fucking my ass for a minute before inserting the second cum-soaked finger.

I moan.

"Ah, my little slut likes that, do you?" he pulls away, "Give me some more, Kitty Cat, and then you can swallow the rest."

I dribble more onto his fingers, and he goes back to fucking my ass. I let the rest slide down my throat and moan again, "Oakley...please!"

"Do you want to come while I fuck my cum into your ass?"

"God, yes!" I'm a desperate slut as I feel the fire build inside me.

"Then come for me..."

The door opens, and my other two Lords walk in. They grin when they see what we are up to, "I hate to interrupt, but we need to borrow Little Saint."

I groan as soon as Oakley pulls his fingers from my ass, "Sorry, Kitty Cat, your Lords need you," his knowing smirk is infuriating, "We'll have to finish this later. At least I know that your holes will be dripping with my cum as you go about your business."

Oakley motions for his friends to come over, and they lift me to my feet, "I'm kind of finding it hot seeing Lovely Lina like this. What do you think, Fynn?"

I glance at Jett and know he's up to something, "Jett…"

"I have to agree, Jett. Let's keep her like this. It will make our little visit so much more interesting," Fynn winks at me.

"What do you say, Kitty Cat? You know what your Lords want, so what should you do?"

Fuck! Why do they do this to me? *Oh, wait, because they know I love it!* I look at Fynn and Jett, "It's my pleasure to remain this way for you if it's what you want."

"Thank you, Little Saint. We appreciate your thoughtfulness," Fynn grips my jaw and kisses me harshly, shoving his tongue into my mouth. When he pulls away, he licks his lip, "Mm, I can taste my best friend's cum on your tongue."

The filthy way he states this would make one think that they have a thing going as well, but they don't. How hot would that be, though? I've never seen man on man, but my Lords aren't like that. They may be sick and twisted, but they love their pussy way too much.

"Quit fucking around," Jett growls, "I'm dying to show our girl the surprise we brought for her."

"Don't forget about the invalid here!" Oakley calls out, "I don't want to miss this," he winks at me, but his smile makes me wary.

Fynn pulls me along, helping me down the stairs and through the halls of the Sinner's house while Jett helps his friend. It's the middle of the day, so most are in classes, but a few linger around and smirk when they see me with my hands restrained.

"What the fuck are you looking at?" I glare at them, and they turn away in a hurry, knowing what I'm capable of.

I haven't had much downtime to be able to think about my actions against Brett. When I think about it, I start to feel bad because he was always nice to me and really seemed like a good guy, but then I remember what he did to me, and my anger rises again. I can't feel bad for a person who chose to be evil, though. Coming back to the present, I know the basement is our destination, and I take a deep breath to prepare myself for what the Lords of Sin have in store for me.

The guys stop us at the basement door, and my stomach does flip-flops for some reason. I know they've been known to torture women for pleasure down there, but that's not all they do in the basement. So, my question is, what is in store for me once they get me there? They won't tell me if I ask, so I don't bother.

When Jett reaches into his back pocket and pulls out a blindfold, chills run through me, "Turn around, Lovely. We can't have you seeing the surprise until we are ready for you to see it."

Jett slips the blindfold over my eyes, and then I feel his warm breath on my neck just before his lips graze my delicate skin. He pulls back and whispers in my ear, "I hope you like it, Lina."

Suddenly, I'm lifted and tossed over his shoulder, and then we descend the stairs. I can feel the temperature change instantly while the slight dampness of the basement permeates the air. I'm then set onto my feet and walked further into the chilled room.

"Kneel, Kitty Cat."

My core throbs at the sound of Oakley's demanding voice. Still needing to come, I do as I'm told, hoping they won't make me wait long. I'm a needy little slut today. Now that we have discussed it and I laid everything out to them, they are balls to the wall, wanting every inch of my soul for their pleasures, and I'm here for the ride.

"Little Saint," Fynn starts off, "What we have for you may come as a little surprise, but we need you to know that we take your safety very seriously, and we will leave no stone unturned in order to do just that."

I jump when I hear Oakley's voice next to my ear, "Especially when they threaten to take what's ours. I've told you before, only we say when we are done with you. Anybody that tries to take you from us will end up six feet under...remember that."

Even though his words build up the flames threatening to incinerate me, they also give me pause. I furrow my brow, but someone's hand caresses my head, and I enjoy the gentleness of it as I smile. Unfortunately, it doesn't last long. A muffled sound reaches my ears, and I freeze. I'm not here for anything sexual. I'm not here to be their whore to play with, and when the blindfold is ripped from my head, my eyes adjust, and a gasp escapes.

"What did you do?" I ask breathlessly.

"He's part of it, Little Saint. We need answers, so he is all yours to question how you want."

My eyes are as round as saucers while I stare at Fynn before returning them to the person tied to the torture chair, "Kaden..."

"What the fuck is he doing here?" I curse as I look at each Lord.

"He's part of this, Kitty Cat..."

"We don't know that Oakley!" I glance at Kaden, "Take the tape off his mouth."

"Lina..." Jett starts, but I glare at him.

"Didn't you say that he was all mine? Then take the fucking tape off!" I look up at Oakley and see that he's pissed, so I take a deep breath to calm down before addressing him, "Please take the zip tie off."

We have a brief staring contest, and then he nods at Fynn, who pulls his pocketknife out and cuts the tie. I get to my feet and start for Kaden to untie him, but I'm grabbed around my waist and pulled back. Jett at least removed the tape from the Lacrosse player's mouth.

"Let me go!" I scowl and try to pry Fynn's hands off me.

"No. He stays tied up until we get answers, Little Saint. Don't press your fucking luck."

"Cat? What's going on? Why did these psychos drag me here?"

My head snaps to Kaden, "Please refrain from name-calling, Kaden. I won't have you disrespecting the Lords."

As pissed at them as I am, I will not tolerate anyone showing disrespect for my guys. I'm the only one who gets to call them psycho, twisted, and depraved, along with so many other things that they are, but they are mine to do so as I please.

"You can't seriously be taking their side, Cat!" Kaden sneers at me, but I hold up my hand.

I'm trying to compromise when it comes to the Lords. Although I disapprove of how they do things sometimes, I will try not to disrespect them in front of others. I will ask the questions that we need the answers to, but then he will be set free unless it's proven that Kaden has something to do with the threats. I will give my guys a piece of my mind about their manners later.

"Please stop talking, Kaden. I can only help you once you answer a few questions," I tell him, but of course, he doesn't listen.

"Are you with one of these guys? Don't you know what kind of guys they are? They are fucking bullies... that's all they are!"

I walk over and stand before all three Lords, "No, I'm not seeing one of them," I glance over my shoulder at my three Lords and then back at Kaden, "I belong to all of them."

"What?!"

"I'm their Lady of Sin, Kaden, so even though I like you, it doesn't mean I will allow you to disrespect them."

"You're as crazy as they are!" He tries breaking the rope restraining him, but it doesn't budge.

I chuckle and look at my guys one more time, "I know, but enough about us. I grab another chair and place it before him, straddling it as I lean against the back, "So, tell me, Kaden. Why don't you go by Kaden Simmons?"

The Captain of the Lacrosse team freezes and gawks at me, disbelievingly, "How..."

When he doesn't finish, I continue, "Your father is Bradley Simmons, one of the three Lords of Sin in the class of ninety-eight. Which brings me to another question. Why are you not living at the Sinner's Fraternity as a Legacy?"

His look turns angry, "You don't know what you're fucking talking about!" Jett steps forward, about to slap Kaden, but I stop him.

"It's okay. He gets a pass this once," I smile up at the Lord, who then dips his head and grabs my chin to kiss my lips. I lick them when he moves away and turn my attention back to Kaden, "We're only trying to figure out if you've been receiving threats as well."

"Threats? What kind of threats?" Kaden asks in confusion.

"A threat is a fucking threat, dipshit!" Fynn growls.

"Fynn, no name-calling until we get to the bottom of this," I wink at him.

Fynn rolls his eyes, "You're asking a lot from us, Little Saint."

"Oh, but I will make it up to you later," I look him up and down, and he automatically steps back, letting me continue.

"Oh wow, the mighty Lords of Sin are pussy whipped! Did hell freeze over?" I can't believe I'm seeing this side of Kaden. Where is the gentleman who drove me to the dorms less than a week ago or the one with whom I enjoyed a pleasant conversation the first night we met?

"Kaden," I say in warning, "They are not pussy whipped, but we have a mutual respect for one another, which did not come very easily. Stop being an asshole. You do want to go home, don't you?"

"Whatever," he scowls, "To answer your question, no. I have not received any threats, and as for that POS sperm donor of mine, I've never met him, and I never want to."

It's my turn to look confused now, "You've never met your father? Then why are you at Helshire?"

"He knocked my mother up and then took off after making promises of marriage. He left the country, and we have never heard from him since. As for coming to Helshire, it's got the best Lacrosse team in the state, and my mother also came here."

"Oh? What is your mother's name?" Oakley asks him.

"Cathleen Miller, if you must know. She's from a wealthy family, but she mainly kept to herself until my sperm donor sweet-talked her into getting into her pants the night after graduation." Kaden's animosity toward Bradley is thick, and I kind of feel sorry for him.

"So, you're telling me that nobody here at Helshire knows you're a Legacy?" I ask him softly.

"No. Not even your father knows. I wanted to come here to play, not get wrapped up in all the drama of the Sinners, and I sure as hell didn't want to follow in my father's footsteps."

"Hm," I'm not sure how to ask this next question, so I'm just going to come right out and say it, "Do you know anything about a rape that took place the year your fath—Bradley was a Lord?"

Kaden scrunches his brows together, "No. I've only heard how he used my mother and left her knocked up." He looks around at the four of us, "I would appreciate it if my parentage doesn't get discussed further than this room. The last thing I want is for others to think differently of me. I just want to be Kaden Miller, Captain of the Lacrosse team. I made it almost four years getting by on my own merits, and I want to make it to graduation this Spring doing the same thing."

I look back at the Lords, and they all shrug. Standing up, I stare at my guys until they reluctantly come over and untie Kaden, "Your secret is safe with us, but you should know, we only figured it out because you are the spitting image of Bradley, and his photo hangs in a room at the Frat House."

His mouth kicks up on the side as he stands, "I'll take my chances."

"Please let me know if you start receiving threatening letters." I briefly touch his arm and hear a slight growl behind me.

"Calm down, Harris. I'm not after your girl," Kaden looks at me amusingly, "No offense, but you're a bit much for me."

I shrug, "I'm not everyone's cup of tea," I jerk my head back toward my Lords, "But I am their kind of whiskey."

"Damn straight..." They all say in sync.

"Well, if that's all, can I go now?"

I nod at Kaden, "Yeah. I will let you know if we have any more questions."

"Can you please just call next time? I prefer not being gagged and dragged out of the locker room again," Kaden sighs his request.

It sounds like a good time to me, but I keep that thought to myself and glare at Fynn and Jett as they snicker, "At least you didn't drag him out naked."

"Oh, we almost did, but then we didn't want you looking upon another half-naked guy." Jett scoffs.

Rolling my eyes, I walk Kaden up the stairs and to the front door, "I'm sorry for their behavior, Kaden."

"Hey, they're only trying to protect you. I get it. I'll see you around, Cat." I watch him walk out the door.

"Yeah, I'll see you around."

FORTY-FIVE

Fynn

I don't like it. The way she walks him to the front door and is a little too friendly with the guy has me itching to beat him down. I don't trust Kaden Miller. Anyone who hides who they truly are shouldn't be trusted, and I will be damn sure to keep my eye on him.

I follow close behind, so when my Little Saint closes the door, I shove myself against her until she's pressed into it. Her hands automatically come up, flattening her palms to the wood as she turns her head to the side.

"Fynn..."

"What are you doing, Saint?"

"I don't know what you mean?"

"You're awfully friendly with Miller..."

"You can't be fucking serious!"

I lean in, so my face is only inches from hers, our eyes burning into the others, "I am dead fucking serious. I don't like him, and I don't like my girl playing nice with other guys."

"Fynn, you know I don't feel anything for him. You Lords..."

I cut her off, "Are all you fucking need. Nobody else can give you what you want..." I slide my hand around and into her shorts, not stopping until I feel the wetness pooling between her legs, "...what you need. This pussy is property of the Lords of Sin, and we don't like others sniffing around what is ours."

I push a finger into her, making her gasp, "It's not like that. He isn't into me..." her voice is breathless as I finger fuck her right here, against the front door.

"Anyone with a dick is interested in you, Little Saint," I bite down on her shoulder, "You're that forbidden fruit nobody can touch. Even before you signed the contract with us, guys talked about the hot piece of fresh meat walking around campus," I push another finger into her, "We wanted to beat the shit out of all of them even before we made you ours," my fingers thrust into her deep, curling and hitting that sweet spot she loves so much, "Now, we will kill them all for trying to touch what is ours."

"Fuck, Fynn..." my needy little slut opens her legs wider.

"Do you want to come for me?"

"Yes!"

I fuck her harder and faster until right before she lets go, and then I pull my fingers away. As she goes to curse me, I shove my soaked fingers into her mouth, making her gag around them. I grind my hardness against her ass, and after looking around, I unzip my jeans.

"What would you do if I fucked you right here, Little Saint?" I yank her shorts down, already knowing her answer, and pull my fingers from her mouth.

"The others..." she pants, but still, she pushes her ass against my groin.

"What about them?" I ask as I pull my cock out and stroke it a few times.

"They may come home and see," her fingers curl as if trying to grip the door's flat surface.

"Reach down and lock the door then," I let her shorts fall to the floor, then lift her left leg, making sure not to strain her stab wound any more than I have to, "Last chance to tell me no, Saint. Otherwise, beg me to give you my cock."

"Fynn...stop fucking around and fuck me already!"

"That's what I fucking thought," I thrust hard, pushing deep into her,

"Oh fuck, Fynn...you're really deep!"

"Good! I want to consume every fucking inch of you...fuck into you deeper than anyone ever has, and I want to cause you that sweet pain that comes with it all."

"God, yes!" she cries out when I bite that sensitive spot where her shoulder meets her neck.

I don't release her until the metallic taste of her blood reaches my tongue. I made her bleed just like I told her I would, and now I'm not only addicted to her sweet cunt, but my obsession now extends to her kiss and her very essence. I need more of it. I won't stop until I can touch her fucking soul.

Pulling out, I spin her around and lift her by her ass, making her wrap her legs around my waist as I impale her back onto my cock. Pressing her back to the door, I lean back, so I can watch my cock take what is mine. Her cunt sucks me in every time I pull back out. It's taking me everything not to come just yet.

When I look back up, I notice the small stream of blood tricking down her neck and soaking into her shirt from the bite I gave her. Like a bloodsucking vampire, I dip my head and take more of her in. Sucking and licking at my bite, I've marked her as mine, and I will never let her go.

Pulling back, her eyes widen at the sight of her blood smeared around my mouth, and I do the only thing my mind tells me to do...I possess her mouth like I have her body. Holding her ass with one hand, I grip her jaw with the other and crush her lips with mine. She fights me for a few seconds before opening and letting me into her mouth.

Saint's arms tighten around my neck as she pulls me in closer. Her kiss is now desperate, and she ends up biting my lip, causing me to bleed. The fact that her blood is now mixed with mine, and I have her essence running through me is too much, and I slam into her two more times before I yank my mouth away and roar, "FUCK!!" as I release my load.

My friends come running, "What the fuck, Fynn?" Oakley stops, panting from the pain of running to see what is wrong.

Saint's cunt clenches around me, and she cries out her own orgasm, so I wait until she's finished before kissing her forehead and turning us toward my friends, "Take her..."

"What?" Jett asks but comes forward anyway.

"Just fucking take her and get her cleaned up. Bandage that bite mark..."

I see the hurt in her eyes, but I can't. I need to get away from her for a little bit. I need to be by myself so I can come to terms with what the hell just took place. I pull out of her and wish more than anything that I could enjoy watching my cum drip from her beautiful cunt, but I have to go.

Tucking myself back into my jeans, I turn and walk upstairs. All three of them call out to me, but I don't respond to any of them, "Fuck you, Fynn!" I hear my Little Saint yell angrily at my back.

I've hurt her, but I can't do anything about it, not yet anyway. I knew I was falling for our girl, but I never realized how deep it went. I will make it up to her if she allows me to, but for now, I need to get my head straight and accept this new revelation.

I've been locked in my room for two days, living off beef sticks, chips, beer, and my favorite smoke. I'm not being useless, though. I've been studying all our information about the Lords of the past, and it's just not making sense. We need that fucking video! Whatever is on it must be able to tell us more, but where the fuck is it?

I grab my phone and dial the number saved in it, "Fynn? What's wrong?"

"I need to see you...alone." I don't have beef with this person, but I know I would piss someone off if they knew I was talking to them.

Silence meets me, but I know they haven't hung up. Finally, a sigh, and they answer, "Where and when are you thinking?"

"Let's say in an hour, and it needs to be secure. Meaning, no cameras or listening devices."

Again, there is silence, but it doesn't last as long, "Do you remember that spot by the lake you used to swim at?"

"Yeah..."

"Meet me at the little hunting shack at the edge of the lake...you know the one."

"Okay, see you then." I hang up and sit back against my headboard.

Photos and papers are spread out all over my bed, and I begin gathering them, returning them to their respective folders. Once I'm done, I am tempted to light up once more before I have to sneak out of the house and drive the twenty minutes to the lake, but I decide against it. I hate to say it, but if I don't get any kind of answers that will be helpful, God help anyone in my path because we have come to a standstill in our investigation, and we can't have that. I'm ready to kill anything and anyone in my way at this point.

I hear music and voices coming from Jett's room. A female giggling goes straight to my dick as it recognizes my Little Saint. I'll talk to her tomorrow and try to explain what the fuck happened the other day, even though I'm still not finished figuring it out myself.

The house is dark when I get to the bottom step. Not a soul is around, which I find weird, but I don't have time to think about it. Suddenly, as I walk through the living room toward the front door, a lamp turns on, and my best friend sits there.

"Jesus, Oak!"

"Where are you sneaking off to?" His angry expression disappears when I put my finger to my lips and jerk my head for him to join me.

"You're driving; let's go," I tell him, continuing to the door.

"Where are we going?" Oakley asks as he starts his Camaro.

"The lake," is all I offer as an explanation.

He accepts it and drives the twenty minutes to get to the little shack by the lake. As soon as he shuts the car off, I jump out and head over to the rundown shack, where I can see a tiny light flicker inside, telling me they are already here. I turn to my friend and stop him from going any further.

"This little visit stays between you, me, and the person inside waiting." I stare at Oak, barely seeing him through the black of night. It's cloudy, so even the moon is under the cover of clouds, but I still see my friend nod.

We continue until we reach the door, and I knock three times, "It's me."

"Come in," the familiar voice says, and I see Oakley stiffen when he also recognizes the voice.

Opening the door, we are met with a friendly grin, "Hello, boys, it's been a long time."

"Mr. Pelletier..." Oakley and I say together.

"Oh stop...call me Blake," He comes forward and hugs us both, "Where is that son of mine?"

"He doesn't know we're here," I tell him, "He would be pissed if he knew," I say to the man who is the spitting image of our best friend.

Jett's dad sighs, "Well then, what can I help you with?"

I glance at Oakley because he doesn't even know why I came here. When I turn back to Blake, I just say, "We need to know what's on the video from the night of your initiation into the Lords of Sin."

Oakley

I sit downstairs in the dark, contemplating whether I should try talking to Fynn since he's been ignoring us all for the last two days, when I catch him sneaking downstairs. I automatically think the worst, that he is leaving to hook up with some chick, but I'm way off.

I'm about to rip him a new asshole when he tells me to come with him, and I know right then that I had it wrong. I'm a lousy fucking friend. I should have checked on him sooner, but I thought he wanted time, and then to imagine the worst and believe he would do Kitty Cat dirty like that...what's wrong with me?

I'm happy to drive, no matter how far it is, but when he tells me we're going to the lake, so many questions start running through my head. However, he remains quiet the whole ride, and I feel like I should, too. He knows I'm there for him if he wants to talk.

Now, standing in the middle of the hunting shack in the dead of night, staring at our best friend's dad, Fynn drops the bomb. I wouldn't have thought to ask Jett's dad because he's been MIA for so long. He hasn't done well since losing his wife five years ago and is now also on the verge of losing his son.

"I don't know what you're talking about," Blake turns away to stare out the window.

I stand back and let Fynn take the lead on this as he goes to stand beside Blake, "You know exactly what I'm talking about. We found the letter in the safe, but the video that was filmed that night seems to be missing."

Blake stares at Fynn, studying the hard look on my friend's face, "You don't want to see what's on that tape anyway, Fynn."

I've had enough of all this secrecy, and I step up to stand beside Fynn, "Who was it, Blake? Who was the girl you, Jakob, and my dad raped during your initiation?"

Jett's dad seems taken aback as he stares at us in disbelief, "You can't be serious. You think that we..."

"Don't try lying about it, Blake. It was all in Devlin's letter that he left. He said how he was the lucky one who had to stay back and record it while his other three friends had more of a physical hand in the rape."

Blake runs his hand through his hair as he exhales, "Yeah, what he said was true. Your fathers and I had to help, but all we did was hold her down," he's quick to say, "Don't get me wrong, holding her down is just as bad, but we weren't the ones to fuck her. Only the Lords did that."

"Then why is this person coming after all of you, or should I say your offspring?" Fynn asks skeptically.

"The letters said that they wanted us to fess up..."

"So why not fess up?" I growl, "Catalina was taken and stabbed already, and then they tried to take us out in the fire! Do we mean so little to our parents?"

"NO! That's not it at all, Oakley. We have been working on this behind the scenes, but you must realize there is so much at stake here." Blake holds his hands out pleadingly.

"The only thing at stake here is losing your kid, which, even if we win, you all can just go fuck off! My parents didn't even come to see me in the hospital..."

"Your mother tried but was stopped," Blake tells me, a look of shame crossing his face, "Your father had his own detail watching the hospital, and they were ordered to turn her away if she had shown up."

"How do you know this?" I ask, "Is that what my father told you because he's been known to lie..."

"Your mother told me...that night. She came to me crying because she couldn't see you."

"But why would she come to you?" I question, completely baffled.

Again, shame crosses his face, "She comes to me a lot, Oakley."

"Jesus, Blake…" Fynn says furiously, and that's when it clicks.

"You and my mom? For how long?"

He sighs, "You have to understand that when Jett's mother died, it broke me. Your mother helped me through it, but it didn't get romantic until about two years ago."

"YOU'VE BEEN FUCKING MY MOTHER FOR TWO YEARS?" I raise my fist, but Fynn grabs me and holds me back.

"What did you expect her to do when her husband has never been able to get over his fucking Lady from college? She never knew who it was, not until recently, and that devastated her. Ashlee was her friend all these years."

"Oh, my dad and the Scotts have been carrying on this affair…"

He cuts me off, "No, just your dad and Ashlee. Devlin is in the dark about Ashlee and Donavan. Yes, Devlin asks Don to join occasionally, but he doesn't know they carry on without him behind his back."

"You all are fucked up, you know that?" Fynn chuckles dryly.

Blake scoffs, "You have no idea. Jakob is the normal one out of us all. He fucks his secretary on the down low like a normal business guy."

I glance at Fynn and see him make a face, "Dad fucks April? Isn't she like ten years older than him?"

Blake shrugs, "It's just sex. Neither one wants to enter a relationship, so they have a deal with one another."

"Wow, I will never be able to look at that woman the same again," Fynn cringes.

"You boys act like you're better than us," Blake glares between me and my friend, "Aren't the three of you fucking Catalina, who should be like a sister to you all?"

It's my turn to cringe now, "Well, maybe if we all grew up together, but from what she was told, it's her duty to serve her Lords."

"I think we're getting off the topic," Fynn states annoyed, "Who is the girl that those sickos raped?"

"If anybody finds out where you got this from, I will be in deep shit…"

"Yeah, yeah, yeah," Fynn rolls his eyes.

"I'm fucking serious, Fynn. The past Lords mean business, and men have been known to disappear when they have given out secrets, but I know this has to be taken care of. Unfortunately, our hands are tied."

We watch Blake walk over to a floorboard and kneel as he works it loose. Reaching in, he pulls out a metal box and opens it but makes a face. What now?

"What is it?" I ask.

Blake looks up at us, "Nothing really. I'm assuming the files you have now came from this box since they aren't in here, but what stumps me is why he didn't give you this file. Maybe I shouldn't give it to you."

He's too busy thinking about it to see Fynn walk behind him and rip it from his hand. I'm still too shocked over my mom and dad to be much help. I mean, good for Mom for not settling and accepting what my father has been doing all these years, but why cheat? Why not just divorce his ass and be free?

"You have got to be shitting me?" Fynn's voice reaches me, and I see him with his nose in the file.

"What is it?" I go to him and look over his shoulder.

I yank the file from his hand, and the moment I do, I understand why he reacted the way he did. I can't believe what I'm looking at right now...this can't be right. The more I think about it, though, the more it makes sense.

I look up at Blake, "This is the girl who was assaulted?"

"No," he sighs, "That is who helped the Lords assault the other girl."

My face twists disgustingly, "Are you fucking serious right now?"

All Blake does is nod.

"So, where is the file on the victim?" Fynn scowls at our friend's father, "If you have these files, you must have hers."

"Well, had you not been so hasty in grabbing that file, I would have given you both," Blake replies sarcastically, handing Fynn the last folder.

He wastes no time opening the folder. He freezes. I can see the rage building in my best friend's eyes as he stares at whatever is in the folder. I'm worried about looking at it myself because if it's having this effect on Fynn, it can't be good. I have to know, though. So, I hold my hand out and wait for Fynn to place it in my hand instead of snatching it from him like the last one.

Keeping my eyes on his until I open the folder, I swallow hard before I allow my eyes to drop to its contents. The face and then the name on the page pop out at me as ones I recognize all too well. I slowly look back up at Fynn, my jaw clenched and the edge of the folder now crumbling inside my fist.

Fynn and I share a knowing look before I say, "This is not going to end well, at all."

FORTY-SIX

Jett

I heard Oakley's Camaro leave a little while ago, two doors closing just before it took off. I didn't want to say anything to my Lovely, but I also heard the creak of Fynn's bedroom door opening, so I know he left with Oakley. I'm not sure what's going on with my friend, but I know one thing, he'll tell us when he's ready.

Lina is humming to some tunes she's listening to through her air pods while I scroll through my social media account. It's just been one of those days where we've lazed around. However, one slight movement from the beautiful girl beside me has a particular appendage stirring to life.

All she does is lay further down on the bed, but it's enough that it pushes her t-shirt up, showing off her creamy flat stomach. The sleep shorts she changed into before crawling into my bed are more like booty shorts. So, what do I do? I move my hand over to her bare thigh and caress the soft skin, giving her goosebumps.

Of course, I don't stop. I toss my phone aside and turn to lie on my left side, propping my head up with my hand. A slow grin pulls at my lips when her body tenses as soon as my hand moves to her midriff. Her breathing becomes shallow, and I bet that if I slip my hand between the warmth of her thighs, I'll find her wet.

I dip my head, running my tongue across the skin that is yearning to be touched. A giggle bubbles from my Lovely's lips when my tongue finds her belly button. Without stopping, I slide across her thigh and make myself comfortable between them. I can already feel the heat radiating from her core.

If she was going to stop me, she'd have done it by now, but it doesn't stop the small shriek that comes out of her when I grab hold of her thighs and spread them wide and upwards. It also doesn't stop the moan that can be heard when my mouth latches on to her covered cunt, licking her up and down until the fabric is soaked. Letting her legs go, they drop down, so I can hook my fingers into the waist and tug them off.

"I'm going to have a little snack, Lina. Do you want to guess what I'm going to do after that?" I toss her shorts and thong to the floor as I stare down at her smoothly waxed pussy.

"You're going to fuck me..."

It's almost as though I can hear her heart thumping out of her chest as I give her a wicked grin and shake my head, "You may call it fucking, but I call it owning you. I'm going to take you how I like because I can, and I know that the slut inside you craves it. Am I wrong?"

She shakes her head.

"Use your words, my Lovely Lina. I want to hear you say it..."

"You're not wrong."

"And why am I not wrong?"

She bites her bottom lip, and my cock jumps, "Because I'm just as sick and twisted as my Lords, and I crave only what the three of you can do to me."

Tilting my head, I study her briefly, "Tell me, Lovely," I run my fingers through her wet folds, "What is it that we do to you that makes you want to whore yourself out to us?"

The little minx slowly slides her hands up under her shirt, lifting it enough for me to watch her play with her nipples, "You find that part of me that I didn't know I had, and you all make it your own, but you never stop there. You dig until you reach the deepest, most private parts of me, and you make me take whatever you do to make it your own, only to leave me craving more when you're done," she pauses for a moment, "But you're never done, are you? You will never be done until you have taken every single piece of my soul…"

"Oh, lovely Lina," I place a light kiss on her clit before looking at her once more, "Even then, we will never be done with you."

I attack her clit, licking, sucking, and biting it, making her scream my name. Pushing two fingers into her, I fuck her hard, pushing them as far inside as possible without fisting her. Maybe someday, but not tonight. I watch her as she arches her back while twisting and pulling at her tits, her mouth forming a perfect O as I make her come for the first time tonight.

I slip out of my basketball shorts and kneel between her legs, "Hold on to something because I'm not liable for the bumps on your head as I fuck you if you slam it into the headboard."

She reaches over her head and places her hands on the headboard, helping to keep her from hitting her head. I reach up, move her shirt, so I have a full view of her plump breasts, then I wrap my hand around her neck, "Oh, my Lovely Lina, have you ever passed out from being choked as you come so hard around a nice thick cock?"

"No…"

I thrust into her hard, "Well, you're about to find out…" I pull out slowly and plunge back into her even harder.

Moving her legs over, I have her so they're both off to my left side, her body twisted as I keep her pinned on her back. This way, I can get in deeper, keep he r choked, and watch as her tits bounce while I fuck her to my heart's content. This is my favorite position to fuck her in because if I decide I want to slap her ass or fuck it instead, it's also right there.

"Oh fuck…" my Lovely cries out as I pick up my pace, "Jett…please!"

"Please, what, Lina? Is this too much for you?" I smirk.

"Yes, but don't you dare fucking stop!"

"Let's fix that running mouth of yours, shall we?" I put more pressure around her throat, still allowing her to get air but not talk, "Much better…"

Gripping her thigh with my left hand while my right is wrapped around her pretty little throat, I thrust my hips repeatedly, penetrating her tight cunt as she keeps her hands on the headboard, so I don't shove her into it. I can already feel her tightening around me, but I'm not ready to come just yet. I push her legs closer to her stomach while keeping them off to the side and find her sweet spot. She tries crying out, rolling her eyes back into her head...

"I'm going to make you come, Lovely," I cut off all her air and watch carefully, ensuring I do it just right.

Biting my lip, I jackhammer into her until her pussy clenches around me, and her eyes begin to close. I release her throat, letting her take in much-needed air, and she ends up screaming at the massive climax that consumes her. I let myself go, too, filling her up nice and full until neither of us have anything left.

I'm just about passed the fuck out from the amazing fuck session with Lina when her phone starts to vibrate. I hear her groan, and I chuckle as she curses at it. Looking at the screen, she tosses it to me and rolls back over.

"You deal with him," she mumbles.

It's a text from Oakley, so I open it, "He wants us to meet him."

"It's fucking midnight! Why can't he just come to us?"

I slap her ass, "Because your Lord told you to meet him, now let's go." I climb from my bed and go to my dresser for a fresh pair of jeans. I don't bother washing myself because I love smelling like Lovely's pussy.

She glares at me the whole time she's getting dressed, but I only smirk. I pin her to the door right before she opens it, which only irks her more, "What?"

I grip her jaw, "Lose your attitude. The last thing I want to do is punish you after the night we just had," my eyes go to the beautiful handprint on her neck, "Just be a good girl, and we can make this quick."

Sighing, her shoulders droop, "Fine."

"Good girl," I press my lips to her forehead and open the door. I lean in as she passes, "In case I didn't mention it earlier, that sex was the best I've had in a very long time." I slap her ass once more when I see the smile appear on her lips.

"You're very welcome, but, you know, I may have to take you for another test drive. Make sure it's just as good the next time as it was this time," she giggles and hurries away as I try slapping her ass again. She calls over her shoulder, "Where are we going anyway?"

"Wherever Oakley tells me to take you. You'll find out soon enough," I grin, knowing that she hates not being told shit.

I wonder why he wants us to meet him at this location, but he must have a reason. I check the surroundings out front before I allow Lina to leave the house. Opening the passenger door for her, I'm watchful because I'll be damned if someone gets the jump on us. Once I know nobody will accost us, I breathe much easier.

"Are you seriously not going to tell me where we are going?" Lina whines as soon as I hop into the driver's seat.

"Nope..." I smile and start the Jeep.

She sits back with her arms crossed, "I was going to be nice and give you road head but fuck that."

I bust out laughing and find that she's having a hard time keeping her smile hidden, "Well, if I wanted you to suck my cock while driving, then your head would be right here," I point at my crotch, "Not all the way over there. And for the record, I'm good to go. You satisfied me enough for now."

I reach over and take her hand, bringing it to my lips, "Aren't you the gentleman," she smirks.

"A gentleman? Not quite, but I do know what a woman needs every once in a while...aside from my cock." I wink at her and put my Jeep in gear before taking off.

"Well, no other women better be getting your cock anymore..." She mumbles under her breath, making me grin. Catalina Scott likes me. She at least likes me enough to get jealous anyway, and that's enough...for now.

I keep her hand in mine and place it on my lap as I drive us to meet my friends. I hope they have a damn good reason to pull us from the warmth of my bed at this time of night. Otherwise, Lina will have their balls. I glance at said ball crusher and see she's turned to stare out of the passenger window. Her head rests back against the seat's headrest, and I can't tell if she's fallen asleep or not. What is so important that they had to pull us out of bed this late? Sighing, I keep my eyes on the road the rest of the drive, and Lina's hand in mine, right where it belongs.

FORTY-SEVEN

Catalina

I rest my eyes as Jett drives through town, taking us to only God knows where. *"Because your Lord told you to meet him…"* I mimic Jett's reply in my head. If he thinks I will jump off a bridge just because he tells me to, I'll push his ass over the edge. The Lords may have me addicted to them, but I have limits. I just need to figure out when to take a stance against them.

I'm most likely overreacting because I'm tired and want sleep, though. I doubt Oakley would call us out in the middle of the night if it wasn't important…right? What about Fynn? Was he ordered to meet Oakley, too?

I get my answer the moment Jett's Jeep slows and comes to a stop. I open my eyes to check my surroundings and stare into big brown eyes through my window. They look apologetic at first but then harden as he opens the door for me.

"Fynn…"

"Little Saint," he smirks.

"I see you could crawl out of your hole for this. I'm glad to know that there's at least one thing you are willing to come out of your room for," I turn my back on him and go to walk away, but he grabs my arm.

"Don't, Saint. You don't understand..."

Hanging my head because it hurts too much to look at him right now, "You're right. I don't understand. That's because you ran away and refused to talk to me about it."

"I just needed time to think, Saint."

"Yeah...fine," I yank my arm from his grip, "So, let me have time to think about whether I'm going to forgive you." I leave Fynn standing next to the Jeep while I walk over to Oakley, who's leaning against his car.

"That was harsh," Oakley frowns.

I shrug, "He'll get over it. Now, tell me...why are we here?"

Oakley stares at me briefly before turning and opening the passenger door, "Get in."

"Oak..."

"Just get that cute ass in the car and look at the folders on the driver's seat. Then you can come out here, so we can talk."

Rolling my eyes, I get in, letting him shut the door before I reach over and pick up the two folders on the seat. Recognizing the name on the top folder, I open it. A graduation photo of Julia Howard stares back at me. I study it briefly before flipping it, stopping at her obituary. Two years after graduating and a little over a year after giving birth to her daughter, Felicia Howard, the former Lady of Sin took her life.

As I read through the article, it never mentions a husband or her daughter's father, but it does mention a sister Charlotte. I remember Felicia telling me about her aunt and how she ensured the rule about Saints and Sinners fraternizing would be implemented. I do not understand why I'm looking at this folder because it's not telling me anything we don't already know.

Just as I think of the latter, I turn the article and find more photos. I'm frozen in my seat, afraid to look at the next one. However, it's like a train wreck, and I cannot look away from the rest, no matter how much it turns my stomach.

Julia had been the one to bring her friend to the Lord's initiation; this we already knew. What we didn't know, and from what these pictures show, the Saint's President participated in the act itself. Until we find that video, we won't know what was said during that time, but I know one thing, Julia Howard does not look like she was coerced into using the different items to fuck her friend with. If the smile on her face is any indication, it seems she was enjoying it immensely.

The anger I feel toward this woman I've never met before is consuming. How can you do this to someone you call a friend? Is this why she ended her life? Because she was feeling guilty over what she had done? We will never know, but I hope this was the culprit.

I don't realize my face is wet until I look out the window, and both Oakley and Fynn stare back at me. I feel my eyes sting at this point and reach up to wipe away the fresh tears. I can't look at any more of the pictures unless I want to lose the contents of my stomach.

Tossing it back on the driver's seat, I take a deep breath and look down at the next folder. I'm confused as I stare at the name at first, but when it clicks, I shake my head back and forth. Simone Richards. Frowning, I glance out the window again, and the guys' expressions tell me I'm right. I may not have heard of the name, but I know only one person with the last name Richards.

I stare at the building behind the Lords, the one that is housing my best friend. Looking up, I notice the light in her room is off. I'm still unsure why we are here exactly, but I'm beginning to think I'm about to find out. Am I ready to see what they want me to see?

Closing my eyes, I inhale and exhale, calming my nerves before looking into the unknown. I open the cover and finally crack my eyes open. It's almost like déjà vu. Simone's graduation photo is first, and then her obituary, only it's a year after graduating, and she had just given birth to a daughter.

My brows furrow. If this is Dani's mother, why is Dani not a senior this year? I push the thought aside for now and flip the article. It takes me a moment to discern what I'm looking at, but then it all comes into focus. I quickly flip through all the photos I've already seen; only these have the victim's face. Dani's mother is the one who was assaulted!

Slamming the car door, not caring if I wake anybody up, I stare glaringly at all three Lords, "So what's the plan? How are we going to do this?"

They all study me, but Oakley is the one who speaks first, "This is your show, Kitty Cat. They went after you first, and she's your best friend," he smirks when I scowl at the term he uses for Dani.

"Before you decide, Lina, you need to think about this. Whatever you just saw in those files may not be what you think."

I go back into the car and grab the folders, shoving them into Jett's chest, "Look for yourself."

"Kitty Cat, Jett is right. Just because her mother was the victim..."

I hold my hand up, "It all makes perfect sense. How Dani was quick to befriend me and why she doesn't like you guys," I put my hand to my forehead and pace, "We were fucking roommates, for Christ's sake! She could have killed me at any fucking time!"

Large hands stop me and keep me from moving. When I Look up, it's Fynn I see, and even though I'm still hurt by his actions, I let him pull me into his chest. I wrap my arms around his waist and revel in the feel of our bodies pressed together. His presence calms me and brings me back from the hysterical ledge I was about to fall over.

"What's it going to be, Saint? Do you want to go home and think this over?"

Images of my time spent with Dani play in my head like an old movie. She seemed so sincere, and trying to find any indication that I missed something isn't possible in my state of mind. She's been a bit possessive and jealous lately, but I just thought it was due to my spending all my time with the Lords. Looking at it from this new perspective, I see it as it really is.

My best friend is my stalker.

There are still holes in all of this, and we need to find out before I do anything too drastic, but I'll be damned if she gets away. So, I pull back from Fynn's embrace and stand up straight. Wiping the last of my tears, I look each of my Lords in the eye and nod.

"Let's do this."

"Kitty Cat?"

"No, I'm good," I tell Oakley when he looks skeptically at me, "We need zip ties, duct tape, and a hood of sorts."

"Damn girl," Jett licks his lips, "You have me ready to go another round!"

"Now is not the time, Jett..." I roll my eyes.

"Oh, but we can make it the time," he pulls me back against him and nuzzles my neck.

"No, Jett...we have work to do first."

"Ugh, you created a monster, Oak...thanks!"

Oakley snickers, "Just wait until we watch her in action. It will be such a turn-on and so much sweeter fucking her after we watch our girl take care of business."

"Hm, that's very true," Jett walks to the back of his Jeep and pulls out a small black duffle bag.

I cock my brow, "You seriously keep items for abducting someone in the back of your Jeep?"

Jett only shrugs, "It's actually from when we went to get Miller, but I may keep it in my Jeep for when I want to get kinky with you." Winking, he passes me as he heads to the door to the Dorms.

Fynn goes up the other set of stairs and takes out the camera on that end of the hall while Oakley takes care of the one on our side. I tap lightly on the door to Dani's room and wait. If she's awake, she'll answer. If not, we'll let ourselves in. After an allotted amount of time, Fynn picks the lock and opens the door quietly.

Unzipping the bag, Jett pulls out a small burlap sack and hands it to Oakley before grabbing the duct tape and giving it to Fynn. Lastly, he pulls the zip ties out and hands them to me. My hands shake a little as I take them, and he looks worriedly at me. I give him a thumbs up and wait for the next move.

It all happens so quickly as Oakley slips the hood over Dani's sleeping form. She wakes up, and he presses his hand against her mouth before she can even scream. Fynn hurries with the tape while Jet holds her down. Once the tape is secured over her mouth and the hood is on, Jett and Oakley flip her onto her stomach.

I won't make it easy on her. I want to play with her...mind fuck her and make her feel how I felt when I was taken. I run my fingers up and down her bare arms and lean in, breathing heavily next to where I think her ear is before running my hand down her back and hiking up her shirt enough to show some skin.

She fights the guys, but it's no use. Taking the slightly pointy end of the zip tie, I let her think it's a knife of sorts, and it must work because she freezes as I run it up and down her skin. The guys snicker as I fuck with her head, but then I finally tie her hands together, pulling the tie tight. I'm beginning to see why there are so many psychos in the world... because I already know this is going to be fun.

I watch over Dani as the guys rummage through her room. She's trying to hide her crying, but I can hear her sniffles. Good, she's scared. Now she knows how I felt when I woke up in a strange place, tied to a chair. At least we haven't knocked her out...yet.

"What do we have here?" Jett whispers in a raspy voice.

He empties a manilla envelope that has a flash drive in it. It tumbles out into the palm of his hand, and I snatch it up. Examining the small black device, I find one name written on the back...Simone Richards. This can't be what I think it is. Up until now, I was really hoping I was wrong, but her having this piece of evidence has changed all that.

I nod at the others and motion for them to grab Dani so we can get out of here. My ex-best friend starts to struggle and cry out, so Oakley does the only thing he can do, he pulls a gun out from the back of his jeans and hits her on the back of the head, knocking her out. I flinch and stare at the metallic black piece in his hand.

"You never know when it will be needed, Kitty Cat," the Lord states.

I'm not a huge fan of guns, but I'm not against people having them to protect themselves. I nod and watch him tuck it away before reaching his hand out for me to take. Walking hand in hand, we leave Jett and Fynn behind, so we can go out and pull the car up to the back door—less of a chance of being seen.

Once the coast is clear, Fynn carries Dani down over his shoulder and tosses her in the back seat before heading back to Jett's Jeep. In no time, we are back on the road, heading toward the Sinner's Frat House. Our prisoner remains passed out for the duration of the drive and then carried straight to the basement.

"I want to watch whatever is on this flash drive before we make our next move," I tell the guys, and they agree.

As soon as Dani is secured to the same chair they tied Kaden to, we leave her and head to the third floor. Oakley heads straight to his door, and we all follow. It's well after two in the morning, but unlike the rest of the house, we're wide awake and ready to take on whatever is on this flash drive. I think we all are hoping for the same thing. We're hoping this is the video my father mentioned.

Oakley takes the drive from me and inserts it into his laptop. We all wait in silence; the only noise is the tapping of keys on the keyboard as Oakley opens up the only file stored on it. Fynn grabs my neck and pulls me over, kissing my temple before tucking me into his side. My anger towards him is melting away as I let him hold me while we wait.

The video starts with Julia coming down the basement stairs with another pretty girl, Simone. Both women greet the guys with friendly smiles, and Julia goes straight to Kevin Douglas and sits on his lap. Simone goes and sits in the corner beside Travis.

"So, you ladies came just in time. We are about to initiate a few of the guys. They will be the new Lords of Sin next year," Kevin grins.

"Oh, how exciting," Simone claps, "I've never been to an initiation before, aside from my own," she giggles.

"Is that right?" Travis lays his arm across Simone's shoulders, "How would you like to be part of the initiation? You can play a vital role in it."

"Really?" the girl's eyes widen with surprise.

Travis shrugs, "Yeah, why not. I think the others will be fine with it," he looks to the other Lords, "What do you say?"

"I think she will be perfect," Kevin grins.

"Yeah, I'm on board with it, as long as she signs the form to participate," Bradley gets up and goes to a desk in another corner. Grabbing a piece of paper from a drawer, he grabs a dagger and stands before Simone, "Give me your hand, pretty girl."

Simone is hesitant and looks over at her friend, Julia, who nods her encouragement. The girl then places her hand in Bradley's, and he pokes her finger, "Ouch!"

"You're okay," Bradley soothes and places the paper before her, "Just sign on the dotted line."

I glance over at Oakley at this point, remembering when they stuck me with the same dagger and said those very words. Chills run through me at the thought of what that dagger signifies. A Blood Oath. No wonder the police were never informed of this incident; she was bound by her Oath, even though she had no idea what she was getting into.

"That's a good girl," Bradley caresses her cheek, "Come, let's get you ready."

Once again, Simone looks at her friend, and Julia nods, but as soon as Simone turns and before the camera moves from Julia's face, a slight frown creases the girl's brow. Julia watches as Bradley places her friend on the edge of a wooden table before he walks away.

Three others enter the camera's view to stand around the table, a blank look on all their faces, "I want you to meet the recruits," Kevin states as he gets up to come stand by the table, "This here is Donavan, Jakob, and Blake. Devlin is the one who will be filming the initiation."

"Kevin..." Julia comes to stand by the Lord.

He stops her from saying anything else, "As the Lady of Sin, you will partake in the initiation as well."

While Simone isn't looking, Julia mouths the word 'virgin' to Kevin, but all he does is grin. Suddenly, it all happens so fast. Donavan, Blake, and Jakob grab hold of Simone and push her down to the table. They hold her, still wearing blank looks on their faces.

The recruits are unhappy with what they are being made to do; that much is evident, and I can now see that Julia isn't entirely on board with this. It makes me wonder if she even knew the Lords of Sin's plans before bringing her innocent friend down to that basement.

"What are you doing? Let me go!" Simone cries out and starts screaming.

"Shut the bitch up!" Kevin tells Bradley, and the Lord unzips himself, using his girth to keep her quiet.

"You fucking bite me, and you will regret it. We will make this a whole lot worse for you. You signed the contract, and now you are ours to do with as we please."

Simone's tears go unnoticed as her clothing is torn from her body. Kevin, Bradley, and Travis laugh as they go about assaulting the poor girl. Bradley is so excited that he gets off fast and releases in Simone's mouth, causing her to choke. This only gets them laughing harder. When Bradley goes to put tape over her mouth, Kevin stops him.

"Wait, I want to hear her scream as I pop her cherry," Kevin positions himself between her legs and thrusts forward, not even preparing her for the intrusion.

"Turn it off! Oh God, I'm going to be sick!" I grab my mouth and run to the bathroom, emptying my stomach into the toilet.

Fynn comes in and holds my hair back, "That was fucked up, Saint. I hope you know that we would never do that."

I wipe my mouth, "But didn't you? You also had me sign a contract, and I had no choice in what you did afterward."

"We gave you time to read over it before you signed it, and I can guarantee that they did not list anything of what she would endure. You saw the same thing we did; Bradley had her sign it without reading it all."

I close my eyes because he's right. I did know what I was getting into. I look up at him from the floor and hold out my hand for him to help me up. He grabs my jaw as soon as I'm standing and stares deeply into my eyes.

"We never did anything you didn't already want, did we?" He waits patiently for my response.

After a brief moment of staring back at him, I shake my head, "No, I wanted it all," my voice is just above a whisper, "Can I rinse my mouth?"

"Fuck, Saint," Fynn's nostrils flare, "I want to taste every fucking part of you. The disgusting parts and all..." His mouth takes mine in a brutal and heated kiss, plundering my mouth as though it's searching for something.

I whimper, this is sick as fuck, but also hot as hell, as I open and give him what he's looking for. Our tongues dance in an erotic tango, if only for a moment. When he pulls away, we remain connected by a thin strand of saliva before it breaks, severing us completely.

"That was so gross, Fynn..." I smile up into his eyes.

"No, that was me showing you I don't care what happens; I want every fucking piece of you, Saint. You are mine, and I'm never letting you go."

My heart thumps so hard, I'm afraid it will burst, "What are you saying, Fynn?"

"I'm saying not to plan for a future without your Lords. I can't speak for the others, but I'm pretty sure they feel the same way. You have burned yourself into our souls' depths and taken our hearts prisoner, but that's okay because I don't want mine back," he caresses my cheek, and I can see it in his eyes; he means every fucking word he's saying.

"Everything okay in here?" Jett asks from the doorway.

We look over at him, and I smile, "Yeah, all good here."

"Good because we have a decision to make about Dani," Jett closes the distance, and as Fynn holds me in his arms, Jett crowds himself in, "I overheard what Fynn just said to you, and you should know...I feel the exact same way. I'm never giving you up, Lina."

He grabs my jaw and kisses me hard. As soon as he pulls away, I chuckle, "What is it with you sickos? Can't a girl rinse her mouth after puking in the toilet?"

Jett grins, "It doesn't bother me any, but go rinse. Hurry up, though. Dani is starting to wake up, and we should question her before we get some shut-eye."

They both let me go, and I watch them walk out. I haven't the slightest idea of how we got to where we are. It was never meant to go this far; it was only supposed to be an agreement, but somehow three depraved men and one equally depraved woman have grown on each other. I'm not sure where we go from here, but first, we must take care of this threat still looming over our heads. Tonight, we're one step closer to ending it all.

FORTY-EIGHT

💀

Catalina

We walk down the basement stairs as a unit, not saying a word. I notice Dani's body become rigid the moment she hears us. Not knowing what the hell is going on but knowing that she's in deep shit, she starts trying to talk through the tape. We let her sweat it out for a little bit and knowing that we are here but not doing anything has got to be fucking with her head.

Oakley pulls something from his back pocket and brings it to his mouth, "Do you recognize this, Dani?"

Oh, my God. It's the voice changer that Brett used when he held me captive! Dani shakes her head vigorously, and it pisses me off that she's denying it. I walk behind her, and grab hold of the hood, pulling it back flush against her face, making it hard for her to breathe.

"Are you sure you don't want to change your answer, Miss Richards?" Oakley chuckles cynically, "Do you recognize this?"

Again, she shakes her head.

Fynn, being the bad boy he is, pulls out his switchblade, and it's open with a flick of his wrist. He presses it by her collarbone until a small bead of blood appears, and Dani screams. He doesn't do much more than that, but it may be enough.

"What about that, Dani? Were those your instructions, too?" Oakley bends down close to her as he asks, making her jump, but she doesn't answer him. Instead, she cries harder, and suddenly a liquid stream starts running from the chair.

She's literally pissing herself. Do I feel sorry for her? Hell no. If anything, it angers me more. The fact that she can stalk me and try killing me not once but twice yet cry like a baby and piss herself when we've barely done anything to her really gets me going.

I point to the chains hanging from the ceiling, and Oakley understands, "Boss says to string her up!"

"MMPH..." Dani screams through the tape, but we ignore her.

Fynn and Jett bring the chains down and transfer her tied hands from the chair to the chains before untying her ankles. Oakley raises the chains until Dani's arms are well over her head, and she dangles; her feet just barely brushing the floor. A pang of guilt passes through me momentarily, but I push it aside and walk over to my ex-best friend.

I hold my hand out to Fynn, and he already knows what I want without me even asking. He grins and hands me the knife after opening it. I was humiliated, made to sit in nothing but a bra and panties, so Dani will too. I slice through her clothing, but since she was already in bed, she isn't wearing a bra, so I leave her just enough material to keep her chest hidden.

After all, it's an eye for an eye.

I take the voice changer from Oakley and raise it to my mouth, "Do you understand why you are here, Dani?"

She shakes her head, no, and I curse under my breath. I slap her across the face over the hood, "Liar. You said your mother was a Saint, and you're a Legacy. Is that correct?"

She nods.

"Your mother is Simone Richards. Isn't that correct?" I question, getting really annoyed.

She pauses but then shakes her head and starts trying to say something, but I'm not having it anymore. I toss the voice changer aside and rip the hood from her head, glaring at her as she looks at me in shock. I take her chin and grip it.

"You fucking lied to me, Dani! You told me you wanted to be friends. You played me this whole time so you could get close to me and then get rid of me," my laughter is more like a sneer as she shakes her head.

"We saw the video, Dani. It was in your room on a flash drive," Fynn scowls, "Deny it all you want, but why else would you have it?"

"MMPH!" She continues to try talking...try denying her part in all this. We need answers, though. So, I rip the tape from her mouth.

"If you scream, you will regret it," I glare, "Now, what the fuck are you going on about?"

"What the fuck, Cat?!" Dani glares back at me pathetically, "You all have gone fucking crazy! Simone isn't my mother..."

"The evidence is stacking against you, Dani," Jett stands back with his feet shoulder-width apart and arms crossed, "Your last name is Richards, you're a Saint's Legacy, and you have the flash drive of your mother's assault."

"W-what are you talking about?" Dani stammers, sniffling as snot runs from her nose.

"The manilla envelope on your desk, Dani," I sneer at her, "It had the video we have been searching all over for! I can't believe you! I should have seen it...the way you act whenever I talk about the guys. Now I know why you dislike them so much, even though none of what was done to your mother was their fault."

Suddenly, Dani starts laughing hysterically. I look at the Lords questioningly, but all they do is shrug. I let her laugh, but when she stops suddenly and glares at me, chills wrack my body.

"You think *I'm* the one stalking you and sending you the threats? You stupid, stupid bitch..."

Fynn's the one to raise his hand and slap her across the face, "Call her that one more time and see what I do next!"

My heart swells with Fynn's actions and words, but I don't have time to think about it now, "Awe, thanks, babe!" I give him a cheesy grin, then step back up to her, "As you can see, you *worried* for nothing. The Lords will protect me from any and all threats."

"You have it all wrong, Cat," Dani argues, "Simone wasn't my mother... she was my aunt!"

The room is silent as we all take in Dani's words. She's fucking with us, right? Doubt fills my head, and I keep looking at the Lords for their reactions. They seem just as baffled as I am, though.

I return my attention to the girl hanging from the ceiling, and in a low, shaky voice, I demand, "Explain."

"Why should I explain anything to any of you? You came into my room and took me without asking questions," she spews.

"That's not the way we work, and you should know that," Jett states, "Everyone knows that we act first and ask questions later."

I scrutinize her, but I can't tell if she's bluffing, so I do the only thing I can think of and call her bluff, "She's lying. Fynn, where is that knife of yours. Maybe carving into her stomach will get her to tell the truth."

"What? No! Please...I swear I'm not lying!" Dani pleads as she eyes the switchblade in Fynn's hand.

"What do you want me to carve into her, Little Saint?" Fynn gives me a devilish grin.

Oakley stands behind Dani, holding her in place, "Try not to squirm. Otherwise, he may go too deep."

"NO, STOP!"

I ignore her, "Let's go with *Liar* first," I tell Fynn.

"SHE'S MY AUNT, I SWEAR! SIMONE...SHE WAS MY DAD'S BABY SISTER!" Dani screams out, and we all stop, going silent once more.

I can't be sure, but Dani seems pretty believable. I don't know if that changes much, though. She could still do this to avenge her aunt if Simone really was her aunt. There is just so much evidence against her.

"The obituary says that Simone left behind a daughter..." I remind her.

"Yeah, my aunt had a baby girl, but she gave her up. She never told anybody how she got pregnant. This is the first I've heard of an assault, Cat!" she looks at Jett and Fynn, "I'm not the fucking stalker!"

"How did you get the flash drive then?" Fynn questions, twirling the blade around in his hand.

"That package got delivered to me today, just before my afternoon class," Dani replies, "I didn't have the time to look at it, and then I forgot all about it."

"Oh, isn't that convenient," Oakley sneers from behind her, "Tell us this then, Dani...why do you hate us so much?"

She remains quiet, but her eyes are glued to me, so I cock my brow, "Are you going to answer the fucking question?"

"What happened to you, Cat? This isn't you..."

"Oh, I don't know. Maybe I'm just tired of being hunted down like prey. I'm tired of looking over my shoulder to see if I'm being followed or wondering if this is going to be the day that the stalker succeeds in killing me."

Oakley yanks Dani's head back by her hair, "Answer my fucking question. If you aren't the stalker, then why do you despise us so much?"

Fynn approaches her and presses his blade to her neck, "Answer, or we will get to see how pretty you bleed."

"Stop...please!" she begs.

"One!" Fynn starts to count.

"Oh, God..."

"Two!"

"Please, don't make me..."

"Three!" Fynn pushes just enough to break the skin and release a small drop of blood.

"BECAUSE I WAS JEALOUS OF YOU!" Dani admits, "I wanted her for myself, but all she saw were you three!"

I step back, feeling like I just got slammed in the gut, "You wanted me? I don't understand..." I stammer.

Dani cries out when Oakley yanks on her hair harder, "I'm bisexual! I like you...I wanted you to like me back!"

"Holy fuck," Jett rubs his hands together, "Now this is getting good!"

I roll my eyes at him, "Seriously?"

"What? I'm a guy, and we all love girl-on-girl action" he grins.

Ignoring his comment, I turn back to Dani, "So, that's your story. You're not my stalker; you just want to get in my pants? Funny, you never told me you were Bibi. You always went after guys when we went out."

Dani swallows hard, "That's because you're the only female I want."

Well fuck. What the hell am I supposed to do with this? A better question...is she telling the truth? If she is, that means my stalker is still out there, and we just assaulted an innocent person. Ugh!

Fynn

None of us saw that one coming. I search Saint's face for her reaction; all I find is confusion. Why wouldn't she be confused after living with this girl and becoming besties, only to find out Dani's got the hots for her.

I can see and feel Little Saint's frustration. If Dani isn't the stalker, then they are still out there, and now we will have a lot of groveling to do, but fuck that. Our Lady will have to realize that we don't grovel. We apologize and try to compensate... but never grovel.

I don't believe it, though. This is probably just another way of trying to get out of it now that we're on to her, "I call bullshit! I don't fucking trust her," I glance at Little Saint.

Her piercing blue eyes meet mine, and I raise a brow, challenging her to find out for sure. I can see the hesitation on her face as she looks over at Dani and then back at me. I move to her and run my hand through the hair on the side of her head before bringing her in close.

"It's okay, Saint. Test the waters. See if what she says is true. It's the only way to truly know whether she's telling the truth." Only Saint can hear my whispered words as my hot breath dances across her ear and neck.

She fists my shirt as her breathing increases. When she looks me in the eyes after I pull back, it only takes the briefest of seconds for me to convey to her that she's got this. Straightening herself, she presses her soft lips to mine, then nods before returning to our prisoner.

"What is it you're jealous of, Dani?" I question her as I step behind Saint, "Is it when we do this?"

I snake my hand around Saint's waist, caressing her stomach as I watch my girl reach up and caress Dani's stomach. Dani sucks her breath in at Saint's feathery touch, and I smile inwardly. It's not like it proves anything, so I keep going.

"Or is it when we do this?" I slide my hand up to cup a breast, and Saint mimics my action, "You know, Dani, Saint's got the softest lips. She's the first girl I've ever kissed on the lips." Turning my Little Saint's head, I capture said lips and force them open, plundering her taste.

"Now, this is what I'm talking about," I hear Jett say from behind us, and I grin. I knew this would be right up his alley.

I pull away and grin at my girl, "Go on. Show her what she's missing."

Saint bites down on her lip, looking nervous, but I see the determination return just before she faces Dani. Oakley lowers the chains enough that Dani can now stand on her feet, and Saint can reach her better. Keeping her hand massaging a breast, Saint pulls Dani's head to her, and their mouths mash together.

Studying Dani closer, I immediately notice her open for Saint and moans when their tongues clash. Little Saint drops her hand from Dani's breast and reaches around to squeeze her ass. I nibble on Saint's ear as she continues her assault.

"That's it, baby. Make her want you. If she is telling the truth, she will come for you without a problem." I slip my other hand between my girl's legs and rub her over her leggings.

Heat radiates from Saint's core, telling me that this show also turns her on. I will let her enjoy it because this will be the only time I will allow her to touch anyone else...male or female...they are all off-limits, but tonight, we have something to prove. We will do whatever it takes to get our answers.

Dani moans and thrusts toward our girl, "I think she wants more, Kitty Cat."

Saint pulls away and looks at my friend over Dani's shoulder. He's just as turned on as the rest of us. Her eyes return to Dani, "Do you? Is this really what you want? Do you like me touching you like this...the way they touch me?"

Dani nods, unable to utter words.

"Use your fingers, Saint. Get her off...make her come for you," I say close to her ear.

Her head snaps to the side to look at me, "But she's pissed herself. Her panties are wet."

"So the fuck what! Do it for us, Saint," I'm finding this situation hot as fuck, "Stick your hand in her panties and finger fuck her. Give her what she wants because this will be the only time she will ever feel your touch upon her body this way."

"Fynn..."

"Fine, we will figure out something else if it grosses you out that much." I tenderly kiss her shoulder and start to pull away, meaning what I said when Dani grunts.

Looking down, Saint has her hand inside the front of Dani's panties, moving them vigorously. My cock jumps at the sight, and I do something I probably shouldn't. I tear the crotch of Saint's leggings and release myself. Pushing aside her thong, I nudge her opening.

"Wrap your leg around her waist, baby."

Oakley grabs her leg when she lifts it, "I've got her, Fynn."

I push inside Saint's hot cunt and groan. My eyes meet Dani's, "Watch me while I fuck her. I bet you will come so much harder."

"Fuck you, Fynn!" Dani spits.

"Nah, I only fuck Saint. Something you will never get to do." Grabbing Little Saint's hips, I pound into her as she now holds on to Dani's shoulder with one hand and fucks her with the other."

"Jesus, how the fuck did this go from torture to porn?" Jett snickers as he adjusts himself.

I ignore him as I continue to stare at Dani. Oakley has to hold her head up to keep her looking at me. She's pissed, but I don't give a flying fuck. She may want our girl, but she will never have her, and I'm reminding her of that.

"Fuck her harder, Saint, but don't let her come yet. Can you do that for me, baby?" I nibble her earlobe as she nods, "Good girl," I lick my lips salaciously as I stare at Dani.

"Tell us, Dani. Are you really not the stalker?" Oakley growls at her.

"I fucking swear to God that I'm not the damn stalker! Whoever sent me that video must think I'm Simone's daughter too..." She stops talking and moans.

"That's finger number three, Dani. Can you take a fourth?" Saint asks, then grunts as I bite down on her shoulder.

"Fuck, Cat... don't stop!" Dani begs.

"Hm, maybe she is telling the truth," Jett snickers.

"Dani," Oakley grips her hair tighter, "Do you know where Felicia is? She seems to have disappeared the day we found Kitty Cat."

She tries shaking her head and grimaces because my friend has a tight grip on her hair, "No, I've heard that she took sick leave, though."

This news is disturbing to me. I assumed the stalker got to the Saint's Prez because of her mother's hand in the assault. This changes a lot. The fact that she's disappeared without a trace worries me...she can be anywhere.

"Oh fuck!" Dani cries out, indicating my girl has shoved another finger into her.

"You are so fucking hot right now, Saint. I'm going to fill you up, and then you will let your other Lords do the same before you allow your little toy to come, okay?"

"Yes," she pants as I begin playing with her clit.

Thrusting into my Little Saint hard and fast, I still. As soon as my cock swells, I empty my load inside her and grin at Dani, "One down, two more to go."

Rubbing my fingers coated in Saint's arousal on Dani's lips, I watch her lick it off amusedly. She really does want our girl. I shrug and move away, leaving Saint dripping with my cum.

Jett is next to step up, "I'm going to enjoy this way too much," he plunges into Saint, causing her to shove her fingers deeper into Dani.

This goes on a while longer. Once Jett relieves himself, I switch spots with Oakley, so he can wet his dick, "How are you doing, baby?" I ask Saint.

"Mm, fucking perfect now that I've had all of you inside me," she looks at Dani, "You will come with me."

Fuck, the way she demands, it tells me that we have rubbed off on our girl, and I'm not sure if that's a good thing, I chuckle to myself.

Reaching over Dani's shoulder to where her collarbone still bleeds, I smear the blood around.

"Lick it, Saint. Tell us how she tastes," I order our girl before grabbing her jaw and smearing blood on her perfect skin.

"Holy shit, she likes that," Oakley groans, "Her cunt just clenched all around me."

"Are you enjoying yourself like my Little Saint is, Dani?" I ask as Saint's tongue snakes out, and she runs it over the small cut I made.

"God, yes!"

"So, if we tell you that we believe that you are not the stalker, we are good, right?" I caress Saint's head as she laps up Dani's blood, "You will not do anything stupid like try going to the police, correct?"

Her body stiffens, and I know that she isn't on board with keeping her fucking mouth shut just yet. Yanking her head, her mouth falls open, "Spit, Little Saint."

My girl does as she's told.

"Just so you know, this whole session is being recorded, so if you try going to the police, we will release it...the fun part, anyway," I snicker, "Now, fucking come for my girl before I make you bleed some more."

"Oh, God, Oakley...yes! Just like that... I'm coming!" Saint moans and tenses as she comes hard, and suddenly Dani is screaming out with her own climax.

I lean in as Dani is coming all over Saint's fingers, "From here on out, you will answer to us until this whole thing is over. Do you understand me?"

She's gasping for air but nods anyway, "Yes..."

"Good," I look at Saint, "Go grab something to clean her up, baby. I think Sean would enjoy a nice wake-up call from his little whore."

Once Dani is all cleaned up, I walk her to Sean's room, "You will remain here for the time being. We aren't done talking with you about your aunt."

"You can't keep me here!" she tries arguing.

I get my face right up into hers, "Want to fucking bet? I'm sure your Daddy would love to see what his little girl gets up to while away at college."

"My father passed away..."

"Oh, well, I'm sure your mother wouldn't want to be embarrassed by your shenanigans," I open the door to my Frat brother's room, "Now, go fuck his brains out. I better hear him bragging about it in the morning." Shoving her inside, I close the door and head to the third floor, whistling.

I love being the bad guy sometimes. It gets my adrenaline going. I'm not too worried about Dani going to my uncle, but if we don't scare her into keeping her mouth shut, we now know that we have a weapon to use against her, and Little Saint doesn't seem to be too upset about getting down and dirty when need be.

I enter my room to find Saint waiting in bed for me, "Go take a fucking shower and get her stench off you. I'm in the mood to fuck again and don't feel like smelling that whore's cunt all over you."

Little Saint grins and hurries to do my bidding like a good girl.

FORTY-NINE

☠

Catalina

What I did to Dani was downright raunchy. I have never considered touching another female intimately, but we need answers. I'll do whatever I need to in order to take back my life. As Jett would say, there's no shame in my game.

Surprisingly, I feel no awkwardness when I come into the kitchen and see Dani sitting with Sean, eating some breakfast. I notice her eyes light up briefly until I cock my brow. I'm still not one hundred percent convinced that she doesn't have a hand in all this shit. I will keep my distance for now.

"Morning," I grumble at the few here, eating.

"Good morning, my Lady," they all say in unison.

I roll my eyes and glare at each of them, "What have I told you about calling me that? You don't call them *'my Lords,'* now do you?"

"They will kick our asses if we call them that," Sean chuckles.

"And you think I won't? How about you ask Brett what happens...oh, I guess you can't." I turn toward the fridge, smirking, as soon as I see the smiles wiped from all their faces.

"Mm, morning Kitty Cat," Oakley leans in and kisses my cheek. His mouth comes to my ear, "You are with me tonight. I need to have you all to myself."

"Why wait for tonight? It's never stopped you from taking me whenever you wanted before." I turn, and he presses me into the shelves of the fridge.

"Are you trying to tempt me, my little slut?" His mouth goes to my neck, and his bite goes straight to my lady bits, "I will fuck you right here if that's the case."

"No, you won't," I challenge him, "You won't allow your brothers to see you fuck what belongs to you." I bite my lower lip and watch as his eyes lower to my mouth.

"Keep tempting me, and I will bend you over the table they are sitting at and show you just how far I will go to teach my little slut a lesson."

I lean in, lowering my voice, "I'm still dripping with Fynn's cum."

He growls, "Do you think that will prevent me from taking that cunt?" His chuckle is sinister, "I will shove my face between those gorgeous thighs and clean you with my tongue, lapping up every drop of my best friend's cum from your cunt just so I can fill you up with my own."

My heart races as I listen to the filth from Oakley's mouth. When did I fall so far that I now crave every sick and twisted thing these Lords want to do to me? I need them like I need air...my body calls out for them just so it can be tortured. I've lost my old self, only to find a new self that cries out for their touch.

"Then do it...I dare you!" I challenge him, hoping he will take me up on it.

He cocks his brow, and just as he pulls me away from the fridge, a voice stops us, "Uh, Cat. Can we talk...alone?"

UGH! I scream inside as I stare at Dani in disbelief, "Um, yeah...I guess."

"You've been saved, Kitty Cat." Oakley snickers, then walks away, and I turn on the person responsible for costing me an orgasm.

"I hope this is important because you just fucking cockblocked me!" I scowl at my ex-friend.

I say *ex* because I will not be friends with her until we can officially count her out of the suspect pool. Some may think I'm being a bitch, but if you were to put yourself into my shoes, you would do what it takes to survive, even if it means cutting people out of your life. I'll cut my own parents out if need be. The only ones who seem to care about my welfare are the Lords. Why do I need anyone else?

"I'm sorry, Cat, but this really can't wait," Dani cuts into my thoughts, "I have to say it before I lose my nerve."

"Fine," I cross my arms and wait for her to go on.

"What you did last night...well, early this morning..."

"I won't apologize, Dani, if that's what you're waiting for. There will be no apology until we know you aren't part of it," I tell her, not caring if it hurts her feelings or not at this point.

"That's not what I was going to say, Cat. Damn it, why are you being such a bitch? The only thing I'm guilty of is being attracted to you. That's it!" She lowers her voice when she realizes that she's attracting unwanted attention, "I enjoyed what you did to me, and I only wanted to see if there was a chance of it happening again."

Un-fucking-believable! Did she not hear what Fynn told her about her never having me? What will it take to make her understand that there will never be anything like that between us? She will be lucky if we remain friends by the time this ends, even if she is innocent.

Being the bitch I'm learning to be, I step into her, causing her to back up against the counter. Not caring that there is an audience, I drag the backs of my fingers down her arms in a soft caress. Licking my lips, I stare deeply into her eyes.

"I bet you want to return the favor, don't you? You want to get me off like I got you off, huh?" I take another step, pressing my body to the front of hers.

"Catalina?" I hear Sean's questioning voice, but I only hold my finger up, telling him to wait.

"It doesn't matter that you have Sean's cock that pleasures you; you want it to be me. You want to feel my fingers deep inside your tight pussy until you come all over my hand again," I glance at Sean, "Did you tell your little boy toy here how I was the first to get you off last night?"

"Saint!" Fynn's angry voice calls out to me, and I'm being pulled away from Dani, who has tears running down her face, and I hadn't even realized it, "What the fuck is wrong with you? Did we give you permission to touch her again?"

I scoff, "I was in the middle of teaching her a lesson because she came to me wanting it to happen again."

Fynn looks over at Dani, "Is that true?"

Dani looks at the floor instead of at Fynn.

"I thought I told you last night that it would never happen again." Fynn looks at Sean, "Take her upstairs and teach her some manners. We will let you know when we need her, but in the meantime, keep her away from Little Saint."

"Yes, Fynn...sorry. I don't know what is going on..."

"I'll fill you in later," Fynn tells his Frat brother, then turns back to me, "I came to find you because there is news on Felicia. Get your ass upstairs, so we can discuss it." He slaps my ass and growls playfully, making me chuckle as I hurry from the room.

"How exactly do we know this?" I ask when Oakley informs me that Felicia has been staying in a small house on the outskirts of town.

"Well, it seems your little boyfriend, Date Rate Rob, has come through for us. It was purely coincidence, but he saw the Saint's President coming out of a liquor store," Oakley explains, "He knew that we were looking for her, and so he followed her back to a house."

"Okay, so do we know why she's there?" I ask, getting a bit impatient.

"Not yet," Jett states and hands me his phone, "But Rob did send us a couple of videos."

I watch the screen and see a guy walk up to the front door of a house. You can't see his face until he knocks and turns his head while watching his surroundings. When I see his profile view, I recognize him, but what's even more disturbing is that Felicia opens the door and pulls him in by his shirt. He grabs her waist and lifts her up, kissing her before shutting the door.

"I don't get it," my brow crinkles, "Felicia is taking a break from school to play house with Chris?"

"We don't know this yet, but watch the next video," Jett says, and my eyes go back.

Clicking on the next video, I watch as Chris exits the house with messy hair, but once again, that's not the part that really gets my attention. The person who walks up to the door after he watches Chris leave is. He glares after the big football player as he pounds on the door.

Felicia opens the door with a smile, but then it falters when she sees it isn't Chris.

Stepping aside to let the newcomer in, it's apparent that they are yelling at her. She flinches a few times before closing the door.

"What the fuck?" I say as I hand the phone back to Jett.

"Those were our thoughts, too," Oakley states.

I look around at all three of the Lords, "I think it's time to pay Felicia a little visit," they all nod in agreement. "We need to find out what is going on with Felicia and Chris, and by how pissed off he looked, what in the world does Kaden have to do with it?"

Oakley

"I did some more digging and found that Kevin Douglas has three children. His oldest is a student here." I stare at Kitty Cat, watching the wheels turn in her head until it finally hits her.

"Chris..." she breathes.

"Yeah, we never knew his last name until we looked it up," Jett states.

"So, we have four students, aside from us," Kitty Cat starts to pace, "Who are all the offspring of the Alumni from that year of the assault."

She looks so cute as she thinks and bites her thumbnail, "Stop that, Kitty Cat," I pull her hand away from her mouth, "And yes, you are correct, and now, we must figure out which ones are the stalkers. It's got to be one or two of them."

"I don't understand why the attacker's offspring would come after us when their parents were also a part of the attack." She stops pacing, "It doesn't make sense. Dani is the only one who makes sense, and I'm beginning to believe she's telling us the truth."

Fynn scoffs, "Why is that Saint? Because you were able to get her off, and she wants more now?"

I furrow my brows, "What are you talking about?"

My friend stares at our girl, "I walked into the kitchen, and our Little Saint here was getting up close and personal with Dani. She claims she was trying to teach her a lesson, but I think our girl loved the girl-on-girl action from last night."

"That's not true, Fynn!" Kitty Cat stands with her arms to her sides, and her hands balled into fists, "I told you the truth. Had you not butted in, you would have seen that what I say is true!"

"Okay, calm down," I walk over to Kitty Cat and run my fingers through her hair until I can get a nice grip, and I tug her hair back, "Don't do that again, Kitty Cat. Not without us knowing about it first. Otherwise, we may get the wrong idea and have to punish you for it."

I can see it in her eyes as they darken at my words, "Ah, there she is. Our little slut wants to come out and play, doesn't she?" Pressing down on her shoulder, I push her to her knees, "How about you make yourself useful while we talk shop."

Kitty Cat's hands are quick to open my jeans and pull my cock out. She strokes it a few times, forcing the bead of precum to form so she can rub it over her lips before devouring me whole. I groan and keep a hold of her hair, letting her control the movements and yet stopping her from coming off my cock until I say.

Jett and Fynn move closer, forming a circle around our girl, and patiently wait for their turn in her mouth, "Okay, so how are we going to play this?" Jett asks, his eyes focused on Kitty Cat.

Looking down at her myself, her hands are gripping my thighs, "Hands behind your back, Kitty Cat. You know better," I tell her and wait for her to obey my command before returning my attention to my friends, "The way the video made it look, Felicia and Kaden seem to have some kind of an alliance. I think Chris is just a plaything for Felicia."

"The whore is probably fucking both..." Fynn cuts in.

"I'm not so sure about that," I say, "Did you see Felicia's face drop when she saw it was Kaden and not Chris?"

"Do you think Kaden is holding something over Felicia's head, and that's why she wasn't happy to see him?" Jett questions as he adjusts himself.

I nod at him, and he pulls himself out of his confines as I pull Kitty Cat off my cock. I maneuver her over and make her take Jett's girth, and his hand replaces mine. She looks fucking perfect on her knees as she pleasures us, and my cock jerks when I watch my friend push all the way down her throat, choking her with it.

"I can't really say, but we can't rule it out," I finally respond to Jett.

"Well, I vote that we grab the big fucker first. Chris isn't smart enough to be the leader in some evil plan. He's the brawn, if anything." Fynn caresses Kitty Cat's cheek as she takes Jett, who is not as nice as I was. Unlike me, he's in control, making her take him how he wants. Fynn gives up the fight, "Fuck this waiting bullshit!"

Fynn lifts Kitty Cat to her feet while still attached to Jett's cock and yanks her bottoms down. Releasing his cock, he lines it up to her glistening pussy and pushes into her as he groans. He doesn't take it easy on her either, as he fucks into her hard and fast. She gags on Jett every time she's shoved into him by Fynn.

Being the asshole that I am, I pull my phone out and record it. I love showing Kitty Cat what it looks like when we use her before deleting it. Sometimes we end up fucking afterward because it's so hot.

"Don't go breaking her on me. I plan on having her to myself tonight," I tell my two best friends.

They are having too much fun doing the Eiffel Tower with my Kitty Cat, but they both wink at me, "She will let you use her regardless," Jett states, "She's a good slut like that."

I'm harder than a rock watching my best friends fuck her right before my eyes. I'm not sure what's wrong with us, but we can't help the way we are. We love our girl and love that she loves what we do to her.

Yeah, I said love. There is no use in denying it, but I don't know if I can say it to her, not yet. Not until I know she won't leave us when college is over. I know we tell her we are keeping her, but I will never make anyone stay where they don't want to be. Well, at least not Kitty Cat, but that's where the whole love thing comes into play; I'll let her go because I love her.

"Oh, fuck yeah...take it, Lovely. Swallow it all down like a good girl," Jett orders as he unloads down her throat, "Fuck, baby. I love your blowjobs."

He pulls out of her mouth, and I'm right there to have her finish me off. Fynn is still pounding away as he also fingers her ass. Jett gives a helping hand as he spits down the crack of her ass, giving Fynn more lube.

Groaning as my cock sinks deep into her mouth once again, I revel in the feeling of her soft lips wrapped around me.

"Jesus, what the fuck does this guy eat?" I grunt as we try carrying Chris's limp body to the trunk of my car.

"I don't know, but all this muscle isn't helping," Fynn growls, "We will have to make sure to use the chains. That way, he can't break free."

Jett scoffs, "He may have the muscle, but he doesn't know how to use it except for in the game. I was able to take his ass in the bathroom at school. Yeah, it took a little bit, but I still beat the fucker's ass."

"That's only because you have a mean right hook," I chuckle.

Chris was a stumbling drunk when he came around the darkened corner to take a piss just outside of the Jock House. The party was going strong when we nabbed him once he was done draining his lizard. Knocking him out with my gun, we let him fall to the ground rather than trying to catch his big ass.

As we near the car, Kitty Cat pops the trunk, and we toss him inside. We have to situate his large frame into the fetal position just so he will fit because there is no way I want some maniac waking up while we are driving down the road. I won't take that chance with Kitty Cat in the car.

Instead of bringing him back to the Frat House like we have the others, we stop just to grab some supplies, then head out to the cabin at the lake. A room was built into it about a decade ago, a replica of the basement at the Frat House. I never asked why our fathers had it made, and quite frankly, I really don't want to know.

"Oh, wow!" Kitty Cat says as she spins around, taking in the room, "This room is..."

"Is not being used for that..." I wink at her.

She sticks her lip out and pouts, "That's too bad...such a waste."

We set Chris down in the torture chair, and then I pull her into me, "I had something installed today that I think you are going to love, but you have to be patient." I grab her ass and squeeze hard, "If you're a good girl, I'll take you down when we get back, and we can play."

She's already panting like a bitch in heat, "Oakley..." She grips my shirt in her fists.

I smirk and lick my lips, "Such a fucking slut." I crash my mouth against hers and kiss her so brutally that I leave a cut on her lip, "I'm going to make you beg for me to do bad things to you tonight, Kitty Cat, but for now, we have work to do."

FIFTY

Jett

"Wake the fuck up!" I slap the big jock across his face.

We have been waiting for over an hour and are getting impatient. I don't want to be here all night if I don't have to be, and by the way, Oakley and Lina can't keep their hands off each other; they don't want to be here either. I'm beginning to think the alcohol is factoring in as to why he isn't waking up yet.

Going to the kitchenette, I grab the biggest glass I can find and fill it with ice-cold water. I head back into the room and dump it over Chris's head. He finally jerks awake, sputtering.

"What the fuck? Where am I?" He tries moving, but the chains holding him in place keep him from doing so.

"Well, it's nice of you to join us, Chris." I pull a chair over and turn it around in front of him before straddling it, "I'm so sorry that we had to ruin your good time, but we kind of needed you here."

The jock looks around the room, eyeballing everyone here, "What kind of fucked up shit is this, Jett?"

Because of the chain wrapped around his neck and chained to the eyehooks sticking out of the floor, Chris has limited movement of his head. I grin as he tries moving it from side to side, pulling at his arms and feet. He is stuck to that chair until we let him up.

"Stop wasting your energy, big guy. We reinforced those chains," Fynn tells him with a shit-eating grin.

"Is someone going to fucking tell me what the fuck is going on?" He glares at me, "Is this about what I said that day about Catalina?"

I look over at her and see that she's listening intently as she scrutinizes the Lineman, "No," I turn back to Chris, "That's not what this is about. I thought we had settled it the day I fucked up your face."

"Me too, bro! So, what the fuck is this?" he scowls.

"This is about you and your own little Saint," Fynn chimes in, "You're fucking Felicia Howard, and we need to know what you know about the shit going down with *our* Little Saint."

The guy's forehead crinkles, "I don't know anything about your Little Saint. Felicia is a piece of ass, that's all."

Either Chris is a good actor, or he really doesn't know what we are talking about, but we will test this shit out, "So you're saying that you don't know anything about who is trying to kill Cat?" I ask as I crack my knuckles.

"I know nothing. I'm telling you the truth!" Chris claims but does it too defensively, so I try another tactic.

"Do you always share your fucks with other jocks?" I question as I pull out my phone.

"Well, sometimes, but Felicia isn't like that. I've already tried." This annoys him if the grimace on his face tells us anything.

"Oh, well, that's funny, seeing as she has you leave and then has another one of your jock buddies coming seconds after you leave, no pun intended." I snicker, then show him the video on my phone, but he's too far away to see her expression.

He laughs, "Felicia isn't fucking Kaden."

"It sure looks that way to me. He actually stayed longer than you did. Maybe you didn't please her enough..."

Fynn grabs Chris's hair and tugs back on it, "Do you not let her come all over your dick before you leave? Maybe she fakes it with you. Is her cunt soaking wet by the time you release yourself?"

"Fuck you, Fynn! You guys are fucking sick if you think Felicia would fuck her own brother!"

The only thing you can hear in the room is the ticking of the wall clock in the other room. We all stand here trying to take in what Chris just said. This is not anything we anticipated.

"You're lying," my Lovely Lina's voice echoes through the room.

"Shit," Chris curses under his breath, "Look, I don't know why they don't want anyone to know, but can you please not tell them that I told you?"

"Why would they tell you but not want anyone else to know?" I ask. Something sounds fishy to me.

"Because they didn't tell me, that's why. I happened to come upon them in a back hall, talking," he pauses as he thinks and then looks at Lina, "It was the same day I ran into you, and you were a bitch to me. Just after that, I came across them talking about their father or some shit. Felicia had tears in her eyes, but Kaden looked pissed."

"So, what? Did they say anything to you at that time?" I lean in a little closer, the chair I sit on going up on two legs.

"No, but Felicia was waiting for me after my next class with a smile. She asked me if I wanted to come over and hang out." The jock shrugs, "She's a hot piece of ass, so I accepted the invite, and we have been fucking ever since."

"Interesting..." my Lovely breathes out.

"What are you thinking, Kitty Cat?" Oakley finally speaks up after all this time.

Lina looks at him briefly and then turns back to stare at Chris, "I'll tell you guys later."

"That's all I know. Can I go now?" The jock tries the chains once again.

Fynn slaps him on the shoulder, "Sorry, big guy, but we will have to check out your story. You just sit tight, but in the meantime..." Fynn pulls his gun out and hits Chris over the head again.

"What's your plan?" I ask my friend.

"Well, you fuckers are going to help me get him into that cell, so we can lock him up. Then we are going to reunite him with his little whore."

"So, Felicia is next on the list?" Lina questions as she smiles.

Fynn grins and nods, "You look like you have something up your sleeve, Little Saint."

She shrugs, "Not really, but I know I'm going to have fun."

"There will be no tongue hockey, finger banging, or coming with this chick," Oakley states, "Do you understand me, Kitty Cat?"

"You act as if I like girls...I don't. I did what needed to be done, and I'll be happy if I never do it again, but I will if the situation calls for it." Our girl moves closer to Oakley and grabs his package, "This is what I crave. Big, fat cock that knows how to fuck me good. That's what I like."

My mouth lifts to one side, and I snicker, "You're grabbing the wrong package for that description."

"Fuck you, Jett!" Oakley growls and grabs Lina as she starts to walk over to me, "Where the fuck are you going? You're mine tonight, so you stick by me."

"Oh, so demanding," Lina says seductively, "Are you going to club me over the head and drag me out by my hair, too?"

Oakley scoffs, "In your dreams, slut. You would like that way too much."

"Hm, that's too bad. It sounded like a hell of a good time." She turns and leans against Oakley's chest as she winks at me.

Shaking my head, I can already imagine what kind of trouble she is in for when we return to the Frat House. Oakley isn't going to give her an inch; I hope she's ready. Just by the look on his face, I can tell she has him rock hard, and after this little stunt, he's probably going to use the ball gag on her so nobody will hear her screams.

"Come on, fuckers! Help me get him in the cage," Fynn already has the chains off Chris and is waiting for assistance.

I jump from the chair and grab the jock's legs while Lina hurries over to the cage and opens the door. Oakley takes one of Chris's legs from me, making it easier for us. Once the big guy is lying on the cot inside the cell-like cage, we place the shackle around his ankle. This enables him to use the toilet inside the cell and reach the food we will provide for him.

"I'll come back in the morning with breakfast and a tote with other snack foods that will hold him over until his next meal," I inform them.

"Will you let your father know that he's here?" Oakley asks me, and I stare at him in disbelief.

"Just because I didn't whoop your asses for coming to see him behind my back doesn't mean all is good between him and me. One of you two can tell him since you're all such besties." I should punch him in the face now for just suggesting that, but I'm trying to work on my anger issues, and punching my best friend would be setting me back.

"Someone's a bit touchy," Fynn snickers, "Just so you know, I'm the one that called Blake, not Oakley. He didn't even know where we were going when I asked him to come with me."

"Whatever, man, I'm over it, but I'm not going to call him," I say and walk from the room.

"Jett!" My lovely Lina calls after me. I stop and turn around just as a small body slams into me.

"Oofta," she knocks the air from my lungs.

"Will you ride in the back seat with me?" she asks, running her hand up my chest.

I know she's only trying to get my good mood back, so I accept her invite with a wicked grin, "Sure, baby. Will you be wrapping those lips around something on the way home?"

She goes up on her toes and whispers in my ear, "I'll wrap whatever you want me to wrap around anything you want." She sucks on my earlobe before nipping it.

Grabbing her hand, I start pulling her with me. Her laughter follows behind us, and I vaguely hear Oakley calling something out, but I don't give a rat's ass. I continue pulling my Lovely Lina behind me until we reach the Camaro. I open the door for her and wait until she crawls into the back seat.

She doesn't realize that thirty minutes is a long time to be in the back seat with me, or with any Lord, for that matter. I can't promise Oakley that I will leave her in good shape for him because she's such a goddamn tease. She's going to deserve everything that's coming to her.

Catalina

Oakley isn't happy with me. Well, maybe it's Jett he isn't pleased with, but he's taking it out on me, and I'm all for it. Our ride home was very eventful for Jett and me. What started as road head turned into him smushing my face into the seat and fucking me from behind, shaking the car the whole way back. Nothing Oakley said would get Jett to stop.

Now, my wrists are tied behind my back, my ankles are tied together, and I have a blindfold and an awful open-mouth gag on me. Oakley is carrying me over his shoulder, stark naked for all to see. Not that I'd know if anyone is looking, but it feels like there are eyes on me, although not a peep is heard. Maybe it's my imagination.

"You're going to find out what it's like to be punished for teasing me the way you did, Kitty Cat. Letting my best friend rail you in the back seat of my car while I'm driving," he tsks, "Such a filthy slut you are."

"MMPH..." I don't know what I'm trying to say, but it is a garbled mess.

Oakley pats my bare ass, "I know it wasn't *really* your fault. The big bad Lord didn't give you much choice, but if you weren't alluring and distractingly tempting, he might have been happy with just the road head."

My head hangs down, not in a defeated way, more like accepting my fate. It makes no difference if I were to plead my case; Oakley will do what he does best, take what he wants because he knows he can. Am I mad? Nope, because I know he will pleasure me in his own way when he is done with me.

The cool, damp air of the basement hits my ass first, and goosebumps scatter across my skin. Oakley descends into the basement, whistling creepily. It almost gives off the sense of being in a horror movie, and the psychopathic killer is about to torture you piece by piece.

Instead of being laid out on a cold metal slab, though, he pulls me off his shoulders and sets me on my feet, "Don't go anywhere, Kitty Cat. I need to get your surprise ready," he snickers and wipes the drool dripping from my open mouth.

I strain to keep my balance while my feet are tied together. The cement floor is cold against my bare feet, and my toes curl up. There is creaking right in front of me, and then the sound of...chains?

"You're going to look fucking gorgeous, Kitty Cat," I can hear the lust-filled voice as he comes close.

His breath is hot, his mouth wet as he captures a nipple. I know there is more to come, so I prepare myself, and he doesn't disappoint. His teeth sink into my sensitive flesh as his tongue flicks back and forth. He then sucks hard, really fucking hard, causing me to cry out, but the pain shoots straight to my core.

Suddenly, his mouth is gone, and I'm bent over. Oakley rests my neck on a smooth, flat surface, and he traps me here by pulling something down over the back of my neck. He next releases my hands, only to capture them in the same way as my neck.

A stockade.

This is my surprise. A piece of bondage furniture to restrain me so he can do all his deliciously filthy things to me. I feel my pussy weep at this. I've never used one; I've never used anything like the shit they have because my sex partners before them were just boys.

The Lords know their kink, but never call them Dominant, because they don't follow the rules. They make their own rules. I just so happen to enjoy their lawless ways in the bedroom.

Oakley yanks the rope from my ankles and spreads my legs as far apart as he can before cuffing them to what, I don't know. I close my eyes because now, he will see just how wet and needy I am. He will somehow use it against me for his own pleasure.

"Wow, Kitty Cat. You're fucking soaked, and I've barely touched you." He slaps my pussy from behind, making me go up on my toes. Doing it a few more times, the room fills with wet, sloppy noises with each contact.

I moan and hang my head.

He leaves me to move around the room. Oakley is up to something; he's always up to something. When the blindfold is yanked from my head,

I blink in the low-lit room before my eyes focus on him. He's smirking as he stands beside a camera on a tripod.

"The others will watch," he moves to stand outside my vision, "They will witness me taking whatever I want from you, Kitty Cat. They will see me use a new toy on you; yes, there is more than one surprise for you."

He leans over my back, his thick, bulging package rubbing against my sensitive pussy. He reaches underneath me and pinches my nipples, pulling them down as far as he can and moving his hands, yanking them back and forth. Slapping them a few times afterward, he straightens up, and that's when I hear the sound of a cap popping open.

The cold drizzle of lube reaches my crack, and he works it all around and into my back hole. Another moan escapes me as he sinks his finger into my ass and starts fucking it. He adds a second and then a third. The squishing sound of the lube would sound disgusting to some, but for me, it's music to my ears.

"Have you ever had an anal hook in your ass, Kitty Cat?" Oakley caresses my back.

I freeze. A what? I shake my head vigorously.

"Well, you will soon find out..."

I shake my head no again.

"Are you fucking kidding me?"

Again, I shake my head. I stand my ground on this one, and surprisingly, he sighs.

"Fine, but I'm getting you some reading material, and some porn, so you can see how it's done because I'm dying to see this ass hooked." He slaps my ass cheek, and then I hear more chains moving away.

Something sharp runs down the center of my back, scraping the skin down the center. Once again, I freeze, but only because I know Oakley holds a knife in his hand. What else can it be?

"I want something from you, Kitty Cat," he brings the knife's point down to my ass cheek, "I need my own mark on you. Will you let me do this one thing, baby?"

I think about what he's saying. He wants to carve me up just like Brett did. Only, he's not doing it out of evilness, and he's asking my permission. How can I deny him this? He's come a long way since we started. In the beginning, Oakley would have just done it. Now, he's asking, so I slowly nod.

"That's my good girl," he says, and I hear his zipper coming down and more rustling of clothes, "Would you like my cock, Kitty Cat?"

I nod happily, and he sinks into me.

"Fuck, you feel so damn good," he pumps into me slower than usual, but I figure out why when a sharp stabbing pain starts at the center of my ass cheek.

I moan when I feel wetness dribble down my cheek. It only stings for a few minutes until he's done carving me. He pulls out and massages the area he's just sliced up. It hurts, but it's not unbearable, and it only feeds into the pleasure he's creating deep within.

"Fucking gorgeous…"

Suddenly, something hard and unforgiving is being pushed inside; it's like it's ribbed for my pleasure. The thrusting starts off slow, and the more I moan and try pushing back on it, the faster Oakley fucks me with it.

The knife handle is long and thick, and Oakley is fucking me with every inch of it, "You've missed this, haven't you, Kitty Cat? Being fucked by all sorts of handles."

He pushes the knife in and leaves it there as he walks around and grabs my hair, "Clench that cunt around the knife so it doesn't slip out as I fuck this pretty mouth of yours."

Oakley pushes his length through the hole of the gag, hitting the back of my throat and groaning. He begins fucking me hard as I clench around the knife, not wanting it to fall out. I realize his hands are full of my blood, smearing it all over my face, and it only turns me on more.

"You're a fucking mess, Kitty Cat…I love it!" He starts driving into my mouth, and he pulls out when he's about to come.

Hot jets of cum spray my face, dirtying it so he can talk about how filthy I am. And I am…I'm so fucking filthy. He smears it all over my face, mixing it with the blood left behind from his hands. He leaves me like this to walk back around and continues to fuck me with his knife. Only this time, he shoves his fingers into my ass again and fucks that too.

"You will soak this handle, Kitty Cat, and then you'll clean it off and thank me for giving you such an amazing experience."

He doesn't have to tell me to come because I'm already there. I cry out through the gag and push back repeatedly, "MMPH!!"

"Hell yes...give it to me, Kitty Cat," Oakley sings in excitement.

By the time I'm done, I'm panting heavily, and Oakley is stroking my back soothingly, "Such a good girl. That's number one..."

FIFTY-ONE

Fynn

My cock is rock fucking hard as I watch my Little Saint get railed by my best friend. I'm a little disappointed that she wouldn't let him use the hook; she would have enjoyed it. If I've realized anything, it's that my Little Saint is a freak and loves everything we do to her, but sometimes we have to use a little bit of dubious consent, using the contract against her. Otherwise, she gets into her own head and denies herself the pleasures we want to give her.

I can't stay in my room longer and watch the show, so I head over to Jett's room. The live stream still going in his room as our girl's muffled scream fills the area while she comes. Jett closes his laptop and tosses it aside; the evidence of his arousal is now in plain sight.

"Thank fuck, I can't watch anymore of that. What's up?" he asks, watching me as I plop down in his chair.

"I'm in the same boat, man. I'm not going to be able to sleep without taking a cold shower, but I figured that maybe if we go over everything we've learned, we can figure out what the fuck is going on...and it will calm my fucking dick down." I scowl down at my lap, the bulge still on display.

My friend chuckles, "Well, let's get to it then."

I eyeball him for a moment as I try to form my first question, "How the fuck did we miss this? I mean, dragon lady looks like her mother, and pretty boy is the spitting image of his father, so I guess it's easy to miss, but we don't miss shit like this." I'm furious that our heads haven't been entirely in the game. They have been on Little Saint for the most part.

"Lovely Lina," Jett simply states, "Our eyes and dicks have been on and in our girl."

"Yeah, well, it needs to stop. Where are we at now?" I wait to see what Jett says before I give him my thoughts.

"I'm not going to lie," his brows furrow, "If Felicia and Kaden are siblings, and I'm assuming it's through their sperm donor, Bradley, why would they be the ones threatening us?"

I nod in agreement, "And where does Chris fit into all of this? His father was one of the Lords, and Julia was his girl at the time."

"I'm stumped too, Fynn. I guess the only way to find out is to get it from Felicia herself."

"What happened to the Lord and Lady after college?" I wonder out loud.

Typically, the Lords and Lady go their separate ways once they graduate, but more often than not, the Lady and one of the Lords end up going on to marry. It makes me wonder what happened between Julia and Kevin and how in the hell they both have kids about the same age with different people.

"You don't think..." Jett lets his question drag off.

"I hope the fuck not because that is just fucking sick!" Knowing precisely what he's thinking, I respond, "Besides, according to Kevin, Kaden is Felicia's brother, not him. I don't know how that would fit into the story, either. Something is off, that's for sure."

"I'm really beginning to hate being a Lord. What transpired back then," Jett says, "It's an embarrassment. We don't claim to be good guys, and our actions may be morally gray, but what they did was against the Lords of Sin's code. If it gets out and seems we covered it up, we will lose everything."

"Well, I guess it's up to us to not let that happen." I say, "We need to take care of this soon before anything else happens to Little Saint. If she's hurt one more time, I'll be done asking questions and just let my gun do the talking. I don't care who the fuck they are."

Jett hops off his bed, "How about we pay the dragon lady a little visit? Now is the perfect time to bring her in."

"You want to take her to the lake tonight?" I ask because I'm in no mood to make that drive again tonight.

"Nah. We can bring her here, then take her to the lake tomorrow." Jett goes to his dresser and pulls a t-shirt out.

Sighing, I stand up, "You do realize that the basement is being occupied, right?"

The sinful grin my best friend gives me is one that I've seen many times before, "That's the best part," Jett opens the door and walks out, "She will be blindfolded, and we can stick headphones over her ears. Felicia won't even know that someone is fucking in the same room."

I snicker, "Oakley is going to kick your ass. You know that, right?"

My friend shrugs, "He can try..." he winks at me before leading us down the steps.

I, myself, would find it hot as hell to fuck Little Saint in front of the dragon lady; no blindfold needed. Just to see her face when she sees the depraved things a Sinner does to a precious Saint of hers would be well worth any wrath I may get from Little Saint herself. Honestly, I believe our freaky girl would also love to rub it in the President's face.

The house and its surroundings are dark as we creep around to the back. Felicia picked the worst place for herself to hide out in but the perfect place for us to break in and nab her. The house is a relatively new build, so there are no squeaks to give us away as I pick the lock on the back door and enter the small space.

We enter a quaint little kitchen that smells of pasta, something she must have made herself earlier in the night. A small table sits in the middle of the room, and we have to slip past it without knocking into it, which is a feat in itself as small as the room is. Of course, we accomplish this task with no mishaps and slip from the room only to stop just outside the doorway.

I point to the right, indicating for Jett to check it out, while I point in the opposite direction in which I will check out. I walk down the hallway and silently open a door on the right side, but it opens to a bathroom; the smell of a recent shower still lingers in the air. Sucks to be her because I have a feeling that by morning she will already be sullied with her own blood.

Closing the door, I walk across the hall and open the only other door, but it's just a linen closet. When I meet Jett at the kitchen doorway, he shakes his head, telling me he found nothing. We both look at the small staircase before walking toward it.

Making our way to the second floor, we realize it's a loft bedroom, an open concept. Lucky for us, the dragon lady is passed out. An empty bottle of wine sits on the nightstand beside the bed. Our target is lightly snoring, and I grin. This is going to be easier than I thought.

With Felicia in a drunken sleep, we are able to gently turn her and tie her hands behind her back. Adding the tape to her mouth, we pull the hood over her head just before she starts moving. Waking up from her slumber and not knowing what is going on must be scary as hell, but they didn't consider this when they took my Little Saint, so I will give her the same courtesy.

Because she has no close neighbors, we don't bother to knock her out. I do pinch her nose closed as Jett carries her to the Jeep, only because it quiets her muffled cries. Had there been neighbors close by, we would have knocked her ass out.

I don't bother to disguise my voice; she will find out who we are soon enough. If she is one of the stalkers, she won't be going anywhere to be able to turn us in any way. If she's not, which is highly unlikely, we will ensure she knows not to open her big mouth.

"Shut the fuck up, Felicia. It makes no difference how much you cry out; we aren't letting you go until we get answers. So, be a good fucking girl and settle down," I tell her as I glance in the back seat.

We didn't make it comfortable for her when we threw her into the backseat. Why would we? From what we saw, they didn't provide my Little Saint with comfort while keeping her tied to a chair and sliced her up. No, fuck that. I'm done being a nice guy. When she doesn't quiet the fuck down, I reach back and tighten the drawstring on the hood, limiting her air access without taking it away completely.

"Keep it up, and I'll take all your air away. We still have Kaden, so your death will be no loss. Remember that, Felicia." I can tell my threat got to her by how her body stiffens. I turn back around and grin.

"So, do we warn them that we are coming or just bring her down?" Jett asks with a wicked grin.

"I think it's easier to ask for forgiveness, don't you?" I chuckle.

Jett's grin matches my own now, "My thoughts exactly..."

Oakley

I don't get it. Kitty Cat won't let me use the hook, but she allows me to carve her? I don't ask questions, though, and I absolutely carve into her soft flesh, but it's not what she thinks it is. She will be surprised when she sees what will remain permanently in place. I'm surprised myself. I could have been a dick, but I let my feelings for her guide me through it.

Afterward, I needed to wash away the mushy shit, so I dirtied her up before fucking her with the knife handle. The sight of her juices dripping from the ribbed handle as it glided in and out almost did me in. My Kitty Cat got off on it, just like she did with the letter opener. Catalina Scott is just as depraved as we are and was made to be ours.

I pull her out of the stockade and walk her to the table. Picking her up, I set her ass on the cold surface, and immediately her skin breaks out with little goosebumps. I push my hand on her chest until she's lying on her back.

"Hands above your head, Kitty Cat. Don't make me restrain you again." My hands caress her thighs as I wait for her to follow my orders, "Mm, you look delectable all spread out like this."

I push her legs up to her chest as I spread her wide. Leaving her open for the cool air, I move up by her head and undo the gag. I want to hear her voice screaming my name now. I want to listen to those sexy as fuck moans when I drive into her tight cunt. Hear her curse me out when I pull out, only to plunge into her fine ass. I want it all.

Tweaking her tit as I move back between her legs, I slip two fingers into her and fuck her fast and hard for about thirty seconds before pulling my digits out and swirling them around in the blood dripping from her ass cheek. I lift my fingers and suck on one at a time as my heated gaze burns into her. She licks her lips and clears her throat before bravely asking me her first question.

"C-Can I t-taste?" She stutters in an adorably sexy way.

"I'm not sure," I smile down at her, giving her a teasing look, "What will I get in return, Kitty Cat?"

She spreads her legs further, "What more do you want?"

An animalistic growl erupts, and I plunge my fingers back into her, sneering as my body burns to take her and make her my very own. She wants to taste herself...she wants the taste of her own cum and blood on her taste buds, and who am I to deny her? Of course, I barter with her, wanting her to offer herself up to me even though I can just take what I want at any time.

"Open up, Kitty Cat. Taste my new favorite flavor of you..." I'm unsure how it happens, but my cock hardens even more as she sucks seductively on my middle finger, "Fuck...Kitty Cat," I drive into her as she continues to suck.

"Mm," she fucking moans, loving the taste of herself.

I hook my fingers into her mouth to help anchor myself as I hammer into her. Her bare back is rubbing up and down against the table, more than likely leaving some type of burn. Neither of us cares, though. She meets me thrust for thrust as though I'm not getting in deep enough.

With my free hand, I spread her right leg open further, my fingernails digging into the creamy flesh of her thigh, "Fucking take it, Kitty Cat. Take every inch of me, baby. It's...all...fucking...yours!" I growl as I empty inside of her.

I let her mouth go and instantly bring my fingers to her clit, rubbing her hard and fast, "Come on, Kitty Cat. Give me what I want. Suffocate me with that gorgeous cunt as you come all over my cock." I spit down onto her clit and continue rubbing it furiously until I feel the tremors of her body break free, and she clenches around me, "There we go. Let it all out, baby."

"Oh, God...Oakley!"

"I'm here, Kitty Cat. Take what you need. Do you want more? I can..."

I'm cut off when I hear the door to the basement open. I try covering Kitty Cat's exposed body until I see Jett coming down. I continue pumping into my girl. Fynn follows our friend, only he has a female body draped over his shoulder.

"Don't mind us. We needed to put her somewhere. She can't hear or see, so proceed," Jett's smirk earns him a glare from me.

"What the fuck?" I pull out of my Kitty Cat, and she goes to sit up, but I stop her, "I didn't tell you to get up."

I instantly see the hurt in Kitty Cat's eyes and regret my tone. I try to take her hand, but she pushes it away, "Don't."

"I'm sorry, Kitty Cat. I was frustrated with them," I glare back over my shoulder at my friends before returning my attention to her, "Here, let me help you sit up."

Hesitating, she finally lets me help her up. The moment she does, I grab the back of her neck and bring her face close to mine. I can't help but take her lips in a brutal kiss. Our teeth clash, and lips get caught in a war of passion, both earning battle wounds from the other. I can taste the metallic in my mouth, but I'm unsure whether it's hers or mine.

When we break apart, her voice is low and filled with need, "Oakley..."

"No worries, Kitty Cat. I'll take you upstairs and finish you off once we are done here. Now, be a good girl and stay right here, sitting pretty."

She nods, and I step away, tucking myself back into the jeans I've yet to take off. Turning back to the motherfuckers I call my best friends, I stomp over to them, "What the fuck is this? Why is she here?"

Fucking Fynn and his nonchalant attitude, "Wasn't in the mood to drive out to the lake again tonight."

"So, you brought her here? What? Did you think I would keep fucking my Kitty Cat with her in the same room?" I ask incredulously. I glance over at our girl and notice that her nipples are harder than a rock, and there are goosebumps all over her body.

Pulling my shirt off, I walk over and help her put it on. I don't need my Kitty Cat catching a cold because of my asshat friends. I'm granted a beautiful smile in thanks before I press my lips to her forehead and turn back to my friends.

Since Jett and Fynn ruined the mood Kitty Cat and I were in, we call it quits and start to question the female, now tied to the chair, "We already know that Kaden is your brother, that Bradley is your father..." This last part is just our assumption, but we must be right when she doesn't correct me, "How does Chris fit into the picture?"

"Fuck you, Sinner! This is why all the Sinners must go; you can't be trusted to be around anyone. You all are ruthless and take what you want, not caring about anybody else's feelings or what consequences there are for those who have no choice but to follow your rules!"

I stare at Felicia blankly, trying to understand what she is saying exactly, but all I see is my Kitty Cat being carved up and then the look she gave me as she climbed out the window of the burning building. No, I won't let Felicia's words affect me how she wants them to.

I give her my most sinful smirk and place my hands on each arm of the chair. Her hands are tied behind her, and her chest heaves up and down as I lean in closer. I pay no attention to her tits practically falling out of her sleep top; they hold no interest for me because she's not Kitty Cat.

"We only take what we want once we are given permission to do so, *Felicia.* Don't get us confused with your father and mother," I catch the wince that she does at the mention of Julia, "Speaking of Mommy Dearest, she seemed to enjoy what she did to Simone. Nobody twisted her arm, so my question is, why are you taking it out on us when all our parents were in on the same assault?"

"I-I don't know what you're talking about. I'm not t-taking anything out on a-anybody," she stammers, and I don't believe a fucking word she says.

Ignoring her little effort at lying, I ask, "How did our good ole buddy Brett fit into this?"

"Brett, who?" She feigns ignorance, and I'm out of patience. I lift my hand, about to backhand her, when another voice stops me.

"Don't do it..." Kitty Cat hops down and comes over to us.

She is sexy as hell in just my t-shirt, and all I want to do is toss her over my shoulder again and take her back upstairs so I can finish doing bad things to her, "What is it, Kitty Cat? Don't tell me you believe this bullshit."

My Kitty Cat steps up to me and grabs my neck like I had done hers and kisses me the same way but only briefly before pulling back, "It's not nice for boys to hit girls. Well, at least not when they aren't spanking them," she licks her lips.

"Thank you, Cat. Finally, you are coming around…"

Kitty Cat cuts Felicia's words off as she swings around and backhands the dragon lady herself, "Unlucky for you, I'm not a fucking boy," she states.

Felicia's head snaps to the side, "You bitch!"

"Oh, you haven't seen bitch yet," Kitty Cat holds her hand out to Fynn, and of course, he knows what our girl wants and grins as he digs into his pocket for his knife.

Felicia eyes the pocketknife with disbelief, and as soon as Kitty Cat takes a step closer, Felicia spills, "Brett was helping Kaden!"

"Why would our Frat brother help a lame Lacrosse player?" I question skeptically.

Felicia shrieks as soon as my girl presses the blade just under her neck, her next words stunning everyone in the basement, "Because Brett and Kaden were together!"

FIFTY-TWO

Catalina

"Wait...what?" I'm having difficulty wrapping my head around what just came out of Felicia's mouth, "That can't be. Kaden flirted with me whenever he was around me."

Felicia glares at me disgustingly, "Have you ever heard of bisexuality? Not that he was really interested in you, but yeah, my half-brother is bi." The way she snarls it at me makes me think she loathes me, but I haven't the slightest idea why.

"Why do you hate me so much? What did I ever do to you, Felicia?" I ask, still holding Fynn's pocket knife to her neck.

"You're just like them, Catalina," she nods towards the Lords behind me, "I tried keeping you on the right path, but you just had to fall for their sick, sadistic ways."

I laugh dryly, "Every Saint needs a Sinner..."

"If you believe that, you're more delusional than I thought!" The Saint's President states, and I add pressure to the blade.

"No, Felicia, I'm not delusional. I'm only accepting who I am...who I've always been," I tilt my head at her, "These *Sinners,* as you call them, have been trying to keep me safe all this time. Keeping me safe from *you!* So, tell me, how are they the bad guys? What does that make you?"

"You still don't fucking get it, do you? You guys are dumber than we thought!" our prisoner spits. The spray of spit hitting me in the face.

I press the blade to her neck, and she shrieks just before I notice the trickle of blood on her neck. I loosen my hold, "Mind your fucking manners. I'm not afraid to stab this knife right through you. It can't be any worse than when I took out Brett." I grind out, starting to lose my patience with the bitch, "Why?" I simply ask.

"Why did we threaten you?" She glares at me.

I've got to give it to her. Felicia is holding up pretty well, even with the knife to her throat. I feel there is more to this bitch than we all thought. She's not just a pawn in this game of cat and mouse. The realization hits me...Felicia Howard is the Cat herself.

I take in a shuddering breath, yanking the knife away immediately. I don't trust myself not to plunge the razor edge of the blade into her neck, draining the life from this bitch. We still have questions, and she has the answers we need. Her death is not possible just yet.

"What is it, Kitty Cat?" Oakley stares at me with concern.

I let my eyes wander over each of the Lords, mainly to give me time to form a coherent sentence, "It's her..."

"What about her, Little Saint?" Fynn takes a step closer to me, and I hold the knife out for him to take.

"I may kill her if I continue holding that," I explain.

"What is it?" Fynn asks, his brows furrowing.

"Felicia..." I glare back at the bitch, "She's the one that started it all."

The Saint's President smirks knowingly but remains silent. The look in her eyes tells me that I'm right. Jett walks over and takes hold of her hair, yanking it back roughly. He spits into her face and glares.

"We should kill you here and now," his voice is deadly and has the effect he wants.

Felicia loses her smirk when she realizes just how serious Jett is, "You w-wouldn't!"

"Wouldn't I, though?" The sinister tone behind Jett's words causes a chill to run down my own spine. "Depending on your cooperation will determine whether you keep your life...or not."

Felicia's round eyes meet mine, "See what I mean? The Lords of Sin are savages, and their offspring are no better!"

Her words anger me, "You're a fucking hypocrite, Felicia! Not only was your father a Lord of Sin, but your mother fucked them as their Lady. Let's not forget her part in raping her innocent friend just to appease her Lords!"

Oakley pulls me back from her. I hadn't realized that I had moved closer to her, but he noticed, along with the rage burning inside me. I nod at him once I have myself in check and watch as he turns to the little bitch.

"Why are you coming after us, Felicia. Stop fucking around and answer the damn question!" Oakley growls out.

Felicia remains silent.

"Why did you send the video to Dani?" Fynn asks a question of his own.

She looks at him, a shadow of a smile playing on her lips, "You were getting too close. We had to try and turn your attention elsewhere. Who better than the one person who bears Simone's last name?"

"Are you telling us that Dani really didn't have a hand in any of this?" Guilt is already rising from the pit of my stomach.

Felicia snorts, "Please, that girl has a brain the size of a pea. The only thing she cared about was how to get into her best friend's pants." The smirk is back on her face as she looks me up and down, "I honestly don't see why everyone is so gaga over you. You ain't shit..."

Jett doesn't give two shits who she is. Still holding her hair, he slaps her across the face, "Catalina is more woman than you can ever dream to be."

Felicia licks the blood from the corner of her mouth, then stares back at me, "Like I said...savages."

I take a few deep breaths to calm myself before asking her my next question. I step closer, my legs now between her spread ones. My face is blank, "Where does Chris fit into all of this? We know he's Kevin Douglas's son, so why are you not going after him?"

"Instead, you fuck him..." Oakley adds in.

Felicia's expression changes to one of what looks like concern, "He's nobody. Chris knows nothing, so you can just leave him alone."

"Kind of hard to do when we have him locked in a cell at another location." Fynn grins wickedly.

"No! You have to let him go. He doesn't know anything!" She pleads as she looks at each of us.

There is no sneer, glare, or angry look toward us...just pure concern for the big football player. I study her as the room quietens, and I know the guys are doing the same. I only come to one conclusion as to why she's pleading with us.

I straighten my back, "You love him, don't you?"

"We need to take her to the lake house," I tell the guys when we file up the stairs, "I don't think we will get any more out of her without incentive."

"You want to use her feelings for Chris in order to get her to talk," Oakley states, and I nod.

"So, we threaten harm to Chris, and Felicia will sing like a bird," Jett grins, rubbing his hands together.

"Yes, but until we know for sure whether he has a part in this, we can't hurt him," I give the giddy Lord a stern look.

"Yeah, yeah, yeah, I hear you. I don't know when you became the boss..." Jett mumbles under his breath, and I hide my laugh.

"When you grow a golden pussy like mine, then you can be boss," I give him a cheesy grin.

"She ain't wrong there, bro," Fynn laughs and pulls me to his chest to kiss my head.

"Fine, you win..." Jett smiles and pulls me away from Fynn, "How about you come to my room and remind me of what that golden pussy is like," he wiggles his brows.

"No way, fucker!" Oakley pulls me into his arms. I'm like a fucking ragdoll, "She's still mine tonight. Kitty Cat and I need to finish where we left off," he smirks down at me as he slides his hand up the inside of the shirt I'm wearing of his, "Don't we, Kitty Cat?"

"Mm, definitely," I gasp as he shoves two fingers into me, "Someone might see, Oakley," I barely try to pull away, not wanting to feel the loss of his fingers.

"It's the middle of the night, Kitty Cat. Everyone else is in bed." Oakley says as he nibbles my ear.

"I just need a taste to hold me over," Fynn steps closer, and suddenly my pussy stretches further as he pushes two of his own fingers inside me.

"Oh fuck..." I grind against Oakley and Fynn's hands as they fuck me.

"What am I, chopped liver?" Jett then lifts my left leg as his other hand joins his two best friend's hands.

The stretch is almost unbearable as my third Lord adds two more digits inside me, "It's too much!" I moan.

"Does it hurt?" Oakley asks with concern.

I shake my head, "No..."

"Good, then take it, Kitty Cat. Let us make you come so your Lords can taste you."

I nod and let them do as they will, right here in the middle of the hallway, where anyone can see if they decide to come down for a midnight snack. I thrash my head back and forth as the pressure builds. With their fingers inside me and their mouths on different parts of my body, my climax builds fast.

"Give it to us, Lovely. That's it...I can see it building in those pretty blues..."

"Come, Little Saint...come now!" Fynn growls and my body listens to his command.

They don't cover my mouth when I cry out; they just watch in awe. I could wake the whole house up, but they don't care. They thrust their fingers in and out, fucking me fast and hard. Each thrust gets slipperier as I come hard.

"Fuck yes...look at her drip all over the floor," Jett grunts.

By the time they are through with me, I feel like a limp noodle, and Oakley lifts me into his arms, "Don't sleep yet Kitty Cat. My cock wants inside you one last time."

I happen to see Fynn and Jett's surprised looks at one another and then at my ass before glancing at Oakley, "Interesting..." Jett smirks as he traces the carving Oakley gave me.

Oakley shrugs, "Is it not the truth?"

They both gaze at me and simultaneously say, "Abso-fucking-lutely!"

Finding Dani in what the guys call the game room, I lean against the door frame, "Can we talk?"

She stands there with a pool stick, contemplating her next move, "What, no torture session this time?" She quirks her brow.

I let out a little snort and look down at the floor, "No, we only reserve those for people we need answers from."

Dani studies me, then asks, "Why does it look like you're guilty of something, Cat?"

I lift my head and push away from the doorway, "Because I am. I came here to say that I'm sorry. We can't take back what we did...what's done is done, but we are truly sorry for putting you through that."

"What brought this on?" Dani sets the pool stick on the table and leans her hip against the corner while crossing her arms at her chest.

"We questioned Felicia..."

Dani straightens up, "You questioned her and didn't think that I'd want to watch?"

I roll my eyes, "She didn't get the same treatment you received." My mouth kicks up on one side as I try not to smile.

"Oh, well, I always knew she wouldn't be your type," Dani snickers.

"I'm trying to apologize here, and you're making jokes," I shake my head and sigh.

"Cat, you said it yourself; there isn't anything that we can do about it. What's done is done. I'm just trying to move on...and besides, I got finger fucked by the hottest chick on campus...I can't be too mad," she smirks.

I stare at the girl who used to be my best friend, "I really am sorry. You just need to understand that I almost died twice, and I wasn't taking any more chances."

"I get it, Cat. Honestly, I'd probably do the same thing," Dani sighs.

I walk over to her and hold out my hand, hoping she will shake it, but she just stares at it disgustedly. When I lower my hand, she pulls me in and hugs me, "You're forgiven," she says softly, "I just want my friend back."

I pull away and smirk, "You do realize how fucked up this friendship is, right?"

"It's one of a kind, sweet cheeks," she jokes, "How about you rack the balls and let me kick your ass at pool?"

"Oh, actually, I need to run an errand with the guys. Can I find you when we get back?" I feel bad, but we have to take care of Felicia before we go after Kaden.

Dani has taken it all pretty well, and I have the distinct feeling that it's only because she has no other friends. This actually makes me feel like shit. Would I do it again if I had to, though? Absolutely.

I give her another quick hug and leave to go find the guys. I have a slight limp this morning due to the minor marking Oakley gave me last night. It's rubbing against my clothing when I walk, even with a bandage on it.

It's fucked up, right? Letting him carve into me after everything Brett did, but I trusted him, and he didn't let me down. I hope it scars up well; otherwise, I will get it tattooed.

When I got out of the shower this morning, I got a peek at it. I remember Oakley coming up to me and smiling. His fingers circling it gently.

"Do you like it?"

"What is it exactly?" I ask because it's hard to determine what it is in the mirror.

Oakley takes out his phone, snaps a picture, and then shows it to me, "It's a heart in the middle..."

I study the picture and realize that it's three people circling a heart. I look back at Oakley, my words caught in the back of my throat. Oakley hooks some of my hair behind my ear and smiles softly at me.

"I know we don't always show it, and we can be major douchebags, but you need to know that we won't just protect you but your heart as well. We are your protectors in all things..."

It didn't matter how sore I was from the night before; I jumped Oakley's bones after he told me this. It's the most he's ever opened up to me, and never has anyone ever said anything like this to me. The Lords of Sin may be sadistic savages, but they are my savages.

Fynn holds my hand as we walk to the lake cabin from the Jeep. Jett has Felicia over his shoulder while Oakley goes on ahead to unlock the cabin. He's carrying a takeout bag for Chris since we are a little late in getting here. We won't make him wait to eat, and that's what would happen if we had to make him something.

Felicia has been non-stop mumbling shit under the duct tape that covers her mouth. Even as she's carried over Jett's shoulder, she's still going on. She's more pissed at us for holding Chris than she is being captured herself, which I find kind of weird. I've always taken the Saint's President as being self-absorbed. I guess I was wrong.

"How did it go with Dani?" Fynn asks as we walk a bit slower than the others.

"It actually went better than I thought. She still wants to be friends," I tell him, "She doesn't have anyone else..."

"Do you think you can return to being friends with her?" he asks.

"Honestly, I don't know. A lot of it will have to do with whether she accepts the three annoying douchebags I have in my life," I grin without looking at him.

"Yeah, that's got to be a deal breaker," Fynn states, "I hear they're very possessive of what's theirs and can be total asshats."

Nodding, "That's a very true story," I say and bite my lip.

Fynn stops and pulls me into his embrace, "Admit it, Little Saint, you love those asshats in your life..." His voice trails off when he realizes that he's said that one word that none of us have yet to reveal.

My own smile drops as I stare into his soft brown eyes. Maybe it's time that one of us admits to it, and what better time than now, "I can't argue with you there..." I say in a breathless whisper.

After gazing into each other's eyes, Fynn snakes his hand around my nape and pulls me in until his lips crash against mine. The kiss is needy and all-consuming. I can feel Fynn's emotions within it, and I kiss him back with all the passion I can muster.

"Can't that wait until after the interrogation?" Oakley calls out.

Fynn and I slowly part, staring at each other, knowing that we both want the same thing...for Fynn to push me against the nearest tree and take what he wants, just like that time on the cliff. A throat clearing is the only thing that snaps our attention back to the present, and we look over to see Oakly still standing in the doorway, a knowing grin on his face.

"The sooner we get the shit done, the sooner you two can fuck," he calls out, then turns and disappears inside the cabin.

"Asshole," Fynn mutters under his breath as he takes my hand once more.

I chuckle and squeeze his hand, "Yes, but he's still your best friend, and you love him like a brother," I remind him.

He smirks, "That's the only reason I haven't beat his ass all these years." He slaps my ass when we get to the door, pushing me inside as he follows.

"Well, are you going to tell us what we want to know, or will we have to take it out on poor Chris, who you swear is innocent?" I ask Felicia as I trace the knife's blade down the front of Chris's shirt.

I have no plans on hurting the guy just yet, but I will do whatever I need to in order to get her to talk. It's up to the Saint's President whether Chris gets hurt.

"I already told you that he doesn't know anything!" Felicia growls as she watches her boy toy swing from his wrists right in front of her.

"That's not what I asked," I remind her, "I want to know why you are doing what you are doing and why you are not going after him?" I stop Chris's swaying body and place the blade under his chin.

After a little glaring match with her, Felicia rolls her eyes, "I wanted your fathers to admit to the wrongdoing because my own mother was also a victim in the assault. She killed herself over the guilt of what she had to do..."

My laugh is cynical, "Did you even watch the video before sending it off to Dani?"

"Kaden made a copy and sent it to her since he's the one that found it among our father's things he left behind when he left Kaden's mom. I could only stomach watching some of it before I told him to turn it off," she informs us.

"Did you even watch where your mother took part?" Jett sneers as he leans against a nearby table.

"T-That's when I had him turn it off. I didn't want to see what they made my mother do." Felicia closes her eyes and swallows.

"Oh? So you never saw the enjoyment she got out of it," I state, "Baby," I glance at Oakley, "Can you play the video?"

We wait for Oakley to return with his laptop and pull up the video, "Watch it," I glare at Felicia.

I don't have to look at the screen to know what's happening. The whole assault is burned into my memory from watching it the first time. Instead, I focus on Felicia and Chris to see their reactions. It doesn't take long to see that Chris really is clueless, at least about the video.

Felicia's face screws up when the parts of her mother's hand in the assault play out. Disbelief shrouds her face as she watches the despicable things Julia does to Simone. She closes her eyes, so she doesn't have to watch it any longer.

I walk over and yank her head back by her hair, and clenching my jaw, I say, "Tell us again how your mother was a victim, Felicia!"

FIFTY-THREE

Jett

This bitch is getting on my last nerve. I probably would have gutted her by now if it wasn't for my Lovely Lina being here. Lina is doing a pretty good job getting the information from her, but it's taking too long. I swear, the bitch loves pain just as much as my Lovely does since that's the only time she tells us anything. Waiting until we deliver some pain before she opens that trap of hers.

"Awe, it looks like someone didn't like finding out how evil her mother actually was," I chuckle evilly as I walk toward Felicia slowly. I pet her head like she's a fucking dog, "Now, how about you be a good girl and tell us everything you know?"

Apparently, she doesn't like my condescending voice by the glare she bores into me, "You already know that I'm the one who sent you the letters..."

"Ah, yes, but you see...you tried killing our favorite person three times..."

"Two..." my Lovely cuts me off.

I look at her gorgeous face and remind her, "No...three. I think you're forgetting about the Toga party, Lovely."

"No," Felecia jumps in, "That was only meant as a warning. It's why it was done over the pool."

My head snaps back to the bitch, "She was tied to a fucking cross and almost drowned!" I snarl.

I hear the small gasp that comes from Lina, now remembering that first incident. Yeah, I will never forget it. How I had to repeatedly swim to the surface to get air for her...it was fucking scary as hell...I won't lie.

"Maybe if you didn't do such savage things, like sacrificing a woman by tying her to a cross, Cat wouldn't have been in that situation," Felicia spits, "I mean, you were going to fuck her in front of all the guests...were you not?"

A slow grin appears on my face, and I shrug, "That's not entirely true..."

"Oh, I'm sorry, you were going to show it up on a damn screen," she glares daggers at me.

"I signed a contract, Felicia," Lina cuts in, "I knew what would happen, so get off your high horse and stop trying to paint the Lords as being such degenerates."

"It's okay, Lovely," I give her my most devastating smile, "She isn't entirely wrong, but we are only as immoral as you allow us to be." I lick my lips as I look our girl up and down.

The leggings she's wearing with the off-the-shoulder sweater don't do anything to keep me from wanting her. I know what's underneath all that clothing, which makes me salivate. Lina really doesn't know what she does to us. She has three grown-ass men willing to worship her at her feet, and even though we haven't quite expressed it yet, we will soon enough.

"Focus, Pelletier," my Lovely Lina smirks.

Doing as I'm told, I return my attention to Felicia, "What's the story behind Chris, Felicia?"

The bitch chooses now to become tight-lipped. With my hand still on her head, I grip her hair and clench my jaw as I get in real close, "Either answer, or you can join Brett because I'm so over your bullshit!"

I feel a hand on my back. Looking over my shoulder, Lina stares at me knowingly, "Take a break, Jett. You're letting her get to you. We still need her for a little longer, so we can't have you killing her just yet."

Letting go of Felicia, I spin around and grip Lina's jaw, "Don't go soft on her, Lovely." I then kiss her hard before breaking it and taking a step back, letting her continue with the questioning.

The sound of cars pulling up draws my attention as I emerge from the soundproof room. I quickly go to the window, my face hardening when I see two vehicles pulling up. I move to the door and open it, taking a stance with my arms crossed at my chest.

"To what do we owe the pleasure?" I scowl as Donavan Harris and Jakob Morin walk up to the porch.

I keep my eyes on the other two climbing from the blacked-out Range Rover. Devlin Scott, and lastly, Blake Pelletier...my father. Devlin opens the back door as my father comes around to the passenger side, and the two of them yank out a trussed-up Kaden Miller with a gag in his mouth.

"What the fuck is this?" I look at Donavan and Jakob.

"You didn't think we would truly abandon you, did you?" Jakob grins.

"Actually, yeah, we did," I reply sarcastically, "The two of you were no help at all. They were the only ones that helped figure some of this shit show out," I say, nodding toward Devlin and my father.

"Our hands were tied," Donavan sighs, "They still are. You don't want to know the hoops we had to jump just to bring this little puke to you without being found out."

"We made it this far. You didn't have to do shit if you were worried about getting caught." I scoff at his pathetic excuse.

"Whoa, what the hell?" Oakley says from the doorway, "Dad?"

"Hey, Oak. We thought we would bring you a present," Donavan says to his son.

"How?" My friend looks confused.

"How did we know you were going to need him?" Donavan points his thumb at Kaden, "Just like the rest of the Lords would have known had we not interfered with the listening devices. You really don't realize how dangerous it was to do half the shit you did."

"I thought we were being tested?" Oakley growls out.

"Yes, but there are still limits to what you could and could not do. Like leaving anyone you talked to alive afterward, even if they weren't guilty," He states, looking between Oakley and me.

"Are you saying that we should have killed Dani and Chris?" I ask, scrutinizing the older version of my friend.

"I'm afraid so..."

"That's bullshit! These are different times, and we are the new generation," I look at all four older men, "With the help of past Lords who want change, we can change these ancient rules."

"Maybe, but it's unlikely," my father chimes in, "All we can do is wait until those who still want the old rules carried out die, but even then, there are still alumni who will carry on with the old rules."

"Whatever. I just want to get this shit done so we can move forward with our lives." I turn and head back into the cabin.

Shutting the door once everyone is inside, I lead them all to the torture room, "We've got company," I scowl at Lovely and Fynn.

Lina's eyes widen as soon as Devlin and my father step in with Kaden, "What are you doing here, Dad?"

"Hey Catty...I mean Cat. I'm sorry..." Devlin gets a sheepish look as his daughter glares at him.

"I think Catty is cute, baby," I wrap my arms around her from behind.

"Use it and see where it gets you, *baby*." She threatens me like I'm scared of her.

"No worries," I whisper in her ear, "I'll only use it when I have my cock buried deep inside that sweet cunt, just the way you like it. I bet you won't do shit about it."

She sends her elbow flying into my gut, knocking the air from me. I laugh and step away from the vicious minx. Turning back toward my father, he and Devlin are carrying Kaden into the cell. They leave him tied and gagged as they come back out.

"You no longer need them," Donavan states as he nods toward our captives, "The only thing you needed to find out was who was sending the threats; the rest of it doesn't matter."

"The hell it doesn't!" my Lovely Lina states angrily, "We didn't come this far...and I didn't almost die three fucking times for us not to get the whole damn story."

"Cat..." Devlin starts, but she stops him with her hand.

"No, Dad. You will not shut me up this time. You shoved me into this world, and we did exactly what we needed to do. Now, we want answers. We don't know why Kaden got into the middle of it, or how Brett ended up being the one to lose his life over a fucking loser...or where the hell Chris fits into all of this. Why didn't they threaten him? That bitch," Lina points to Felicia, "won't fucking tell us!"

Lina is so pissed that she walks over to Felicia and backhands her, splitting the President's lip. When she goes to hit her again, I wrap my arms around her and lift her up and away from Felicia.

"Calm down, Lovely girl," I whisper into her ear.

She's panting hard as she closes her eyes and tries to take some deep breaths. I want to leave this place with her and hide until all this bullshit disappears. I've already been looking into traveling over the holidays, just the four of us. As soon as I talk to Fynn and Oak, I want to surprise her with it, but this shit show needs to end beforehand.

"You know," Jakob speaks up, "That little shit over there was trying to spew shit out of his mouth earlier, but we were in a hurry and needed to leave, so we gagged him."

We all focus on Kaden, who glares back at us from the cell, "You have something you want to say?" Fynn asks as he walks over and leans against the bars.

Kaden nods, so Fynn enters the cell and takes the gag off. Kaden coughs, and then his eyes meet our impatient ones, "You wanted to know why Chris wasn't threatened...well, aside from my slutty little half-sister fucking him, it's because he's the most innocent one here."

I scoff, "I wouldn't go that far," I glance at Chris, remembering what he said about my Lovely, but he seems to be hanging on Kaden's every word.

"You all were looking for the daughter of Simone because her obituary said she had a daughter who was given up for adoption, but that couldn't be further from the truth," Kaden glances at Chris, "Simone had a baby boy who was taken from her shortly after birth by his biological father. It wasn't the rape that caused her suicide. It was Kevin Douglas taking her baby from her."

The whole room is silent as we all take in what this little fucker is saying. Chris is staring wide-eyed with disbelief at Kaden. I now see just how innocent this big mother fucker is, and to be honest, I almost feel sorry for him.

Catalina

Another shocking revelation has us all reeling, but what surprises me most is the stunned look Felicia has on her face as she listens to Kaden rattle on. Her half-brother has been keeping things from her, and she's only now realizing it. While Felicia's expression is a mixture of shock and anger, Kaden wears one of utter enjoyment.

I've never seen Kaden look like this. The sinister look on his face is all wrong. Gone is the all-American-boy-next-door look, and in its place is one of malicious amusement when he reveals more information, "According to letters I found among my sperm donor's things he had left behind, Simone was threatened and even held against her will for the last month of her pregnancy, so as soon as the baby came along, he was taken straight to his father."

Kaden explains more, "Julia and Kevin were still an item even though she was pregnant by one of Kevin's best friends...my father. Turns out Julia was a hypocrite because even though she had no plans on giving her child up, she hated that Kevin was keeping his bastard." His eyes move to Felicia's, "Your mother didn't commit suicide because of guilt. She did it because Kevin had enough of her shit and broke it off with her."

"Those are lies!" Felicia shakes her head in disbelief, "Why wouldn't you tell me this?"

"You came to me with your plan after discovering we were siblings. I wanted nothing to do with it at first...I didn't fucking care," Kaden's eyes meet mine, "Not until I met Cat and realized she was into the fucking Sinners. I didn't give a shit about your problems, Felicia."

"What about Brett?" I ask, scrunching my brows and ignoring what he implied, "I thought you had something going on with him?"

His wicked smile tells me that I probably won't like what he will say, "I did, but look at you, Cat. You're a hot piece of ass…"

Fynn, being right beside him, punches him in the face and breaks his nose. Blood pours from it instantly as Kaden curses, "Say shit like that again…I fucking dare you!" Fynn growls.

"Fynn, let him talk," I tell him, "We need to hear it all."

The brooding Lord glances at me, then nods, addressing Kaden, "Finish before I finish you, Miller."

I roll my eyes at Fynn but then turn back to Kaden, "Please, Kaden."

He glares at Fynn before his eyes meet mine, "Brett caught me jerking off as I watched you changing in your room at the Sorority House…"

I jerk back, "What? How…?" I trail off.

Kaden smirks and stares at Felicia, "Sister dearest installed a camera to keep tabs on you."

I walk over to Felicia with murder in my eyes and cock my arm back. Before anyone can stop me, I swing, my fist making contact, and now both siblings have a broken nose. Oakley grabs me before I can get another hit in, so I will have to be satisfied with the one punch…for now.

"Brett shouldn't have been your guard after you were taken," Kaden continues, "But for some reason, my sister hates you with a passion, and she used Brett's jealousy to manipulate him…"

"Shut the fuck up, Kaden! You don't know anything…" Felicia glares at her brother.

"Oh, don't stop now," I muse, "It's getting really fucking good."

My father steps in, "Why don't you take a break, sweetheart, all of you? You are all worked up. We will work on them, so we will have the whole story when you return."

"No fucking way! I love you, Dad, but I don't trust you at the moment." I see the hurt flash across his face, but he only purses his lips.

Oakley comes to me, "Go. I'll stay here and make sure nothing shady goes on." He nods at Jett and Fynn.

"I'm not going to leave…"

"You will, Kitty Cat because I'm telling you to." He caresses my cheek. His stare bores into me, not angrily but more sternly than I'd like it to be.

After a few seconds of eye contact with Oakley, I break contact, "Fine, but I won't be gone long."

Turning, I walk out of the room, Fynn and Jett following close behind. When I go to spin on them, I'm stopped by rough hands. Hot breath caresses my cheek and neck as Fynn's low baritone voice gives me an order that sends chills down my spine.

"Run, Little Saint. Run fast because if we catch you, we're going to fuck you without mercy." His teeth nip at my lobe as I hear Jett snicker in the background.

Fuck. I need to be back in that room. I want to make sure we know everything, and we need to figure out what we're going to do with our captives once we're done. But for now...I run.

I shoot for the woods the second my feet hit the front porch; there are more hiding places to be found. My core is already throbbing with the thought of them catching me. Of course, I'll let them find me, but not until they work for it.

They give me a little head start, but the moment I enter the tree line, about fifty feet from the cabin, I hear their snickers and taunts, "Run, baby, run..."

As the trees get denser, I stop briefly, looking around for the best course of action. About a hundred feet in front of me is a large tree with an enormous trunk. I race for it and throw myself behind it just as I hear the light footfalls of my Lords.

I'm breathing hard; I'm not used to this kind of physical activity. I cover my mouth with my hand so they can't hear me. My eyes search the surroundings and soon fall on another large tree with branches hanging so low that they touch the ground. My first thought is to run to it, but then I realize it's too obvious, so I keep searching.

A stick breaking not too far off catches my attention. Fynn and Jett are cocky, thinking they will catch me regardless, so they don't bother silencing their footsteps. I, on the other hand, will prove them wrong...hopefully.

I glance around the huge tree and see Jett's white hoodie through the trees. Maybe, just maybe, if I stay here, I can just circle around the tree as they pass, and then I can make a break for it, running back toward the cabin.

Waiting patiently, I hear them close in on me, and I start to inch around the trunk. They are discussing what we will eat when we leave here, and I want to giggle but keep it to myself. Their voices start to fade, and I wait a little longer before peeking out to see if they are near.

When I see nothing but trees, I breathe out a sigh of relief and smile. Stepping away from the large tree, I jump as hands grab my waist, "Or we can just eat Lovely Lina. What do you say, Fynn?" Jett laughs out loud.

"I have to agree, Jett. Saint's pussy is the best meal around," Fynn grabs for my legs, and I begin to kick out.

"Let me go," I cry out, trying to break free but only because they love a good struggle, "Please...I want to get back!"

"I told you to run, Little Saint. Now, we are going to fuck you right here, and you'll take it like a good girl, won't you?" Fynn pulls my leggings down, yanking my ankle boots off and then the leggings.

Jett grabs the hem of my sweater and pulls it over my head. I'm left in just a thong in mid-November, but I can honestly say I'm not cold. A fever burns through me as my two Lords ravage my body like men possessed.

I hear a zipper and watch as Fynn pulls his cock out, "Hold onto our little slut, Jett. I'm going to teach her what happens when she tries tricking us."

Jett sits on the ground, bringing me with him. He holds me by bringing his arms around and grabbing hold of my breasts. Fynn spreads my legs and lines his throbbing hardness up to my slit. His eyes meet mine, and his mouth curves into that wicked grin that I love so much.

"Beg me, Saint," he says, "Beg me to fuck this cunt; you know the drill."

I'm already becoming delirious with desire, so it takes nothing to open my mouth and beg, "Please, Fynn...I want you deep inside me. Fuck me like you mean it."

All the air from my lungs escapes when he surges into me. He doesn't stop and wait for me to adjust. He pulls out and drives into me again and again. He pushes my knees to my chest, where Jett takes over, holding me open for his best friend.

"Mm, pound that cunt good, Fynn. Make her come so fucking hard that she can't see straight," Jett orders as he watches me get fucked. I can feel how hard he is, himself, and it excites me more.

I feel it. The climax that Fynn has made his mission to pull from me is beginning to build. Knowing what it needs to do, my body doesn't listen when I try to hold my orgasm back. Instead, it closes in on the cliff's ledge that I will tumble over as Fynn clenches his jaw and fucks into me roughly, playing with my clit.

"ARGH!!!!" My scream echoes through the woods as he pulls my first orgasm from me.

What surprises me is that he doesn't come. Instead, he pulls out, and I'm manhandled until I'm turned around. The side of my face is pressed into the cold ground, and my ass is pulled into the air. Fynn switches places with Jett, who now lines himself up to my entrance.

"Hold on, Lovely Lina. It's about to get rough." Jett drives into me, and I lose all sense of myself.

FIFTY-FOUR

Fynn

I needed to get out of that fucking cabin before I killed that little fucker. My blood is boiling after how Kaden described my Little Saint. Only we, as her Lords, can describe and sexualize her that way. Had it not been for my fiery Little Saint, Miller would be dead by now.

Teaming up on our girl the way Jett and I are doing will help calm the raging storm inside me. I wasn't ready to let go when I made her cunt weep around my cock, so I switched places. I want us to fill her fully before giving her what I know she desperately wants.

I never thought I would love watching the one person that has captured not only my heart but my whole fucking soul be taken by another right before my eyes. However, it's a gorgeous fucking sight, and I can't help but stroke myself as I help hold her down. Her eyes are on my hand as it wraps around my hardness, gliding back and forth.

"Do you want my cock, Little Saint?" I taunt.

She tries moving her head, but my hand restricts her, and I chuckle. The mere fact that I'm driving her crazy and knowing that I have one of the things she wants most right now...well, let's just say that it does something to my ego. I may blow at any second if I continue to watch her salivate for my cock, so I stop stroking myself, earning me a displeasing groan from her lips.

"Now, now, my little slut. You need to learn to be patient," I smirk as I grip her hair.

"Fuck, this pussy feels so fucking good!" Jett moves his right leg, planting his foot flat on the ground to get better access before driving into my Little Saint even harder.

Moving some of her hair from her face, I give our girl a devious grin, "Look at you... you're such a slut, Catalina. Even in the middle of the woods with our fathers not too far away, you love getting fucked. Your cunt weeps for us every fucking time."

"Say it, Lina," Jett orders as he uses her hole for his own gratification, "Say that you are a filthy slut for our cocks, and I'll let you come again."

"Jett..." Saint pants, her body shoved forward continuously. She may very well have a few cuts on her cheek by the time my friend is done with her.

"Fucking say it!" He slaps her ass.

"Do as your Lord says, Little Saint," I growl and slap her face with my hardness.

Our little slut sticks her tongue out, wanting a taste of it, so I reward her, slapping it a few times on her tongue before thrusting just a little. I don't allow my shaft to enter her mouth because I will lose it if I do. I don't want her to know she has me unhinged, so I make it look like I'm only teasing her.

"Fuck, Saint...you are the perfect little plaything for us..." I growl and pull away, "Now...say it!"

"I'm your filthy little plaything, your slut to use and abuse...to take pleasure from. Please...let me come," she moans, and I can see her straining to keep her orgasm at bay.

"Good fucking girl..." I smirk, "Now, reach down and rub that pretty little clit for us."

She bites her bottom lip as her hand disappears beneath her, "Uh..." she breathes.

The little sounds coming from her as she plays with herself while getting fucked is almost my undoing. Ever so slowly, I run my hand down her back, my fingers running through the crack of her ass. Jett slows down so I can insert two fingers into her warmth beside him.

"Oh God..."

"There is no God here, Little Saint...only your Lords," I begin fucking her with my fingers, keeping the tempo with the thrusts of Jett's cock.

"Uh...oh fuck... I'm coming... don't stop!" My Little Saint sings, and just as her body begins to tremble, I plunge a finger into her tight little ass hole.

Jett spits down her ass crack, adding lube for me, so I can insert a second finger, "That's it, baby...take us both."

When her body stops shuddering from her climax, we pull out of her and yank her to her feet, "T-That was..." she stutters, but I stop her from talking.

"We aren't done with you yet, Saint," her eyes widen when she sees my wicked grin.

Jett lifts her and impales her onto his cock once more while I come behind her and line the head of my cock to her cute little pucker. She's whimpering, but not because she doesn't want it. Saint is a fucking butt slut, loving how we fuck her deep and feeling it as we empty ourselves into her.

Too bad Oakley isn't here so we could fill all her holes. Two of them will have to suffice. Before I enter her, a thought comes to me, and I bend over to pick up her leggings. I then wrap them around her neck, taking half her air supply as I enter her. She's going to scream this time, and I think it's best to keep the noise down just a bit.

I moan as I sink into her tightness, and I have to stop to take a few breaths before I start fucking her. With Jett inside her cunt, her ass is even tighter. I nip her ear lobe until I taste a hint of metallic, then I suck.

"Fuck, baby... you're so tight. No worries, though. We are about to stretch the living shit out of this cunt and ass." I pull out slowly before slamming into her, making her cry out.

"Damn, Fynn," Jett says, "I don't think I will last very long."

"Keep it in until our pretty little slut comes all over your cock again," I tell my friend.

Reaching around to her front, my hand dips between my Little Saint and Jett, and I rub her clit vigorously. I pull out little moans and whimpers from her, and when Jett pulls her ass cheeks further apart, allowing me to go deeper, the sound that comes from deep within her is music to my ears.

"Fuck Fynn...Jett. Faster...I need you to fuck me faster!" It comes out whispered with the leggings still tight around her neck.

"Don't fucking tell us how to fuck you, Saint. You take what we give you," I slam into her repeatedly, knowing her ass will be sore for days, but I'm looking forward to seeing her walk a bit wonky.

"Come for us, Lovely," Jett tells her, "My cock is waiting for your floodgates to open..."

No sooner does Jett have the words out his mouth, our girl is coming, and she's coming hard. It almost feels like she's pissing on us, and I grin. I love it when my Little Saint squirts.

"Oh damn, hold on," Jett says through clenched teeth, his nostrils flaring in and out as he tries breathing while shooting his load deep inside her.

I'm the last to release myself, and as I spray the inside of her ass, it drips back out. I can't stop. My cock has a mind of its own as it gets milked of every last drop.

I'm the first to reluctantly pull away and instantly feel the loss. Cum seeps down her thighs from both mine and Jett's releases, putting the biggest smile on my face. Before she can move, I shove my hand between her legs and scoop the cum that Jett left behind and shove my fingers into her mouth.

"I'd let you taste mine, but even I'm not that fucking sick and depraved..." I don't need to tell her to suck because our girl knows better. "You will pull your leggings back on as your cunt and ass drip with our seed," I pin her to the tree that Jett was bracing himself against, "Then later, Oakley will fuck our cunt, adding his cum."

"O-Okay," she stammers, still in a daze.

It takes us another fifteen minutes to return, mainly because Saint's legs are like Jell-O, and we take it slow. Yeah, we're proud fuckers at the moment; no apologies for pleasing our girl the way we did.

The cabin comes into view, and Oakley is stumbling out the door. My brows furrow, and the next thing I notice is that our fathers are gone. I'm not liking the uncertain feeling that is starting to creep in.

I scoop my Little Saint into my arms and quicken my pace, "What the fuck is happening?" I ask as soon as we are close enough.

"I'm going to fucking kill them!" Oakley growls, holding his head.

"Who?" Jett asks.

"Our fathers... that's who!" our friend scowls fiercely, "My father put me in a sleeper hold, knocking me out! I just came to, and everyone is gone! I must have bumped my head when I fell to the floor."

"Wait," Saint becomes alert, "When you say everyone..."

"Fucking EVERYONE! Our fathers took Felicia, Kaden, and Chris with them!"

"Son of a fucking bitch! I knew they were up to something," I curse as I set Saint back on her feet, steadying her until she can stand alone, "Let's go..."

"There's more!" Oakley hands me a piece of paper, and I skim over it before I curse again and pass it to Saint.

Sorry, kids, but this is how it has to be. Just know the three will be cared for, but not here. Don't ask us what will become of them because it's safer if you do not know the answer. We are doing what is best for all parties involved, and this way, no more lives will be lost.

We have not given any of you a reason to trust us, but we hope you can do so just this once. Everything we have done has been out of love for you, even if you don't see it as that. Take care of each other, and we will see you soon.

Love,
Your Fathers

"Un-fucking-believable!" I put my hands on my hips and tilt my face toward the sky, trying to calm myself down.

"What will they do with them?" Saint asks, looking just as pissed as the rest of us.

"I don't know, but we sure as fuck are going to find out," I growl, "Let's go."

I walk towards Oakley's car, and everyone else follows suit. I'm not sure what's going to happen when we find our fathers, but I'm not leaving until we find out what the actual fuck is going on. I hold the door open for Saint and wait until she gets into the back seat before climbing in after her. Whatever is going on is not going to happen without us being there. We are fucking adults, and it's about time they started treating us as such, even if it means we must implicate ourselves.

FIFTY-FIVE

Oakley

To say I'm beyond pissed would be putting it mildly. I can't believe my father would do this to me. Wait, actually, I can. Was this their plan all along? Bring Kaden to the cabin just to appease us, then snatch all three? I couldn't care less about what happens to Kaden and the dragon lady; they were part of the threats, but if it's to be believed...Chris is innocent in everything.

"What are we going to do now?" my Kitty Cat asks as she gently places an ice pack on the bump on my head.

"We find our fathers. They won't hide from us, but by the time they show themselves, it will mean that they've already disposed of Chris, Felicia, and Kaden," I tell her, "We need to find them before they do that."

We came straight to the Frat House to grab a few things from our stash. Not knowing what we will be up against, I want to be prepared for anything. My Kitty Cat is refusing to go anywhere until I ice my bump. It's sweet of her, really, but we don't have time for me to be coddled. The look she gave me when I told her this a moment ago actually put me in my place, if you can believe that shit. I sighed and sat down so she could play Nurse Kitty Cat.

"Where do you plan on looking for them first?" she asks.

"Jakob and Blake have warehouses and empty buildings throughout the town, so I figure we'd start there," I inform Kitty Cat.

She crinkles her forehead, "Why don't you just call your mother and have her check your father's location. They share a phone plan, don't they?"

I stare at her in disbelief. Why the fuck did I not think about that? After everything that has happened between my parents, my mother will happily give up this information. My Kitty Cat is a smart cookie and has made me incredibly proud. She's pissed just as much as I am that our fathers bested us, but she's still thinking straight.

I pull her close, so she stands between my legs, "You, my beautiful Kitty Cat, are amazing."

She shrugs as a smirk dances on her lips, "I know."

I grab the front of her shirt, pull her down to eye level, and then confiscate her mouth, giving her an earth-shattering kiss. I want her here and now, but there is no time. Ripping our lips apart, reluctantly, I gaze into her pretty blue eyes. My heart skips a beat.

Before I know what words are coming out, I already say, "I fucking love you, Kitty Cat."

Her eyes widen as she stares at me like a doe in headlights, "I..."

I've made her fucking speechless. Good.

Moving her hand away from the bump on my head, I stand up and look down at her, "I don't expect you to say it back..."

Kitty Cat cuts me off, "No, it's not that. You surprised me, is all," a smile slowly grows on her face, "I love you too, Oakley. I love all my Lords. I'm in love with all three of your crazy asses."

I close my eyes briefly, "I don't want to disappoint you. I'm afraid I will follow in my father's footsteps."

"You won't. If you start to act like an asshole...well, more than you already are," she chuckles, "I'll put you in your place."

My mouth kicks up in a half grin, "I believe you will do just that."

It's just as I thought; my mother comes in clutch for us and informs me of my father's whereabouts. Currently, they are at Fynn's father's empty warehouse on the outskirts of town. So, Jett and Fynn hop in the Jeep while Kitty Cat comes with me, and we race off toward the warehouse.

"How are we going to play this?" Kitty Cat questions, her eyes on the road before us.

I reach over and take her hand, bringing it to my lips briefly, "Honestly? I'm not sure yet," I tell her, "I really don't care what they do to Felicia and Kaden, but Chris shouldn't suffer the consequences of his father's actions, nor Felicia and Kaden's."

I notice her brows knit together, "What exactly did Kaden do? I mean, aside from knowing what Felicia was doing and sending Dani the video," I can see the wheels turning in her head as she thinks everything over, "Brett is the one who was mainly helping Felicia. How dirty are Kaden's hands in all this? That's what I wanted to find out. Without knowing his whole part in this, I don't feel right with condemning him to the same fate as Felicia."

I think about what she's saying, and as much as I dislike the guy, once again, she's right. "I guess it's something that we will have to find out before deciding to leave him with our fathers."

"Can I ask you something, Oakley?"

"Of course..." I tell her as I glance her way momentarily.

"Well, when this is all over with, does that mean the contract will be null and void?" I can't tell what she's thinking because her face is a blank canvas.

My brow quirks, "Do you want it to be null and void? I mean, have we really followed the rules in it anyway?" I snicker.

A sly smile creeps onto her face, "Yeah, I guess we haven't, but...I don't."

"You don't what?" I know what she means, but I need to hear her say it.

"I don't want the contract to be up. I like knowing that we have it on paper that the Lords of Sin own me. It makes me..." she trails off.

"It makes you what?" I furrow my brows.

She licks her lips, her face turning an adorable pink as she blushes. Suddenly, she just blurts out, "Wet."

My knuckles turn white as I grip the steering wheel, "Oh yeah? How wet, Kitty Cat?"

"Very…"

My cock stirs inside the confines of my jeans, causing extreme discomfort, but I will deal with that later. Keeping my eyes on the road, I order my Kitty Cat, "Pull your leggings off and turn toward me; I want to see how wet you are, Kitty Cat."

Like a good girl, she obeys, peeling her leggings off but keeping her panties on. Before I can instruct her to remove the barrier, she turns, spreads her legs, and pulls the fabric aside, showing off her glistening pussy. Her lips are still swollen from my best friends using it, and there, on the inside of her thighs, is evidence of their release, dried and stuck to her creamy skin.

The sight makes my dick even harder.

My hand automatically goes to her cunt, and I plunge my fingers into her, "Ride my hand and get off, Kitty Cat."

"But…" she looks at the traffic on the road.

"I don't give a fuck about them, Kitty Cat. If they see, they see. This is mine, and I want my prize. Now, fuck my fingers."

Her pussy clenches around me, liking my command, and she thrusts her hips. I add a third finger, making her moan loudly. When I add a fourth, she cries out and starts to go wild.

"That's my good little slut. See, you need your Lords to give you what you want. You love how we use and abuse this gorgeous body, and we will gladly keep doing so for as long as you want. To be honest, I don't think we will ever allow you to go free."

I tell her this because I know it turns her on to hear it, but I will if I have to. Even if it does rip my fucking heart out. I don't think I would live a good life without this woman by my side. I don't know when she became my everything, but I can finally admit that is precisely what she is.

Her head is thrown back against the window, her mouth in a perfect O as she comes, and she looks fucking perfect. I'm enthralled by the sight of her. I keep my eyes on her longer than I should, and a horn blares at me. Looking back to the road, I swerve back into my lane just in time.

Fuck…

Kitty Cat is breathing hard as she comes back to earth. My fingers continue to fuck her until the last of her climax is gone. When I pull my fingers from her, a slurping noise is heard due to how wet her cunt is, and I bring my hand to my mouth.

One by one, I stick a finger into my mouth, groaning as her essence coats my tongue. She's my favorite fucking flavor, and I savor every...last...drop. I want to bury my face between her thighs and drink from her until nothing is left, but that will have to wait until later.

"You have three minutes to put your bottoms back on, take out my throbbing cock, and fucking suck me off, Kitty Cat." I use my stern voice, so she knows I'm not joking around.

"We are almost there," she says as she hastily pulls her leggings back on, covering her beautiful legs.

"Then I suggest you get to sucking, baby."

Catalina

We pull up to a dark warehouse. Our father's vehicles are parked right outside, along with a black van that reminds me of a pedophile vehicle. Its windows are tinted, most likely with illegal tint, as black as they are.

I glance at Oakley as he pulls up and parks behind the van, blocking it in. A smirk dances across my lips as I watch him button and zip his jeans. I wipe the corner of my mouth, making sure there are no remnants of what I just consumed.

"Who does the van belong to?" I ask, as the Lord grins at my actions.

Oakley shrugs, "It could be for transport. Let's hope that's the only thing it's for."

I knit my brows together, "What else would it be for?"

His expression darkens as he stares back at me, "Clean up."

I freeze.

"They wouldn't just kill them outright...would they?" I swallow hard, a knot forming in my throat.

"I would like to think not, but then again, if the past Lords of Sin are involved, they may not have a choice." Oakley grabs my hand and strokes his thumb over it, "Like I said, let's hope it's for transport. Although, that may not be a good thing either if they're sending them to their deaths elsewhere."

I open the door hastily, but Oakley grabs my arm, stopping me. I try to yank free, "Let me go," I say, "I will not let them be killed unless it's in self-defense," I plead with my eyes, "I may have taken a life, and I may hate them for what they did to me, but it's obvious that past actions have fucked them up. They have their whole lives ahead of them, and they deserve to get the help they need, so they can move past all this."

Oakley's gaze burns into me, "Are you telling me that you are willing to forgive them for trying to kill you...for trying to kill us?"

I shake my head, "No, I can't forgive Felica or Kaden for their roles in this, but Chris is innocent," I lick my lips, his eyes drop to watch as the tip of my tongue glides across my lips, "That doesn't mean that I want them dead."

He hauls me over, so I'm draped across the center, "You have a good heart, Kitty Cat, but you need to consider the fact that they weren't concerned about your life. They were willing to take it without a second thought."

He runs his thumb over my bottom lip, and I suck it into my mouth briefly. Lust rolls into the depths of his eyes, and I smile before letting it pop out of my mouth. However, it drops when I see the emotion behind it all.

Clearing my throat, I push away, "Let's see the situation first, then we can decide."

Jett and Fynn pull up beside us, blocking the van even more. Cutting the engine, they climb out and meet us on the driver's side, waiting for us to get out ourselves. I start to get out, but his voice stops me this time.

"Open the glove box, Kitty Cat."

I glance over my shoulder at Oakley before doing his bidding. A small pistol sits nestled inside. Pulling it out, I eye the Greek God with a raised brow.

"You never know what we are going to walk into," he shrugs and opens his door.

It's then that I see his Glock tucked away in the back of his pants. Sighing to myself, I ensure the safety is on before tucking it in the back of my bottoms. Fynn stands near as I get out and shuts the door for me, winking and giving me his devilish grin.

None of us say a word as they surround me, and we head toward the only door on this side of the building. I glance around the parking lot to see if anyone else is around, but all seems quiet. It isn't until we open the door and make our way down a narrow hallway that voices can be heard.

The closer we get, the more distinguishable their words become, "It will take two hours to get there. If you leave now, you can make it there just after dark," Oakley's father is speaking.

Garbled murmurs sound throughout the space. The three prisoners are obviously not happy with whatever plan our fathers have for them. At least they are still alive.

"Are you sure you don't want to just *get rid of them?*" An unfamiliar voice speaks up.

"If they give you any problems, then do what you must..."

Before Donavan can finish, I rush through the door in front of us, the Lords cursing behind me as they hurry to follow. Our abrupt appearance startles our fathers and three other faces I've never seen before.

"You will do no such thing!" I call out, making my way toward the group, huddling in the center of the empty space.

"Catalina, you don't understand..." my father tries to say, but I don't want to hear it.

"No, Dad. For one, Chris is innocent..."

"It doesn't fucking matter now, Catalina," Jakob steps forward, "If we don't send them away, the Lords will take it upon themselves to get rid of them."

"Where do you plan on sending them?" Jett moves closer to the other group.

Blake sighs as he looks at his son, "There is an Institute just across the border. It's where we have sent others who have stepped over the line and would have been taken out by the older Lords had we not stepped in."

"What kind of Institute?" Jett growls at his father.

"A Reformatory. It will teach them how to move forward in the real world when they are set free. It teaches them the History of the Lords of Sin and why it's important to follow their rules and keep their secrets."

"Chris did nothing wrong!" I step forward, and Fynn tries to keep me back, but I shake him off, "Why should he be sent away?"

"Unfortunately," my father responds, "Kevin never taught him about The Lords. He was afraid that Chris would learn the truth about his mother."

"How do you know this?" I knit my brows together, and then another thought occurs to me, "You never taught me either."

"I called Kevin personally about this. He knows that we are holding his son and has given his consent for us to send Chris to the Institute. He wants him to know now that the secret is out," my father gives the football player a sympathetic look, "I think it's because he doesn't want to deal with his son's wrath. As for you, it's different for a Lady."

"Chris is an adult. Why would you need his father's consent?" I ask.

"Because Chris refused to go on his own." Donavan states, "If we let him stay, the Lords *will* take care of him themselves. They never take chances."

"How long will they serve?" Fynn questions.

"Chris will only have to spend a year at the Institute. Felicia and Kaden will spend three, possibly longer, depending on how well they do."

"Are you fucking serious?" I scowl, "I may not want them dead, but they did try to kill us! Brett is dead because of them!"

I notice Kaden shaking his head vigorously, and I walk over, ripping the tape off his mouth, "No! I had nothing to do with his death! That's all on Felicia. She was blackmailing him so he would help her."

I turn my gaze on the one that started this whole shit storm, "Oh really? What exactly did she threaten him with?"

"She threatened to spill that he was into men; told him she had evidence that she would show the whole school and send it to his parents. His father is very strict, and so he did her bidding. Then, when he found out that I really was interested in you, he was happy to go along with it." Kaden isn't having any issues spilling everything or answering our questions.

"What about the fire?" Oakley asks, "How did anyone know we would be there?"

"There's a bug in Cat's phone. Felicia had Brett install it. She could always hear everything," he informs us, and I feel my face heat.

"Everything?" I croak out.

"Yeah..." Kaden nods.

I look over at Oakley and see the anger etched in his face, "You fucking bitch!"

I grab him when he lunges for her, and she begins to laugh behind the tape. She knows he's pissed about her listening to our little tryst in my father's office. She has no remorse. I can tell by the gleam in her eyes that she isn't sorry for anything.

Ripping the tape from her mouth, I ask her straight up, "Are you sorry for any of it?"

I'm hoping she will say yes, because maybe there is still hope for her. Her ominous look tells me I won't like what she's about to say. I send up a prayer, asking for forgiveness on what I may have to do if she proves that she isn't remorseful.

Felicia's eyes squint at me, "I had no plans to harm you, but your fathers left me no choice. Then, when I realized that you were *letting* them use you, to treat you like their own personal whore, and that you were enjoying it...I knew there was no saving you. They're the worst Sinners of all..."

She doesn't get to finish her sentence as a bullet flies right through her forehead. The smoke plumes from the barrel of my gun as the room goes silent. I stand here and watch a trickle of blood roll down her forehead as it lulls forward. I'm a fucking hypocrite. I just killed her... and it wasn't in self-defense; she was just a shitty person.

"Jesus Christ!" I turn my attention to Kaden when I hear his outburst, and his eyes widen.

"Sorry, but your sister was a fucking bitch," I bring my hand to my side and look at our fathers, "I want to be updated on their progress at the Institute."

Once I see their nods, my eyes linger on my father, and I notice the pride in his. Turning, I head for the door, not needing to check and see if my Lords are following. I can feel their presence close behind. I know they will follow me anywhere, just like I will follow them.

It's not until I step outside that my body begins to shake in the aftermath. Strong arms wrap around me and lift me as warm breath tickles my neck, "I've got you. I'll always have you, Lovely Lina."

FIFTY-SIX

Jett

Staring down at the beautiful woman in my arms has my heart stuttering. Catalina just killed someone...put a bullet in her head, but that's not what has the beating organ going haywire. It's the reason behind it. Sure, we could all see that Felicia wasn't going to change; that much was clear, but her last words solidified her fate.

That bullet through Felicia's head was because she insulted my Lovely Lina's Lords. So, when she almost collapses just outside the building, you better believe I'm there to catch her. My words are the truest I've ever spoken... *I've always got her.*

This woman can drug me as many times as she wants, because, if I'm being honest, I feel high on her whenever she's around. That will never change. Catalina Scott is a fucking siren, calling out to not just me, but also to Oakley and Fynn. She has us all enthralled by her beauty, brains, and fucking delectable body. There will never be another woman like my Lovely Lina.

Tossing Fynn the keys to my Jeep, I climb into the back seat, so I can hold onto Lina for as long as possible. She's a badass when she needs to be, but it doesn't mean she likes it. I have the feeling that she isn't going to take this kill well. Unlike with Brett, this wasn't self-defense, and she will fight her demons over this one. It will be our job to ensure she stays afloat and doesn't sink down into a dark abyss.

"Hey, baby. Talk to me," I urge, brushing some strands of her blonde hair from her face.

Her head lays against my shoulder as I hold her across my lap, "I don't want to talk right now, Jett."

"Don't shut us out, Lovely. We are all here for you," I tell her before pressing my lips to the crown of her head.

"I won't," she whispers, "I just need some...time."

"Okay, baby, but if you overthink it, your feelings will worsen. Just know that any one of us would have done the same thing. You just got there first." I squeeze her gently, but all she does is nod.

I take my Lovely Lina straight to my room once we get to the Frat House. On the way up, I'm stopped by Dani, "What's wrong with her?" she asks, frantically.

"She's fine," I try to appease her, "At least, she will be."

The audacity this pint-size of a woman has as she glares at me, "What the fuck did you guys do to her?"

Rolling my eyes, I turn toward her, "We didn't do anything, and if Cat wants to tell you when she's ready to talk, then she will. Otherwise, it's not our story to tell anyone."

I turn my back on her once more when Fynn joins us and unlocks the third-floor door. When Dani tries following us, Fynn stops her, "No. She needs to rest right now. You can talk to her in the morning," I hear him tell the feisty woman as I carry Lina upstairs.

I lay her on my bed, and when I start to move away, her voice reaches me, "Thank you for getting rid of her. I'm not in the mood right now."

"I know, baby," I sit on the edge of the bed, "Can I get you anything? Something to eat, a drink..." my voice trails off as she shakes her head no.

I stand, but she grabs my hand, "Actually, there is one thing you can do."

"What is it?"

"Lay here with me?" The way her eyes plead with mine makes it impossible to say no, even if I wanted to.

I let a grin grow on my face, "Sure, I can, but you're not going to take advantage of my kindness, are you?" I tease.

Lina scoffs, "Oh, please, Jett. Haven't you ever heard the saying that *you can't rape the willing?'"*

Smirking, I lean in, "Oh, but you can when you drug them... can't you, Lovely Lina?" I use my most intimidating voice, and I notice the slight quiver her body makes.

My cock stirs, and I move away before I do something that I really shouldn't. Kicking off my shoes, I pull my shirt over my head, but keep my jeans on. Climbing in on the other side, I scoot my body up behind Lina's and pull her into my chest, so her back is against me. I hear her sigh in frustration, and I grin.

"I'll do it again in a heartbeat if you piss me off..." her voice trails off softly.

I chuckle, "Get some rest, Lovely..."

She doesn't respond, but I don't need her to as she settles into me, and I feel her body relax. It doesn't take long before her breathing evens out, and I know she's asleep. I don't leave her, though. That's the last thing I want to do. I want to be here when she wakes up in case she needs something. Anything she needs, I will give her...

I must have fallen asleep, because I wake up with a start when I feel a warm mouth wrapped around my length. After Lina had fallen asleep, I thought it was safe enough to pull my jeans off, leaving me in only my boxers. I'm so fucking happy that I did!

I groan and thrust my hips gently as Lina begins to take me deep, "Fuck, baby. You should be sleeping..."

I hear a throaty chuckle, which vibrates against my cock, and I curse. It feels so goddamn good. I want nothing more than to take control and shove myself all the way down her tight throat, but I don't. I want to see what she does.

"I asked you if you needed something to eat before you went to sleep," I snicker, teasing her a little.

She responds by sliding her teeth against me, making me hiss and jerk my hips. I glance at the clock and see it's a little after eleven. Apparently, my Lovely didn't need as much rest as I thought she did.

I frown when she pops her mouth off my cock and climbs up my body, but again, I want to see what she will do. When she straddles my thighs, her wetness smears across me. My hands grip her thighs as I clench my jaw, barely holding on to my sanity at the moment.

"I wasn't hungry. All I wanted was a little snack..." she smiles down at me.

I look at my throbbing cock, and raise my brow, "Careful, or he might get insulted. He's far from little..."

She bites her lower lip as she rises onto her knees and scoots closer until she hovers just over my tip. She gazes into my eyes in the darkness as she lowers herself, impaling her hot cunt onto me. She's got to be sore from Fynn and I taking her earlier.

"Oh, God, Jett..." she sinks all the way down until my whole length is buried deep inside, "Fuck, you're big."

I can't help the proud grin that crosses my face, hearing her say this, "That's right, and it's all fucking yours, baby."

I want her to fuck herself on me. I want her to take control... take what she needs to make herself feel better. I grasp her breasts, kneading and massaging them before twisting and pulling until she gives me her little cries. I repeat.

"Jett..."

"Yeah, Lovely?" I watch her grind down on me.

"I need..." her words trail off as she pants.

"Tell me what you need, baby."

Her eyes bore into mine as she licks her lips and says, "I need you to fuck me like you love me."

Oh fuck...no, she didn't.

I let out a loud animalistic growl and flip us over, "There is no need to ask twice, baby, but know this...I fucking love the ever-loving shit out of you, and every time we fuck, know that I'm loving you just as much, if not more."

Lifting her leg, I drive into her repeatedly. My name echoes through the room as she screams it over and over. The headboard pounds against the wall, waking the whole house, I'm sure, but I don't fucking care. My girl asked me to fuck her like I love her, so I'm doing just that.

"Oh fuck...oh fuck...oh fuck!" Lina chants as my cock owns every fucking crevice of her pussy.

"Tell me, Lovely...are you feeling my love now? Do you understand the depths of my love for you?" I say through clenched teeth, my neck straining as I take the woman beneath me.

"Yes, Jett...yes! OH, GOD..."

My hand snakes to her throat, wrapping around it just before I pull her toward me, "Look at how my cock shows his love for you. It's a gorgeous fucking sight, isn't it?"

We both look between us and watch as my cock owns her fucking cunt like it's been doing it for years. My cock will never see another pussy again. It will never want another pussy ever again.

Shoving her back down, I lift both her legs until they're up by her chest, and hammer into her faster. Her eyes roll to the back of her head just before a whine starts low in her throat and grows until she's coming like a fucking freight train.

"Fuck, baby..." It's all I have time to say before I start jerking, ropes of cum spurting out, and painting her insides with my fucking baby batter.

It isn't until every last drop is out that I drop down and roll us back over. When she tries to pull herself off me, I growl, "Don't you fucking move, Lina."

Like a good girl, she listens. I need to feel connected to her for as long as possible, so I don't pull out of her. We're both falling fast asleep all too soon and I... I'm still buried deep inside the woman I love.

Catalina

Where do I start? Oh yes... I'm a fucking hypocrite. I didn't want our fathers to kill any of them, but I had no issue with doing so. Felicia sealed her fate the moment she insulted my Lords...it was the last straw for me. How fast I raised that gun and pulled the trigger makes me sick to my stomach. I hadn't even given it a thought before I did so.

Jett, being here with me the way he is, calms the demons and settles my soul enough that I don't drown in the violent waves of the storm brewing deep within. He doesn't take advantage of me in my weakened state, though I wouldn't stop him if he did... I'd welcome the distraction.

When I wake up, due to my nightmares painted in blood red, I need something to shake off the remaining thoughts running through my head. I look over my shoulder and gaze at a sleeping Jett. Moonlight filters in, showing me his slightly parted lips as he breathes evenly. I wish I could sleep like that.

I wake him in my own way, knowing he won't be upset about it. It's the best thing I could have done because not only does he allow me to use him to chase my demons away, but I also now know the depth of his love for me. The way he savagely takes me and fucks me harder than he ever has, touching places that, for some, may be painful, but I welcome all of it.

Loving someone is painful, both in a good and bad way, and I'm finding out just how much my Lords are sacrificing by loving me the way they do. I know of their pasts and what they have endured growing up, and still, none of it kept them from placing their hearts in my hands and trusting me to keep it safe for them.

When Jett and I are sated, I become trapped on top of him, his cock still inside me as we both find our peaceful slumber. I'm not sure how he did it, but Jett chased away all the demons trying to consume me just a short time ago. I sleep better than I have in days.

"Fuck...uh!" I moan as Jett thrusts into me, waking me up this time, "God...don't stop..."

"Not a fucking chance, baby."

The first rays of light stream through the curtains' cracks as sunrise approaches. There is enough light to see the need etched into Jett's face. His jaw is clenched, and he bites down on his lower lip. He's restraining himself.

"Damn you, Jett...you are way too good at fucking." It's not meant to be a joke, and he knows it.

"I'm trying to take it easy on your poor cunt," he states, "But I had to have you again."

He rolls us and lifts my leg. I hook it over his hip and grind against him as he thrusts into me. He takes it slowly this morning, but it feels as good as last night. Like the other two Lords, Jett is a phenomenal lover, and I will never deny him when he needs inside me.

"God, yes!" I toss my head back as his head dips, and he takes a nipple into his mouth.

I hear the door open, but I don't bother to look. I already know it's either Fynn or Oakley coming to get their piece of me, most likely. I'm definitely okay with either of them joining; we all need to let off as much steam as possible.

It isn't until Jett rolls us again that I open my eyes, but still, I don't look to see who has joined us. Suddenly, a tongue runs through my crack and down to almost where Jett's cock is stretching me out. The tongue comes back up as hands spread my cheeks. It dips into the tight pucker that will soon be filled with another cock.

When I try to turn my head and look, Jett grabs my face, shaking his head, "You don't need to know who it is that's going to trash that ass of yours. All you need to do is let them."

He kisses me, and that's when I feel it. Lube is drizzled onto my back hole. Fingers begin to work it, pushing in and out as they prepare me to take their girth. Jett's tongue is dominating mine, and when I start to grind against both him and the fingers behind me, I get a slap to the ass.

Jett rips his mouth away, "Stop being an impatient slut, Lovely. You will get it when we decide," he grins and then pulls me down and bites into my shoulder.

"Fuck..." I curse, his sharp teeth digging into my sensitive skin.

It doesn't last long, as he growls and glares over my shoulder, "Take her ass already, so I can fuck her!"

The fingers pull out of my ass and are replaced with the head of a cock. Slowly, they work into me, soft whimpers leaving my mouth as I try to relax enough to let them in. They pull out a little and slide back in, going a little further.

"That's it, baby. You are doing so good...take it all," Jett's voice coos at me as he caresses my head.

The door opens again, and now, all my men are here with me. My head is turned in the opposite direction, so I'm still unable to see anything. The scent of leather hits me, and I know that it is the ever-present musk of Fynn, which means Oakley is the one who has made my ass his home.

"Damn it, Oakley... you're too fucking big for my ass..." I pant.

A chuckle sounds behind me, "It's nice to know you can tell whose cock is inside you, Kitty Cat."

I won't spoil his way of thinking by telling him that I knew it was Fynn who walked in. Let him believe that I'm capable of telling them apart when they are all so much alike. I smile and open as Fynn steps forward, his cock already in his hand.

"You look like perfection, Little Saint," he bites his lip while watching me take him deep into my throat.

They don't use me like they usually do when we are together. No, they are lavishing my body, ever-so-slowly, with theirs. Intoxication takes hold, and it feels like I'm sinking deeper into a euphoric bliss as they all begin thrusting in and out.

"Fuck, Kitty Cat...how does your ass feel so tight when we fuck it all the time?" Oakley groans.

"The same way her cunt feels just as tight," Jett responds, "This body was made for us. Lovely Lina was made to be ours, and we would be fools if we ever let her go."

"Well, there is no way in hell that I'm ever letting her go," Fynn growls, "Little Saint will always be our Lady, and we...her Lords. She will never know another fucking cock. Will you?" He stares down at me as he pushes all the way down my throat.

Tears spill at how deep he is, and I hum my agreement.

He grins and swipes at the wetness, "I love your fucking tears, Saint."

Hands grip my hips, and thrusts become harder as I open up for them. I can't move as they stir the storm building inside me. Waves become more turbulent the faster and harder they all fuck me. I can't stop it when the biggest wave hits and sucks me under before spitting me out and tossing me into the air. I then free-fall and crash back into the stormy waters.

It happens a few more times before my guys groan and grunt their pleasure, pulling one last one from me. I feel Jett and Oakley come inside me a split second before Fynn is spurting down my throat. I swallow every last drop, not wanting to waste any of it.

None of us move for what seems like hours, but then Fynn is the first to pull away. Bending over, he grabs my chin and kisses me hard. I'm sure he can taste himself on my tongue, but he doesn't give a shit; none of them do.

"Thank you, Little Saint," he steps away and pulls on his boxers, "I'll go start breakfast."

I drop my head to Jett's chest, still trying to catch my breath. Oakley slaps my ass as he pulls out, his seed dripping out as he does. He chuckles, spreading my ass as he watches the mess he made in my ass.

"You should probably take a shower after this," he's smirking as he comes around so I can finally lay my eyes on his dark blue ones.

Gripping my hair, he yanks my head back and steals my lips just like Fynn did before moving away, "Thank you," I surprise myself by blurting those two words out.

"What are you thanking me for? Fucking your ass?" Oakley raises his brow.

"No, asshole," rolling my eyes, I smile, "I'm thanking you for being here for me. This is what I needed. All of you here with me at once."

He sobers and gazes into my eyes, "We are always here for you, Kitty Cat. Don't ever think we will abandon you."

He helps me off Jett, and they walk me into the bathroom and shower with me. After being under the hot spray for a few minutes, I look between them both, "So, what now? It's kind of weird knowing there is no more looking over our shoulders or playing Nancy Drew," a little chuckle slips out.

"Well, us Lords still have another full year of ruling over Helshire," Jett states, "And our Lady still has three years. All we can do is make the best of it and do what we do best."

I run the loofah over Jett's bare sculpted pecs, "And what exactly do you do best?"

Jett's wicked grin has my heart skipping before he's looking over my shoulder as Oakley washes my back, "Instill fear into the student body, and fuck our girl senseless every chance we get."

"You're forgetting one important thing, Pelletier," I can hear Oakley's grin in his voice.

"What's that, Harris?" Jett replies.

Suddenly, I'm being pushed down to my knees, "Making sure our Lady knows her fucking place at all times."

I glance up at Oakley, who smirks while stroking his cock. Licking my lips, I grab hold of Jett's girth with one hand and turn my mouth to Oakley, "Make it good, Harris," I give him my own smirk just before I open my mouth nice and wide.

FIFTY-SEVEN

☠

Fynn

"Here you go, gorgeous," I hand my Little Saint her Sex on the Beach drink as she lazes in the lounge chair in our rented private cabana.

Her smile goes straight to my heart and groin as she says, *"Thank you,"* before winking and sipping the drink.

After everything went down with Felicia, Kaden, and Chris, my best friends and I decided it would be good to take Catalina away. Because Helshire University shuts down from Thanksgiving, until after the New Year, we whisked her away to a little all-inclusive, private resort in the Caribbean Islands. We have a small villa that suits the four of us perfectly.

Jett and Oakley ran into the small island town to grab a few things we can't get from the resort. Mainly *toys* or items that we can use as toys for our beautiful little slut. So, it's up to me to entertain her while they're gone.

"You know, this part of the beach is private. Why are you wearing a swimsuit?" I eye her string bikini warily. Not that it really counts as clothing, anyway.

Her chuckle floats away on a gentle breeze, "Just say it, Morin. You want your toy naked, so you can enjoy the view."

I shrug, "Fine. I want you naked. You should always be naked around us. We want to be able to use you whenever the need arises." I sit in the lounge chair beside hers and stretch my legs out.

Putting her tall glass down, my Little Saint stands and steps up beside my chair, "If you want me naked, then undress me yourself."

I raise my brow, and a slow grin forms, "You know you just got yourself a little punishment for that."

It's her turn to shrug, "Do you worst...*babe.*"

Reaching my hand up to rip her bottoms away from her, she slaps my hand away and shakes her head. I'm baffled at first, but then I notice the glint in her eyes, and I know exactly what she wants me to do.

Sitting up and twisting, so my feet are on the ground with my legs spread wide. I pull her closer, and with my hands gripping her hips, I take the fabric of her bottoms between my teeth, and yank on it as I growl, tearing it all from her body.

When she goes to move away, I hold her in place and shove my mouth against her bare mound, my tongue flicking back and forth over her clit. Sliding my hands to her ass cheeks, I squeeze them and pull her closer. Her hands grab hold of my hair as she shrieks and tries to move away, but it's no use; I'm not letting her out of my grasp.

"Fuck, Fynn... it's too much... it's too sensitive!" she cries out.

"Like I fucking care. You'll come for me before I bend you over and fuck you right here." I feel her hands pull at my hair, but then her hips grind against my face.

I hook one of her legs over my shoulder, opening her up, so I can have better access. Saint tastes so fucking good; I can never get enough of this sweet cunt of hers. We began this whole thing to see the mighty Saint fall, and even though she's fallen to where we wanted her to, she's also risen. My Little Saint has risen to be the biggest Sinner of all, just because she fell for the worst of all the Sinners.

Catalina Scott may be our Lady of Sin and will answer only to her Lords, but she *is* our downfall. She's somehow found a way to capture our hearts and now holds them prisoner. I don't mind, though. To tell you the truth, I had a feeling that my Little Saint would be someone special the moment I saw her peeking through the curtains at the Saint's Sorority House.

It seems so long ago, but it's only been three months. So much has happened in this short time, but the four of us have grown from it all. The Lords of Sin will do whatever it takes to protect our Lady; now we know she will do the same for her Lords.

"Oh, God...yes!" Saint cries out.

"I'm not your God...but I am your Lord, and I order you to come all over my *fucking* face, Saint!" My voice rumbles against her pussy, and as soon as I use my fingers to pull apart her lips and I shove my tongue deep inside, her gates open, and she gives me everything I have been waiting for.

I eat her pussy like a starved man...like it's the last fucking meal I will ever have. I'm lifting her off the only foot she has planted on the ground. As I do so, her body balances on my face as her one leg dangles. Her cum covers my tongue, and it's like sweet ambrosia, the food of the fucking Gods.

I don't waste any time in making good on my threat as I flip us and put her on all fours on top of the chair before shoving her head to the seat, "Don't fucking move," I warn her as I lift her ass high in the air and drive into her.

I suck my thumb, lubing it up before entering her ass. I love seeing her ass plugged. I've ordered a special one just for her. I repeatedly slap her ass with my free hand to hear her little whimpers. I rarely go easy on my Little Saint, but she loves how I use her body.

"Who are you?" I growl out, almost at the point of coming myself.

"Your filthy little slut..." she cries out as I drive deeper into her.

"That's right, baby. Will you ever leave us?" I ask as I reach around and pinch her clit between my thumb and forefinger.

"No, never!" She squeals.

"Such a good slut. Now, milk me, Saint. Make me fill you with every drop that's bursting to unload inside of this filthy cunt." My jaw is clenched as I hold back until she gives me what I want.

"Use me, *my Lord.* My body is all yours for the taking..." Saint pleads like the nice little whore she is for us, and I let myself go.

I slap her clit multiple times and jerk my seed inside her, "Fucking come like a good little whore, baby. Give your Lord what he wants... what's his for the taking."

And she lets herself go with a guttural cry...

"Looks like we missed a hell of a good time," Jett chuckles just as I'm pulling out of my Little Saint.

"Oh, I'm sure she's got enough in her for the two of you," I smirk and slap Saint's ass, "Don't move, baby. It looks like Jett wants a piece." I eye my friend, who is already pulling his cock out.

Glancing over his shoulder, I see Oakley nodding, wanting me to accompany him. I bend down and place a kiss on Saint's temple, "Perfect as always." I watch as my best friend comes up behind her and pushes into her, "How does that feel, baby?"

"Fuck...like Heaven..." our girl states and closes her eyes.

Chuckling, I straighten and fist bump Jett just as he continues to thrust into her. Call us fucking pervs, but we love our girl's pussy, and it may make us act like horny teenagers, but she still loves us. Maybe we will grow up one day, but today isn't the day, and tomorrow isn't looking good either.

"What's up, Oak?" I ask as soon as I step into the villa.

Oakley motions for me to close the door, and my eyes meet bright blue ones when I do. I smirk as I watch our girl get railed by Jett, and all I do is raise a brow and tilt my head, and she's coming all over his cock. I mouth the words *good girl* before giving Oakley my full attention.

"My father called me while we were out," he starts, "It seems as though Felicia's aunt is starting to stir shit up, demanding to know what happened to her niece."

"Jesus, fuck!" I run my hand through my overgrown hair, "So, what's going to happen?"

"My father will be sending the jet in two days. You and I will fly back to New England while Jett stays with Kitty Cat. We'll take care of the aunt and fly back. Everything we'll need will be on the jet, along with the file on the aunt," Oakley informs me of all this but forgets one minor issue.

"Little Saint will never be on board with this," I deadpan.

My best friend sighs, "I know. Which is why she's really going to get pissed off when we drug her up." He shakes a little bag of pills between his fingers, and I now know why it took them so long in town.

"You really are a glutton for punishment, aren't you?" I hold my hands up, "I'll go back with you, but I'm not having any part in drugging that little hellcat," I snicker.

"Pussy," Oakley huffs at me, "It's the only way unless we take her with us, and I will not put her in danger."

I watch as Oakley places the pills on the top shelf in one of the cupboards, and I shake my head back and forth. This will not turn out well, and I hope Saint doesn't hold it against me for too long.

Oakley

After talking with Fynn, I make myself a drink and walk out to the cabana. I slide a chair over, place it right in view of my Kitty Cat, and take a seat. Our eyes hold one another's as Jett fucks her from behind.

"A package came for you, Fynn," I call over my shoulder, "It's on the counter."

A minute later, I hear a loud *"WHOOP,"* and a few minutes after that, Fynn steps out carrying his package and a bottle of lube. I know what it is right away and grin deviously at Kitty Cat. She may not like it at first, but she will take it for us, and if I know anything at all about my little Kitty Cat, she will learn to love it.

"You're going to want to relax, Kitty Cat," I pull out my cock and start stroking myself, because, come on, this is going to be hot to watch.

Fynn drizzles the lube on her ass hole, and Jett rubs it in, fucking his finger inside to help stretch her. I hadn't seen Fynn carry out the cleaner, but he pulls it out of the back of his cargo shorts and cleans the shiny metal object before coating it with lube.

Jett holds my Kitty Cat's ass cheeks open while Fynn slowly starts to push the plug into her cute little ass, "Eyes on me, Kitty Cat. Watch what the sight of what they are doing to you and what you are taking for us does to me."

Her whimpers make me even harder, and then, it's in, and she moans, which causes Jett to curse and release his load, and it couldn't have been better timing. I need inside her in a bad fucking way.

As soon as Jett pulls out, I order her to come over to me. Kitty Cat's legs are wobbly as she stands and slowly approaches me. I make a circle with my finger, indicating that I want her to turn around, "Bend the fuck over, Kitty Cat. Show your Lord what you're hiding inside your ass."

"You don't have to be a dick, Harris," She hisses but bends over as soon as I slap her ass.

"You're going to be riding this dick in a minute..." I smirk and spread her ass cheeks to get a better view.

Peeking out of her ass hole is a blood-red gem attached to a silver butt plug. Inside the gem are the words *Our Lady, Our Slut*. My cock jerks, and I can't hold back anymore. Grabbing her hips, I pull her cum-dripping cunt down onto my pulsating cock.

She grunts, most likely from the soreness due to my two best friends already using her well. I lean into her ear as soon as she's fully seated on me, "Does it hurt?" I nip her lobe.

She nods, "A little... I'm so...full."

"Good," It's all I say as I start thrusting into her from below.

Jett, being a funny guy, has his phone out and is recording it as I fuck our girl out in the open, her tits bouncing hard while having her ass plugged. We'll watch it later and get off again. Kitty Cat will come the hardest, as she always does after watching one of our videos.

"My Lady, My Slut," I say out loud, "Fucking come for me, Kitty Cat. Show me just how slutty my Lady really is by coming all over my cock."

It only takes the filthy words leaving my mouth to make her body tense up, and an animalistic cry leave her lungs. Down on the beach, a ways away, a couple walks hand in hand, and they turn when they hear our girl. They're far enough away that they can't see her nakedness, but it doesn't take long for them to figure out what we're doing.

I chuckle, "You're gaining an audience, Kitty Cat, but don't you dare keep quiet," I growl as I fuck her even harder before a roar rips from my lips as I come deep inside her cunt.

Catalina never complains about how often we take her. Sure, we let her rest, but we can't help ourselves if we walk in on one of the others fucking her. It's just too damn hot, and it makes us want her just as much. If she decides that she wants to fuck tonight, then we will fuck, but most likely, we will only have her suck us off, giving her poor cunt a reprieve. We aren't total deviants.

"Who am I?" I ask after our fuck session.

She's still on my lap, only sideways, as I hold and caress her. Catalina is a treasure; any man would be a fool not to keep her. We will never let her go. I know I keep saying that I will if I have to, but the more we are together, the more my thought process changes.

"My Lord, and one of the men I love," she sighs, contentedly, as she replies.

I grip her chin, not roughly, but enough to turn it up toward me. I gaze into her eyes and see the truth in her words, "And I love you, Kitty Cat. Don't ever doubt that. Everything we do is because we love you, and if there is ever a time that we do something that may be unforgivable to others, know that we do it for a reason."

Her brows knit together, "What aren't you telling me, Oakley?"

Shit. I'm trying to make her understand why I will be doing what I have to do without telling her what that something is, and I'm failing miserably. I know she will be pissed about being drugged, but it can't be helped. We just can't risk her coming with us if things go south. Her father is the one who told us to drug her, so at least he's on board with it.

I smile, "Nothing, Kitty Cat. I'm just trying to tell you how much you mean to us, and I'm fucking it all up."

She cups my cheek, "I already know how each of you feels about me, Oak. You don't have to try convincing me."

When she tries to get off my lap, I growl, "Where the fuck are you going?"

"To get dressed, silly," she chuckles, but I hold firmly to her.

"No. Unless we leave the villa to go to town or sightseeing, you will not wear anything." I challenge her with my stare.

"Fine, but the same goes for all of you," she huffs as she crosses her arms.

"That's not the way it works, Kitty Cat." I grin, loving the way her eyes burn into mine.

"Just try wearing clothes, Oakley, and I will throw every article of your clothing in a pile and light it on fire," The gall of her to make that threat only hardens me below.

I groan, knowing I can't have her again, "Don't try making demands of me, Kitty Cat. You know the rules. You wanted to keep the contract in full force, so you have to play by *our* rules."

"Hell, I don't see anything wrong with being naked here," Jett stands a few feet away from us, grinning and gloriously naked.

"Me neither..." Fynn pushes his shorts down and tosses them aside before lounging in the chair next to us.

Kitty Cat giggles and lifts her brow at me, but I glare at my two best friends, "Whose fucking side are you on?"

"Well, the way I see it is unless you're willing to take it up the ass or drop to your knees, I'm on Lovely's side," Jett winks at our girl.

My ass clenches at the thought, and I grimace at him, "You're fucked in the head, you know that?"

He only shrugs, but to my surprise, Fynn chimes in, too, "He's right, Oak. You're not the one we are fucking, and even though Jett went about saying it the way he did, he isn't wrong."

Fynn taps his lap, and before I can stop her, my Kitty Cat flies off my lap and onto my best friend's, earning them both a death stare from me. I study all three of my people. I say my people because that's who they are. They are the only ones I go to, and are there for me regardless.

Rolling my eyes, I give up my fight, "Fine, but know that you will probably get fucked a lot more this way," I warn my Kitty Cat.

Her giggle gets me in multiple areas, but her words do the most damage below, "Who says I will have a problem with that?"

I groan and toss my head back against the chair. This woman will be my death, but I guess I wouldn't want it any other way. My Kitty Cat is my life now, and no matter what, she will always be my first priority. I will give her whatever she wants for the most part, even on the days when she tests my patience...I will only love her more.

FIFTY-EIGHT

Catalina

I love all three of my Lords, I really do, but they sure do know how to test me. Not only that, but they also continue to underestimate my learning abilities. I know they don't just see me as a fuck toy, even though that's what it must look like to most, but they forget that they have been training me, and I've been watching for the last few months.

When the guys surprised me with this trip to the Caribbean, I was speechless. We fucked all night long that night, with me being the initiator. I've become a certifiable slutty nympho for those three, and I'm not ashamed to admit it.

Now, what they do outside the bedroom raises the question of whether I want to stay with them sometimes. I know they mean well, but I hate that they still keep shit from me, like two days ago when Oakley and Jett returned from town.

I knew something was up when Fynn closed the door. Those eyes...dominating me with just a simple look and a tilt of his head. He had me coming all over Jett instantly. I could see through the French doors that they were having an intense conversation, and then afterward, when Oakley said the things he said, I just knew.

With everything that has happened, I knew that my guys wouldn't come on vacation and not worry about danger. So, while all three were passed out after a long night of insatiable sex, I was able to take Oakley's phone into the bathroom and go in to find the security feed from the cameras that they had secretly set up throughout the house. I find the app immediately and click on it.

"*Un-fucking-believable!*" I say to myself as I listen to the conversation between Oakley and Fynn. At least Fynn is the smart one out of the two. I'll have to reward him for it, but it doesn't get him out of what I now must do. I tap the phone against my chin as a plan begins to form. Biting my bottom lip, I grin.

"Good morning, gorgeous," Oakley places a kiss on my head as he walks by on his way to the fridge, "Mm, something smells really good!"

"I figured my Lords would be ravenous after the night they had with their Lady," I giggle, "A nice breakfast should fix that right up. Will you be a doll, pour the orange juice for me, and take it to the cabana?" I ask with a smile.

"Of course," he says and heads to the cupboard for glasses.

It just happens to be the same cupboard in which he stashed the pills. I make sure I don't turn around; that way, he has time to mix the drugs in my drink. If I'm not careful, I will drink a glass of juice with double the drugs mixed into it.

Oakley grabs the jug of already-made juice from the fridge and pours it. I can hear glass clink against the glass jug as he does. Just when he's lifting the tray of glasses to take out to the table where Fynn and Jett are already sitting, I stop him.

"Hold on, babe. I'm thirsty. You can leave mine here," I smile and let him hand me a glass.

I pretend to take a drink in front of him before placing it on the counter and go back to humming as I start plating the food on two separate platters. Eggs, bacon, and sausage on one, and pancakes and toast on the other.

Once I know he isn't looking, I quickly dump my juice into the sink, grab the already poured glass I had hidden in the fridge, and place it on the tray to take with me. I try not to tremble as I carry the tray, but I'm worried this will backfire on me. I'm about to do something that I can't turn back from.

When I listened to the conversation between Oakley and Fynn, I knew what I needed to do. This is my mess to clean up, not theirs. I'm the one who pulled the trigger. Apparently, Felicia's aunt isn't accepting the story of her niece being in a fiery car accident, and because of it, the Lords want her taken care of...or at least, our fathers do before the others find out.

"Eat up, boys! I'm afraid I might have made a bit too much," I chuckle as I look at the heaping platters.

"Hm, you worry too much, Saint. Take a load off," Fynn pulls me into his lap and feeds me a piece of bacon before kissing me thoroughly.

I pull away, grinning, "Enough of that! You need to eat because I want to go hiking this afternoon."

Silence covers the area briefly before Oakley clears his throat, "That sounds like fun, Kitty Cat." He winks at me, and all I want to do is smack the ever-loving shit out of him.

I'm not sure how strong those pills are, and I didn't know if he knew how many pills were in the baggy, so I had to be careful with how many I used. It isn't until we are finishing up with breakfast that I notice them start yawning.

Oakley's been eyeing my glass throughout the whole meal, so just for shits and giggles, I guzzle the rest of my drink, and see relief cross his face. I want to smile smugly, but I hold off for now. I can't have them suspecting anything, not until I have them where I need them.

The jet touches down at a private airport in New Hampshire. I am only fifteen minutes away from Felicia's aunt Charlotte's house. According to the file I found waiting for me, the woman lives alone and works at her own little bakery in town. It also has Charlotte's schedule from the time she wakes up until the time she goes to bed. Our fathers were very thorough.

There is a car waiting for me when I step off the jet. A burner phone begins to buzz in the center console just as I get in, and I just stare at it, looking dumbfounded. How would anyone know that I'm inside the car? I look around the cabin of the blacked-out Sedan to see if there are any cameras, but I find none.

The phone stops ringing. When the buzzing starts back up immediately, I gasp, *"Calm down, Cat. They are probably tracking the jet,"* I tell myself, but it still doesn't help me decide whether I should answer the phone.

Finally, taking a deep breath, I swipe right on the screen, answering the call, "To whom do I owe the pleasure?" I answer, proud that I'm able to keep my voice even.

"Catalina?" Donavan's voice comes over the line, "What are you doing answering this phone? Where's my son?"

"Oh, you know, they're tied up at the moment and can't come to the phone right now," I smile smugly even though he can't see me.

"What is that supposed to mean?" I can hear the concern in his voice, and I have to roll my eyes.

"Do you honestly believe that I would hurt Oakley? That I would hurt *any* of the guys?" His assumption pisses me off, "They are safe...back at the villa. The next time loose ends come up on a job that I did, I will be the one to take care of it."

"Catalina, this isn't what a Lady of Sin's job is," he sighs on the other end, "Your father isn't going to like this..."

"Do you think I give a rat's ass? He told your son to drug me! How can I be okay with that?" I pause and wait for him to respond.

He curses under his breath, "Fine, but if anything happens to you, I will never forgive myself."

"Don't worry, Donavan. This should have been a woman's job to begin with. Standby, because I will need someone to help carry her out of the house," I inform him, knowing that he's going to be confused.

"What do you mean? You go in, get the job done, and get out. The clean-up crew will be there shortly after," he says.

"I am not killing her, Donavan. Charlotte is innocent, but I understand certain measures must be taken. Just trust me on this, will you?" I ask in annoyance.

It is beyond me why it takes so much to get it through a guy's head that a woman is just as capable of doing the same things they can do. My guys are going to learn fast not to fuck with me. If being drugged, then chained and gagged back at the villa while I'm out playing villain doesn't teach them, then maybe they're a lost cause.

A chuckle reaches my ear, "Damn, my son is going to have his hands full with you."

"I think you're forgetting Fynn and Jett..."

"No. It's been discussed. We want you and my son to marry. Our families will be a force to be reckoned with once the union occurs."

"Discussed by who?" I ask angrily.

"Your mother and I did. We plan on bringing it up with your father this weekend," he states matter-of-factly.

"Was this while the two of you were fucking behind my father's back? Are you planning on telling him that as well?"

There is absolute silence on the other end.

"Know this, Donavan," I continue, "I will never marry, because my future plans include all three of my Lords. I will never choose one over the others, only to sneak behind my husband's back with them." I take a deep breath and exhale, calming myself, "Be on standby..."

I cut off the call and toss the phone into the passenger seat. Putting the car in drive, I take off like a bat out of hell, heading to take care of business, so I can get back to my guys. Before I turn them loose, I have plans for them, and I need to have my head on straight to do so for those plans. Once I free them of their chains, I have a feeling that I will be in a heap of trouble.

FIFTY-NINE

Jett

I wake up groggy as fuck, and feeling like I partied hard last night. Only when I open my eyes do I notice that I'm outside in the cabana and the sun is setting. I'm confused as fuck.

"What the hell?" I ask myself and look around.

I spot Fynn a few feet away, to my right, on another lounger. He's passed the fuck out, and I take note of the tape over his mouth. My eyes travel down the only arm I can see from this angle, and it's tied to the lounger.

I'm only just realizing that I also have tape over my mouth and can't move my limbs. When I turn to my left, I see Oakley in the same state. Panic begins to rise as my thoughts go to my Lovely Lina. I look around, searching for her, but she's nowhere to be found.

Scrutinizing both my friends to see if they have any kind of injury, relief fills me when I don't see any blood or bruises. So, who the fuck could have done this, and where the fuck is our girl? Only when Lovely's face pops into my head again do I start putting two and two together. She's been very considerate, wanting to please us at every turn. Now I know why.

If I didn't have tape over my mouth, you would see the slow grin that appears and hear the chuckle that tries bursting out at the realization that Catalina bested us. The little minx drugged me again...drugged us! She was onto us. How? I haven't the slightest clue, but I know our girl is a clever little bitch, and we underestimated her...again.

Fynn is next to wake up. It's been about thirty minutes, give or take, since I woke up, and I've been working on trying to get the tape off my mouth, but it's harder than fuck when something is shoved in my mouth. Fynn glares at me, relaying how pissed he is, and I try to smile to let him know that all is good. The look he gives me is a baffled one, and I throw my head back and chuckle even though it's muffled.

After about another fifteen minutes, I'm able to tuck my gag into the side of my cheek and wet the tape enough to get it unstuck from my lips. I give my tongue a break before continuing. Once I have enough of it away from my mouth, I can finally speak. Well, as much as I'm allowed with the gag still tucked in my cheek.

"Our little minx is in so much trouble..." I say to Fynn, his eyes widening, "Yes, she figured it out somehow."

He throws his head back, and I can hear his muffled laughter, and so does Oakley, because he begins to groan. I watch as he tries to move, only for his body to tense when he realizes he can't. I want to laugh at his reaction, but I know this really isn't a laughing matter. Not when my Lovely Lina could get hurt doing this task on her own.

"Don't bother, Oak. She tied us up good," I tell him as clearly as I can speak, "All we can do is wait, and hopefully, she gets back before housekeeping arrives in the morning."

We all settle in for the long wait, hoping our Lady comes back to us unharmed. As proud as I am of her for besting us like this, it doesn't take away from the fact that I am terrified of something happening to her. Do I think she can handle the task at hand? Hell yeah, she can, but in her own way. If I know my Lovely Lina like I think I do, she will ensure all is well without bloodying her hands, but damn if she isn't hot when she does bloody them.

Catalina is the one that I will spend the rest of my life loving in every way possible. I don't mind sharing her with the others...it's how we are and how we will continue being for as long as *she* wants. My Lovely Lina...will always hold my heart as well as keep me on my toes.

Fynn

I must have fallen asleep, because a noise off to my right startles me awake. Only when a figure walks over and enters the cabana do I see who it is, but I already know it's *her*. Unlike Jett, my mouth is still taped, so all I can do is watch her move closer.

I look over at my two friends. They are both sleeping. I'm not sure how long we've been tied to these damn chairs, but I know that I'm going to need a fucking massage after I'm freed. Eying my Little Saint curiously, I'm relieved that she is back in one piece, but now that I know this, I let the anger take hold. What she did was dangerous, and I'm going to punish her for scaring us the way she did.

I yank on my ties, and I glare at her, indicating that it would be in her best interest if she were to untie me right fucking now. To my utter surprise, her lips turn up into a wolfish grin. She lifts a leg and throws it over my waist, so she can straddle me.

My Little Saint runs her hands up my chest before leaning close to my ear, "If you're a good boy and can stay quiet, I'll fuck you right here."

I jerk my head back and stare at her in disbelief, but my dick doesn't know any better as it begins to harden. I'm too mad and shake my head while pulling on my arms with no success. I have no problem fucking my Little Saint, but I want it to be on *my* terms, which does not include any pleasure for her.

Her grin widens, "What's that, Fynn? You want me to fuck myself on your cock?" She taps her finger to her mouth, "You know, I'm very disappointed in you for not stopping Oakley from drugging me. I know you weren't on board with that part, *but* you still went along with it. Lucky for you, I will reward you for not *wanting* to drug me."

Fuck! How the hell do I stop her from doing what she's about to do? That's easy...I don't. I may be upset with my Little Saint, but I will still enjoy her using me, and then, I will punish the shit out of her once she finally frees me.

I thrust upwards, and she begins to dry hump me. She's wearing a mini skirt, and from what I can feel rubbing against me, no panties. I groan.

"Shh, you don't want to wake the others. Otherwise, I will stop, and you won't get to come." She licks up the side of my face.

We are still all naked from before she left us. It was a good thing that we were under the protection of the cabana all day, or else our cocks would be burnt to a crisp. Catalina had planned this well, which means she found out pretty early on. These lounge chairs are bolted into the cement, so they don't blow away during tropical storms. She chose to tie us to them, so we couldn't tip and break them to free ourselves. Such a sly little bitch.

Saint sits up and spits on my cock before raising herself ever-so-slowly and impaling her cunt on my length. As she moves up and down on me, she closes her eyes and, in a low voice, asks, "Do you want to know what I did all day long?" before opening those pretty blues and peering at me.

All I can do is nod.

"Well, after drugging you all, I left to catch the jet that Donavan sent. After the almost five-hour flight, I drove the fifteen minutes to Charlotte's house and waited for her to come home."

I feel myself getting closer to coming as she fucks me harder. Gritting my teeth, I try to hold back and concentrate on her words simultaneously. When my cock swells with the tell-tale sign of a release, Saint pulls herself off me.

"That was a very naughty boy, Fynn. I didn't tell you that you could come yet." Then she does something she has never done before and flicks me in the dick, "Bad boys don't get to come."

As I stare at her in disbelief, I can't help but be in awe of her. My Little Saint, who started as a shy but sassy-mouthed little vixen and turned into a little bird before finally spreading her wings, has now become her true self. No longer the prey but the fucking hunter.

Catalina has surpassed everything we ever wanted her to be, and even though she will still be punished for this little stunt, I can't help but be proud of our lady of Sin. We wanted to see the Saint fall, but we never thought we would see her rise from those ashes like a fucking phoenix and reign over the Lords of Sin, but she's done precisely that. She's not just the Lady of Sin, but the Queen of all us Sinners.

"Fynn," her seductive voice captures my attention, "Be a good boy and stay hard for me, because I'm going to wake up your friends and show them that only good boys get to come." With that, she moves away from me and rips the tape the rest of the way from Jett's mouth.

"Son of ..." Jett curses as he wakes, but then sees our girl standing over him.

She tsks him and then looks over at me, "Looks like someone was a naughty boy and didn't keep his gag in place." She gives me a devilish smile, and I know that Jett's going to be really sorry.

Oakley

I've been awake since right before my Kitty Cat returned. Listening to her talk to Fynn in a hushed voice has me feeling all sorts of fucked up. I want to be pissed at her, but I'm proud as fuck of what she did. I mean, look at us. She drugged us, restrained us, and left us outside, naked, all day long while she took care of loose ends.

Hearing what she said to Fynn has me acknowledging just how right she is for doing what she did. She is our Lady, after all, and I shouldn't expect anything less than what she has done. Oh, but is her ass going to be a pretty red once we are all released? Most definitely.

I turn my head and watch as she sucks off my friend, bobbing down on his cock a few times before pulling off and slapping the throbbing appendage. She repeats her actions again and again. I wince each time, but this is our punishment for doing what we did, so I will take mine when the time comes.

"Tell me what happens to naughty boys who try to escape their restraints," my Kitty Cat orders Jett.

He groans, and I smirk. The tape still covers my mouth with what I now know is a pair of Kitty Cat's panties inside, being used as a gag. I wait for him to answer her, "They get their dick slapped," he grunts as she slaps it again.

"That's right. How does it feel to be on the receiving end, Jett? Not very good, huh?"

"No, Lovely. I'm sorry for everything, just please, let me come…" Jett fucking begging has a chuckle slipping from me.

Catalina snaps her head in my direction, "Ah, looks like sleeping beauty has finally decided to join us, boys." She pats Jett on the chest and walks over to a table a few feet away, grabbing something before approaching me.

When I see that she has my favorite hunting knife in her hand, apprehension stirs inside. I watch as she begins to pace beside my lounger. Kitty Cat glances at Fynn, and then at Jett before her eyes settle back on me.

"I'm most disappointed in you, Oakley," she states, and just hearing those words leave her mouth crushes me, "Fynn and Jett are the two that I always thought were the harder ones. Especially after the last time I was drugged, and you didn't want any part in fucking me while I was under the influence."

I try to tell her I'm sorry, but it's all muffled.

"What was that? Oh, well, you can tell me later, because I think it's best that we leave the tape on while you take your punishment." Kitty Cat straddles my waist and drags the knife down my torso.

My breath hitches at the feel of the sharp edge, and yet, my dick gets hard when her wetness rubs against me. I don't drag my eyes away from her, though. I gaze into her pretty blue eyes, challenging her to do whatever it is she has planned for me.

"I love you, Oakley. I love all of you, and that's why when your father told me that he and my mom discussed the two of us getting married in the future, I pretty much told him to fuck off." She bites her bottom lip and stares at me.

I swallow hard. So, what does this mean? Is she going to leave us for this little stunt? Did we go too far this time? Panic begins to take hold. I haven't felt like this since she was taken from us.

"I will not give you a fake marriage, where I go off and fuck the other two behind your back. You don't deserve that, and to be honest, I can never choose between the three of you. We are all in this together until death do us part," she ends in a whisper.

Lowering herself, she presses her lips against the tape and kisses me hard. My hips thrust on their own, and Kitty Cat snickers. I love that evil little titter from her. It makes me smile. That is until she places the point of the blade right above my heart.

"You have marked me, Oakley. Now, it's my turn to mark you." With that, I feel the tip puncture my skin, and the burning of the blade gliding through it.

The pain only lasts a couple of minutes, but it seems longer. Suddenly, the tape is ripped from my mouth, and she slowly pulls her panties from inside. I can only pant heavily as she dips her head and flattens her tongue against my skin before dragging it through the blood.

"Fuck, Kitty Cat..." I groan, "I need inside you, right fucking now..."

She cocks a brow, and then does the last thing I thought I would see. Deep throating the blade handle, she leans back, straddling me, and pushes the handle deep inside her. She keeps her eyes on me as she fucks herself.

"I'm going to come all over this handle and then smear it all over you," she says before biting her bottom lip and moaning.

"Fucking harder, Kitty Cat," I order her as I watch her masturbate with the knife, "Fuck it like it's my fat cock, and come all over it, baby."

As she does what I tell her to do, she explains what took place back in the States, "As I said before," she pants, "I waited for her to come home, and then I pretended to be one of Felicia's friends from school...oh..." she moans, "She let me in without issue."

"Fuck, Kitty Cat. I may come just watching you..."

Our eyes meet, and she continues, "We chatted while drinking tea. I tossed one of your pills into her cup when she wasn't looking," Kitty Cat's eyes roll back, "Oh God..."

"I think this is the hottest fucking thing I have ever witnessed..." Jett grunts, and when I look over at him, cum is spurting from the tip of his cock. The fucker came without even being touched!

"That's a naughty boy, Jett, but I'll let it slide this time..." Kitty Cat smirks and returns her attention to me, "I contacted your little doctor friend on my way to the aunt's house. Dr. Halsey had another doctor friend in the psych ward who agreed to help."

She pulls the handle from her, coated in her juices, and rubs it in the blood on my chest before sucking it all off. She reinserts it inside her and continues, "Your father came and helped get her into the car, and then we took her to Halsey's friend...oh fuck, I'm going to come!"

Her hips start thrusting harder as she fucks the knife like her life depends on it, and suddenly, her head falls back, and she screams out her climax as she fucking squirts all over my chest. It not only gets my chest but also hits my chin, and a few drops shoot up my nose. I open my mouth, trying to catch some of it, but it's over all too soon.

"Jesus, Saint!" Fynn growls from over on his chair, and my Kitty Cat winks at him.

When she moves, I think she's going to ride my cock, but instead, she stands up, "You won't want to miss this, *babe*."

The little slut leaves me and returns to Fynn, where she slides down on his shaft and starts fucking the shit out of him. I glare at her, but I can't help but be proud of her once again. She's giving us exactly what we have dished out to her. She's the perfect fucking Lady for us.

Glancing down, I look at the carving she gave me, and my heart swells. There on my chest, just above my heart, is *Kitty Cat*. I'll wear her name proudly, and if it fades too much, I'll fucking tattoo it on me. Catalina doesn't know just how much she is a part of all three of us, but I will happily inform her of it, just as soon as she releases us.

Catalina

I stand before my three Lords after I fuck Fynn into a much-needed climax, rewarding him for not wanting to drug me. Jett and Oakley look like they are hurting something fierce, even though Jett already came on his own. His cock is still throbbing and looking very angry. It's not their cocks that have me gazing at each of them, but the bloody names now carved into each of their chests.

Kitty Cat, Lovely Lina, and *Little Saint.*

I am theirs, and they are mine. Nobody will take them from me. Not any of their groupies, and definitely not our families. I smile at the thought, and then I strip down.

"Before I release you, I have something to say, and I want you to really fucking listen to me," I stare each of them in the eye, making sure they are paying attention before I continue, "Never again will you pull something like this. I will be your Lady, but I will not remain idle while you three go off and do stupid shit without me."

"Saint..." Fynn tries to say something, but I send him a look that shuts him up instantly.

"You don't have much faith in yourselves, do you? You have all taught me well over the last few months; now you have to let me join you." I begin to pace slowly, "This job was one for me, not you. Not only was it *my* loose end, but it was a female's job. I was able to take care of it without bloodshed. Charlotte will be in that ward, undergoing some form of memory treatment. They will make her forget about her suspicions while still remembering her niece and that she was killed in a horrific car accident."

"I can't believe you were able to pull this all off," Jett smiles proudly at me, making me blush.

"Well, believe it. There is a lot that I can do if I'm given a chance," my smile grows slightly seductive, "You were all very bad boys, but you have accepted your punishments. Now it's time for you to do one more thing..."

I take the knife I fucked myself with and start with Fynn's ropes. I release his limbs one by one before moving over to Jett and doing the same. When I reach Oakley, I cut the ropes around his ankles before starting on his wrists.

"What's that one thing, Kitty Cat?" Oakley grins up at me, wickedly.

The knife slices through the last of the rope as I gaze into his stormy blue eyes. The blade clatters to the cement, and I stand before him with my brow cocked and a matching grin, "Be good boys and punish the fuck out of me."

SIXTY

Epilogue:

Catalina

Had you asked me when I first started Helshire University if I had any plans for when I graduated, I would have laughed in your face. I only came to this University because I was a Legacy. I thought that by doing so, I'd make my parents proud after putting up with my rebellious attitude the last few years of high school. Now, I'll not only be graduating with honors, but I've already got a spot waiting for me at the Law Firm here in town.

I know what you're thinking. How can a girl like me, who has not only killed, but has added a few more felonies to the list over the past three years, turn out to be a Defense Attorney? Well, that's where connections come in. It helps when you're part of a polyamorous relationship with the Mayor and the new Police Chief. The Senior Partner in the Law Firm I'll join is also part of our happy little tribe.

Because of his family's status in this town, Oakley is the youngest Mayor this town has ever had, but he does his job well. We all figured that if we were going to have to get down and dirty at times, we might as well work in the fields that would help the most, so long as we never get caught, that is.

Things did calm down once we returned from the Caribbean that year, so it's not like we've broken numerous laws. Chris had served his one year at the Reformatory and came out a totally different person. He now runs a high-end security business in Helshire, refusing to return home. He's cut ties with his father, Kevin, but still talks to his other siblings and is close with his cousin, and my best friend, Dani.

As for Kaden, we were informed that he served three years. He was released a few months ago, and nobody seems to know where he went. Like his father, Kaden has disappeared off the face of the earth, and it had nothing to do with us. Oakley has sent out Private Investigators to find him, mainly to keep an eye on Kaden and ensure he isn't up to no good.

Donavan, and Oakley's mother, finally called it quits, and she is now happily married to Blake. As for my parents, they have gone from a couple to a throuple after Mom and Donavan came clean. Dad was pissed more over the fact that they lied to him but forgave their transgressions. Everyone is now happy.

So, as you can see, life has been good so far, at least for me and my Lords. I'm no longer the Lady for the current Lords of Sin; I haven't been one for two years. Not since my Lords graduated, but all three make sure I get treated like one every chance they get. I, for one, like to make them work for it, but as always, I make sure they are well rewarded.

"Are you ready for this?" Dani asks as she places her cap on her head while we get ready in one of the restrooms.

I have to grin, because my friend, as is her style, has a big ole middle finger painted on the top of her cap, which she has covered up for the time being. I'm so glad we got past the whole misunderstanding from freshman year, because Dani has turned out to be irreplaceable in my life.

"I'm more than ready," I have her turn to ensure her cap is secured correctly, "What are your plans for after the ceremony?"

"Don't know yet. Tara wants to hang out at some point, but I have Kurt coming over," my friend's sly grin tells me exactly what she's thinking.

My eyes widen, and I gasp, "Are you seriously going to try and get Tara to join in on a threesome with you and Kurt?"

Dani and her boyfriend, Kurt, have been dating for almost a year now, but recently, they have met a cute little blonde that they are both interested in. I try not to think about the fact that Tara kind of reminds me of myself, but it's hard to miss it every time you look at our matching blonde hair and blue eyes.

Dani shrugs, "We've been subtly dropping hints when she's around. Maybe it's time we're just direct."

I laugh at my best friend, "I'm surprised it's taken you this long to be direct. You never have an issue with it any other time," I tease her.

Suddenly, I'm being grabbed and lifted from behind, "Have time for a quickie? I want our cum dripping out of this sweet little cunt of yours as you cross the stage," Fynn's breath is hot on my neck before his teeth catch my ear lobe.

"That's my cue to leave," Dani chuckles, "Kurt and I will stop by later, Cat."

I wave my hand since I can't talk while Jett has his tongue down my throat. I moan and thrust my hips when a hand slips under my dress and between my thighs. If I wasn't horny before, I am now.

"Damn, Kitty Cat... you're fucking soaked already!" Oakley pulls his fingers out and sucks on them as he walks over and locks the door, "We've been searching everywhere for you, woman..."

I'm whirled around and then bent over the vanity, "One more gang bang at Helshire University," Fynn chuckles as he holds me down by my neck and flips my skirt and robe up over my ass, "What do you say, Little Saint?"

"Only if you're going to make it rough, *my Lord*," I grin, "You know how I like it to hurt. Did you bring your handcuffs, Chief?"

He presses down on my neck harder, "No, but you're going to remain still and take it like a good girl, aren't you?"

I hear his belt buckle jingle, and then his zipper just before he thrusts into me hard, "Oh fuck!" I cry out.

Fynn reaches around and plays with my clit, "We don't have much time, Saint, and you have two more cocks to take before you have to join your fellow graduates." He pinches my clit as he pounds into me.

It's not long before I start to come, and he joins me. As promised, Oakley steps up next and fucks me just as hard. They use me as their personal cum dumpster like they usually do before any kind of event. They have to mark their territory every fucking time.

"Fuck, Kitty Cat. How is it your cunt never loses its tightness?" Oakley growls, and I feel his seed filling me up before he slaps my ass and pulls out.

"Saving the best for last," Jett teases, and his two friends scoff.

"Jett, hurry. I have to get out there," I remind him.

He grabs my hair and yanks my head back, "Don't fucking rush me, Lovely. You better get used to me taking my time with you, because once you work at my Law Firm, I'll be taking all the time I want with you," he slams into me repeatedly, and I know I will have bruises from the edge of the vanity, but I don't mind war wounds. They are a reminder of how much my guys love me.

Once they are through with me, Jett helps me to stand while Oakley and Fynn pull up my panties and yank my skirt back into place. They all wear proud grins as they walk with me out of the bathroom. A group of students stand just outside, smirks covering their faces when they see us emerge.

Everyone knows about Lady Catalina and her three Lords. We are respected and feared by all, but it doesn't stop the catcalls that are echoed through the hall as we walk past them all. I walk with my head high, knowing I'm wanted by all the guys and hated or envied by most girls. Does it bother me? Not one fucking bit.

I've earned my place here, and I'll be damned if anyone tries to knock me from my throne. This will be the last time I walk through the halls of Helshire with my three Lords surrounding me, but it won't be the last time they will hear our names. For those who remain in the area, our names will be etched into their memory, because we plan on owning this town.

Our families may have been big contributors to Helshire, New Hampshire, but we will be the ones to run the town. Don't get me wrong, we aren't the Mafia, and we don't do bad deeds that aren't necessary...and we never hurt the innocent. That's why we want the town. We want to ensure corruption doesn't touch this place we plan on making a home in.

I want a family in the future, but before that can happen, the garbage needs to be taken care of, and that's what we plan to do. Only by making this town safe for our future children will I be able to give my boys their heirs. They all want a Legacy, and it's up to me as their Lady to provide each of them their own.

"Are you ready, Lovely Lina?" Jett looks over at me.

I raise my brow at his question, "Ready for what?"

"Don't tell me you've forgotten all about the contract being up the moment you accept your diploma, Little Saint," Fynn pretends to be crushed, and I roll my eyes at his theatrics.

"It's all good; I've got it covered," Oakley states as he pulls two items out of his inside pocket. Unrolling one, he holds it out to me as the sacrificial dagger is held in his other hand.

I look at the two items he's holding and smile wickedly at the Greek God, "Seriously?" I ask excitedly.

Nodding, Oakley licks his lips and turns his own devilish grin on me, "All you have to do is sign on the dotted line, Kitty Cat."

THE END

ACKNOWLEDGEMENT

First and foremost, I want to thank my family. Putting up with my long hours and my being absent a lot was not easy, but they took it in stride, knowing this meant a lot to me. Thank you for loving me enough to put up with me while I'm in the 'zone.'

Next, I want to thank my ARC readers for taking the time to read this title and give me their feedback, they truly are an amazing bunch!

I can't forget Sky, my new proofreader, who has become a new friend of mine. I trusted her with my baby, and she took care of it even better than I would have, so thank you for offering to help me out with this title. I look forward to working with you on future titles.

Last, but not least, I would like to thank Prince at CentralCovers for designing an amazing cover for me. I love his work and plan on using him on many more upcoming titles.

That being said, I would also like to send a huge thank you to Painted Wings Publishing for formatting and giving my book a kickass look with their edge designs and inside graphics. They were amazing to work with, even on the tight deadline I was on. I appreciate them willing to work with me, so I had my files in a timely manner. I highly recommend them if you're looking for a little something extra to bring your baby to life.